D0423294

THE
BLACK CAT

Forge Books by Robert Poe

Return to the House of Usher
The Black Cat

THE

BLACK CAT

ROBERT POE

A TOM DOHERTY ASSOCIATES BOOK

NEW YORK

This is a work of fiction. All of the characters and events portrayed in this novel are either fictitious or are used fictitiously.

THE BLACK CAT

This book is printed on acid-free paper.

A Forge Book
Published by Tom Doherty Associates, Inc.
175 Fifth Avenue
New York, NY 10010

Forge® is a registered trademark of Tom Doherty Associates, Inc.

Library of Congress Cataloging-in-Publication Data

Poe, Robert.
        The black cat / Robert Poe.
            p.   cm.
        "A Tom Doherty Associates book."
        ISBN 0-312-86013-7 (hardcover)
        I. Title.
        PS3566.O34B58   1997
        813'.54—dc21   97-14683
                                                CIP

First Edition: November 1997

Printed in the United States of America

0 9 8 7 6 5 4 3 2 1

To the cats:

General Stonewall Jackson and Cleopatra,
who allow me to share their home;
Dizzy, Wild Child, and the rest of the gang
at the Midway Veterinary Hospital;
and the strange, shadowy Black Cat
which haunts Edgar Poe's gravesite in Baltimore

ACKNOWLEDGMENTS

I would like to send a special note of thanks to Yvon Owen, Robin Skelton, and Petty Officer Dave Pell, followers of the Wicca religion who shared their knowledge, spells, and insights with me and my research assistants.

I would like to thank Anne Theis, Pat and Fred Wallenberg, Sheriff Lewis Jones III, Carol Butler, J. R. Furqueron, Richmond Poe Museum, and Breck Montague for their kindness in helping with our research in the environs of Richmond, Virginia.

For their help in researching veterinary practices in rural Virginia, I would like to thank M. W. "Tookie" Myers, D.V.M., and Ruth Ann MacQueen, D.V.M., and the entire staff at Midway Veterinary Hospital in Chesapeake, Virginia.

ONE

The earth felt soft and yielding underfoot as I stepped outside on that day in early April. Spring had come to Crowley Creek. The air had a bite in it still and I shivered as I walked along the garden bed. Tiny green spears poked their sharp green pointed leaves above the soil, but many, caught under the mold of the last winter leaves, still clung to the damp black earth.

A light breeze rattled the lilacs and the sweet, cloying smell mixed with the scent of young green shoots and of the newly turned earth. I took a deep breath.

Then I heard a distant muffled sound, a harsh reproachful cry. I looked up. High overhead I saw crows, a black swoop of them. They circled over me, cawing, crying out, as if trying to tell me something. I had a sudden instinctive desire to put my arm over my head, to huddle down. I felt as if a dark shadow had passed over me, and a chill ran up my spine.

Perhaps you think it strange that when I heard those crows on a bright spring day I took it as a bad omen. But consider my heritage.

My name is John Charles Poe and I am a descendant of the famous writer, Edgar Allan Poe. I live in a big old house outside of the town of Crowley Creek, Virginia, where I work as a journalist for the *Crowley Creek Sentinel.*

My life hasn't been the same since my thirtieth birthday, last fall. On that day I inherited the Poe papers.

Ambrose Prynne, the family lawyer, invited me over to his office. The firm, founded by his great-great-whatever-grandfather, had inhabited a gloomy suite of paneled offices above the Crowley Creek First National Bank for generations. From their headquarters he and his forefathers had summoned members of my family from time to time to lecture us about our management of family affairs, so I did not look forward to the meeting.

But, to my surprise, Prynne had called me in for a different purpose. He gave me a decrepit, brassbound oak casket and told me that my ancestor, Edgar Allan Poe, had instructed that the casket be passed along to the first son of each successive generation on his thirtieth birthday. Old E.A. apparently began the tradition when he willed the box to his illegitimate son, Montgomery Alexander Crowley, my great-great-whatever-grandfather and the illustrious founder of Crowley Creek.

"Be advised, John Charles," Prynne said, looking at me intently, "this casket has caused harm to your father and to all your forefathers. I regret deeply that I have no choice, under the will, but to hand it on to you."

I must have looked skeptical, because old Prynne frowned, lowered his voice, looked around as if to be sure no one was listening, and said: "Now, you mark my words, John Charles. Whatever is in this casket has brought darkness into the lives of your forefathers. Take care, the world needs that blithe spirit of yours."

I'm not sure what he meant by *blithe spirit.* He might have been talking about my fondness for Blanton's single-barrel whiskey. In any case, I paid no attention to his dire warnings. It is true that the heavy oak casket and its contents of moldering papers gave me a bad feeling the moment I took possession of it. This is the kind of feeling it is best to ignore, and not long ago I decided to put the casket into a secret hiding place in the library at Crowley House and not take it out again.

How could I know that a flight of ravens would single me out for a message that only the casket papers could interpret?

"John! John Charles!"

"Edith!" I called out. "I'm in the yard out back."

Edith Dunn came out the back door of my antebellum house, down the steps, and out onto the lawn. Lovely looking as ever, she wore a navy blue dress with a long, calf-length skirt and a navy blue straw hat. The dress had tiny white flowers on it, and she picked up the skirt so she could step over the damp sod.

"How are you doing?" I said, glad as always to see her. It sounds funny to say that Edith is my assistant, because she is eight years older and much much wiser. But as a divorcée with two teenage sons, Edith needed work and I jumped at the chance and hired her. Three days a week she works as my research assistant. She has an office in my house. So, while I slave away as a journalist and jack-of-all-trades at the *Crowley Creek Sentinel*, Edith works at my house, doing research for my just-barely-syndicated historical column.

"How come you're all dressed up?" I asked.

"I just got back from having tea with your boss," Edith said, smiling at me.

"Boynton?" I said. "Tea with Mrs. Boynton? You had to have a good reason. Nobody'd do that kind of thing for fun."

"Come on, John Charles," Edith said, smiling mischievously. "Fanny can be so charming when she takes a mind to."

"Is that so? I wish she'd take a mind to be charming to me sometime. Well? Why?"

"Why? I wanted to talk to her about my cousin, Margaret."

"Oh," I said. I looked out past Edith, past the carriage house and beyond it, to the tall stand of oak trees, their tiny green leaves glistening in the soft sunlight. In one of the fields beyond the hedge that marked the edge of my property, I could see a bulldozer digging up the earth. Huge rocky piles of black sod and torn-up tree trunks marked the spot where another house was going up in the Laburnum Estates. They had a passel of houses there already. I never should have sold the land. Why had I? I didn't need the money. The mayor, that toad Jackson Lee Winsome, had promised me that the housing would be for needy folk. But something got lost in translation because imitation Georgian mansions with strange columns and porte cocheres were sprouting up on the property like weeds. They do that kind of thing around Richmond. But who'd have thought it would ever come to Crowley Creek?

"You know, my cousin Margaret . . . John Charles! Are you listening?"

"Of course." There they were again, that dark flight of crows. I couldn't hear them calling, they were too far away. But I could see them, high overhead, circling and circling. I turned and walked toward an iron bench, dusted it off with an old proof sheet I found in my pocket, and gestured to Edith to sit down. She did, smoothing her skirt over her legs. Edith has lovely legs. She also has smooth shiny brown hair, a long graceful neck, and intelligent deep gray eyes that can look right inside you. They were doing that now.

"What is it, John Charles?"

"Why nothing," I said nonchalantly, sitting down beside her. I didn't need to wipe off the seat for myself. After all, it was Saturday. I had on an old pair of jeans, some tired muddy sneakers, and a flannel shirt that had been around forever. Maybe my grandfather, Alexander Crowley Poe, wore it. I can vaguely remember him standing outside in a similar-looking shirt, watching the servants pull his big Pontiac into the carriage house, and grousing that they would scratch it. Crowley Poe had a nasty temper, as did my father, Crowley Poe. That's why I try to keep a lid on mine. I've got the moodiness, the irrational sense of the uncanny, the love of good whiskey, the money, and the house. That's enough. I can do without the black rages that my grandfather inflicted on my father and he on me. "Just . . . for some reason, I saw some crows and they got on my nerves."

She frowned. "Crows? What are you talking about?"

I didn't see how I could explain that I had the feeling the crows were some kind of a bad omen, so I changed the subject. "Don't worry about Margaret. Dr. Cully said she went to see her folks in Durham."

"Well, John Charles, I can tell you one thing. Fanny Boynton doesn't believe it. She says Margaret has left Dr. Cully. Left him for good."

"She should mind her own business. Why can't Margaret go away if she wants to?"

"What is with you, John Charles? You sound like you know more than you're saying."

"I do?"

"Yes, you do. And why aren't you more curious? You know perfectly well that Margaret and Dr. Cully have the perfect marriage. She'd never leave him without a word to anybody."

The way Edith said *perfect marriage* I could tell she thought the idea ridiculous. Maybe the breakup of her own marriage had made her cynical, but I imagine she was just too smart to believe in the myth of "happy ever after." "So what do you think, Edith?"

"I'm worried, John Charles. Real worried. It's not like Margaret to take off without telling anyone. Even if she was angry at Dr. Cully, she's too responsible to do a thing like that. You know how he counts on her down at the vet clinic. She's always got a few animals she's nursing. How could she just go away and leave the whole veterinarian practice on his shoulders? When he's visiting 'round to the farms, who will mind the clinic for the small animals?"

I shook my head.

"You're acting funny, John Charles," Edith said, giving me one of those sharp looks of hers.

"I think you're about to ask me to help find her," I admitted. "You've been leading up to it since you came out here."

She put a hand on my arm. I wished she wouldn't do that. Edith knew how I felt about her, but I wasn't supposed to talk about it. Usually she didn't take advantage, but I guess she was really upset about her cousin. "Yes, I am. You're a great investigator, John Charles. Look how you helped your friend Rod Usher last year."

"That took the two of us."

"Right! Exactly. And the two of us, we can find Margaret."

"Maybe she doesn't want to be found."

"Fine. We won't tell anybody. We'll leave her alone if that's the case. But I don't believe it for a moment; I think something's happened to her."

"I doubt that, I really do," I said, confident that I was right. "Trust me on this. Margaret is fine."

"Oh, I hate it when men say *trust me*," Edith said, exasperated. "I didn't think you would stoop to it, John Charles. If you don't want to help find Margaret, you need to tell me why."

"I'm afraid I can't do that."

"John Charles, I don't understand why you're acting like this," Edith said. She looked like she was getting angry. Her cheeks flushed, her jaw set, she glared at me, challenging me to explain myself. "Didn't Dr. Cully save the life of that dog of yours, that old golden retriever? I know you don't know Margaret that well, but you and Dr. Cully, I thought you two were buddies."

"Oh, we are. We are. Great pals."

"Well—"

Whatever she was about to say was drowned out by the sudden roar of loud rock music. A mechanical synthesized shriek blared into the garden. We both turned to see two kids, one carrying a boom box, forcing their way through the hedge.

"Hey!" I yelled. "Watch it!"

The kids didn't hear. The air reverberated with the throbbing of drums and the wail of electric guitars. I strode toward them. They saw me coming and grinned at me.

Just as I got close enough to grab them, I saw, out of the corner of my eye, a shadowy form, taller than either kid, streak through the bushes in the direction of the house. But my entire attention was focused on putting an end to the hellish din that was polluting the peaceful spring Saturday in my garden. "Cut that out!" I yelled, trying to be heard over the racket.

They just stood there, laughing—a skinny energetic-looking boy of about thirteen and a little girl, obviously his sister, about ten. The boy, a blond with his hair cut short and ears that stuck out, had bright intelligent blue eyes, a sprinkle of freckles, and a sneer. He wore baggy blue jeans that looked two sizes too big and a black Orioles baseball cap, bill pointing backward. He held the boom box on his shoulder with an effort, and kept it pointed in my direction. The little girl, her blond hair in two pigtails tied with big Day-Glo orange puffs, had on a similar outfit and a similar sneer, though hers lacked her brother's bravado.

"Turn that thing off or I'll turn it off for you!" I yelled even louder. No use. Either they couldn't hear me or they didn't want to. I reached over and grabbed the radio from the little twerp. For a moment we tussled for it. He was strong for a kid, but at six feet with the strength that wiry guys come by naturally, I had the jump on him and it was no contest.

I clicked the sound off and took a deep breath. Peace descended upon the garden. I could hear the wind in the oak leaves and the chirping of the robins. "What the heck do y'all think you're doin', coming on my property and blasting me practically out of my socks?"

"Mr. Poe, don't you remember us?" the boy said.

"Can't say I do." I looked closer at him. His arms were covered with scratches, probably from pushing through the hedge. He had a smear of jam in the corner of his mouth. His eyes sparkled with pleasure, as if at a secret joke. He looked as if he were about to burst out laughing.

"What's so funny?" I said, holding the boom box away from him.

"You know who we are," the little girl said. She took a tiny skip and dug her dirty pink sneakers deeper into the mud.

"Are you the Beebee kids?"

"That's us. I'm Travis and this here's Sue Anne. You came to our open-house party."

"You were all dressed up then. So you live in that new house just over my hedge?"

His sister darted a look over my shoulder. Then she pumped a fist in the air and whispered something to her older brother. A long whispered conversation ensued, with the kids glancing at me and then at the house.

"I'm sorry if we made too much noise. Can I have my boom box back?" Travis Beebee said. "We better get on home."

"How's about you leave the radio behind next time and come to the door instead of through the hedge?"

"Cool," Travis said, snatching the boom box away from me. Then the two of them slipped back through the hedge.

"That was kind of strange," I said to Edith as she and I headed back up to the house.

"Cute kids," Edith said. "Who are they?"

"Neighbors. Their parents, Mort and Barbara Jane Beebee, bought that new house in the Estates. The one that looks like the antebellum South meets Disneyland. Kind of a Georgian Pepsi generation."

"Come on, John Charles, it's not that bad. Not everyone inherits a historic Gothic Revival house."

"Right. Mort Beebee is the president of Crowley Creek First National Bank. The kids look real bright. But they acted kind of funny."

We came in through the back door, into the kitchen. "John Charles," Edith began, "about Margaret . . . "

"Excuse me a moment," I said. "I have this funny feeling. Let's go check out the library." We went along the hall. After the big fall hurricane I'd done a lot of renovations. Instead of the familiar smell of dust and old mold, the hallway smelled faintly of paint and varnish. The tall double doors leading into the library were open. Surely I had left them closed? I went in, with Edith right behind me.

What a mess. Muddy footprints on the faded old Turkish carpet. Drawers open, their contents scattered on the floor. Chair cushions flung around. I hurried across the room to the bookshelves, removed a moldering copy of *The Narrative of Gordon Pym*, and opened the deep concealed cupboard behind.

I took out Edgar Allan Poe's casket, brought it over to my father's desk, and set it down.

At midafternoon, light streamed in through the tall library windows. Swirling with dust motes, like channels of energy, the rays shone upon Edgar Allan Poe's ill-fated casket. It was about three feet long, eighteen inches wide, made of blackened oak and strapped with pitted, tarnished brass bands. A large ornate lock, shaped like a two-chambered heart, secured the center band. I pulled out the center drawer of my father's desk, slid back the panel concealed behind it, and removed a tiny key. I opened the casket. Lying within, a heap of yellowed manuscript covered with faded nineteenth-century copperplate handwriting. The papers were tied with shreds of ribbon, the color of pallid skin. I hesitated for a moment. It felt as if my hands resisted my will, but I picked up the top sheaf, studied the ribbon and the knots, removed each sheaf of papers in turn, examining each. Then, with relief I replaced them, carefully relocked the lock, returned the key to its hiding place and the casket back into the dark depths of the bookshelves.

"I don't think whoever broke in here found the casket." I began to walk around the room, examining the disarray. "If not the casket, what could they have been looking for?"

Edith picked up a sofa cushion and, for a moment, held it to her chest, examining the room. "You sure they were looking for something? Maybe it was just some sneak thieves or troublemakers having fun?" She replaced a cushion on the sofa, plumping it as she did so.

"No, I don't think so. And look at that." A big blue and white Chinese bowl stood on a side table. Mrs. Slack, my housekeeper, had filled it with sprays of willow, now opening into tiny green fuzzy catkins. Caught in one of the branches, something glinted in the sunlight. Edith went over, pulled it loose, and held it out to me. We both stared at it.

The object in Edith's hand glowed, as if lit from within with a faint, pulsing white light. She turned her hand so that I could see it was a smooth, luminous stone, perhaps a moonstone, on which a strange design had been inscribed.

At first the design appeared to be simply a few elegantly curved lines, but as I looked closer, I saw an eye.

"I think it's a Wicca talisman," I said.

I put out my hand and Edith dropped the talisman into it. It felt cold and heavy, and for a moment I had a powerful instinct to fling it away, but I resisted the impulse. The stone had been crudely set into a silver oval to create a brooch. A shred of purple silk clung to the shaft of the closure, as if the pin had been ripped off something. I slipped it into my pocket.

Now I saw something else. Across the library floor, mingling with the muddy footprints, were other markings. Tiny, three-pointed footprints. "Edith, look at that."

"A cat," Edith said.

"And look there." The pawprints led directly from the library door to the bookshelf, right to the spot beneath the casket's hiding place. But the other footprints did not follow. They crisscrossed the room, from the desk to the side table, from the door to the sofa. Could it be that the animal knew what its master sought to discover?

"You have a bad feeling about this, don't you, John Charles?" Edith asked.

"Don't you?"

Edith shook her head. "Well, I admit, it's puzzling. But look on the bright side. They didn't find the Poe papers and nothing is really damaged and nothing has been stolen."

"Of course," I said. Of course.

When I got to the office, Buzz Marco, our intern from the Columbia School of Journalism, hadn't shown up. On the other

hand, the proprietor of the paper, Ma Boynton, appeared to be
lurking in her office, and the moment I walked in I knew she
was in a foul mood.

"Is that you, John Charles?" she demanded, coming out of
her private inner office and stalking over to my workstation. No
privacy for John Charles Poe today, it seemed. The *Sentinel*
had a subscription to the Nexis database. Nexis contains most
of the major newspaper and magazine articles printed in the
U.S. It's expensive, so I haven't subscribed at home. Strictly
speaking, I'm not entitled to use the office access for my column. For that reason, I tend to hit Nexis on Saturday or Sunday, when the office is officially closed. Of course, Boynton is
a workaholic, so this plan rarely pans out.

The only person with a private office at the *Crowley Creek
Sentinel* is Mrs. Boynton. Buzz and I, the two ad salespeople, the
typesetter-designer, and the bookkeeper all share the big open
storefront room that looks out onto Central Avenue, right in
the heart of downtown Crowley Creek. That way we are avail-
able to be hassled at any time by Mrs. Boynton. And should
anyone have a story they want published, they can just drop
right in and lay it on us.

"Hello, Mrs. Boynton," I said, taking off my windbreaker
and hanging it on the coat tree. "What are you doing, working
on a nice spring Saturday? Why aren't you out on the links?"

Mrs. Boynton sniffed. Her husband, Roger Boynton, the
original proprietor and official editor of the *Sentinel*, had spent
most of his working life on the golf course, at the races, or
drinking with his town cronies. A great friend of my father,
he'd ended up in the sanatarium with a stroke and gout just
about the same time my father succumbed to heart failure. But
for as long as I could remember, Mrs. Boynton had been the
one who really ran the paper, and now, increasingly, she has become the center of a powerful cabal that dominates town poli-
tics. She knows everything that happens in town, often before
it happens. She is a short, stout woman with a helmet of thinning russet curls, a pugnacious jaw, and little brown eyes that
stare out balefully from under puffy eyelids. She wears a choker

of pearls with a flashing diamond clasp, shapeless silk dresses in summer and shapeless wool suits in winter. Because my family has been in Crowley Creek as long or longer than hers, she tends to assume I am her ally and it infuriates and surprises her each time she realizes she has miscalculated.

"On the links? Young man, I have a paper to run, as you well know. Nobody else is going to do it for me, that's for sure. Didn't you say Buzz would be here today? No sign of him. Not that that's any big surprise. New Yorkers, all flash, no stick-to-itiveness."

"Maybe he logged in from home."

Mrs. Boynton looked at me suspiciously. She hasn't quite grasped the new computer technology and whenever I mention it she suspects I'm pulling her leg. "More likely he went home to New York City for the weekend. One less stranger in town, so it's not all bad. The place is going to the dogs, all the new folks in town."

This surprised me. I felt pretty sure Mrs. Boynton was a major investor in the Laburnum Estates. New people meant more profit for her. I wondered what she had on her mind.

"I haven't heard about any new folks in town aside from the Beebees," I said, sitting down at my terminal and firing it up.

"You haven't? You mean you haven't met that Noir girl yet?"

"What new-war girl is that?"

"Not new-war. Noir, like black in the French language. Julie Noir. Now *she's* someone Crowley Creek can do without."

"How's that?"

A shadow crossed the room. Someone walking along the sidewalk outside the window. I looked out, but the sun shone full into the room now and all I could see was a black shape. Beyond, cars drove slowly by, their paintwork reflecting the sun.

"You mean you haven't seen Crowley Creek's newest citizen? Now there's one strange girl, I can tell you that, John Charles."

"Strange? How?"

"Everybody's talking about it. She wears a ring in her nose, this ugly cross around her neck that has a hole in the top, and her hair hanging all over her face. She's an odd one, and no mistake."

"How old is she? Lots of teenagers in Richmond have their noses pierced. Kind of harmless, to my mind."

"Harmless? John Charles, you don't know what you are talking about. This girl is one nasty piece of work. Seems she got a job working for Dr. Cully and not long after, his wife Margaret just up and disappeared."

"I've heard about that. But how could this Noir girl have anything to do with Margaret's going away?"

"Well, people are suspicious. There's those that say that thing around her neck is an ankh."

"Say what?"

"An ankh, John Charles. A witch charm. They say she's a witch and she wanted Margaret's job at the clinic, so she did her black magic and Margaret disappeared."

"Oh come on, Mrs. Boynton. Who are you kidding? Surely you don't believe that."

"Of course I don't," Mrs. Boynton said, not meeting my eyes and fingering her pearl necklace as she tends to do when she's plotting something. "But Margaret *has* disappeared. Nobody knows where she is. Your friend Edith Dunn doesn't believe she'd leave on her own. Edith is worried, I can tell you. And there's little Miss Mysterious, working at the clinic. That girl is making lots of enemies in this town. I, for one, won't be sorry to see the back of her."

Fingering her pearl choker and smiling nastily, Mrs. Boynton walked back to her office and shut the door.

I stared after her, and I thought I felt that moonstone talisman, cold and heavy, move slightly in my pocket.

TWO

"You okay, John Charles?" Cully leaned over the table and looked closely at me, as if I were an animal exhibiting curious symptoms in need of a diagnosis.

"Right as rain," I said.

Cully looked unconvinced. He smoothed his hair over the top of his head and looked around The Old Forge, Crowley Creek's premier watering hole. There was plenty to see. Ten years ago, Tommy White, the owner and an old friend of mine since we beat each other to a draw on the playground at Jefferson elementary, hit the jackpot on a trip to Las Vegas, took his winnings, and bought a boarded-up old tavern on Central Avenue. He cleaned it up, covered the uneven walls with brass horseshoes and brass bugles and brass coach lamps and brass warming pans and . . . well, you get the idea. The place still shows its age though, the floorboards uneven and darkened with resin-based stain and spilled beer, the paint along the cornices and on the tin ceiling thick and discolored with cooking grease that obscures the detail. But the brass rail along the bar shines with many polishings, and reflected in the mirror be-

hind the bar you can see the shelf of town trophies for best
baton twirling in the Independence Day parade. And Tommy
never stops adding things. On the wall right behind Lawrence
Cully's head, I noticed that Tommy had put a little light under
his brass-framed litho of Patrick Henry's famous "Give me lib-
erty or give me death" moment. The light beamed upward so
you could see Patrick clutching his heart and pointing outward,
gesturing toward Tommy's wall of brass colonial memorabilia.
It made you wonder what Patrick thought of the row of ketchup
and hot-sauce bottles, the jukebox, and the gum-ball machine.

Early on a Saturday evening, the place hadn't started to fill
up, and Cully and I had been talking softly, so as not to be over-
heard.

I hadn't yet really gotten into my first glass of Blanton's
single-barrel, but Cully had finished his Jack Daniel's and I
watched as he restlessly stirred the melting ice cubes left in the
glass with his little plastic spear. He ate a few peanuts and
looked around for Tommy. "Hey, Tommy, you forget your
friends in time of need?" he called out. Behind the bar Tommy
nodded and reached for a bottle to pour us a second round.
Cully didn't usually get ahead of me, and I looked more closely
at him.

The fellow had been down the last few days, but tonight he
looked different. Tense, wired. Younger. Dr. Lawrence Cully
had to be fifty, maybe even in his mid-fifties. He had thinning
gray hair, which he combed carefully over his bald spot; sweet
brown eyes, like an aging cocker spaniel's; and full lips, which
tended to curve into a gentle caring smile.

I have known Cully ever since, as a kid, I had trusted my
beloved golden retriever, Maybelle, to him, and he—then a
young vet, new in town—had stayed awake for thirty-six hours,
fighting to save her from a seemingly incurable bout of acute
gastroenteritis. Now his kind eyes were bright with nervous
energy as if he had found his second wind. Maybe he had heard
good news from Margaret.

Tommy brought over our drinks and Cully picked up his in

both hands and pressed the glass against his lips. He put it down without drinking. "You okay, John Charles?" he said again.

"Edith came to see me this morning," I said. "She wants me to help find Margaret. Said she's worried about her."

Cully sighed. "Maybe we didn't handle it right, Margaret and me. Lord knows, I'll never understand women. But I promised Margaret I wouldn't tell anyone that she'd left. And I have to keep my promise, you know that. I have to give her time."

I nodded. Though, of course, strictly speaking, Cully broke his promise to Margaret when he told me.

I'd gone by his house, late, day before yesterday, to drop off a proof of an ad he'd put in the *Sentinel* for a new treatment of cow mastitis.

Cully had greeted me at the door, mumbling a hello, not able to look me in the eye. To my surprise, he smelled strongly of bourbon and his stained knit shirt hung out over his khaki pants, which looked creased and grimy. Cully enjoyed his whiskey but I never remembered seeing him overdo it before— and normally he was a spick-and-span sort of fellow.

The Cullys lived in a renovated frame farmhouse, about a mile out of Crowley Creek. They'd built an addition, where Cully had his small-animal clinic. He led me back to his den. We walked through the hall, past the living and dining rooms and the kitchen. Everything looked neat as always, but the lights were off and the rooms seemed strangely deserted.

Once he opened the door to his private hangout, I saw that he must have been living there for several days. He had plates of take-out leftovers stacked on his desk, the wastebasket over-flowed with empty whiskey bottles, and the room smelled of stale sweat, bourbon, and moldering pizza.

"Cully! What's going on?"

"Margaret and I . . . ," he mumbled. He sank down on his La-Z-Boy chair, stretched out his hand to a glass sitting on the side of the table, and tried to pick it up. But his hand bumped the glass and it spilled onto the rug. "Oh, Lord. . . ."

I knelt down next to his chair, picked up the glass and the

ice cubes, and set them back down on the little cherry table beside his chair.

"Troubles?" I said. How sad and pathetic he looked. The hair usually combed over the top of his head hung down over one ear and his bald spot shone in the lamplight. Two days' growth of gray stubble shadowed his chin and his eyes were sunken in and bleary.

"Promised not to talk about it."

"You can trust me," I said, my heart going out to him.

"But I couldn't have her here, not after the way she acted. She didn't leave me, John Charles, you've got to believe that," he said, looking at me for the first time. " 'Why'd you do that?' I said to her. 'How could you bear to hurt poor helpless creatures? They can't fight back. They only understand love. Not pain.' She didn't used to be like that, John Charles. Something went wrong in her head. See, going away, it was mutual, you've got to believe that. She said she just needed some time, time to pull herself together. Time to think. See things clearly. And that's what I've got to do. See things clearly. Know what I mean?"

I had no idea what he meant. What poor helpless creatures?

"You can't tell a soul, promise?"

"Of course I promise."

"Anybody asks you about Margaret, where she is, when she's coming back, you just say you don't know. That's best. 'Cause you don't know, John Charles. I didn't tell you she went away to get her head straight, did I?"

"Of course you didn't," I said, not understanding, only seeing an old friend, sad, out of control, and wishing I hadn't.

"I can't see her shamed in front of everyone. I couldn't bear it, the whole town talking about her. Saying she's had a breakdown. She's always been so respected in town. Everybody loves her, isn't that right?"

"Yes, that's right," I said gently.

" 'Kind Margaret Cully, give you the shirt off her back,' that's what they say about her. Never let down the church folks, takes the Brownies on a special tour of the clinic, always something for the bake sale, spends hours cooking for it, salt of the earth, Margaret . . . that's true, that's real, nothing changes that, right?"

I didn't answer fast enough, because he suddenly sat up in his chair, swung his legs around, stared at me belligerently, and shouted, "Right? That right?"

"Yes. Right," I said quickly. "Loved by all."

He leaned back. "After the fire, every lady in town brought a casserole. They wouldn't do that if they didn't love her, would they?"

"You need a good night's sleep," I told him. "Things will look better in the morning. Why don't you go upstairs, lie down."

"Can I count on you, John Charles?" he said, getting up carefully, putting a hand on the wall to steady himself.

"Yes, yes, of course," I said. "You can count on me."

Now, as we drank together at The Old Forge, I could see that Cully was studying me closely, maybe trying to decide if he could still trust me with his secrets. Being a sensitive fellow, he probably saw how much it bothered me to keep things from a close friend like Edith.

"I hate to see Edith worrying so, but I understand why you don't want to talk about it," I said. I drained the last of my drink and shoved it aside. It slid along the varnished wooden table until it came to rest against the paper-napkin holder. Talking about private things had always seemed to me a bad idea. The less you thought about them, the better. "How's it going at the clinic?"

"Now there's a piece of luck!" Cully said. He grinned, as if at a secret. "Just about a week before Margaret, uh . . . you know . . . took her . . . uh . . . vacation, this girl came 'round looking for a job helping in the clinic. Poor thing. Dead broke. Lots of experience with animals, willing to work cheap, like a gift from God, John Charles, because Margaret—to tell you the truth—well, she hadn't been pulling her weight for a long while. So I hired her and she's worked out real well. A bit strange, but then, the animals don't care. They just need a gentle, patient hand and she's gifted that way. Julie. Julie Noir. She's coming by in a bit for a drink, you can meet her for yourself."

I didn't feel it would be appropriate to tell Cully what Mrs. Boynton had said about Julie Noir. Fact is, I'd take Cully's judgment before Boynton's anytime. We drank quietly for a while. The place had started to fill up. Someone had turned on the jukebox and k. d. lang crooned out her sorrow over lost love. Woman had a voice like warm honey. Every time I glanced over at Cully I felt sorry for him. Here the man's wife has left him and he's getting tanked on a Saturday night. That's OK when you're my age, but at fifty, it seemed sad to me. Then I slipped my hand into my pocket and touched the cool, etched surface of the talisman we'd found that morning in the willow wands.

My fingers closed around it and I pulled it out of my pocket and put it on the table. "Ever see anything like this before?" I asked Cully. He reached out for it, then pulled his hand back and stared at it more closely. Just as he was about to speak, a woman's voice, soft and tentative, said, "How did my talisman get there?"

"Julie!" Cully said, getting up and gesturing in a courtly fashion. "How you doin'? This here's my old friend, John Charles. Works for the *Crowley Creek Sentinel*. Will you join us? Have a seat."

I could see right away how Julie had got on the wrong side of Fanny Boynton. She had to be one of the strangest-looking girls I'd ever seen in Crowley Creek. Or woman. Hard to tell. She could have been anywhere from fourteen to twenty-four. Small and fine-boned, she stood beside the table slightly hunched over, her head down, staring at the talisman. Raven-black hair tumbled in waves halfway down her back and, parted in the middle, over most of her face. What I could see of her face showed her to be very pale, with long black lashes, an upturned nose with a tiny gold stud in it, and a soft little mouth.

She had deep purple circles, like bruises, under her eyes, and when she turned her head to look more closely at the talisman, her hair fell forward and I could see a row of thin gold rings along the rims of her ears. Stuck through the lobes she wore earrings of sharp multifaceted crystals which dangled down, twisting and fiery at her throat. She must have had eight or nine holes pierced into each ear.

On her shoulder sat a large, black cat who stared unblinkingly at me out of brilliant slanted green eyes, its tail slowly moving back and forth. As I looked back at it, it slowly stretched out a paw, as if to shake hands, then it extended its claws. For a moment I thought it might be trying to scratch me, but then I had the strange idea that the cat had taken my measure and warned me: *Don't fool with Julie.* As soon as I thought that, he retracted his claws and turned his head and his unblinking green stare to Cully.

"Sit down? I don't know . . . sure I won't be interrupting your time with your friend?" she said in a whispery, hesitant voice.

"Not at all, not at all," Cully said, his voice kind, obviously picking up on her shyness. "I'd love for you to meet John Charles. After all, you're part of the Cully family now. Slide right in there next to him and go ahead and have a look at that pin. I thought it looked familiar. Yours, isn't it? Where'd you say you found it, John Charles?"

I moved over and Julie sat down on the bench next to me. For an instant I thought I felt a chill emanating from her, and I moved farther away.

Our table was one of the booths that run along the back of The Old Forge. High-backed red-leather bench seats provide some privacy, but they are bolted in place, making it hard to get in and out. Julie sat down on the outside edge of the bench and her cat turned and looked at me again. He had a faint white streak on the side of his chest. It reminded me of something but I couldn't think what. Julie turned toward me and brushed her hair back out of her eyes with a gesture I found strangely sexy. "Hello, John Charles," she said. I saw that she had green eyes, the same color as the cat's, and that her skin was so translucent you could see fine blue veins beneath it. "This is Asmodeus, my best friend. Say hello to John Charles, Asmodeus."

The cat jumped gracefully onto the table without upsetting a glass or moving a piece of cutlery. I had been holding my tumbler of bourbon with a view to taking a sip. Asmodeus reached out a paw and gently ran it down my sleeve. Thankfully, his claws stayed retracted.

"He likes you," Julie said.

I'm a dog person but I have to admit that being liked by a cat, especially one that looked as arrogant and domineering as Asmodeus, felt flattering.

"Hello, Asmodeus," I said, playing along.

The cat stared at me and I was mesmerized. As if the cat were transmitting a message to me—but I had no idea what was in it. Then he seemed to go into receiving mode and I could not drop my eyes from that hypnotic stare as he looked deep into me. Finally his eyes released me, and he turned his brilliant gaze to Julie, as if to pass along what he had learned. I blinked, grabbed my drink, and took a deep gulp just as the cat bounded back onto Julie's shoulder.

The Blanton's single-barrel bourbon did its usual magic and the strange feeling passed. Asmodeus now looked just like a big black cat, not like a . . . whatever.

"You said this is your talisman?" I asked Julie, my voice surprising me by sounding perfectly normal.

"I lost one like it. . . . I'd need to touch it to be sure," Julie said. She pointed to the design graven into the stone. "That's an *udjat* carved on it. The eye of Ra. You really need a pair, the Eye of Ra and the Eye of Aah, to be sure you are protected from evil. I can't understand how I could lose one and not the other. May I hold it?"

I had no idea what she was talking about. "Sure, go ahead."

She reached out and picked it up. "Oh!" she said.

"What?"

"It's yours now." She took my hand, which was lying on the table next to my glass, her fingers cool and almost limp, her touch delicate, and dropped the talisman into my palm. "I can feel that it has left me and become yours," she said. "I'll get another, don't worry." But I could see she looked puzzled.

"What's the matter? What do you mean it's mine?" I asked her.

Her hair had fallen over her eyes and she brushed it back. Now I saw that, fastened to the silk shawl, patterned in scrolls of black, gray, and purple, which she wore wrapped around her shoulders, she had a pin carved with the same design as on the one I had found. But on her pin, the eye shape had been carved onto an oval piece of jet, set into silver. Our two pins were virtually identical, except mine was white and hers black.

"Julie," Cully said. "How about a drink? Would you like a beer?"

"I'll have an iced tea, thank you," Julie said.

"Julie is a witch, or so she tells me," Cully said.

"I am a follower of the ancient religion of Wicca," Julie said. "It's very helpful for my work at the clinic since it is a nature religion." For the first time she smiled, and I saw that she had shiny white teeth and a rosy tongue, like a cat's.

"Of course it is, Julie," Cully said.

"Hello there, my friends. Mind if I join you for a moment?"

"Hello, Fairchild," I said. I hoped the fellow could not hear my annoyance. The Right Reverend Rowland Fairchild was a fool, in my opinion. He led the town's Episcopalian church. Most people in town were Baptists, although we had a small crew of Methodists and various Pentecostals. And now one Wiccan. Not that it mattered what religion you are. I wouldn't like to say that Fairchild was a snob because he was an Episcopalian—maybe he was Episcopalian because he was a snob. My folks had been Episcopalians but I regard myself as a skeptic. All men of the cloth, no matter what denomination, tend to get on my nerves. Someone once said it's because I think they are judging me. That might be right. Or it might be that most of them are jerks.

"Sit down, Rowland, sit down," Cully said, patting the seat beside him. "Join us."

"I hope I'm not interrupting anything," Fairchild said.

Yes, you are, I thought. You're interrupting something real bizarre.

"Have you met Julie Noir, my new assistant at the clinic?" Cully said. "Julie, Rowland Fairchild, he's the minister at St. George's, just past the four corners. You know, that pretty old colonial church?"

"I've seen it," Julie said in her soft little voice. She tilted her head down so that her hair fell over her face and took a sip of her iced tea.

"Beautiful cat you have there," Fairchild said in his phony sweet voice.

"Asmodeus, say hello to Reverend Fairchild," Julie said. The cat hunched its shoulders, stared at Fairchild, and hissed.

"He doesn't like you," Julie said.

Fairchild laughed nervously. "Cats are very independent, they say."

"Yes, they are," Julie said, tilting her head so that her hair fell back off her face and staring for a moment at Reverend Fairchild. "I apologize for his rudeness."

"Think nothing of it."

"Have a drink, Rowland. The next round's on me," Cully said jovially, trying to cut through the tension that had overtaken us all as soon as Fairchild sat down. "John Charles and I are having bourbon, what will you have?"

"Nothing for me, thank you. I'll just have a glass of ice water," Fairchild said. He took a large white-linen handkerchief out of his pocket and carefully wiped his forehead. Fairchild is a tall slender man, late thirties, with a long pale face and long straw-colored hair swept back from his forehead and styled into waves.

The man got on my nerves. "Come on, Fairchild, loosen up. Have a drink with us. We won't tell on you."

Julie smiled. "We won't tell on you," she repeated in her soft little voice. She ran her hand through her hair and shook it off her face. Every time she did that I felt it. Maybe Fairchild felt her strange sex appeal too. Or maybe her peculiar remark got to him, because he stared at her for a moment, then he looked at his watch.

"Heavens! I had no idea it was so late. Please excuse me. Nice to have met you, Miss Noir. Good-bye John Charles, Dr. Lawrence, take care and have a good day." Awkwardly, he extricated himself from the table, and in a moment, he had worked his way past the crowd clustered around the bar and vanished out the front door.

"What a sanctimonious pain in the butt," I said. "Let's have that other round you promised, Cully. That man makes me real thirsty."

"I'm with you there, John Charles," Cully said, looking after Fairchild thoughtfully. "I'm with you there."

Asmodeus jumped from Julie's shoulder to the floor. He gazed up at her. "I have to go now," Julie said.

Cully and I looked at each other and Cully smiled. "Best you go right home. It's probably not a good idea to be walking around alone on a Saturday night. Some of the boys may be feeling like mixing it up and a young woman alone . . . "

"I need to pick some herbs tonight," Julie said. "You know that slow-minded sweet red setter, belongs to Sue Anne Beebee? The one that got run over?"

Cully nodded, a worried look crossing his face.

"He's not getting better like he should. So I have to get out and find some special herbs to help him, while the moon is full. Asmodeus and I think now is the time to go, Dr. Cully." She didn't look at him. She slid off the bench with a graceful movement, adjusted her long silk shawl around her. It fell in sensual folds, the fringe waving slightly as she wove her way through the crowd and the smoke and out the door. We both looked after her.

"I hope you don't mind me saying this," I said, "but boy, is she strange. And her cat is strange too."

Cully took a deep swig of his bourbon and looked around for Tommy. "I know, John Charles. But that girl arrived in town without a penny or a friend. When I hired her, she was darn near starving with hunger. I needed help and she turns up, you know?"

"What does Margaret think of her?"

"Just what you'd guess. Margaret felt sorry for her. Margaret said she'd had a real tough life and if we just showed her some kindness and kind of ignored her weirdness, she'd get better. They got along great."

"Everyone gets along with Margaret," I said. I looked at my watch, looked out the door. "I wonder where Marilyn is? She was supposed to meet me here half an hour ago. If you'll excuse me, I think I'll just wander over to The Cutting Edge and see what's keeping her."

"Sure thing. And on your way out, how about you send Tommy over with another round?"

The Cutting Edge, Marilyn Larue's beauty salon, is only five doors down Central Avenue from The Old Forge. At six-thirty, light still streamed out from the windows, and when I opened the door, I heard Crystal Gale telling the ladies that her heart was breaking, breaking, breaking. Not that anyone was listening. Blow-dryers roared full blast, and ladies' voices competed, talking shrilly above the commotion. Bright lights reflected off mirrors and I smelled hairspray, shampoo, perfume, and that cosy odor of heated hair. Marilyn sat at the reception counter, her face twisted into a scowl, filling in an order form.

"Hey, Marilyn!" I said, loud enough to be heard over the din.

She looked up, saw me, and her face broke into a happy smile. "John Charles! Thanks for coming by. Just what I need to get me over my mad."

Marilyn Larue and I had been dating off and on for about seven months. Yet every time I saw her I felt the same tense, nervous little thrill of pleasure at my good luck. Marilyn has bright blue eyes; a tall curly mass of blond hair, which never looks quite the same but always suggests that somehow she has mussed it getting out of bed; a lush inviting body, which she enjoys showing off; and a wide, generous smile. She likes to play the dumb blonde, but Marilyn is one of the sharpest people in Crowley Creek. She sees right through to the core of things and has one of the best bullshit detectors of anyone I know. The problem between us is my drinking. Marilyn thinks I should cut back. I don't agree.

"What's the trouble? What's got you mad?"

"I'll tell you as soon as we get out of here. I'm ready to go. Tiffany can close up."

Outside, the action had picked up. Cars cruised slowly down the street, rock music blasting from their open windows into the evening air. Most of the stores had closed and last-minute shoppers could be seen packing their trunks with bags and loading their kids into car seats before taking off into the night. The air had grown cool and the breeze picked up, scudding torn newspapers and bits of grit down the street.

"Teenage girls!" Marilyn said, as we walked down Central Avenue. "I don't know what the world is coming to, I really don't. Used to be, teenage girls either giggled and talked about boys or cried and talked about boys. Now more and more they *act* like boys, know what I mean?"

"No, I don't."

"These two girls came in this afternoon for perms and streaks. We spent pretty near four hours on the little vixens and then they didn't like their dos. Not what they wanted. Uncool. Too hick. So all of a sudden the little witches just let loose, go on a rampage, and smash a whole row of color products. Just straighten their arms, swing, and *boom*. Then *crash crash crash*, bottles hitting the floor, and they're screaming fit to beat the band. Then they let out this dirty-mouth foul stream of curses and take off. Laughing. Leaving behind one heck of a mess. About three hundred dollars' worth."

"Marilyn, that's terrible. What did you do?"

"Both their mothers are hardworking women. On their own. Husbands left 'em. Trying to raise kids on part-time salaries, you know? I need to think about what I'm going to do.

Besides ordering a whole new supply of russet red and ash-brown hair color, that is. Anyway, I feel better now that I have that off my chest. What's new with you?"

We'd reached the little park across from the town hall. Near where the memorial statue of the Confederate Soldier stands on guard, we sat down on a bench. Marilyn opened her handbag and took out a bag of unshelled peanuts, which she loves. She started cracking them open and handing the nuts to me.

"You met this girl, Julie Noir? Works for Dr. Cully?"

"That is one sad little girl, John Charles. She's left some big trouble behind her, I'd say."

"She says she's a witch."

"Well, I don't put much stock in that myself. Teenagers like to act up. They're all witches or punkers or hip-hoppers or something. I don't follow the different flavors. But whatever she's into, she's sure thrown a scare into some people in town. I hear they were talking about her over at the Emmanuel Baptist last Sunday after church. How she's a pagan and an evil influence. You know Crowley Creek, John Charles. They don't take too well to Comeheres who are different."

"And that cat . . . "

"Yeah, I saw the cat."

"Didn't it give you a funny feeling, that cat?"

"How so, John Charles?" Marilyn asked, turning toward me. Now I could smell her perfume. When she handed me a peanut, she gently touched my hand and I felt her skin, warm and caressing.

"Let's drive out to Murphy's Steak 'n' Ribs and have dinner," I said, thinking that the sooner we had dinner, the sooner I could invite Marilyn back to my place. "My Bronco's parked back down the street in front of The Old Forge."

"Okay," Marilyn said, pleased. She was always disappointed if we ate in town. She liked to go to one of the nice restaurants between here and Richmond.

We got into the Bronco and headed out of town. But about a half mile out, as we were driving by one of the fields that had been left to fallow, I saw two muscle cars parked helter-skelter by the side of the road. The windows were down. I could hear shouts and laughter and something about the sounds, loud and mocking, disturbed me. "Hang on a minute, Marilyn," I said, jamming on the brakes and screeching onto the shoulder. I jumped out and ran over to the cars.

Three teenage boys had gathered around a slight figure. As I got closer, I saw Julie Noir, a small shadowy presence surrounded by the taller boys, and I could hear Asmodeus, hissing.

"Let's see you do a spell, get yourself out of this!" a mocking male voice said. "Fly away on a broomstick! Your shit not working tonight, huh? What you got there? Weeds? Let's see that!"

"No!"

"Come on. What is it? Grass? Can I have a smoke? Ha-ha!"

The boys' voices sounded a mixture of bravado, fear, and menace. "Give it over, give it over, or we'll take it!" one of the boys said, lunging at Julie.

"Cut it out!" I shouted.

The boys turned, their faces white in the beam of my headlights. I didn't recognize any of them, but I saw that they looked to be in their midteens. They wore baseball caps turned backward, windbreakers, and faded jeans. As I got closer, I smelled beer on their breath and I saw that they stood in that cocky, menacing way young men do when they want trouble and don't care what form it comes in.

"What are y'all doing?" I said, my voice calm, even. "Why are you bothering this lady?"

"She a friend of yours? You one of those witches too?" one of the boys, the shortest and the most belligerent, sneered. Good-looking, about five feet seven, black short hair slicked back, little black eyes and ears that stuck out, he contorted his face into a tough-guy mask. "She don't like it, why don't she vanish in a puff of smoke?"

"She's been picking poisonous weeds. We're gotta take 'em off her, protect her," one of the taller boys said.

"It's just wild thyme," Julie said in her soft, vulnerable voice.

"Wild time, wild time," mocked the black-haired boy.

"Yeah, let's have a wild time. Where's your car?"

"I don't have a car, I walked," Julie said.

A moment of silence while the three absorbed this further evidence of total weirdness. Nobody walked any farther than a block in Crowley Creek.

"Come on y'all, lay off," I said. "Get back in your cars and go on to wherever you were going on to, okay?"

"No way. I want to see this witch fly out of here the same way she flew in," the tallest boy said. About six foot three, he had carroty-red hair that hung down over his eyes and wore his jacket with the collar turned up. I could see they were working their way up to a confrontation and I tensed. The three of them circled around me. The short one in front, his dark little eyes staring angrily at me, his mouth tight.

"I said, go on, go on home." Now I, too, was getting angry.

"We don't go without her. I think she needs a ride," the short black-haired kid said. His fists came out of his pockets and he began to rock back and forth on the balls of his feet.

"Yeah, she needs a ride," the third kid said, stepping menacingly toward me. The most muscular of the three, he had about twenty pounds on me. His jacket stretched tight across his back and his pale face, pocked with acne on the cheeks flushed red. "We say she wants to come with us. You gonna stop us?"

The redhead grabbed at Julie. Asmodeus, hissing, jumped on him and began to scratch at his face. Blood ran out of the scratches, but I noticed Asmodeus did not go for his eyes. The kid struggled, grabbing at Asmodeus, trying to pull him off. "Hey! Get this freaking cat offa me! Get him off!"

I started toward him, wanting to help. But the acne-faced boy who had moved in on me swung a punch. I stiffened my arm and straight-armed him. He hadn't expected it. He over-balanced and fell into the brush by the side of the road. I ran toward Julie. Asmodeus had not let up on the redheaded boy who had grabbed her. He fell to the ground and Asmodeus jumped onto him, hissing, but the black-haired boy now had Julie. He held her close, in front of him, and screamed at me, "Call the cat off! Call him off!"

"Let her go!"

"Call that devil cat off, or you're dead meat!" The kid's face twisted with rage and he started to drag Julie toward his car. I came up behind him and grabbed his arms. I broke his hold on Julie and he let her go, turned on me, his fist slamming into my shoulder.

"Run Julie, run! Get to the car!" I yelled. I heard Marilyn shouting, "Come on, come on Julie honey!"

Julie took off toward the Bronco, Asmodeus a black shadow behind her. The black-haired kid swung at me, his breath coming in short angry gasps. I ducked, backed off a few paces, looked him in the eye. "Let it be, son," I said.

I could hear the kid who had been attacked by Asmodeus sobbing and swearing, and now the one I had knocked down was up and coming toward me. Then I heard the Bronco door slam, and the motor rev up.

"Your friend is hurt, you need to get him looked after."

"I need to get you . . . looked after," the black-haired kid gasped. He swung a right at my jaw. He had a lot of spunk, and that nasty, choked-down aggression you sometimes see in shorter guys. I ducked low, then punched him in the gut. I heard the air go out of him and he fell backward, landed with an ugly thump, then rolled over and began to make retching sounds. Just beyond where he had landed, the moon lit up a patch of thistles. I gave him a good shove in the butt and he lurched into it.

The redhead sat huddled on the ground, wiping trickles of blood from long, shallow scratches on his face. The muscular, acne-faced kid stood a few paces from me, watching. I turned and our eyes met. He put up a hand and backed off. "No trouble, I don't want any more trouble, okay?"

"Okay," I said. I slouched back to the Bronco. Marilyn leaned over and opened the driver's door. I got in and drove off the shoulder onto the road, gravel spurting up behind the wheels in an angry hiss, as the adrenaline drained away. "What a stupid . . . "

"It's okay, John Charles," Marilyn said.

"That the best you can do, beat up on a bunch of kids?" I said aloud to myself, accelerating so the tires screeched. "Let's get you home," I said to Julie. "Looks like Dr. Cully was right when he told you Saturday night's not the best night for finding herbs in Crowley Creek."

"Oh, I don't know," Julie said. "After all, I got my herbs and you obeyed the Eye of Aah, didn't you?"

I took a hand off the wheel and reached into my pocket. The talisman slid into my grasp, as if it had a will of its own.

THREE

should of come out and helped you. I'm sorry, John Charles," Marilyn said. She sat over on her side of the Bronco, her face looking drawn.

"Oh no, Marilyn," I said.

"What did they want?" Marilyn asked Julie.

"Their spirits were in turmoil and the moon drew them, but they did not understand," Julie said. "Like many, they fear the Goddess."

"She's shivering, John Charles. We need to get her home."

"Yes, Asmodeus and I would like to go home. Thank you," Julie said from the backseat. "Those men disturbed the peace of our Mother Earth, and I am afraid that their negative energies have spoiled the wild thyme." She leaned forward. "John Charles, you are no longer angry, are you?"

"I don't know," I said.

"Will you hold my wild thyme to try and cleanse it from the male anger that those three unleashed upon it? Sue Anne's red setter was run over by two drunken teenage boys, and anger has gotten into his bones so that he cannot heal. I wanted so much to pick wild thyme in the peace of the Goddess and the full moon so that I could make a poultice. . . . "

"I hate it when men fight, I just hate it!" Marilyn burst out. "John, you pass my house on the way back to the Cullys', right?"

"Yes, they're out on Highway Twenty-two."

"Would you mind dropping me off? I've lost my appetite. It's been a rotten day and I just don't feel like going out."

"Of course, if that's what you want."

"I do," she said, turning her face away from me.

"I am sorry for your bad memories," Julie said. "If you would like, I could make you a tisane of—"

"What do you mean, bad memories?" Marilyn snapped. "I've had a miserable day and I just want to go home, okay?"

"Sorry," Julie said. In the rearview mirror I saw her drop her head so that her black hair fell over her face. She held Asmodeus close to her breast and stroked him and the cat pressed up against her.

I dropped Marilyn off and walked her to her door. "Forgive me, John Charles," she said, putting a hand on my arm. "You were great back there. Call me tomorrow. I'll find a way to make it up to you." She stretched up and gave me a gentle kiss, then slipped inside. I sighed, went back to the Bronco, and drove Julie home.

Julie lived in a little apartment above the detached garage out at the Cullys'. I drove her up to the garage and got out to open her door. As I did, Asmodeus bolted past me, streaked up a heavy gnarled vine that grew up the side of the garage, and vanished into a partly open window. Stepping down, Julie turned away from me and looked at the Cullys' house. The breeze blew her black hair off her face and the moon shone down on her so that her skin glowed white as my moonstone talisman. She reached inside her shawl and drew out a small pouch from which she took a handful of weeds. "Here, John Charles, hold them a moment. I want them to feel your positive male energy."

What the hell? I thought. But I took the weeds from her.

"This long enough?" I said, wanting to get out of there and head on back to The Old Forge for a drink and some food. Maybe a burger and hush puppies would cheer me up. "Just a moment more," she said, her voice pleading.

Long strands of cirrus clouds passed slowly over the full moon, now high in the sky, so that I could see changing shadows on the ground. A chill wind ruffled the leaves in the trees and fluttered the fringe on Julie's shawl. "Look," Julie said, "Dr. Cully's house is still dark. I wonder if he is out on a call? Maybe I should check to see if he left me a note."

We walked closer, to a small door set in the side of the garage. We both saw a piece of paper stuck onto it with a thumbtack. Julie removed it and held it out so that the moonlight illuminated it.

"Oh, poor Dr. Cully. Gleason's cow is having a bad birth and he's gone over there to give him a hand. The Gleasons have the farm down that way about two miles. You know them?"

"Not to talk to," I said. "I think I've seen Zak Gleason around, though. He's trying to breed some sort of fancy new species of cattle, right?"

Julie stared off past the darkened Cully house to the shadowy fields beyond. "You should go and give him a hand, John Charles," she said. "We've been worrying about that cow. Dr. Cully thought the calf might be a breech. Something's not right with it. But Zak didn't want a cesarean."

Oh brother, the last thing I felt like. I just wanted a beer and a burger and to go home and call it a night. My shoulder ached where the kid had punched me, my knuckles were bruised, I felt hungry and cranky, and I missed Marilyn.

"Oh, all right," I said. "Good-bye, ma'am." I handed her back her weeds. "I hope these are okay now."

She lifted them to her cheek, sniffed them, then held them out in her hand so that the moon shone on them. "Yes . . . they feel much better now. And if you will go on and help Dr. Cully that would make them even stronger, I'm sure."

What a weirdo the girl was. She was starting to really give

me the creeps. I could hardly wait to get away from her. I gunned the Bronco and sped down the driveway and off toward the Gleasons. At this point, even a cow in labor sounded good.

"Hold her, John Charles, hold her!" Cully shouted. I leaned over and pressed my arms down on a ton of struggling, suffering cow. At the other end, Cully, soaked in sweat, struggled, his hand up inside the cow, blood pooling around him. The cow gave a giant convulsive shudder, straining against her rope restraints, and her huge belly contracted. The stench of manure and hot blood and sweat surged over us, despite the piles of fresh straw that had been brought in and placed under the poor, wretched animal. With each contraction, blood, water, and feces spurted out over Cully, soaking him, soaking the straw, the stench overpowering.

"How long you goin' to keep tryin', Doc? Four hours—don't you ever give up?" Zak Gleason gasped out. He leaned over the other side of the cow's shoulders, pressing down, but the muscles in his arms jumped with fatigue and I didn't think he could go on much longer. "This calf is just too big. It's my fault for breeding her to the mayor's Charolais bull. Greedy, I was just too damn greedy, that's all."

"No, I'm hoping it's just . . . a transverse presentation. I can turn it . . . I hope. . . . We're going to get it. . . . We're not going to give up. . . . Come on girl, you can do it . . . come *on* . . . don't quit on me now . . . push that little baby out . . . come on . . . help me. . . . I can turn it . . . ," Cully panted with exhaustion. "There you go, sweetheart. . . . Hold her, John Charles, hold her, Zak. . . . I'm getting you, baby, you're gonna be okay. . . ."

The sound of his voice, warm, resonant, loving, gave me courage. As he pulled and wrestled to turn the calf trapped in its mother's womb, it felt as if he pulled on all of us, the calf's mother, Zak, me, to release our last reserves of energy. I could hear the wheezing breath of the cow, its fur soaking wet with sweat and blood, its eyes rolled back so only the whites were visible.

Zak looked exhausted. He had monitored the cow's labor for hours, then called Cully on his pager. The two had been working to turn the calf into the correct birth position so the mother could give birth, and now the struggle was coming to a climax.

"It's coming! It's coming," Cully cried. He had both arms deep within the cow. She gave a last, despairing, violent convulsion. Cully heaved and we saw, emerging from the cow, the two tiny hooves and the blood-smeared muzzle of the calf's head. Now more was coming out. Gooey with mucus, smeared with blood, splotched brown and white, the calf slowly emerged, a bundle of fur, a muddle of head, thick twisting neck, long fragile legs. Cully, his face bulging, pulling so hard that his entire body was rigid with the strain.

The cow convulsed, throwing Zak and me onto our backs.

"Lord God, poor thing!" Cully cried.

Zak struggled up and staggered over to where Cully bent over the just-born calf. "My God, what is it?"

I gathered myself together and stumbled across the mucky floor to the two men, who knelt staring down at the baby calf. Cully swabbed it with clean rags, wiping it dry. But right before our eyes, the calf was dying. It quivered convulsively, its matted fur trembling, then shuddered more and more slowly. We could see its ribs sharp against the fur as it gasped out its last breaths; then it lay still, its legs rigidly outstretched. But it was not at the stiff legs, the now flaccid belly that we stared, but at the two horned heads on the poor, misshapen abomination that we had struggled so hard to bring to birth.

A long groaning sigh came from the exhausted cow, and turning toward her we saw her breathing subside too, as her eyes filmed over and she lay still.

"Lord God above," Zak said. "I never saw anything like. Did you, Doc?"

Cully got slowly to his feet, his face sad, his eyes distant and withdrawn. "I've seen many, many terrible things," he said. He began to put his veterinary tools back into his large black bag. "I'll call the Jacksons to come pick them up tomorrow. I'm sorry, Zak, these mutations happen. No one knows why."

"Not your fault, Doc. I'm real grateful for all you've done," Zak said. "But I just lost a bundle, so I hope you understand if I pay you as soon as I can. Kind of a blow, I was counting on this calf. And this cow here, that's two thousand dollars down the drain. Poor thing."

"Of course, of course. Pay whenever you can, that will be fine," Cully said, his voice exhausted, his entire body limp with fatigue. He patted Zak Gleason on the shoulder. "Don't blame yourself. We did all we could. Thank you, John Charles. I really appreciate your coming by to help. Don't feel bad, the calf could never have survived, no matter what we did. And he killed his mother being born, there's no way around it."

We all averted our eyes from the horned two-headed beast that lay dead in the straw. I slid my hand into my pocket and fingered my talisman, and I pricked my finger on the pin.

Tap. Tap. Tap. The keys on my PC hummed away as I wrote up the story of Doc Cully's heroic battle to save the calf, and about the strange mutated two-headed thing which he had brought forth. I had this vague memory that two-headed calves were a bad omen, and for a moment, I thought of including a reference to the swirl of crows I had seen that same day, but the idea was absurd.

"What you working on there, John Charles?" Mrs. Boynton came out of her office and looked over my shoulder at my computer screen. "Oh no you don't. We're not running any story about that two-headed calf. Just leave that part out, you hear?"

"Why's that, Mrs. Boynton?" I know that Boynton believes that bad news, real scandal, or in fact, painful truths of any form have no place in the *Crowley Creek Sentinel*, but I didn't see how the two-headed calf fit into any of her no-no categories.

"Two-headed calf?" Buzz Marco said, swiveling in his chair, where he had been desultorily keying in the results of the weekend high-school baseball games. As a real live journalist intern from Columbia University, Buzz still hoped for the big, investigative story that would catapult him into the major leagues. "Hey, that's bizarre. Do you think it has anything to do with the witch in town? That Julie girl? I heard she had some trouble this weekend with some high-school kids. Maybe she cast a bad spell."

"What it doesn't have to do with is lowering the value of Mayor Jackson Lee Winsome's Charolais bull, that's what," Mrs. Boynton said. "He's getting a thousand bucks for a vial of its semen right now because the calves that bull gets are top notch. Word of a two-headed monster would be real bad for business. And let me remind you gentlemen that Winsome has been advertising regularly in the *Sentinel*." Buzz and I looked at each other and I started hitting the Delete key.

"Who had a bad spell?" Edith said. She had come in just in time to hear Buzz's last remark. She knew Buzz wrote the news column about who had gone to the hospital in Richmond, what for, and when they were coming home.

"Uh, nobody," Buzz said, catching Mrs. Boynton's warning look and swiveling back to his terminal.

"John Charles," Edith said, "here's those books you wanted for your column. I ordered them through interlibrary loan and went over to Richmond to pick them up this morning."

"Thanks," I said, putting the books on the floor. I didn't want to reinforce the idea Mrs. Boynton had that I worked on my column on her time.

"John Charles, about Margaret . . . "

"I want to see that article about Dr. Cully and the Gleason calf when you finish it," Mrs. Boynton said. She walked slowly back to her office and shut the door. But I noticed that she then opened it again, just a crack, so she could listen to our conversation.

"I told you not to worry about it, Edith," I said. "I had a drink with Dr. Cully last night and he's sure Margaret will be back soon."

"That's what he's telling everybody, but I just don't believe it. Where is she, John Charles?" Edith said.

"How would I know where she is," I said, irritated.

Edith stared at me. "You're acting real funny, John Charles. Not like yourself at all. I think you know something you are not saying."

How do they do that, women? "Why do you say that?" I said weakly.

"Isn't Lawrence Cully a good friend? What reason could you have not to want to find his wife? I think she's in trouble, John Charles. Nobody else does, but I do. Isn't that enough for you?"

"Edith, you're putting me in a real bad position here."

She gave me a cold look. "You have every right to keep secrets from me. I understand," she said, her voice making clear that not only did she not understand, she did not accept and she didn't intend to forgive me. Having Edith angry with me and not being able to explain, hurt. But I had given Cully my word. "What I can't understand is, how you can not care about Margaret. You'll never forgive yourself if something happens to her, John Charles. And neither will I."

She gave me another glacial look, then turned and went out the front door. I watched through the window as she strode angrily away from me, down Central Avenue. Then I swiveled back to my computer and began to type. Now my fingers moved more slowly and it didn't seem to matter so much what I wrote.

Nothing went right after that. It turned into one of those Mondays. Marilyn phoned to say she couldn't see me until the weekend. Doc Cully phoned to say that he'd gotten a note from Margaret, she'd be gone at least another week, maybe longer. And Julie phoned to say that the Beebees' red setter had recovered, thanks to the wild thyme, and did I want to stop by and see him?

I had no idea why Julie would invite me over to see the setter. I suspected it was an excuse and that she had taken to me. Certainly her cat had. Having a teenage girl attracted to you can be a real problem. You have to treat them with kid gloves, and even so, you can end up hurting them without meaning to. All my instincts told me that Julie was trouble and I should stay away from her. Yet I couldn't help but feel sorry for her, she seemed so alone and vulnerable. Surely it wouldn't do any harm to stop over at the clinic after work. After all, I had nothing better to do.

"Leaving exactly at five, John Charles? I hope you're not turning into one of those clock-watchers," Mrs. Boynton said as I turned off my computer and began filing my notes.

"I'm going to check on Mort and Barbara Jane Beebee's red setter," I told Mrs. Boynton. This was the kind of hard-charging news story she liked. "He got knocked down by a hit-and-run. Seems he was close to death and now Julie has saved him with some herbs she picked at the full of the moon."

"You're not going to write it up like that, are you, John Charles?" Mrs. Boynton said, peering at me to see if I was serious.

"Holistic medicine is big time, Mrs. Boynton," I said. "I hear there's talk of a herb and candle store opening up on Main Street where Miller's antique store closed up? They'll sell crystals and unicorn posters, things like that."

"Lord save us," Mrs. Boynton grumbled. "But with businesses going under right and left, I guess we can't be choosy. It's not good to have empty storefronts, that's for sure."

Mrs. Boynton always puts business before principle and I could see she was sticking to her guns.

"Just leave out the full moon part," she called to me as I left.

I didn't answer, just climbed into my Bronco and headed out. Trying not to think about the strange pull of Julie's green eyes, I turned on the radio. It seemed loud rock stations were taking over, but I found a new country station and sang along with Dwight Yokum while I drove out to Cully's. Soon I was bumping over the ruts in his gravel driveway.

A one-story addition covered with new white-painted siding extended out from the east side of the house. I went in through the screen door. The reception area was empty, so I banged on the little silver bell on the counter and Julie came through.

I had forgotten how tiny she is. Today she had her hair pulled back from her face, so when she looked up at me, I could see those uncanny green eyes and the fine, arched black eyebrows, shaped like the wings of a raven. "Gomer's around back. You can come with me," she said, opening a door and leading me down a hall into the part of the place they used as a kind of animal hospital.

"Gomer?"

"I think the Beebee kids named their dog after someone on TV, someone stupid. Sue Anne told me that he's not very bright, but he has a kind heart. Asmodeus has no patience with stupid dogs, so I told him to wait in the apartment. Otherwise he'd be here to say hello. Asmodeus likes you."

"Yeah, you told me."

I hadn't been there two minutes and already she was getting on my nerves. Why couldn't she talk like ordinary people?

She opened the door to a long narrow room. One side had been divided into pens with flaps allowing the animals to go outside. A few of the pens had animals in them; I saw a couple of small dogs and a cat. Julie led me to the far pen. A red setter lay curled up on a tattered blanket in a cardboard box. As we approached he lifted his head and watched us with that sweet, goofy look setters get.

"Hello, Gomer, hello. I've brought John Charles to visit."

Gomer had three of his legs splinted and bandages wrapped around his middle. I went over to him, patted him. "How you doin' fella?" I asked him.

He thumped his tail and gazed up at me.

"I didn't know you lived down the road from me, old boy," I told him.

He pressed his muzzle into my palm affectionately. I've never been a big fan of Irish setters. They mean well, but they are overbred and do tend—as Julie said—to be stupid. Crazy and irresponsible as puppies, they have a few good years as hunting companions and then they lose their zip and prefer to lie around.

"What's that?" I asked Julie.

In the corner of the pen stood an old potato crate. On it had been placed a shabby black velvet cloth with strange cabalistic symbols embroidered in gold all over it. On the cloth I saw a lump of jasper, a piece of black cord, and a pile of dried weeds.

"Oh . . . healing things. Gomer was hurt in his heart, John Charles. Kids ran him down, they didn't care. He likes to wander in the middle of the road and they thought it funny to knock him down. The bloodstone eases pain and it is good for the heart. I use the black cord in my knot magic, which soothes and comforts. I have some real good knot spells in my Book of Shadows. The herbs I gather keep the air sweet and soothe him and some I use to make poultices. I put my power in the bloodstone, but of course it isn't as good as the *udjat* I had here. Still, the Goddess must have wanted you to have the *udjat* or she wouldn't have sent it to you."

"How did the Goddess send me the *udjat*?" I asked, gently stroking Gomer's head.

"I think she must have used Sue Anne Beebee. Maybe my crystal would know? I could look, if it is important to you."

"Sue Anne? Why do you think that?"

"Well, Sue Anne came here to visit Gomer, and then after she left, I saw my *udjat*, that I'd put here to protect him, had disappeared."

"That's real interesting," I said. "Did you tell her about the *udjat*, say it was magic or anything?"

"No. She asked about it, but I just said it was a special pin. I don't talk about Wicca to everyone. Just to people who have the right aura." She ran her fingers through her hair, not meeting my eyes. Gomer gave a contented little snort and thumped his tail again. "See how happy you make Gomer? It's important that a grown man come to visit and be kind to him. Thank you."

"Glad I could help," I said, suddenly desperately anxious to

get away from her. "Have to go now." I walked rapidly down
the corridor, waved good-bye, and hurried out of the clinic.

Why would Sue Anne Beebee take Julie's talisman? What
had she been looking for in my library? Sue Anne and her
brother, Travis, seemed mischievous to me. I wondered if they
had intended to get Julie in trouble. Kids are cruel to strange
people, so it wouldn't surprise me. Still, luckily, it was none
of my business. Julie was fine. No harm done in the library,
after all.

I got into my Bronco and took off. I had done my duty by
Julie, I decided. Best to avoid her in the future. Being a Poe
means I have enough problems without a weird teenager on
my case.

But when I got home, Edith was waiting for me, looking
angry and frightened. She sat in my kitchen, drinking tea. Because Edith has her office in the house, she comes and goes as
she pleases. But usually she is very careful about it and normally she doesn't come over after working hours without making sure it is ok. Even though I could see she was upset, I felt
happy to see Edith. Someone who would talk sensibly, rationally, logically. Someone who saw the world the way I saw it—
or, at least, the way I wanted to see it.

"Hey, Edith, how you doing?"

"Hello, John Charles. Please forgive me intruding like this.
I just had to talk to you."

"What's on your mind?" I said, pouring myself a Blanton's
from the bottle I keep in the kitchen for that purpose. I filled
another glass with ice, topped it up with tap water, took a glass
in each hand, and sat down at the kitchen table across from
her. Twilight was falling and the kitchen growing dim.

"I heard something today, John Charles. I need to tell you
and hear what you think."

"Sure, fine."

"It's about Dr. Cully."

"Okay." I took a sip of Blanton's, letting it slide down and
ease the strange, queasy feeling I had gotten from Julie. The
feeling that there was something I ought to be doing, some-

thing I knew but wasn't facing. Reminded me of how my daddy always said, "That's the problem with you, John Charles. You'd rather run than fight. Know what that makes you? It makes you a coward, John Charles. You don't face up to things, they sneak up behind and get you." Yet the truth is, my father spent his life running from his troubles: from my baby brother's death, from my mother's suicide, and from his own business failures. He lived off the money he inherited from my granddaddy and slowly drank himself to death. But he figured he had the right to tell me how to live my life and I have the scary feeling that somehow, maybe because he had lived it, he knew what he was talking about, and his words stayed with me, like curses.

"Remember that fire at the Cullys' a little while ago?"

"Kind of. Wait a minute, didn't their whole house burn down? Holy Moses, I'd completely forgotten about that. But they rebuilt and you'd never guess, now."

Edith's face had drawn up, tight and white. Her intelligent gray eyes looked hard.

"The house caught fire in the middle of the night. It was so fast, and the flames so high, people could see it for miles around. You know everyone loves Dr. Cully and Margaret and people headed over to help, soon as they saw."

"Of course they would. It must have happened when I went to Bull Run with Marilyn."

"Could be. Otherwise, I think you'd remember the strange thing about it."

I didn't ask her what strange thing. I could see she was going to tell me.

"Margaret and Dr. Cully just got out with the clothes they had on. The house was falling in all around them. The animals in the hospital were all ambulatory, and they got out through those flaps they had. First thing, Margaret and Dr. Cully got them safe away from the house."

"Yes, I'm sure that's what they'd do."

"Flames roaring, the heat something terrible, or so they say."

"Yes."

"But then, they found poor Cyane's body."

"Cyane?"

"The Cullys' big, old black tomcat. The one that loved Dr. Cully so, followed him everywhere. You know, the one that had only one eye? Someone gouged one out and Cully nursed him back to health. No one wanted that cat, so Cully kept him around."

"I don't think I knew about that," I said. "Not that I would. None of my business."

"John Charles, that cat was found hanged, with a noose around his neck."

"How come you never told me that before?"

She dropped her eyes from mine. "Margaret didn't want me to talk about it. She knew Dr. Cully held it against her, because she was supposed to take care of the small animals at the clinic. Anyway—that's Margaret. Always feeling responsible for everything."

"Maybe she *was* responsible," I said, remembering Cully's hints about Margaret and "defenseless creatures."

"John Charles, something is very wrong. Think about it. First the cat is murdered, then the fire almost kills the Cullys, then Margaret . . . disappears."

" 'The Black Cat,' " I said. I took a deep drink of my bourbon, trying to still the feeling of dread that rose up within me.

"What?" Edith said.

" 'The Black Cat,' " I repeated. "Edgar Allan Poe's story."

"I don't understand," Edith said.

"Well, someone does. I guess I have no choice."

"What do you mean?"

"I have to open Edgar Allan's casket."

FOUR

I told Edith that my ancestor, Edgar Allan Poe, had written a famous story called "The Black Cat" and that the events in the Cullys' life had begun to echo this story in an eerie way. Both of us recalled that, once before, notes left in the casket had thrown light on my ancestor's stories and also upon strange events that threatened to put people we loved in danger.

Edgar Allan Poe combined profound intuition, brilliant intellect, and a tormented artistic vision in a way that gave him unusual insight. But I had never thought of him as prophetic, and found it hard to believe that anything he wrote could help us. Rather I feared that someone, knowing the story, might be toying with me. When I thought of the "break-in," the mess left behind so obviously, the careful cat footprints, and the talisman, I knew something ugly had begun and that someone intended to get me involved.

Edith agreed to come by early next morning to discuss what I might find in the papers. Soon after she left, I took my bourbon and water along to the library. Before facing up to the casket, I took my worn paperback edition of E.A.'s stories from the shelves. My family has never owned any of the first editions of his collected works. Instead, each of us, as our interest in our ancestor grew, would buy our own copy, read it, and write our comments in the margin.

Mine is the 1975 Vintage paperback, the one with the lurid silver, black, and orange art-nouveau cover. I had bought it as a kid and thrilled to the dark tales, read under the covers late at night by flashlight. Then I had seen them, as young people do, as doors into the darker realities that no one wanted to talk about—confirmation that debauchery, "nameless horror," evil, and inexplicable madness were as much a part of life as small-town self-discipline, cheerfulness, neighborly kindness, and our responsibility to others. And when my father lit into me, telling me I was useless, hopeless, a blot on the family honor, I hugged to myself the secret knowledge that, no matter how low I fell in his esteem or mine, I could not fall lower than my famous ancestor, out of whose despair and degradation had come works of genius.

I knew the story of "The Black Cat" well. I had always loved the sentence: "Who has not, a hundred times, found himself committing a vile or a stupid action, for no other reason than because he knows he should not?"

Now as I turned the pages, immersed in the hypnotic rhythm of the master's prose, I felt again the power of this tale of a man's descent and the terrible dark powers he unleashes by his cruel acts.

"The Black Cat" tells the story of a kind man who turns evil. In a rage, he gouges out the eye of his beloved cat, then hangs him. The man's house burns down, he drinks too much, and eventually murders his wife and then goes mad. I did not believe Dr. Cully could have gouged out the eye of his cat, or hanged it—or murdered his wife. I had known Lawrence Cully since childhood and never seen him show anything but kindness to man and beast. I believe the reputation a man has built through his deeds ought to stand for something, ought to protect him against unfair suspicion.

Instead, I suspected that someone wanted me to think ill of

Dr. Cully. Someone who knew the story "The Black Cat" had picked up on the resemblance between it and what had happened to Cyane, and was using it to turn me against my old friend.

Why? Then, a line in the story—a line I had never paid any attention to before—struck me. "In speaking of this cat's intelligence," Edgar Allan Poe has his narrator say, "my wife, who at heart was not a little tinctured with superstition, made frequent allusion to the ancient popular notion, which regarded all black cats as witches in disguise. Not that she was ever *serious* upon this point. . . . " *A witch*, I thought. *Julie.*

I topped up my tumbler of Blanton's single-barrel bourbon and began to read.

*Reflexions upon the mysteries of "The Black Cat"**

They who dream by day are cognizant of many things which escape those who dream only by night.

In their gray visions they obtain glimpses of eternity, and thrill, in awaking, to find that they have been upon the verge of the great secret. In snatches, they learn something of the wisdom which is of good, and more of the mere knowledge which is of evil. They penetrate, however rudderless or compassless, into the vast ocean of the "light ineffable".

Those who dream by day are the artists and I am one.

What I see and what I know I cannot tell in intelligible words, for the truth is so terrible that all who see it—in daydreams—are mad.

You say, then, my beloved descendant, who alone reads these words, that therefore I must be mad. But I grant you only this: that there are two distinct conditions of my mental existence—the condition of lucid reason, not to be disputed, and belonging to my memory of events and my true perceptions of this visible daily world—and a condition of shadow and doubt, appertaining to the compassless ocean of the night.

---

*This and subsequent fragments of the casket papers are excerpts from Edgar Allan Poe's letters and stories, combined with some additions of my own—Robert Poe.

These two conditions make visible to me what is hidden to others: the terrible links between virtue and vice.

When you look around you and you see the comings and goings of the Virtuous, do you feel a corresponding echo in yourself? Do you say, "That is good"?

Or do you say, "That is a lie"?

And if, my descendant, like me you say, "That is a lie", who lies? You or your darker self, who cannot bear his reflection? Where is the truth? In the horror of your nighttime terrors or in the disgust of your daytime lucidity?

Look with the white, daylight eye and look with the black, nighttime eye.

And the two eyes, together, are your protection against evil.

Beware, my descendant, for the Story of "The Black Cat" is a story of blindness. The witch and the demon, the power of magick and of illusion, will blind you if you do not dream awake.

All around you, your enemies will try to enshroud you in fog. But dream in the day, dream in the night, and you will see true. Read my story, for it is a message to you about the blindness of illusion. If you are too pure you will be blind to the truth. Embrace evil and you will be destroyed.

This is the moral of "The Black Cat."

I awoke the next morning with a blinding headache. I had closed my bedroom curtains before falling asleep, but had not done so completely. Not surprising considering how blitzed I had been. A beam of brilliant golden sunlight shone on my eyes, dazzling me. I got out of bed, staggered down the hall, turned on the shower, cold, and stood in it, letting the icy water shock me awake. Toweling off, I felt the bands around my head tighten and through my barely open eyes I saw that the air appeared full of fog. The outlines of familiar objects were blurred. It seemed I had the hangover from hell.

I know better. Yet I never seem to learn. That's what my father always said and it looks as if I am bent on proving him right.

Shivering, a damp towel around my waist, I swallowed three aspirins and choked down several glasses of water. My stomach heaved but I managed to quell it. Scraping away at my chin with a dull disposable razor, I saw in the mirror a pale, confused-looking fellow staring back at me. His brown eyes looked bleary, his wavy brown hair stuck up in a cowlick in back, and his skin had an unhealthy pallor. Hadn't old Ben Franklin said, "Early to bed and early to rise, makes a man healthy, wealthy, and wise"? Did it follow that late to bed and the worse for bourbon, made you unhealthy and stupid? The evidence pointed in that direction.

As I padded back down the hall from the bathroom to my bedroom, I heard faint noises from the kitchen, the chink of dishes and the sound of running water. Edith had arrived to hear what I had learned in the Poe papers. What would I tell her?

I found a pair of clean khaki trousers and a sunny yellow crewneck sweater that hurt my eyes, but maybe would cheer up Edith. I had just finished dressing when the bedroom phone rang.

"Hello?" I said, hearing my voice sounding thick and grumpy.

"Hello? Is that John Charles?" The mellow, smarmy tones of Rowland Fairchild caused me to hold the phone away from my ear. After all, I already felt queasy.

"Yes, that's me."

"John Charles, this is Rowland Fairchild. I, uh, I need to talk to you. As soon as possible."

Why doesn't the fellow call me at work, like a normal human being, instead of at seven-thirty in the morning? I thought irritably.

"Sorry to bother you at home, but I thought we could meet for breakfast at Shelton's. We could talk there. I have to go to Richmond today, so if you agree, we can talk before I go."

Much as I disliked Fairchild, this looked like it might be an excuse to avoid telling Edith I hadn't a clue about what I'd read the night before, but that it had frightened me. For some reason Edith seems to look up to me, and I hate to disappoint her.

"Right now?"

"Say, half an hour? That way we could talk and you'd still have plenty of time to get to work."

"Sure, okay. . . ."

The pain in my head had started to subside as I walked down the stairs, but I still felt a little rocky. When I came into the kitchen, I saw Edith standing at the screen door, looking out.

"Good morning, John Charles," Edith said, turning as she heard my step and smiling at me.

I walked over to the stove, saw the pot of coffee she had made, and poured myself a cup.

"That was Reverend Fairchild on the phone," I said. "He needs to talk to me right away. Want to come along?"

"Rollie Fairchild?" Edith said, brightening. "He a friend of yours? I've been getting to know him since Bobby and Jase have gotten involved in the church youth group."

Bobby and Jase were Edith's sons.

"A friend? Not exactly."

"He's a real nice man," Edith said, enthusiastically. "I'm hoping he'll be a good influence on the boys. Right now, all they seem to think about is baseball and rock music. They need a spiritual element in their life."

"Sure," I said. Edith worried a lot about her boys. Since her ex-husband had moved to Roanoke he had neglected them badly, and I knew Edith had been having her troubles with them. My own experience suggested that teenage boys were not too spiritually inclined, but I was not a father, so what did I know?

"Come on, we can talk on the way," I said, finishing my coffee.

"I'll follow you in my car," Edith said. "I just need to . . . comb my hair."

I looked at her in surprise, but she avoided my eyes, picked up her purse, and headed down the hall for the powder room.

"Morning, John Charles." "How y'all doin'?" "Hey, John Charles, good to see you."

As I walked through Shelton's coffee shop, the morning regulars all greeted me with a smile. Everyone looked relaxed and easygoing. That's how they played it, these boys who had coffee and honey buns and gossip here every morning, had done so for as long as I could remember. The fellows who sold real estate and farm equipment, who fixed cars over at Earl's body shop, who did plumbing and electrical work, who rented out big tractors and combines and balers. At one table, you can often find Mayor Jackson Lee Winsome, banker Mort Beebee, lawyer Ambrose Prynne, and the sheriff, Carter Rumpsey. When I see them together, I can't help wondering what back-room deal they're cooking up and what fun it would be to eavesdrop and then write it up for the *Sentinel*. Dream on, John Charles.

Shelton's has looked the same since I was a kid. A big room, the front window often fogged with a combination of cooking steam and grease, a counter running along one side, behind which they fry up eggs and sausages and cook grits in the morning. The rest of the day, they kept greasy hamburgers and mounds of french fries coming to stoke up the cholesterol count of the town teenagers.

However, their breakfast honey buns and dunkin' sticks, hermetically sealed in plastic, are trucked in from Richmond once or twice a week. Even microwaved hot and smeared with butter, they taste like sweetened cardboard to me.

Fairchild jumped to his feet when he saw Edith. He looked his usual stiff self in his highly polished black penny loafers and a navy-and-red paisley tie. "Good morning, Miz Dunn, Edith. To what do I owe the honor . . . ?"

"Hello, Rollie," Edith said, smiling up at him. She had put

on lipstick, powdered her nose, and even rubbed on something to cover up the circles under her eyes. "I hope you don't mind. John Charles suggested I join you."

Fairchild looked perplexed for a moment, as well he might. Then he smiled graciously, gesturing for Edith to sit down. Fairchild had a bowl of those canned pink-grapefruit sections and a cup of black coffee in front of him. "Hope you don't mind if I started breakfast. I'm on a tight schedule today." He looked at his watch. "I give a class at U.Va this morning on Faith and Superstition and the traffic report suggests I should leave no later than, let's see"—he studied his watch, furrowed his brow—"eight forty-five. That gives us a good twenty-two minutes."

Edith smiled at him. "I didn't know you taught at the university," she said, her voice admiring.

Fairchild gave a self-satisfied smile. "We all must give of the gifts that the Lord has seen fit to bless us with." He looked around for the waitress and gestured to her. Edith ordered tea and whole-wheat toast and I ordered a black coffee. My stomach still felt very unreliable and Fairchild wasn't helping any.

"So what's on your mind, Fairchild," I said.

"You know I work with our young people here in Crowley Creek," Fairchild began.

"You do important work," Edith said.

He smiled. "Thank you, Edith. And now I am turning to John Charles—and perhaps to you—to help. You see, John Charles, the young people are all talking about Julie. You know, we met her together Saturday night?"

"Right."

"John Charles, they're saying she's a witch. That she practices strange Satanic rites. That she witched a cow so that it brought forth a monster and that she killed the cow."

"Well, that's ridiculous," I said.

"Of course," Fairchild agreed, smiling his sanctimonious smile. But I saw the unease in his eyes. "If that were all, I wouldn't pay it any mind. But the kids have decided they need to get powers to counter Julie's. Edith, you know that rock group, The Dead Souls, that your sons have been talking to you about?"

Edith sighed. "Only too well. I hear that noise night and day."

"Edith, that rock group, they're Satanists. They call on the kids to believe in the Dark Lord, to follow his practices, and they promise special power in return."

"So what?" I said. "That's how they get the kids. Teenagers rebel. Always have. Always will. Taking their fads seriously only makes the kids like them better."

"I don't agree," Fairchild said. "They urge our youth toward ungodly practices. Sexual rites, truly evil things. We cannot take these threats lightly. It is our duty to speak out. By our silence, we signal our assent."

"Where do I come into it?"

"I am going to preach an important sermon on the evils of Satanism, on the Devil and all his works, this Sunday. But as you know, our congregation is small. Many of the worst offenders either go to other churches, or in most cases, go to no church at all. I wanted to ask you to report on my sermon, to print it in the *Sentinel*."

Oh boy. "Well . . . Mrs. Boynton assigns the stories. It's not up to me. You need to talk to her."

"Mrs. Boynton? I thought Mr. Boynton ran the *Sentinel* and she's just holding the fort until he recovers from his stroke. Surely you can write what you want."

"Oh no, Rollie," Edith said. "You don't want to underestimate Fanny Boynton. She runs the paper—and a lot of other things. She's a good person to have on your side."

"You need to be careful," I said to Fairchild. "We don't want to rile people up against Julie Noir. She's obviously had a rough time and she needs her job at Cully's."

"He shouldn't have hired her, John Charles. You may call it harmless, but the Bible warns us against the practice of witchcraft—warns us for good reason."

"Dr. Cully has lost that cat of his that he loved so much,

Cyane. And now Margaret . . . ," Edith said. "I think he's real lucky to have someone like Julie to help him out."

"Cyane?" Fairchild said. "Oh, that's right. Dr. Cully's cat. What a tragedy, his getting his eye gouged out like that—then killed."

"I thought that story was a secret," I said, looking at Edith.

"Oh it is, it is," Fairchild said, looking uncomfortable. "I shouldn't have mentioned it. Please forget I said anything about it."

"Do you know who tortured the cat?" I asked Fairchild.

"Uh, no," Fairchild said, not meeting my eyes. "Dr. Cully sure took it hard, though. I was there when he heard about it. He must have really loved his pet."

"What happened, Rollie?" Edith asked.

"You remember when that hurricane was on its way to Crowley Creek last fall? That terrible wind and the rain?" He sighed, looked at his watch. "Well, my parakeet went into some kind of a panic, got loose, started flying around the house. I couldn't catch him and I was frightened. Thunder booming, rain coming down like the heavens had opened up. The poor little thing went crazy in all that racket . . . flying into windows, mirrors . . . completely terrified. Even in that wind and rain, Dr. Cully came over to help. What a chase we had trying to catch that little bird. It would have been funny if the little thing hadn't been frightened to death. You should have seen Dr. Cully. So gentle. Caught my little budgie, calmed her, got her safely back in her cage. And while Dr. Cully was here, Margaret called, hysterical."

"Why? What happened?" I asked. Fairchild's pale blue eyes glistened, and I saw something in his expression I didn't understand. As if he had something to hide.

"Margaret was sobbing when she asked to speak to Cully," Fairchild said. "I handed him the phone and when he heard what she had to say his face went absolutely white as a sheet. When he got off the phone he was just so upset—close to tears. He looked at me like any moment he would start crying and he said, 'Never, never till my dying day will I understand how a human being can be cruel to a poor, defenseless animal. All they want is our love. Isn't that right, Rollie?'

"Of course I agreed and I asked him what was wrong, what had upset Margaret so. You should have seen him, he looked so pale. He just stared at me. At first I thought he wouldn't tell me, but then maybe he saw the sympathy in my eyes, because he said, 'Margaret put Cyane out right after I left and he just came back with one eye gouged out, gouged right out of his head. Margaret says it looks like someone took a knife and cut his eye right out of its socket.' "

Fairchild put on a sad expression to show his pity and continued his tale. "I tried to comfort Dr. Cully but he was absolutely grief stricken. I couldn't console him. He rushed off to see to his poor cat, to try to save his sight. And you know, the damage went deeper than the physical. Even though Dr. Cully managed to stop the bleeding and save the cat, Cyane changed. From being Cully's closest companion and most beloved pet, he just withdrew, got vicious. As if he were possessed. Sometimes, when he saw a human being, he'd just streak off and hide and it took hours to find him. At other times, he hissed and spat whenever anyone got near him.

"And Margaret—to think that it happened right when she was in the house— I don't think, to this day, she's gotten over it. Why, she hasn't been able to look me in the eye."

"You know the story about Cyane being hanged the night of the fire?" Edith asked.

"Yes, and to tell the truth, it doesn't surprise me," Fairchild said. "That cat had gotten so mean it seemed as if he had the spirit of the Devil in him. I myself saw him try to attack Dr. Cully when Dr. Cully went to change the bandage on his eye a few days later. Maybe he attacked someone who came to help put out the fire and that's how he ended up getting hanged. Dr. Cully and Margaret looked everywhere for the cat during the fire, and Margaret told me it must have happened right while they were looking. They were together when they saw him alive and then . . . they found him hanged."

"Is that right," I said. Strange the way Fairchild told the

story about Dr. Cully and the attack on Cyane. He almost seemed to be implying that Margaret had gouged out Cyane's eye and Dr. Cully had protected her. Yet I thought Fairchild was hiding something and lying to cover it up. I gave Edith a look to see if she felt the same and saw her gazing at Fairchild raptly.

But then, Edith hadn't read the Poe papers and "The Black Cat" story. She didn't know that in Edgar Allan's story, the black cat, Pluto, has his eye gouged out by the evil narrator, who torments the animal in a sudden drunken rage. And then that cat is hanged. And then the house burns down.

Maybe Edith saw more clearly than I did, because truly, I felt blind. I had the sensation that events were moving inexorably toward a terrible conclusion that the old story foretold. As if no one saw it but me. As if I could do nothing to stop it.

FIVE

What did Reverend Fairchild want?" Mrs. Boynton demanded, practically before I had come in through the
front door of the *Sentinel.*

"Good morning, Mrs. Boynton. Lovely spring morning
today, isn't it?" I said jauntily. I walked over to the coffeepot
and poured myself a cup, though I already felt coffeed out.
Then I sat down at my workstation, fired up my computer, and
logged in to see if I had any electronic mail. Since my column
now appears in twelve community weeklies below the Mason-
Dixon line, and it has my E-mail address in it, I sometimes get
useful feedback, or interesting letters, as well as the occasional
hate mail of the "Live free or die" variety.

"Reverend Fairchild?" Mrs. Boynton said. Buzz swiveled
around to watch the action.

"Breakfast, I think. Yes, that's it, he wanted breakfast," I
said.

Mrs. Boynton glared at me. "Don't mess with me this
morning, John Charles. I'm not in the mood. I have a lot on my
mind."

I relented. "I'm sorry," I said, giving her my best smile. After all, my job means a lot to me and she who issues the pink slips calls the plays. "Fairchild is worried about Satanism in Crowley Creek. He is going to preach an important sermon on it this Sunday and he'd like me to write it up for the *Sentinel*."

Mrs. Boynton frowned. "That wouldn't go down well with the other churches in town. Pretty soon we'd have to cover everybody's sermons. What did you say?"

"I said it was up to you."

"Well, that's right. And I can't say as I favor it." She fingered her pearl choker nervously and took a few paces around the room. Passing the desk of Millie, her best ad salesperson, she stared at a form on her desk. "Ad-space sales down again this week? How many inches we looking at, as of today?" The answer didn't please her and she twisted her choker gently. Turning back to me she said, "No, I don't see us covering a sermon, but on the other hand, we can't sit back and do nothing when there is witchcraft in town."

"Right here, right here in River City," Buzz Marco hummed under his breath, giving me a meaningful look.

"I think we need to come out against it. Come out most firmly," Mrs. Boynton said. "Denounce it."

"How is that a news article, Mrs. Boynton?" I asked her.

"I hear tell that Julie has been practicing disgusting rites. Black masses. Dancing naked in the moonlight waving a knife."

Buzz raised his eyebrows and made "screw loose" gestures with one finger.

"It's disgusting, that's what it is," Mrs. Boynton said.

"Naked dancing should sell papers," Buzz commented.

"The mayor called me just yesterday to say that he was outraged. That was his very word—outraged—and I think you could quote him."

" 'Mayor outraged,' " I said. "Not a grabber as a headline."

"All right, get serious now," Mrs. Boynton said. "You can joke all you want, but this is a small town with decent people and something like this Julie is upsetting. Especially to parents with young kids. The older generation needs to show leadership." She nodded, agreeing with herself.

"I think I'd rather not," I said. "We shouldn't start a witch-hunt—no pun intended. That little gal is real delicate. And strange. It won't take much for the kids in town to turn on her. I don't want to be a part of that."

"You saying she could have a breakdown if we write an article denouncing pagan practices?" Mrs. Boynton said, fixing me with those sharp, beady little eyes of hers.

"Lawrence Cully won't like what he sees as an attack on his assistant," I said, shifting ground. "And he's a big advertiser."

"You have a point there," Mrs. Boynton said. "I need to think on this. Damn that girl anyhow." She stamped back into her office and banged the door.

"She's not at her folks' place in Durham," Edith said. We sat at the wrought iron table under the big hickory tree in the garden behind my house. On the barbecue, chicken sputtered and dripped onto the foil-wrapped baking potatoes buried in the coals. I had my hands wrapped around a cool tumbler of Blanton's single-barrel and Edith sipped a glass of white wine.

I picked up my glass and chinked the ice cubes against the side. I didn't know how to begin.

"Did you read the Poe papers?" Edith asked me.

I nodded, swirling the bourbon in the glass, not looking at her.

She saw I didn't want to talk about it yet and changed the subject. "Well, today I called Margaret's parents in Durham. You know, Margaret is my cousin. Aunt Elizabeth told me she hadn't heard one word from Margaret for over a week. Margaret had called to say she was coming last Sunday. But she never arrived."

"What?"

"That's right, John Charles. Aunt Elizabeth called Dr. Cully, but all he would say is that Margaret has gone away for a while, said she needed some 'space.' He wouldn't say where.

John Charles, Aunt Elizabeth pleaded with him. She told him she was real worried, that Margaret hadn't sounded like herself, and that if she—Aunt Elizabeth, I mean—could just talk to her daughter, be sure she was okay, she'd stay out of it and leave those two to sort out their problems."

"Oh boy."

"Dr. Cully was real sweet and all, but he said he had promised Margaret he wouldn't say where she was and he was bound to keep that promise."

"Makes sense."

"Does it? I don't think so." Edith leaned forward, and those gray eyes of hers, so wise and perceptive, looked deep into me. "Why would she tell her mother she'd call and then not do it? If she wanted some time to herself, she'd tell her mother that. They are real close. She'd never say she was on her way home, then not come and not call. Something's wrong. You know it."

"No, I don't know it," I said irritably, fearing that she might be right and not wanting to think about it. What could I do, anyway? What business was it of mine? I took a long drink of the bourbon, slid an ice cube into my mouth, and sucked at it, feeling it press against my teeth. Then I crunched it up and swallowed it. I walked over to the barbecue and basted and turned the chicken. "Five minutes more, we'll eat, okay?" I said.

"John Charles," Edith said gently. "I know you are Dr. Cully's friend and I respect that. I really do. I get the feeling you're in a difficult position. There's things you feel duty bound not to tell me."

"He's my friend," I said. "He's a good guy."

"I know that. But did you ever think that maybe I know things I can't say too?"

"Do you? Do you know something you can't say?" I asked, looking at her.

"Yes, I do."

What if Cully had been lying to me? People lie all the time. Especially, men lie about the women in their lives. Even when we try to be truthful, we lie. We lie to our friends and we lie to ourselves.

I got up, picked up the long barbecue tongs, and took the chicken off the grill. I put a few pieces on our plates, along with the potatoes and some of the salad.

"What do you want me to do?" I said, seeing in my mind's eye Cully's troubled face as he pleaded with me to keep his secret, realizing I might have to break that promise.

"You can't tell me what you know about where Margaret is? What Cully told you?"

"It wouldn't make any difference. It doesn't change anything." I peeled back the silver foil from my potato, cut a cross into it, squeezed it so it opened up, and put butter and salt on it. Then I mashed up the insides. Mashed it and mashed it.

"Oh, stop mashing that!" Edith said. "Don't look so upset." She smiled at me. "Relax. We'll think of something."

I smiled dutifully. "Did I tell you that Mrs. Boynton and Mayor Winsome want me to write an article denouncing witchcraft?"

"Are you going to?"

"I don't know. I don't want the whole town focusing on it, making a scapegoat out of Julie."

"There's a big difference between witchcraft and Satanism, you know that, John Charles? Witchcraft is an ancient nature religion. It's about getting in harmony with natural things."

"Is that right?"

"Yes. I think you could write an article explaining the difference between witchcraft as an old religion and Satanism. You might help Julie if you did that."

"That's an idea. And you know what? If you did the research for it, you could talk to Julie. Ask her to tell you about witchcraft. She worked at the clinic before and after Margaret disappeared. If you hit it off with her, she'd probably tell you stuff that would help us figure out where Margaret went."

"I like that. That should work well," Edith said, her eyes brightening with enthusiasm.

"Truth to tell," I said, "that gal gives me the willies and I'd just as soon stay away from her. But she's taken to me since I kind of rescued her from some punks last Saturday. This way you could be the one to deal with her. And I'll see what I can find out from other sources."

"And what about 'The Black Cat,' the Poe story you read? It's so strange—the black cat that has its eye gouged out, dies in a fire, just like the Cullys'. And then, there's the talisman in your library. What do you think is going on?"

"No idea. I reread the story and looked at some of the Poe papers, but it made no sense. There's no way what my ancestor wrote a hundred years ago has anything to do with what's happening now."

She looked at me and I saw she didn't believe me. She knew I hadn't told her my real fears.

"I still wish Fairchild wouldn't preach a sermon against witchcraft," I said.

"Well, he's going to. You could tell that this morning."

"I know. I have a feeling that man intends to make Julie's life a misery. He doesn't like her. In fact, I think he's afraid of her."

"That's ridiculous. Rollie is just worried about her spiritual well-being."

I felt like saying, "Oh yeah?" but I restrained myself. My take on Rollie Fairchild suggested that the boy was real repressed, that he felt attracted to Julie and hoped that denouncing her would help him stifle his desires. A few drinks and the true Rowland Fairchild might just show himself. "Hey," I said, "I'm taking Marilyn to Richmond for dinner at The Frog and the Redneck restaurant this Saturday, to make up for wrecking her evening last week. How about if I invite you and Rowland to join us? We can talk about his sermon, maybe we can come up with some way to avoid making trouble for Julie." And maybe a night out with Fairchild and a few drinks and Edith will see what a fool he is, I thought to myself.

"Oh, that would be lovely!" Edith said, smiling.

After Edith left, I stayed out in the garden. The coals had burned down so that just a faint red glow came from the barbecue. I turned off most of the lights and sat letting the cool evening settle around me, listening to the background noise of the tree frogs, the chirping of the crickets, and the soft noises of animals—squirrels, field mice, night birds moving in the shrubberies and in the tree branches. From time to time I could hear the hoot of an owl and the bark of a fox and, in the distance, the steady muted sound of cars on the interstate. The moon, on the wane, sailed through long streamers of silvery cirrus clouds.

I felt restless. I didn't want to go back in the house. I craved another bourbon yet I didn't want to do that either. So I got up, walked down the lawn, where it sloped away to the fields and woods beyond, and then just kept on walking. I passed through a space in the hedge that I had used since I was a kid, and made my way along a path through the blackberry brambles until I entered the woods. Moonlight filtered down through the canopy of branches overhead as I walked slowly along the path. I felt at home here. I had walked this way often in my childhood. Sometimes hunting with my daddy, but more often alone, practicing listening to the sounds, learning to see animals camouflaged in the underbrush, pretending to be a knight on a holy quest, an animal on a search for prey, a native scout seeking an enemy. It was here that I had first composed imaginary stories, created imaginary worlds, and begun to dream that someday I would write stories and novels that others would read. That dream had taken me to the University of Virginia, where I had studied literature, and brought me back to Crowley Creek and to a job that meant a great deal to me.

I still dream of writing a great novel, but I think of it less and less. Now, walking deeper into the woods, I remembered my dream and wondered if I could ever find the willpower and confidence to sit down and face that first, blank page. Sometimes I feel so close. A first line will appear, tantalizingly in my mind's eye and I will swear that as soon as I get to a piece of paper I will write it down, and begin. But I always find an excuse not to.

The earth continued to slope downward. The path I had chosen led to a pool and stream, a favorite destination of mine.

I realized that, feeling troubled and confused, I somehow wanted to go to a place that had been a comfort to me in my childhood. Soon I heard the rustling of the stream, swollen with spring runoff. Then I heard another noise—splashing. Perhaps an otter or mink or raccoon?

I walked as softly as possible, wanting to see what was bathing in my special pool, not wanting to frighten any creature that might be there.

But when I came out of the trees I saw something totally unexpected, and for a moment, I could not make sense of what I saw.

The white naked figure of a tiny beautiful woman with long dark hair, sparkling with water droplets, emerged from the place where the stream widens into a pool. Julie.

She reached up to a branch and took down a deep blue hooded robe hanging there, which she wrapped around herself and tied at her waist with a thick, black-green sash. Then she walked into a circle, about nine feet in diameter, defined by flowering branches of dogwood and marked at four points by candles, burning inside globes of blue glass.

In the circle, facing north, stood an altar. A crate covered with a white satin cloth, upon which I could see a censer of burning incense. I could smell the incense too, and see a fine tendril of smoke ascending. On the left side of this altar burned a tall white candle in the shape of a woman, its flame quivering in the faint breeze. Beside it stood a brass chalice, a silver bell, a sphere of crystal, and a black iron basin. On the right side of the altar, I saw a thick red candle, a long straight branch, and two very large knives, shaped like daggers. One had a carved white handle and the other a black handle studded with smooth black gems. The large objects cast shadows upon the table and hid from view several other small objects lying there. In the center stood a wicker basket holding flowering tree branches and willow wands. The light of the candles flickered, casting shadows on the ground and on the altar.

Julie entered the circle on bare feet and, reaching the center, bowed first to the east, then the south, then the west, then the north. Then she approached the altar. Suddenly she froze, and turned in my direction.

At the moment I first saw her, I had stepped back into the shadows of the trees and I knew I could not be visible. The setting she had created was both beautiful and terrible and so mesmerized me that I could not think or truly grasp what I saw. I tried to tell myself that the scene before me was absurd and silly, but I did not believe it. I could feel my talisman, suddenly heavy in my pocket, and my fingers sought for it. I did not know what to do.

It seemed clear that Julie had sensed my presence. She stared toward me, like a pointer when it scents prey, her face pale and intense in the moonlight. Then she turned back to the table and picked up the white knife. She swung it upward until the blade pointed directly at the moon, then her arm arced downward until the tip of the blade pointed straight at me. I felt as if she had spoken a clear, unequivocal command and my confusion vanished. I turned quietly, and walked away from her, back through the wood in the direction from which I had come. The woods closed in around me, welcoming, familiar and dark.

SIX

The Frog and the Redneck, a trendy new restaurant in Shockoe Slip, is housed in an old redbrick warehouse that has been turned into a restaurant meant to combine Gallic flair with southern hospitality, and you feel welcome and relaxed the moment you walk in. We arrived at twilight, and the strings of little golden lights in the windows glittered like jeweled curtains.

The waiter seated us so that Marilyn and Edith could look out over the restaurant and watch the action, while Fairchild and I got to study our reflections in a mirrored pillar. The music was loud and people talked even louder over it. Dishes clanged, waiters shouted orders back to the open kitchen, and a small terrier ran from table to table begging for scraps. A lively place. I could see it made Fairchild uncomfortable.

I felt happy to be having dinner with two such lovely women. Marilyn had put her hair up so that it looked like a tower of gold curls, with some falling out in a sexy way. Edith wore a black linen dress with a high little Chinese-style collar that drew attention to her graceful neck and the way she held her head.

Fairchild looked like he had just stepped out of a board meeting in an office tower. He had on a navy blue suit, a white shirt, and a yellow tie. He had been surprised and pleased when I invited him on this double date and happier than I would have wished when I admitted that Edith had welcomed the idea. I saw him watching her as she ordered her drink and realized that things were worse than I feared. She may have liked him, but *he* was infatuated. When had this thing started? How had I missed it? How could a smart woman be so blind?

"You should try the margaritas here," I said to him. "They're excellent." A patently absurd suggestion since the restaurant specializes in French and local wines, but nobody noticed.

"Good idea," Marilyn said. "I'll have a strawberry margarita."

"I'll have a tequila sunrise," I told the waiter. "How about you, Rowland?"

"Uh, I'll have an iced tea."

I gave Marilyn a look. "Come on, Rollie, live a little," she said.

Edith smiled at him. "You work so hard, surely you deserve to enjoy yourself," she said.

He smiled back at her. "Okay . . . I'll have, what's that you're having, John Charles?"

"A tequila sunrise. But hey, why don't we just have tequila? I'll show you how some guy from Texas taught me to drink it." I said to the waiter, "We'll each have a tequila, straight up, and bring us a plate of salt and limes."

Marilyn gave me a sideways look. "*You're* in a good mood," she said. I realized Marilyn suspected I was up to something. But I didn't care. I felt as if I had a devil in me. I intended to get Fairchild drunk and lead him into making a fool of himself, and nothing and nobody was going to stop me.

I showed Fairchild how to chug the tequila, then lick the salt off his wrist and suck on the lime. I did it quick and neat and he wanted to do the same, so he concentrated on the gestures. Of course, I pointed out, practice makes perfect. He'd had three by the time our food arrived.

Perhaps the drinks had gotten to me more than I realized, because I heard myself saying, "I saw Julie the other night down by our stream in a magic circle. She had flowers and candles and incense. I came upon her suddenly, by chance, and it was like the old stories, where you see a fairy in the woods."

Edith smiled indulgently. "She's young for her age."

Fairchild frowned. "It may seem like a child's game, but it's dangerous to play with these powerful forces. You never know what you may raise. The fathers of our church warned against it and they were right."

"Oh, come on, Rollie," Marilyn said. "It's just teenagers acting out. We all sow a few wild oats. If you don't go through it when you are young, you're doomed to do it at middle age, when you have a family and kids. Better to get it off your chest when you can't hurt anybody but yourself. Right?"

"You don't understand," Fairchild said.

"So explain. . . . "

"It's difficult. . . . "

"Bring another round of drinks," I told the waiter. "We have some difficult understandings to master here."

"Coming right up, sir."

Fairchild chugged his tequila. He was definitely getting the hang of it. His face flushed and his usually neat hair had fallen over one eye. He had loosened his tie, removed his jacket, and rolled up his sleeves. Unfortunately, this appeared to please Edith. As he got more disheveled, she gave him admiring looks and hung upon his every word. Not at all what I had intended.

"What do you mean, 'You don't know what you will raise'?" I said to him, sucking on my lime.

"There are Dark Powers out there just beyond the Gates," Fairchild said, squinting his eyes shut and rubbing them vigorously, as if to wipe something off. He then opened them into slits and looked around, lowered his voice. "The witches believe that they deal with beneficent forces. But only by allying with the Evil One do you open the Gates to the old powers. Have you read the witch-hunter's handbook, *The Malleus Maleficarum*? It's all in there."

"The what?" Marilyn asked, giving him that smile I knew meant she was humoring him.

The little terrier that had been roaming between the tables trotted up to Fairchild, looked up at him, and sat up in a begging posture, his front paws outstretched. Fairchild paled. He stared down at the little dog. "Get away! Get away!" He made shooing motions, but the dog, sensing his weakness, just begged harder, gazing winningly at Fairchild out of his liquid brown eyes.

"What's the matter, Rollie?" Edith said. She saw, as I did, that he looked frightened—scared to death. And of what? A cute little dog. The man, as I had suspected, could not hold his drink.

Fairchild mumbled something under his breath. I have very good hearing and I thought he said, "Get thee hence, thou foul familiar." He stared at the dog, shrinking back in his chair.

"Come on over here, little doggy. I'm the sucker you're looking for," Marilyn said. We had ordered desserts and now Marilyn pulled a piece off her chocolate Bavarian and tossed it to the pup. He gulped it down and came over to her, putting a paw on her leg. "No more, that's as good as it gets, go on," she said, indulgently. The dog believed her, dropped back on all fours, and trotted off to another table.

"I've had too much to drink," Fairchild said suddenly. He still looked very pale. "Excuse me, sir," he said politely to the waiter, "I would like a cup of black coffee please." He looked at Edith. "Please forgive me, Edith," he said, his voice gentle. "I'm not used to drinking and I've had too much."

Edith gave me a reproachful look. I feared she had figured out what I had done and didn't think much of it. Actually, I had started to regret it myself. The fellow looked kind of beaten down all of a sudden.

"You mustn't take the Dark Powers lightly," Fairchild said, looking from one to another of us. "I know you are humanists, that to you the spiritual world is tenuous, doubtful, unreal. But your skepticism blinds you and puts you at risk. You can have no idea what the Dark Powers may drive you to, once you summon them into your life. I urge you to take care."

Edith put her hand out and touched his, where it lay on the table. "We *are* listening, Rollie," she said, "don't think we aren't listening."

Marilyn stared at him, respect in her eyes. She felt his sincerity too, it seemed. Only I saw hypocrisy and lies. And guilt. I thought he was hiding something.

The waiter brought us all coffee. Fairchild took a big drink of his. He must have scalded his tongue because he started at the first sip, and I heard the cup rattle as he replaced it in the saucer. He ran his long fingers through his blond hair and then let it fall back over one eye. His face still looked pale and drained, but his watery blue eyes regained their focus. "That girl has let foul evil into our small town and she must be stopped. Innocent children's souls are at stake." He looked at us, one by one. As each of us met his gaze, we failed to sustain the challenge and dropped our eyes, chastened.

The next day I didn't feel very good. Not because of the tequila—three straight tequilas then a long evening of food and talk were neither here nor there. But because I felt ashamed of my attempt to sandbag Fairchild and humiliated by the realization that it had boomeranged. The person who ended up looking like a fool appeared to be me. Both women had seen through my ploy, I was pretty sure, and it didn't elevate me in their opinion. Fairchild had looked better drunk than he did sober and had come off as more interesting too, in a kind of crazy way. I think Marilyn suspected that my feelings for Edith went deeper than just a business relationship and wasn't thrilled.

Sunday morning dawned overcast and gloomy, to match my mood. I spent the morning going through a pile of old books on witchcraft that I'd ordered through interlibrary loan.

I found *The Malleus Maleficarum* among them and tried to read it. I couldn't get into it. Written in the 1480s and headed by a papal bull, it had chapter headings like: "Of the way a formal pact with Evil is made"; "Of the several Methods by which Devils through Witches Entice and Allure the Innocent to the Increase of that Horrid Craft and Company"; "Here followeth how Witches Injure Cattle in Various Ways"; "It is Shown that, on Account of the Sins of Witches, the Innocent are often Bewitched, yea, Sometimes even for their Own Sins"; and "Whether Witches can Sway the Minds of Men to Love or Hatred." My edition had two scholarly prefaces, one written in 1928 and another in 1948. Each praised the book as a true and important insight into the real evils wrought, even in modern times, by these witches.

On the other hand, pro-witch books in the pile included New Age descriptions of how nature-loving, ecologically minded types could get in touch with the beneficent forces of nature by following ancient rituals suppressed by narrow-minded, misogynist Christians. Well and good, but why did they need to dance naked by the light of the full moon waving knives? Chapters in the witchcraft book included, "The Solitary Witch vs. the Coven," "Magical Techniques," "The Power of Talismans," "Spells," and "The Days of Power."

After several hours of this, I decided what I needed was, first, some lunch. Then I'd assemble a chilled six-pack and a bag of nachos, turn on the TV, and watch a baseball game. I stacked the books on the library table and headed toward the kitchen. But in the midst of building a sandwich, I must have been subconsciously thinking about some of the things I had read, because as my knife cut into the tomato and the red juice ran out, I suddenly had an idea about what the intruders in my library had been up to and decided that I had better go next door and talk to those kids.

I made short work of the BLT, then headed over to the Beebees'.

Although they lived on the property next to mine, the distance by road had to be at least a quarter of a mile. So as not to shock them, I drove.

The house had been set back from the road. A curved driveway led to the front portico and on to the three-car garage. A Mercedes and a Grand Am were parked in front of the house. The Mercedes had a golf bag sticking out of the open trunk and both doors were open.

As I reached the top step the front door opened and Mort Beebee came out. He was talking to someone behind him. "Then we'll meet at the club at six-thirty, okay, hon?" He turned and saw me. A puzzled look crossed his face.

"Hi, how you doin'?" I said. "I think we met at your open house? I'm your neighbor, John Charles Poe."

"Of course, of course, right, right, nice to see you . . . but . . . " He looked covertly at his watch. Obviously the man had a golf game and my arrival had put him off his stride.

Mortimer Beebee wore dark red trousers and a white V-necked sweater with a little golf player on the breast. A thin man with sparse, faded strawberry-blond hair, his hazel eyes had a kind of sadistic sparkle that surprised me and put me on my guard.

"Sorry to intrude on you uninvited like this," I said in my politest tone. "Please don't let me keep you from your game. I've actually come to talk to Travis and Sue Anne."

Two little vertical lines appeared between his orangish eyebrows. "Travis and Sue Anne?"

"Yes. Are they home?"

"They haven't gotten into any trouble over at your place, have they?"

"I hope not. May I see them?"

"Of course, of course, I'll get Barbara Jane." He turned so that his rubber-soled shoes squeaked on the marble floor of the foyer. "Hon!" he called. "Someone here for Trav and Sue Anne."

Barbara Jane Beebee came hurrying toward us down the hall from the back of the house. The entry foyer where we stood opened into a huge living room on the right and a formal dining room on the left. Directly in front, a grand circular stairway ascended to the second story. At the top, I could see a landing with a white-railed balustrade running along it. Two little grinning faces looked down at me from between the posts. I winked at them.

"John Charles!" she said, her voice cooing and overly friendly. "Well, isn't this just wonderful? Mort and I have been saying how we have to get to know our neighbors better and here you turn up! Can I offer you a drink? It's just so sweet. . . . "

"He's come to see Trav and Sue Anne, honey," Mort Beebee said, giving her a husband-to-wife "listen up" look. "I hope they haven't been causing him any trouble. Please forgive my rushing off, but as you can tell from this getup, I have a golf game and I'm running late. Bye, hon," he said, leaning over and giving her a perfunctory peck on the cheek. "See you later."

"Travis and Sue Anne?" Barbara Jane Beebee said. "Is there something I should know?"

Thud thud thud, their feet pounded down the carpeted stairway and the two kids came hurtling toward us. Of course they had heard everything.

"Travis, why don't you take Mr. Poe on down to the family room and I'll be right along," Barbara Jane said.

Travis and Sue Anne sat down on the sofa. I sat down on a chair facing them. "I've come to talk to y'all about what you were doing in my library," I said.

"That wasn't us," Sue Anne said.

"Well, then how did the talisman you took from Julie Noir end up in my house?"

"Say," Travis said, looking at me, "I bet you're the guy who beat up on Tiny."

"Julie is *we-e-eird,*" Sue Anne said, bouncing energetically on the sofa. She jumped up and began twirling around the room. "She dances down by the crick without any clothes on. Tiny saw her and he said she's built. But too we-e-eird."

"What do you mean, 'I beat up on Tiny'?" I said. It seemed I was losing control of this meeting.

"He was with some kids from town and they were hassling Julie and you came along and totaled them. Tiny says you must be a black belt. Are you a black belt?" Travis said.

"Tiny says you must have black magical powers and secret spells that you inherited from that famous writer you came down from," Sue Anne said.

"Who's Tiny?" I asked Travis.

"Lookit this!" Sue Anne said. She danced over to a desk and took a studio photo of three children posed before a painted backdrop. Sue Anne, Travis, and a third kid, dressed in a blazer with a school crest on the breast pocket, his carrot-colored hair neatly styled. The six-foot-three redhead Asmodeus had attacked the night I "rescued" Julie. "That's our big brother, Tiny. He pitches for James River Collegiate."

"He's cool," Travis said proudly. "He's going to run for class president next year."

"But he can't fight black magic," Sue Anne said. She came over, squatted down in front of me, and looked up. Her eyes were a very clear, luminous blue. For a moment I forgot I was looking into the eyes of a child. "Some bad kids are trying to wreck everything. They go to Richmond and do Devil-worship and have Dead Souls rock posters and can witch you so you get sick and die. If they go against Tiny, then what? Or if they go against us Beebees, then what? They want Tiny to not run. But I know you have big powers in your daddy's library."

"You have a magic box, a casket," Travis said. "Everybody knows that."

"Hey, wait a moment."

"Tiny didn't take anything and he left you a present," Sue Anne said, putting a small hand tentatively on my knee. "I know he made a mess when he looked for the casket. We're sorry. Our di-diversible didn't give him enough time, so it was kind of our fault. I could come 'round and clean up something for you. I can make real good corners on a bed so you can bounce a coin."

"Tiny said you shouldn't keep black magic in your house," Travis told me. "We're your closest neighbors. It could leak out on us. You should get that casket ex-ex-exorcized over at the church, Tiny said."

"I think I need to talk to Tiny," I said, looking back and forth between the two little terrors.

"You lose," Travis said, sitting up straighter. "Tiny is traveling with the team. They have a game this afternoon at Fork Union. He's the pitcher."

"Well, guys, I don't appreciate you and your brother breaking into my house and messing up my library. And your brother was treating a young lady very badly when I had that little run-in with him. Not to put too fine a point on it, he was asking for it."

"*You* say," Sue Anne said to me. She hopped up and did two quick and wobbly *tour jetés*. "Daddy says there's never no excuse for grown-ups to strike children."

I could hardly say that at six-three, and aggressive with it, Tiny had lost his child's immunity. "How old is Tiny?"

"Fifteen going on sixteen," Sue Anne said.

"Well, I think your daddy's right about grown-ups hitting kids. But I think you were very wrong to break into my house. Now, listen up. I don't have any magic in there. I have an old box that my great-great-great-etcetera-granddaddy put some stories in. He was a writer who believed he would be famous and the early drafts of his papers would have historic importance. And they do. But that's all. There's no magic to it. As for Julie, she has a right to her ways, she . . . "

"She's in league with the Devil, sir," Travis said. "Bad things are happening and it's her fault. She has no right to mess with the Devil—call him to Crowley Creek."

"Where did you hear that?"

"And so are all those kids in town who wear earrings in their noses and big boots and funny hair and do bad stuff. She's let something bad get in around here. We have to fight back."

I shook my head. "Julie hasn't done any harm to you or to anyone. You remember I said that," I said, looking straight at each kid in turn. Two determined little faces stared back at me, unconvinced.

As I left, I looked back at the Beebee house. In an upstairs window I saw two faces. One, with pigtails, was sticking out its tongue. The other just stared at me fixedly and I thought I read pity in his expression.

SEVEN

Monday morning Fairchild caught me coming out of the office on my way to interview the mayor for my witchcraft story. "You never came to cover my sermon, John Charles," he said, looking at me reproachfully.

"I didn't promise I would," I said, looking past him, wishing he would go away.

"True enough."

"Did you preach your sermon against witchcraft?" I asked him.

"No, I didn't. I want you to be there when I do it, John Charles."

That's good, I thought to myself. He'll never preach it then.

"Do you have time for coffee?" Fairchild asked me.

"I guess so, but we have to make it quick. I have an appointment with the mayor."

We walked down Central Avenue to Shelton's. The overcast had begun to thin out. The sky had a soft gray film over it and you could see the sun behind it like a burning silver coin. I opened the door to Shelton's and smelled the familiar smells:

scorched acidic coffee that had been on the hot plate forever, boiling grease, and stale cigarette smoke. We started to the back when the door opened again and Edith came in, a plastic shopping bag in her hand. She headed for the counter and handed the sack to Bunny Shelton, who stood behind the counter. "The book on roses I told you I'd order for you, I got it," Edith said, smiling. "It came in the mail on Friday. Sure you don't want me to put you down for the gardener's catalog? The seeds they have are special."

"I get a ton of junk mail as it is," Bunny Shelton said. "You don't want to have your name on any more lists than you can help. Government can track us from birth to death, they say." A woman in her midforties, she has a fat jolly face and hard little eyes. "But thanks a bunch, Edith."

Then Edith saw Fairchild and me. "Edith!" Fairchild said. "Good morning. John Charles and I are about to have coffee. Will you join us?"

We took the same table in the back where we had had our breakfast together the previous week. Right away, I could feel the attraction between Edith and Fairchild, and it really riled me. Stupid. Why couldn't Edith like whomever she wanted? She'd made it clear there could be nothing between us, and anyway, Edith was eight years older and I was seeing Marilyn.

"I enjoyed your sermon on Sunday," Edith said, smiling at Fairchild. "I'm real glad you didn't preach against witchcraft or against Julie."

Fairchild frowned. "I just postponed it until I could convince John Charles or Mrs. Boynton to cover it. I have to get the message out. John Charles, I saw Dr. Cully this morning. He doesn't attend our church, so I haven't been able to tell him how concerned we are about Julie. I asked him to send her back to wherever she came from. I warned him."

I felt myself getting angry. "You did wrong then, Fairchild. That little gal needs that job. Dr. Cully tells me she's alone in the world without a penny to her name. You shouldn't speak against her to her employer." Edith glanced worriedly at Fairchild. Score one for John Charles.

Fairchild's face tightened up. I saw his hands tense around his coffee mug. But he kept his voice gentle, condescending. "You don't understand. Haven't you noticed how Lawrence Cully is changing? How he's drinking more and more? How the atmosphere in town is getting poisoned? Don't these things mean anything to you? How can you deny the evidence before your eyes?"

"I think you are looking for a cause to make yourself feel important and you've found it in a poor defenseless little girl."

"She's not a little girl. She's an evil woman!"

We glared at each for a moment.

"Evil? What are you talking about?"

"She casts spells, she calls upon the Evil One. That cat . . . that's her familiar."

"Oh, what a load of crap!"

"John Charles, Rollie, you're shouting," Edith said. "Everyone is looking at us."

I leaned forward. I could feel my fists balled up in my pockets. The right one closed around my talisman. "You don't have a single scrap of evidence of that. You think because you're a minister and teach a course at U.Va that gives you the right to bad-mouth a helpless teenager?"

"You are wrong. I do have evidence. I have seen with my own eyes that girl consort with the Devil, call down terrible powers into the cone of her magic circle."

"You have not seen it!" I said, staring at him, willing him to tell the truth.

He dropped his eyes. "It's been seen," he said. "You can take my word for it. I've been told things. Margaret told me . . . "

"Margaret told you what?"

"It's confidential. But the girl is an evil influence. You can trust me on that."

"Not in a million years."

"Boys, boys," Edith said. "Now you stop this. It's ridiculous. What are you arguing about? Rollie, I'm surprised at you. And

John Charles, calm down. Can't you men have a difference of opinion like civilized folk without losing your tempers?"

We both turned and glared at her. Just when things were heating up she had to butt in. Then we looked at each other and I felt myself starting to smile. It *was* a bit ridiculous. Actually, more than a bit. We had been acting like fools. "Sorry, Fairchild. I kind of lost it there for a moment."

He gave me a cold look. "I wonder about you, John Charles," he said. I think he meant to sound superior and "more in sorrow than in anger," but I heard jealousy and resentment. He touched Edith's hand tenderly. "I'll see you tonight, Edith," he said. "Good-bye. Good-bye, John Charles. God bless." He put down a five-dollar bill and walked out.

Edith and I looked at each other. "That man is a liar and a hypocrite," I said, before I thought.

"No, John Charles. You're wrong about him. You're not acting rationally. We may not agree with his ideas, but he has only the best intentions."

"Oh yeah?"

"John Charles, I'm going over to visit Julie tomorrow evening. I want you to come."

"I'd rather not. I told you, I want to avoid her."

"I am glad you defended her," Edith said gently. "Somebody has to. I've talked to her a couple of times as we agreed. I'm not done interviewing her yet, there's a lot more to learn. But I think she's a sweet little thing behind all that New Age jargon. And she really knows a lot about witchcraft. She's studied herbal lore and holistic medicine too. Half the time I'm not sure what she's talking about, but the more I listen, the more I think there's just plain common sense behind most of it. And she loves animals and gives herself heart and soul to helping them."

Julie? A sweet little thing? Didn't Edith feel the darkness around her? It was one thing for me to defend her against losing her job. But calling her a "sweet little thing"? "Did you ask her about Margaret?"

"Yes. That's why I need you. It's clear to me that something funny's going on and Julie knows more than she's saying. She's told me a few things that really worry me."

"Like what?"

Edith shook her head. How had it come to this, that Edith and I were keeping secrets? We'd always been so open with each other.

"But, Edith, how can I help find Margaret if you know things and don't tell me?"

"It's Julie you need to talk to, John Charles. She has things to say to you. I pressed her to tell them to me but she said she wanted you there before she'd say anything. She's really taken to you, John Charles."

I started to protest.

"I'll meet you at eight o'clock at Julie's, okay?"

I sighed. "I'll be there."

"Nobody trusts that little gal anymore," Cully said. "Nobody human that is. But you should see her with the animals. I would never have thought folks in this town could act like this, would you, John Charles?"

We sat in his den. I'd arrived early and dropped in to have a drink with Cully before going to Julie's. Knowing he was lonely, I thought it might look rude to drive in and just go on over to Julie's apartment above his garage. But just like the time before, I arrived to find him way ahead of me.

"I hate to say it, but in a way, the town turning against her doesn't surprise me."

Cully took a big swallow from his bottle of Jack Daniel's. It bothered me to see him drink direct from the bottle. He had a big bowl of chips. He dug his hand into it, scooped up a handful, and tipped it into his mouth. I heard a scrabbling noise and turned. Something moved in the corner of the room.

"That's Tantalus," Cully said around his mouthful of potato chips. "He's a ferret. Was a sick ferret. Looked like a dying ferret. All better now. Couldn't figure out what was the matter with him. Julie steamed some herbs and made him breathe them in and he perked right up. Family's coming for him to-morrow. She said he needed company and Asmodeus didn't like him, so I agreed to keep him here at night. Julie tells me ferrets need lots of affection." He burped.

I walked over to the corner and saw, on the floor, a large cage lined with newspapers. A sharp-nosed, narrow-bodied, sinister-looking animal prowled around the cage. When he saw me, he poked his nose through the bars and gave me a thoughtful look. Asmodeus had a point.

"How are you doing?" I asked Cully.

He got up carefully and poured me a Jim Beam, straight up. "Sorry, outta ice cubes. I forget to fill the tray. Margaret never forgot to fill the trays. Look here." He walked over to a sideboard that had Jim Beam bottles lined up on it and shelves above. On the shelves he had mementos, souvenirs of trips to Disneyland and Petersburg and Cumberland Gap National Park and Manassas. He had silver cups won at county fairs, ribbons, and silver-framed pictures. He took one of these down, gazed at it tenderly, and handed it to me. I saw a beautiful teenage girl wearing a sixties-style prom dress. She had long brown wavy hair and lips curved into a sweet tender smile.

"Is that Margaret?" I said. "Wow, she was beautiful." I took a sip of the Jim Beam. Kind of sad, when you saw a picture like that. The Margaret I knew, who looked in her late forties, had frizzy permed reddish brown hair, a pudgy shapeless body, and a soft anxious face, like a puppy who wants to please. She had always looked to me like someone's mother, but the Cullys had no children. How had this bright, eager girl turned into the retiring, always-ready-to-help Margaret Cully? I walked over to the shelf and found a recent picture of Margaret and Lawrence Cully standing by a prize-winning Charolais bull. Mayor Winsome stood behind them, an arm around each, beaming. I looked back and forth between the two pictures of Margaret Cully, and suddenly, I felt a chill go up my spine.

"What are you staring at?" Cully said suddenly, very loudly. "Are you blaming me because she got old and tired? You blaming me for mortality and death?"

I put the pictures back and sat down in a chair across from his La-Z-Boy. He climbed onto it with difficulty, picked up his bottle by the neck, and waved it about. "Folks get old, they change. You think you're gonna stay young and handsome forever?" He glared at my hair. "You watch, pretty soon you'll be combing it over the top of your bald spot just like the rest of us and it won't be so easy to date sexy women and have it all your own way. . . . "

"Hold on a minute. . . . "

"Things change, you'll see. You're on a roll now but it won't last. You like the bottle, just like me, and that thing comes out of the bottle at you and gets right into your gut and starts chewing on you. They lied to us when we were kids, John Charles. They lied through their teeth."

"What do you mean?"

"Nothing's like they promised. See a sweet young thing like Julie and now everybody's after her just because she believes in going her own way." He reached out and took the picture of the teenage Margaret from me. He stared at it. "Only thing you can trust in this world is God's dumb creatures, John Charles. He made them without sin. You know?"

I inadvertently glanced at the ferret. It stared out at me from its shadowy corner, its eyes glowing.

"It's a sin to be cruel to helpless creatures." His voice sounded belligerent. "Isn't that right?"

"Whatever."

"I've been drinking too much and missing appointments," Cully said. "And Julie covers for me. She doesn't need to do that, but she does it out of the goodness of her heart. Got to pull myself together."

"You miss Margaret, I bet," I said. Cully had passed into the maudlin-drunk stage, but I could feel his anger boiling away under the surface. Whoever was around would get the brunt of it. I thought I should get out before something happened between us that would be hard for both of us to get over when he sobered up.

"Don't get any ideas about mixing up in my business, John Charles," Cully said. He drained his bourbon bottle and struggled to sit up and get out of the La-Z-Boy so he could go and get himself another. He waved to me to hand him a fresh bottle from the sideboard, but I pretended not to see. "I have to protect what is mine or what will happen to them? Margaret. Julie. The animals. And I don't need any help. Not from you, not from anybody."

"Of course you don't. I better be going now. See you tomorrow."

He squinted at me, as if suddenly not sure who I was. "No offense meant. Old buddies got to stick together. But I got a rat gnawing at my insides and it makes me cranky. Forgive and forget, okay?"

"Sure. See you. Take care," I said, grabbing my jacket and making my escape. I could hear Cully stumbling over to the sideboard to get another bottle as I opened the door and hurried out into the night.

I saw Edith's green Taurus parked outside Julie's garage apartment. I walked over and knocked on the door. A second-story window slid open. "That you, John Charles?" Edith called down.

"Yep, it's me."

"Come on up. The door's open."

Edith's voice didn't sound right. I took the stairs two at a time and bounded into the room.

The garage apartment had two little poky rooms, a living room and a bedroom. Plus a tiny bathroom. A kitchen ran along one end of the living room.

In the living room a saggy old sofa with a faded madras spread draped over it faced the door and on it I saw Edith sitting, her arms around Julie, hugging her like you hug a child. Julie looked extremely pale. The only color in her face dark greenish circles under her eyes. Julie's head tilted down and she clutched a crystal ball in her hands. I remember seeing that crystal when I had last seen her in the woods. Something moved near her feet. Asmodeus twined around her legs, rubbing against them as cats do, his tail erect and curling sinuously, his ears pointed forward.

A quick glance around the room revealed a pentagon on the wall, candles everywhere, and a chest covered by a black cloth with strange shapes embroidered on it. By the door stood a twig broom and a black cauldron. "Julie's not well," Edith said.

I saw that Julie had begun to shiver. She had sat calmly when I entered, not really seeing me, but now she opened her eyes, took me in, and began to tremble.

"Can I get you a sweater or a blanket, honey?" Edith said, stroking her arm and looking at me as if to say, "something is seriously wrong here."

"What's the matter? Is she sick?" I asked, avoiding Julie's eyes and looking at Edith.

"Tell Asmodeus we will not go back," Julie said.

"Say what?"

"I don't know what to do . . . ," Julie said, her words barely a murmur.

"Julie, you must tell us what you have on your mind," Edith said. "You promised you would when John Charles came. He's here now."

"Yes . . . but first I will ask the crystal." She passed her hands over the crystal, then looked out the window. The moon, veiled behind floating wisps of cloud, hung in the dark sky.

"Wise One of the Waning Moon," chanted Julie in her soft breathy voice,

> "Goddess of the starry night,
> I call upon your power within this crystal
> to transform that which is plaguing me.
> I call upon you, reverse the energies
> From darkness, light!
> From bane, good!
> From death . . .

"From death, rebirth and purification . . . no . . . no . . . she won't hear me, will she, Asmodeus?" Julie's voice sounded agonized. "She won't help us until we heed her call."

At the sound of his name, the cat jumped up on Julie's lap, put a paw on her arm, and stared up at her. Then he gave the most curious, the most sad and plaintive, yowl I ever heard issue from the mouth of man or beast. The hairs stood up on my arms.

A tear ran down Julie's cheek. "Yes, beloved friend, I accede. I shall do as you bid." She looked up at me and Edith. "Asmodeus says the Goddess will not protect me unless I show you what Asmodeus revealed to me at the Goddess's behest." She looked out the window. "The moon is high, we can go now."

I looked at Edith and she shook her head. She didn't understand any better than I did, but we both saw that Julie had worked herself up into such a state that neither of us dared question her.

Julie gently placed Asmodeus on the floor, put the crystal on a table, and wrapped herself in her long purple-and-black fringed shawl. She went out the door of the apartment, down the stairs, and out the ground-floor door. We followed.

She opened a garage door. Inside, in the dim light, we saw rakes and shovels hanging from nails along the side wall. She stretched up and took down a spade, turned, and set off toward the woods behind the house. Edith and I followed.

Asmodeus had jumped up onto her shoulder. Julie followed a path into the woods that led downward, probably toward the creek. But after about two hundred feet she turned off and began to walk directly into a dense thicket. Sumac twisted around her, but I noticed that many branches were broken. She had come this way before. She took ten or twelve paces and vanished into the underbrush.

Edith and I followed, to the sound of cracking branches and rustling foliage. Moonlight penetrated the interwoven canopy of branches, and the air under the leaf cover glowed with a silvery luminosity. We caught up with Julie in a tiny clearing.

The ground was spongy, covered with rotting leaves and small ferns. I saw at once that someone had been digging. The ground cover had been disturbed.

"Asmodeus found this glade and this spot and told me to dig here," Julie said in a breathy whisper. "Please, you've got to believe me, I swear by the Goddess herself, Asmodeus showed me this . . . ," she said. She handed me the spade and pointed to a spot in the mulch. I dug in and immediately struck something metal. I dug around it, then under it, then put my heel on the spade and tilted. The buried object came up suddenly, tipped over, and fell flat upon dug-up soil and rotting leaf mold.

For a moment, we stared, uncomprehending, at the gleam of metal in the dark earth. Then we grasped what we saw. Lying on the damp wormy upturned soil, a long-handled ax. The blade spotted and clotted with dark earth and dried blood and reddish brown curled hair and fragments of cloth and chunks of something that looked like black decomposing maggoty flesh.

"Asmodeus found it!" Julie cried, her shivering now violent. Edith put her arms around Julie. Over Julie's shoulder, Edith looked at me, her face drawn and agonized. I returned the look. I took off my jacket, removed my shirt, and put my jacket back on. Using the shirt, I picked up the bloody ax and carefully wrapped it in the shirt. I marked the spot where it had been dug up with a stake made from a branch.

Then, holding the wrapped-up ax, I followed Edith and Julie back. Edith had her arm around Julie and supported her, for Julie could barely walk and kept stumbling as if her ankles were giving way. Asmodeus rode on Julie's shoulder. He turned and looked at me, his eyes glittering green and full of vengeance.

EIGHT

The sheriff sent the ax to Richmond and the results came back: The hair and blood matched Margaret's. The fragments of clothes corresponded to those Cully remembered her wearing the day she left Crowley Creek. But I already knew all that. I knew it the moment the ax came out of the earth.

Maybe I knew it before that. Maybe I understood the night I drank too much Blanton's single-barrel and opened the casket of Poe papers. Margaret dead, her skull cloven in with an ax. Cully's black cat, his eye gouged out, then hanged, then a fire. All of it in Edgar Allan's story, "The Black Cat."

But there was more. Cully's drinking, his anger, even that was in the story. If you believed in the power of the occult, in reincarnation of evil forces, you would be sure that Cully had murdered Margaret with the ax in a drunken rage, because that is how it happened in the Edgar Allan Poe tale. In the story, the narrator kills his wife with an ax, after venting his growing rage upon his hapless cat. You might even think that evil forces had been unleashed—forces we were powerless to combat.

I didn't know what to believe. I can't say where I stand on

the occult, but it seems to me that it is arrogant to believe that we can understand everything about the world we live in. We need to be humble. The men of the church as well as the believers in other realities.

But I had the feeling I was being manipulated. The Beebee children may have admitted to breaking into my library, but I thought someone had put them up to it, filled them with ideas about my casket and the Devil. Who? Why? What about the pressure from Fairchild and Boynton and others to demonize Julie? And Julie herself. What part did she play in all of this?

Because even though the old story pointed to Cully, all the evidence pointed to Julie. She had appeared in town and then Margaret had disappeared. *She* had found the ax. How did she know where it was unless she put it there?

What possible reason could there be for Cully to have murdered his wife? He had been devoted to her for thirty years, he had proved himself over and over to be a kind, caring man.

But if Julie had had problems before, they were nothing to those she would experience when public opinion in Crowley Creek convicted her of murder, without waiting for indictment, trial, or verdict. Cully had an alibi for the cat torture. Fairchild, the Right Reverend Dr. Fairchild himself. How much better could you do? If Cully hadn't killed his cat, he didn't match the villain in Poe's story. And if he hadn't mutilated and killed his cat, he didn't match the profile of evil either. And could I really ignore the feeling, growing in town, that Julie had released evil forces previously held at bay?

I drove through town and out to the long low one-story redbrick building that housed the offices of the sheriff and his deputies.

The most important thing to know about our sheriff, Carter Rumpsey, is that he is a second cousin once removed of Mayor Jackson Lee Winsome. Carter Rumpsey had been a year ahead of me in school, and I remembered him as a good guy. He was the best fullback that Jefferson had while I was there, tough, extremely stubborn, and not too bright—he hung in when a smarter player might have eased off to avoid punishment.

Rump, as we called him, had a loyal streak. If you did him a favor, he never forgot and you could always count on him. Sometimes it seemed as if the Lord created him as the perfect tool for Jackson Lee.

The sheriff came out and led me to his office. There, sitting back and surveying the desk and computer and the empty bookshelf, sat the mayor himself, smiling his famous oily smile.

Our mayor, Jackson Lee Winsome, likes to play the southern gentleman role. We all let him go to it. Nobody reminds him that his ancestors had been carpetbaggers, Comeheres who arrived in our part of the world intent on taking advantage and looking to be still at it. Jackson Lee rewarded his friends and never forgot an enemy.

Jackson Lee sat back in the corner of Sheriff Rumpsey's office, beaming at me. He wore a light brown suit, the jacket unbuttoned to allow his swelling paunch breathing room. "John Charles! How ya doin'?"

His grip felt firm and enthusiastic but I noticed that as he pumped my hand his sharp little blue eyes studied me, as if calculating my current position on all the issues of importance to him.

"Jackson Lee, didn't expect to see you here," I said, acting surprised.

The sheriff stood up from behind his desk and leaned over to shake my hand. "Hey, Rump," I said as he mangled my hand. "How's it goin'?"

Sheriff Rumpsey sat back down and shook his head. "It's not going, John Charles, that's how. We got the ax and we got a suspect, but we don't have a body. We've had a special team of bloodhounds and their handlers down here. They searched over what seems like the whole county. No sign of Margaret's body. It's been real hard on Dr. Cully. When we showed him the ax, he just about had a coronary. I've never seen a man so brokenhearted. Cried like a baby."

"Did he recognize the ax?"

"We all did. Most popular seller at Dilbey's, right here in town. Just about everyone has one like it. He has a couple, different sizes, couldn't say if the one we found was one of his or not."

"So, do you have a suspect?"

"Oh come on, John Charles," the mayor said. "It's clear as black flies on a white bull that gal Julie took an ax to Margaret. Wanted the vet and wanted the job and took a shortcut to get 'em. Only have to look at her to know, girl's obviously disturbed."

"Now, Jackson Lee," the sheriff said. "I can't go along with you there. It's too soon to say that. Especially to the press." He winked at Jackson Lee.

"Especially since Julie's about five foot one and barely a hundred pounds and Margaret must have been at least one-fifty, one-sixty," I said.

"Long-handled ax," the mayor said. "One swing and it's game over for the vet's wife."

I took out my notebook. "So the situation is, we have an ax with hair and blood that matches Margaret's and you consider her dead, murdered, right, Rump?"

Rumpsey darted a glance at the mayor, who nodded.

"Yep, missing, presumed dead. Presumed foul play," Rump said. "Hair matched what we found in Margaret's comb."

"You want to be quoted that your prime suspect is Julie Noir?" I asked, praying he'd say no.

The sheriff looked at the mayor.

"Hell no," Jackson Lee said, smiling his overly genial smile. "Rump won't say that. Wouldn't be right. But no harm in you *implyin'* it, now is there? Just so folks know that pervert don't think she's pulling the wool over anybody's eyes."

"Uh-huh," I said.

"Don't take on like that, John Charles," the mayor said. "If folks think we aren't on to her game, we could get a vigilante mentality going. We have to handle this real delicate while we look for the body."

"The mayor is right," Rump said. "Soon as we find the body, we'll move. In the meantime, she's promised not to leave town and we're keeping an eye on her to be sure she don't. Slow and steady wins the race."

I wrote in my notebook, "Sheriff at sea—baffled—can't find body, not sure what to do next." "Okay, gotcha," I said. "Any other suspects?"

"Nope," said the sheriff.

"How can you be sure?"

The mayor leaned toward me. "What you implyin', John Charles? You don't think Julie is our perpetrator?"

"I'm interviewing, you're talking," I said, smiling at the mayor.

He stared at me, trying to understand where I was coming from.

"What's on your mind, John Charles?" he asked.

"There's no real evidence against Julie," I said, trying to convince myself as much as him. It didn't feel right, the way they suspected Julie so easily, with so little evidence, just because she was different.

"Is that so?" the sheriff said. "Well, give us time, we'll find it. I'd say you'd be all alone in this town if you hang on to that point of view."

"Yep," the mayor said, smiling his famous crocodile smile. "I doubt you want to print that, John Charles. I doubt it very much."

"Julie wants us to come to a magic-circle rite, tonight," Edith said to me. Her voice sounded hesitant. "I don't know what to tell her. She says that her powers aren't strong enough if she is alone and she doesn't know who else to ask. She says the rite will help us find Margaret's body."

"No way," I said.

I sat across from Edith in her office at my house, Crowley House. She wanted to talk about the sheriff's investigation, why the mayor had been mixing in, what would happen to Julie. I felt restless. I had this strong desire to go to the library, to get out the Poe papers, an inexplicable feeling that something waited for me there, something I hadn't been ready to read before, but now needed to know. I didn't feel much like talking to Edith.

"Is it because you think her witchcraft ideas are evil?" Edith asked me.

"Of course not," I said quickly.

Edith looked at me.

"I don't understand how I feel," I said, half to her, half to myself. "Logically, I don't think much of her ideas one way or another. Yet, sometimes the things she says make me feel downright queasy."

"You're picking up on something hidden," Edith said. "That's your gift, John Charles. You don't need to explain. Sooner or later it will come clear to you. But in the meantime, Julie needs friends, and really, it's not a lot to ask, to support her in this rite. It's kind of like a play, you know. If it will help her get over her shock of finding that ax, it will be a good deed."

The phone rang. I picked it up. "Hello?"

"Hello? John Charles?" Fairchild again. The very last person I wanted to hear from. "I heard you saw the sheriff today. Any word on the ax?"

"The news isn't good. The hair and blood type match Margaret's. Hair isn't conclusive, but it's pretty clear. It's her."

"Lord have mercy upon her, may she rest in peace. Uh . . . who does the sheriff suspect?"

Why did Fairchild sound so worried. Frightened, almost. "No one right now, is what he says." I looked over for Edith, but she had gone out of the room. I heard her footsteps descending the stairs. The imp of mischief came over me, and lowering my voice I said, "Edith and I are going to a rite of Julie's tonight. Why don't you follow and watch? Then you'll be able to have real evidence to back up your allegations—or find out that she's harmless."

Silence. Then Fairchild said, "Wouldn't a man of God spoil the ritual? Wouldn't it prevent her from calling on the Devil's minions?"

"I don't know about that. You're the expert. But if it did, all the better, right? Anyway, I'm just letting you know. But as you're not officially invited, you come at your own risk. If you decide to follow along, I recommend you do it inconspicuously, know what I mean?"

"That doesn't seem right. . . . "

"We'll be leaving from Julie's at nine. You could keep an eye out if you waited behind the garage. So let your conscience be your guide," I said.

"Always," Fairchild said.

In silence Edith, Julie, and I walked through the woods down toward the stream. I could hear Fairchild slinking along behind us, so I made more noise than usual to camouflage the sounds. Neither Edith nor Julie noticed.

When we arrived at the same place where I had seen Julie performing her rite last time, Julie led Edith and me to a flat place by the stream, and gestured for us to sit. Working quickly, she created a circle around us with flowering branches. She made an altar in the center, facing north, and put a bowl and candles upon it. She filled the bowl with water and placed her knives next to it. Clouds thickened and passed over the waning moon until we could barely see. Only the four candles flickering at the four points of the compass cast any light. The air was chill. I felt the cold and could see Edith did too. Julie moved freely and sometimes her black robe swung open, so that you could glimpse the whiteness of a naked leg or arm. From time to time Julie glanced at the moon, and when the clouds had covered it completely, she sighed and turned to us.

"I will begin, if you are ready," she said in her soft voice.

"I'm ready," I said, trying to hide my unease.

"I'm ready," Edith said, in her matter-of-fact voice.

"Let your minds and hearts be open so that no ill will clouds our work tonight. We have much to do."

Three times Julie walked around us, around the circle. As she walked, she chanted. Her voice, growing in intensity, lost its

soft, diffident tone and became increasingly clear and incanta-
tory.

> "I draw this circle around us
>   to protect us with love
>   in the power of the first name of the Lady.
>
> I draw this circle around us
>   to join us together
>   in the power of the second name of the Lady.
>
> I draw this circle around us,
>   this is endless,
>   in reverence of the third name of the Lady.
>
> In the three names of the Lady, this circle is made!"

Now Julie walked to the south and taking the white knife
from the pocket of her robe, she made a cutting gesture, as if
making an opening.

"Hear me, Lady, the Gate is open!"

Julie walked to the altar and raised her face upward. "The
power of the Goddess enters the circle!" she chanted. Asmodeus stood by her side, unmoving except for his tail, which
arched slowly from the earth upward and back. "It rises from
the earth through my legs, it fills my sex, it rises through my
belly, through my breasts, out my arms like sap rising through
a tree, it flowers and fills the air about us like branches of a
tree. Do you feel it? Are you ready?"

Julie now looked at us. Not knowing what to do, I nodded.
Edith nodded too. She had a wondering expression on her face
I could not remember ever having seen before.

Julie scribed a pentagon in the air with her knife.

> "I know by the powers of Air
>   By the powers of Water I dare;
>   By Fire I wield my Will
>   By Earth I am silent still,

And in their heart and hight
I tread my road aright,
Blessed be!"

The air seemed to quiver around us. Julie's voice rose.

"You who surround us,
Guardians, Watchers, the spirits of the unquiet Dead,
The Dead we were and are
And the unborn
Help us! Guide us! Bless us! Teach us! Approach and
speak!
For we are one in spirit, in death and in life."

Now Julie turned to the east, then the south, then west, then north. A wind had risen. Around us, the leaves rustled in the forest. The sounds had grown more distinct. We could hear the creek running over its pebbly bottom, the rustle of night animals, perhaps the uneasy movements of Fairchild crouched in the underbrush. Outside the circle. Unprotected from whatever Julie was about to summon. Did that frighten him?

Julie's voice now had a high, piercing, keening note.

"From the East, I call upon
The powers of Air;
From the South, I summon
the tongues of Fire;
From the West, I invoke
the singing of Water;
From the North, I command
The Wisdom of the Earth!

In the name of the Goddess,
We call upon you, the ancient powers!
Guide us! Protect us! Watch us!
Blessed be!"

Now Julie picked up the bowl of water on her altar.

"The Goddess has hidden her face and the water is dark," she chanted. "Earth, fire, air and water, in your presence I bow my head and serve Her power." She stared into the water for a moment. Then she stepped back and raised her white knife.

"You have given me the power to speak with spirits.
I accept.
You have given me the power to find what is hidden.
I accept.
You have given me the power to hear voices on the
wind. I accept.
You have given me the power to perceive truth in
cards. I accept.
You have given me the power to heal the body and
mind. I accept."

Her voice grew louder, the sound vibrating—high, intense, keening. It seemed to rise above the trees into the black, lightless, night sky.

"You have given me the power to bless, to ban, and to
curse. I accept.
You have given me the power to speak to restless
spirits. I accept.
You give me the power to unearth what is hidden.
I accept.
You have given me the power to change water into
wine—"

"Blasphemy! Shame!" Fairchild burst out of the underbrush, stumbling, his face red with rage. "The soul that goeth forth to wizards and soothsayers, I set my face against!" He was shouting. "Stop this sacrilege in the name of our Lord!"

"What the . . . ," I said.

The man charged at us, his face frenzied.

"Fairchild!" I shouted.

Julie held up her ankh, while Fairchild, clutching the cross around his neck, raged at her. "Sacrilege! Blasphemy!" He ran to Edith. "Edith, Edith, you must not do this! She has opened the Gates! She is about to call forth the Dark Spirits. . . . Break the circle!"

"*Margaret!*" Julie called, her voice high, thin, penetrating, overwhelming the hoarse, baritone cries of Fairchild. "*Hear me, Margaret!* The circle has been broken and profaned. You must depart. If you are near, I release you. I release you. I release you. The time is not now. We will call you again. Go with our blessing. Go, fair friend. Rest. Wait. Fare well."

She turned to Fairchild. Asmodeus, his tail flicking back and forth, his back arched, his green eyes blazing, stared at the minister as if about to spring.

"No, Asmodeus, no. He is frightened. Blessed be. Reverend Fairchild, we meant no harm. We call only the spirits of love."

"Love!" shouted Fairchild, his voice rasping, his breath panting. He staggered around the circle, blowing out the candles. He grabbed at the bowl of water and flung it outward so that the water, a gleaming sheet of black, sprayed out, splashing Julie.

But she stood her ground, gazing at him, her green eyes bright. "Reverend Fairchild. We meant no disrespect to your gods. They are ours too."

"What's gotten into you, Fairchild?" I said, collecting my wits. "Settle down." He had been staggering around the circle, pushing the branches aside, kicking at the candles, panting. I gave him a gentle shove and he collapsed, falling on the ground.

Edith hurried over to him. "Rollie, what's the matter?"

"She was going to talk to spirits," Fairchild said, trying to rise, but failing. But now he sounded slightly ashamed. "She was going to let them reveal the secrets . . . "

"Rollie," Edith said. She sat gracefully down on the ground next to him and stroked his arm tenderly. "Julie's ritual, don't let it worry you. She's so young. Just a child. It's nothing. It's not serious."

"What secret are you afraid she'll tell, that's got you so upset?" I demanded.

"May God forgive me," Fairchild said. "I did it out of love."

"Did what?" I said.

"Cully asked me to say he was at my house that night, the night Cyane . . . got hurt. I didn't see any harm in saying it. Poor man. Distraught, succumbing to drink. Needs loving kindness. I offer succor, yet he goes on drinking, he repents but God forgive me, he backslides."

"But you lied. Cully never came to your house the night of the storm, the night his cat was tortured, did he?" I said, staring at Fairchild, my fingers clutching my eye talisman.

"No, no, not that night. He came the night before. I confused the two nights. Surely, no harm done, a little white lie."

"No, it's a big black lie. You hound this girl while you yourself try to blind us all so we can't see the truth. If there's evil here tonight, it's in you!"

"John Charles! What's the matter with you? Look at him," Edith said, giving me a look of disdain.

Fairchild half sat, half lay on the ground, his eyes wet with tears, twigs sticking out of his hair, his face scratched and dirty. He looked truly beaten and pathetic. I knew the man would never forgive me for trapping him into this, for seeing him like this.

"You had no right to bring him here, to put him under this kind of pressure, to talk to him like that," Edith said, her voice colder than I had ever heard it. "It seems like you did it to get him to break Cully's alibi for Cyane's torture. Surely you could have found a better, kinder way. This was cruel and heartless." She helped Fairchild up and the two of them began to walk back toward the house.

I turned away. Despite all my rationalizations, had I conned Fairchild into coming because I thought he'd get upset and tell the truth about Cully? Did that mean that I suspected my old friend after all?

Julie muttered incantations under her breath as she collected her bowl, candles, knife, and other paraphernalia. I helped her. In silence we headed back up the pathway. The clouds above began to thin out and stray rays of moonlight filtered down through the branches. One fell upon Julie's face. She looked calm and far away. For a moment, I thought I saw a sly, satisfied smile cross her lips. Then the look vanished. I must have imagined it.

Later, well fortified with Blanton's single-barrel, I removed the Poe casket from its hiding place and found the paper I remembered, that I knew—somehow—I needed to read.

Ratiocination, intuition, and delusion

My dear descendant,

I write to you today, July 1, 1849, in a quiet moment, a moment of peace, when the storms that have so beset me are at bay and for a moment I am calm. Rare and rarer are these moments, when I am not buffeted by unbearable suffering. Like the narrator of my story "Manuscript found in a bottle," I move unseen through a ship of wraiths, bound for a terrible destination, and nothing I do will alter my inevitable fate.

Death grows ever nearer, the ship, drawing closer and closer to the whirlpool . . .

I must grasp those gleams of light, of clarity, set them down, here, like beacons from beyond the grave. . . .

How strange, when I reflect that no person is less liable than myself to be led away from the severe precincts of truth by the ignes fatui *of superstition. Yet, that said, there are moments when, even to the sober eye of Reason, the world of our sad Humanity may assume the semblance of a Hell—but the imagination of man is no Carathis, to explore with impunity its every cavern. Alas! the grim legion of sepulchral terrors cannot be regarded as altogether fanciful—but like the demons in whose company Afrasiab made his voyage down the Oxus, they must sleep, or they will devour us—they must be suffered to slumber, or we perish.*

And yet—and yet! I assert that the higher powers of the reflective intellect will conquer. Have I not kept madness at bay with the strength of my analytical will?

Do you, my dear descendant, fear blindness yet dread to open your eyes? Are you tormented, wondering how to descry the difference between the Hell of our Humanity and the Demonic caverns we dare not enter?

Are you cursed with the same dreads as have shadowed my life, because my blood runs in your veins?

I have little comfort to offer. But hold on to this: The ingenious are always fanciful, and the truly *imaginative, never otherwise than analytic.*

Yes, analytic. This is the charm that may save you.

First, observe. See what is before you! Do not be deluded by what you wish to be true but direct all your attention to what is. Second, remember. To observe attentively is to remember distinctly.

Consider a player at whist. The winner is he who has the knowledge of what *to observe. Do not reject deductions from things external to the game. Examine the countenance of your partner, comparing it carefully to that of each of your opponents. Note the variation of face as the play progresses, gathering a fund of thought from the differences in the expression of certainty, of surprise, of triumph or chagrin. A casual or inadvertent word; the accidental dropping or turning of a card; embarrassment, hesitation, eagerness or trepidation—all afford, to the apparently intuitive perception, indications of the true state of affairs. By such observation you will know the truth and the terror of the unknown may be kept at bay.*

Fancy, imagination, intellect, analysis. My descendant, I urge you, master the power of imagination by the discipline of intellect. Then you may risk much, so long as you do not wake the demons of the voyage of Oxus.

NINE

Everyone wanted to help look for Margaret's body. To hear folks talk, they'd all loved her, they all grieved for her, they wouldn't rest until she had been found and given a holy burial. All around me, in the Jefferson school gym, I could hear them whispering to each other.

The sheriff briefed us all on how he wanted the search to go, then picked out search-team leaders. He put me in charge of a group that included Edith, the Beebees, Bunny Shelton, her husband, Woody, and their son, Billy. Unfortunately, Billy was the short dark kid who I had gut-punched during the set-to over Julie. Catching sight of Edith in my group, Fairchild joined us. However, when he saw Julie heading in our direction, he gave me a look and departed.

I knew most of the people gathered together to search for Margaret's body. Of course Lawrence Cully had come, along with Julie. All three teenagers who I had routed: Tiny Beebee, Billy Shelton, and the acne-faced muscular one had come. There were other teenagers too. They clustered in groups. Some wore jeans and school jackets. Others wore army fatigue–style pants, long baggy black coats, and clumpy black boots. This group had strange hair, tattoos, and rings in unexpected parts of their bodies. The two groups of teenagers stayed away from each other.

People's faces looked white and strained in the harsh fluorescent light of the gym.

"She shouldn't be here," Tiny hissed, as Julie approached us. "It's not right." The kid towered over all of us. I had watched him and his friends while the mayor and the sheriff spoke. They had not sat on the rows of folding chairs. Instead they had leaned against one wall of the gym, ignored the mayor's speech, glaring alternately at the weirdly dressed kids and at Julie. Tiny's friends had come over with him to our group, but seeing Julie, their easy demeanor changed. From looking like charming young citizens, the next generation of Crowley Creek "establishment," they metamorphosed into threatening adolescents in thrall to a sudden testosterone surge.

"No way I'm going to search with that crazy witch," Billy Shelton said, giving Julie a look of disdain.

"Now, Billy, that's not polite," Bunny Shelton said, without much conviction, and I noticed she had put as much distance as she could between herself and Julie. Julie did look strange, but no worse than usual. She wore a long floppy black-velvet jumper over a black short-sleeved T-shirt, big chunky black boots, long crystal earrings, and a strange-looking pentagon pendant. Asmodeus sat on her shoulder as usual. The color of his short glossy black fur blended into the velvet of her jumper, so it looked almost as if the cat and Julie were one being.

The sheriff wound up his instructions and people began to stream out of the gym. A fine rain was falling. The blacktop in the parking lot glistened with water and I saw oil rainbows in the puddles. Cars had begun to peel out of the lot. The sky, heavy with ominous gray clouds, hung low over the town, so you could not see very far into the distance.

My group divided up our "quadrant" and agreed to rendezvous at Shelton's at five. "You want to come in my Bronco with me and Edith?" I asked Julie, hoping she'd say no. After finding the ax and attending her aborted witchcraft ceremony, I trusted her less than ever and feared her more. I couldn't shake the feeling that she knew too much about Margaret's death. Too much for an innocent person. And no matter how often Edith told me that Julie was just a confused teenager, I couldn't help but feel she had some power over me that I didn't want to examine too deeply and that I resented.

"No, that's okay. I'm going with Dr. Cully. He knows the fields that you assigned us better than I do."

"So Asmodeus doesn't know where Margaret is?" I said to her. It came out nastier than I had intended.

Julie fingered her pendant. The crystal beads in her earrings glowed in the filtered light. "Asmodeus loved Margaret," Julie said.

"Margaret was kind to him?" I asked, despite myself. "Even just before she disappeared?"

Julie tilted her face toward me. Her green eyes narrowed and grew murky. Her face looked pinched. "Margaret was kind to everyone in this world, blessed be," she said. She tugged at her hair and an expression of pain crossed her face. "But looking for her will do no good. It will not help her." She turned away and climbed into Cully's pickup. He leaned out, waved at me, and drove off with Julie.

All that day Edith and I searched our designated area for Margaret's body. We tramped through fields looking for freshly dug earth, we searched through abandoned barns, uncovered and stared down disused wells. We inspected melancholy, partly built houses, checked out discarded car carcasses, and prowled around one large car graveyard. Nothing. By four that afternoon, damp, discouraged, and tired, I dropped Edith off so she could clean up, went home to do the same, then, dry and clean, but still dispirited, exhausted, and needing a drink, I headed over to Shelton's.

I opened the door expecting the usual commotion and noise. Instead, a dull muted sound greeted me. The jukebox was silent. People sat around, barely talking, drinking coffee or beer. Even Mayor Jackson Lee Winsome looked sad and de-

flated. Edith leaned over the counter and chatted with Woody
Shelton, who had returned and taken up his station. I headed on
back to the mayor's usual table, where he sat with Mrs. Boynton, Mort Beebee, and the sheriff.

"How y'all doin'?" I said. "Any luck?" Although I knew the
answer. You could tell from people's demeanor.

"Nope," the mayor said. "A terrific effort. Commendable.
Commendable. These good folks searched their hearts out. But
no sign. Whoever did it hid her real good. Looks like we're
not going to find her."

"Hey, Rump, surely you're not giving up?" I said, pulling up
a chair and sitting down. "If we don't find her body, Cully will
never know what happened to her. And how can we figure out
who did it?"

The sheriff shook his head. He had a mug of coffee in front
of him. He picked it up with both hands and took a long deep
sip. "You know this county as well as anyone, John Charles.
You and your daddy hunted it all, some time or other, right?
You think, if someone wanted to hide a body in some thicket,
some brush, some swamp, and bloodhounds couldn't find it, we
would?"

"You might," I said. My voice sounded unconvinced.

"Yeah, we might. So that's why we looked. And we'll be
keeping our eyes peeled, you can count on that. But for now,
there's nothing more we can do. Mayor says we've spent
enough money looking."

I turned my attention to the mayor, who did not meet my
eyes. "Dr. Cully says this searching, it's hopeless, it's like salt in
a wound. He's all tore up about losing Margaret. Rump told
you how it near broke his heart, seeing that ax. But now, he
needs to move on. He wants us to let it go. Told me that himself this afternoon, after we finished searching all over his property. Dug it up something awful." The mayor shook his head
and looked at me. Seeing my expression, he smoothed a hand
over his bald spot. "And we got to watch the taxpayers' money,
John Charles," he said. "Nobody's going to thank me come
election time if I just throw it down the sewer."

"Sewer?" Edith had come up behind me and had been listening. "I don't believe I'm hearing you right, Jackson Lee," she said. "We can't stop looking. We have to find Margaret's body. We have to!"

"Dr. Cully's right, we need to move on," Mrs. Boynton said. "This whole thing's not healthy for Crowley Creek."

"A downer," said Mort Beebee, smiling his easy smile, while his cruel little hazel eyes looked at me as if intending to turn me down for a loan. "In a precarious economy like this one, we must do everything we can to keep up an attitude of optimism. Look to the future."

"You're talking about a woman who may have been viciously murdered," Edith said, standing tall and staring down at Mort Beebee as if he were a bug. "Not a business deal. A kind gentle woman who met a terrible end. We owe it to her not to give up."

"I know how you feel, Edith, and it does you credit," the mayor said, smiling his synthetic oleaginous smile. "Sit down, join us, let's talk this out."

"I don't think so," Edith said, her eyes moving from one to another with the same cold, judging expression. "No, I don't feel like it."

I stood up. "See you later, people," I said. I walked Edith over to another table and we sat down. I saw that she was in a rage. I had never seen her so angry. Her mouth turned in so tightly I could see the tension in her jaw muscles. A vein throbbed visibly at her temple. "It's another one of the mayor's cover-ups, John Charles!" she said. "He knows something, that son of a . . . son of a . . . "

"He just thinks it's useless, Edith," I said gently. "I know you loved her, but don't you think . . . ?"

"No! No, I don't. Margaret gone, an ax with her hair and flesh found, and we just forget about it? And he says—remembering, searching is bad for business! I don't believe it. *Bad for business.* Forget that Margaret had her head cloven in and we don't know what happened? I'll never never never accept that. Wait a minute. I get it. He's trying to protect Dr. Cully!"

"What makes you think that?"

She turned to stare at me. Her cool, wise gray eyes looked deep into me. "You still trust Dr. Cully, John Charles?" she asked.

I thought about her question. I didn't want to answer quickly. The question was too important. I *had* trusted Cully. All my life I'd seen his kindness, his willingness to go that extra mile for any human or any animal in pain. And Margaret had been loyal and loving toward him and he toward her—as far as anyone knew. In a small town like this, wouldn't folks know if there had been trouble between them? Could a man change that much? Could a man that kind murder his wife?

On the other hand, he had lied about the night his cat, Cyane, was tortured. The man had changed and couldn't be trusted. He might have fooled Fairchild into alibiing him. He had fooled me for a while, but I could no longer hide from the fact that I didn't trust him anymore. I thought he had gone bad in some way I didn't understand.

And I didn't trust Julie either. I thought she had some part in everything that had gone wrong. She had brought something ugly to Crowley Creek. Yet I didn't go along with Fairchild and his cant about demons and devils. In fact, I found Fairchild's behavior suspicious. Why was he trying so hard to turn the town against Julie?

I didn't agree with Edith when she called Julie's practices childishness or theater. No, if I had to choose between a man who had been good all his life and a girl who spoke to spirits in the moonlight, I'd go with the tried and true.

"I'm not sure what to think anymore," I said. "But it seems to me that Julie is involved somehow. She is lying and she's scared to tell us what about. And so are you," I said. "You know things about Margaret. You worried from the moment she disappeared because you know things."

"John . . . " Her eyes, piteous, pleading, looked back at me.

"Okay, I'll investigate. I'll spy on an old friend. Just don't tell me Julie gets messages from her cat, okay? Just don't tell me that." I got up suddenly, shoved my chair back against the table, and stormed out of the coffee shop. Outside the light rain had turned into a downpour. A vicious slashing fork of lightning lit up the dark sky and then in the distance I heard the long, sinister, pulsing drumroll of thunder.

The next day the clouds began to break up and thin rays of pale spring sunshine struggled through the front plate-glass window of the *Sentinel* where I sat at my computer terminal trying to psych myself up to "investigate" Margaret's disappearance as I had promised Edith. But how?

"Almost done with your article on witchcraft and Devil worship?" asked Mrs. Boynton. She had come out of her office and taken up her favorite spot just behind my right shoulder, where she could read off my computer screen. I hoped she enjoyed looking at the blank screen and blinking cursor.

"It's going great. Just great," I said.

"You plan to include the attack on Sue Anne Beebee?"

"Absolutely," I said. I had no idea what she was talking about. But I couldn't admit that to my boss. "Just on my way out to the Beebees' right now." Anything to escape Mrs. Boynton watching me not working.

I went outside, got into my Bronco, and drove out of town over to the Beebees'. What could Boynton have meant, an attack on Sue Anne? How did that woman know everything that happened in town before anyone else?

At the Beebees', the door was shut, curtains drawn, and no cars in the drive. When I rang, the door opened almost immediately and I saw Barbara Jane Beebee, looking tense and unhappy. "John Charles!" she said. Her smile flickered and vanished. Her hair had been pulled back in a ponytail, she wore no makeup, a sloppy white sweatshirt, jeans, and bare feet.

"Please excuse me dropping in like this, Miz Beebee. . . . "

"Oh, Barbara Jane, please," she said, smiling harder, but her smile looked forced and did not reach her eyes.

"Barbara Jane. I've come to find out how Sue Anne is doing."

Barbara Jane frowned. "She's not real well right now, John Charles. I'd rather not, if you don't mind."

"The *Sentinel* needs to find out what happened to her," I said. "It's important."

"Important? To who?" But she wasn't used to confronting people and she couldn't maintain her resistance. "Oh, all right, I guess we can't hide it." She led me back to the kitchen and seated me at a polished colonial-style maple table, then bustled around getting me some coffee and cookies.

"Be right back," Barbara Jane said. She retreated while I sipped my coffee and munched on a peanut-butter cookie. A few minutes later she returned, her face made up, her hair neater, wearing a pair of loafers. "Excuse my appearance, I've been mostly staying home with Sue Anne since it happened. Trying to, you know, help her. I just hate for anybody to see me like this." She smoothed her hand over her hair and gave me a weak smile.

"You look as lovely as ever," I said politely.

"Oh, go on," she said, but I could see she had begun to perk up.

"What exactly *did* happen, Barbara Jane? I hear so many different stories."

Lines appeared around Barbara Jane's mouth and between her eyes. She leaned forward. "Someone attacked my little girl, right here in this house. Can you believe that? Climbed up the drainpipe and attacked her in her bed!"

"How terrible for you. You must feel so vulnerable. Who would have thought anyone could get up one of your drainpipes? They don't look strong enough."

Now her pale, frightened eyes looked at me. "That's just it, John Charles. No one could. Those drainpipes wouldn't support a person. But we found muddy footprints around the bottom of the pipe, mud smears on the pipe, and mud on her rug the next morning. And the footprints . . . " She put a hand over her mouth. "I can't say any more about it, please. Okay?"

"I understand, I surely do. It must have been absolutely terrifying," I said. The idea of someone getting into a little girl's room, going up a flimsy drainpipe that couldn't support more than fifty, sixty pounds at most, gave me a chill. "May I have your permission to talk to Sue Anne? She's such a bright, lively little thing. I bet it would cheer her up to be 'interviewed' by a reporter. I'll be careful not to frighten or push her. You can listen and stop me if I say something you think I shouldn't. I'd like to put her picture in the paper too. I bet she'd love that."

"She surely would," Barbara Jane said, looking undecided. "But I don't know. . . . "

"I'll be careful," I said with my best smile. I got up and started walking back toward the stairs. "You'll see, she'll love being in the paper. Fifteen minutes of fame in Crowley Creek will help her recover."

Of course I still had no idea what had happened. I could see that Barbara Jane didn't like talking about it. I hoped Sue Anne would be more forthcoming.

We walked up the curving stairs and along the second-floor gallery that overlooked the entry to a doorway. Barbara Jane knocked. "Sue Anne, honey? It's Mr. Poe come to interview you for the paper. What do you think of that?"

"Mr. Poe?" Sue Anne's voice sounded high and much younger than the last time I had heard it. Barbara Jane opened the door and I entered into a dimly lit pink boudoir. Pink-checked gingham curtains waved gently beside an open casement window. A small glass-topped dressing table with a ruffled pink gingham skirt and a Pocahontas lamp sported bottles of toilet water and piles of Barbie and Ken dolls. Shelves held toys and games. Dolls and CDs were strewn across the white and pink-flowered carpet. Propped up in bed on two large pink pillows, huddled under a pink comforter printed with mauve and light blue miniature bouquets, I saw the wan face of Sue Anne. "Did you hear what happened, Mr. Poe?" Sue Anne said in a tiny little-girl voice. "You said you had no black magic in your house but looks like you lied, don't it?"

I came over to her bed, looked around, then took the stool from the dressing table and pulled it up beside the bed and sat down. "How are you doing?" I said gently.

"I'm doing real good for a little girl who got chopped up with an ax, right, Mommy?" Sue Anne said.

"Yes, you are, dearest thing," Barbara Jane said, coming over, leaning down and kissing her daughter. She smoothed a hand over the little girl's forehead then gave me a look that went right to my heart. "Sue Anne's restin' and recoverin' from her ordeal," Barbara Jane said. "You can write that up in the paper and put it alongside her picture."

I took out my notebook and wrote in it. "I'll say that she showed courage . . . ," I said, pausing and holding my pen above the page, looking at the two of them expectantly.

"Them devils chopped up my whole bed," Sue Anne said. Her voice sounded a little perkier now. "This here's a 'tirely new bed. New sheets, new comforter, brand-new. Mommy went to Richmond to buy all new stuff. She bought me chocolate candy in a box shaped like a heart and a scuba diver Barbie too. I slept in the guest room until the new bed came and Daddy slept in the other bed to protect me. And Daddy got workmen to take down the drainpipe too. Water might rain right into my window."

I wrote busily. "How many devils came into your room, then?" I asked.

Sue Anne's face got paler and she gulped. "I saw the horns! They had an ax. They went *chop chop chop.* Mama had to call a carpet man to rub it out—their dirt! That was from the pig feet."

"They were pigs?" I asked.

"They were devils. But the doctor said it was a miracle. I didn't get a mark on me."

"Because you were so brave and didn't move," Barbara Jane said, kissing Sue Anne's pale cheek. "Mort and I heard her scream and came running. We found her sobbing, the bed practically chopped to pieces and muddy marks on the carpet, on the sill, leading down the drainpipe. We looked out, then Mort got his shotgun, ran downstairs, but no sign of anybody out there."

"Doesn't sound like devils to me, if they leave footprints,"

I said, hoping to calm the little girl's terror, which I could see just below the surface of her returning bravado. Barbara Jane was right. Sue Anne was a brave little girl. She wanted to surmount her fears and I thought she soon would get the better of them. Strange that she hadn't been hurt. Even assuming the little girl's story suffered from childish misapprehensions, exaggerations, and confusions, it did appear she had been attacked by one or more assailants, one wielding something like an ax—I noticed she had only mentioned one ax—who had left curious footprints behind.

"Mr. Poe? Can I tell you a secret?" Sue Anne said, looking at me anxiously.

"Sure you can, honey. I'll be right outside if you want me," Barbara Jane said. She walked to the door and stood there, watching.

"I got to whisper. Lean close," Sue Anne said, whispering herself.

I leaned close.

Sue Anne pressed her fresh little face against my ear. I smelled flowery lily-of-the-valley toilet water and her cotton pajama top, covered with little pink rabbits, brushed my cheek.

"Tiny couldn't find your powers casket when he broke into your den, but he took a little picture of your grandfather what wrote all the books and a magic glass ball and a statue of a bird you have."

The magical objects in question in fact consisted of a little miniature of Edgar Allan Poe, an old paperweight I had given my daddy for Christmas one year—you turned it upside down and snow fell on Santa and his reindeer—and a tiny brass figure of a raven. All inexpensive little pieces of bric-a-brac that had been around so long, mixed among so many other such things, that I had never noticed that they had been taken.

"Tiny buried them by where we come through your hedge and put a teeny cross in the dirt so the witch couldn't use them. We're sorry. But don't dig 'em up, please?"

"Okay."

"I'm a good girl, really."

"I know, Sue Anne."

"Will you promise to put my picture in the paper and write that I was brave?"

"You have my word on it," I said.

Walking down the stairs, I asked Barbara Jane about the "pig" footprints. She didn't answer until we reached the door. She opened it, and we both stepped outside into the chill, damp air. "Nobody understands the footprints," she said. "At the bottom of the drainpipe and in Sue Anne's room, crossing back and forth between the bed and the window. Sheriff photographed 'em and showed 'em to lots of people. Smaller than a human foot, too big for an animal, cloven . . . "

"Like . . . "

"Yes, John Charles. Like devil's footprints." She attempted a derisive, ironic smile but did not succeed. "Good-bye, thank you for calling," she said, as politely as if I had come for tea. Then she turned her back on me, went inside, and shut the door. I stood there for a moment, staring out into the empty driveway, astonished, frightened, and angry. Then I got into my Bronco and drove back to town.

TEN

I knew it was time to talk to Julie, really talk to her. I couldn't go on avoiding it, asking Edith to do it, or sabotaging my encounters with her like I had by inviting Fairchild to watch her witchcraft ceremony. I tried to figure out what it was about her that troubled me so. After all, she couldn't be more than seventeen years old. She'd had a tough life in those few years, you could see it in her eyes, in the dead pallor of her skin, in the way she walked most of the time, hunched slightly, as if avoiding a blow. In the way she pierced her body, those holes she'd made for rings around the rims of her ears and in her nose. But the Poe in me sensed something else, something dark, something that threatened me.

Much as I didn't want to admit it, I knew that Fairchild felt it. Cully seemed oblivious and that worried me. I remembered Fairchild saying Cully had begun to have trouble with drink after Julie arrived in town. I had dismissed the remark, but it was true.

I'd see what Edith had to say first.

Edith and I met for lunch at The Old Forge. I ordered a

beer, a burger, and a side of hush puppies and Edith had barbecue and salad and iced tea. I told her about the attack on Sue
Anne.

"What do you make of it, John Charles?" she asked me.
"After all, Sue Anne's only a little girl. How old is she, ten?
Eleven? Obviously something happened to frighten her half to
death. But horned devils swinging an ax?"

"I know. And going up a drainpipe that wouldn't support a
person? And cloven hoofprints?"

Edith smiled. "Of course it all makes sense if you believe in
the occult. She was attacked by two devils and it happened in
some other dimension, so her body was untouched."

"Right. They leave footprints, devils. I think I read about it
in H. P. Lovecraft when I was a kid."

Edith looked uneasy. "You're not saying you believe that
stuff, are you?"

"I don't want to. Remember what Sherlock Holmes said.
When the impossible is eliminated, you accept what's left, no
matter how improbable. Well, lots of possible explanations are
still lying around. Maybe her brothers sneaked into the room,
left marks on the carpet, scared her with a pretend ax."

"She'd know her brothers—even disguised—don't you
think? And what about the marks on the drainpipe? And didn't
she say they came in the window? And why would her brothers
want to scare their sister half to death and trash her bed? Don't
forget, that was a real ax. You said the bed was practically destroyed."

"When you interviewed Julie, what did you find out?"

Edith pushed her salad around with her fork. "It's a trou-
bling situation in town right now," she said. "I don't think I've
even skimmed the surface of what's going on."

"What do you mean?"

"Well, to put it in context, there's witchcraft, like Julie practices. The people involved call it a religion and try to do good.
It's a worldwide movement with lots of decent people involved,
yet I'm sure some folks—especially religious people—think that
Wicca is evil. It's pre-Christian, it's not dualistic, they don't

see good and evil as two battling powers, and they don't think sex or promiscuity is wrong. They believe in magic and spells and ancient gods, you know?"

I nodded. When I studied American literature at U.Va, I learned about a gnostic thread that runs through American life. We studied Thoreau, Emerson, Whitman and learned about their love of nature and their bias against established religion. Wicca fit right into that.

"Then there's the Satanism," Edith said. "That's a different matter altogether. Followers often seem attracted to cruelty, to pain. There's a rock group out of Richmond called The Dead Souls that has drawn a lot of followers. Some kids in town are big fans and my kids were getting into it, which is one reason I want them to spend time with Rollie Fairchild. Religion can be a powerful antidote and Rollie is charismatic."

Not to me, I thought.

"I know you don't like him, John Charles, but Rollie helped my boys see how wrong the Satanism ideas are. Now that baseball's in full swing, and Bobby's so good at it, I think my boys have turned away from this Devil-worship stuff. They'd rather fit in with the popular kids if they can pull it off. And another thing, I get the impression from what my boys say that they can no longer play both sides against the middle. They can't follow The Dead Souls, wear the clothes, and still keep their old friends. They have to choose. Because what looks to be happening is that the kids around here are dividing into cliques. The straight kids, the athletes, the popular kids on one side. Then the oddballs, the misfits, the troubled kids, they are drawn to this Devil worship. And somehow, the straight kids see Julie as an enemy. They think she's a leader of the others, though in fact, she doesn't have much to do with either group. She's an outsider to both."

"Teenagers," I said. "Maybe that's all it is."

"We don't want to underestimate the situation, John Charles. I've got the feeling the problem in town goes deeper than normal conflict between teenage cliques. Ever since Julie came to town, things have gotten a lot worse. She's polarizing feeling in Crowley Creek. It might have blown over, but with Margaret disappearing, and now it looks like murdered, people are really scared. I've heard people say the Devil is afoot in town, doing his evil work."

"Oh, come on," I said, uneasily.

"Who will the Devil get next, they want to know."

"Oh boy. And I'm supposed to do an article on this? Whatever I write, someone will want to lynch me." I felt like saying that Fairchild had to take a big responsibility for stirring people up. Who had put out the idea that the Devil was at work through Julie if not him? It made me angry that Edith could not see how much evil the man did under his sanctimonious cover.

Thinking of Fairchild reminded me that he had implied that the Cullys' cat, Cyane, got hurt while in Margaret's care. "Edith," I said. "Do you think it's possible that Margaret was having some kind of nervous breakdown? That she tortured Cully's black cat? He hinted she'd been treating animals badly, and so did Fairchild."

"That's ridiculous," Edith said, flushing.

"I asked Julie about Margaret, but she avoided the question. Something about that girl really bothers me. It's going to be hard to write an article, with her in it, that doesn't make things worse."

"Julie has a strong desire to heal," Edith said. "She knows so much about herbs and plants. Maybe if you write up that side of her, people will see her differently. Lots of people in town like the idea of herbal medicine. And her love of animals—John Charles, she's helped lots of people's pets. Look what she did for the Beebees' setter. Dr. Cully had given up on him and he's pretty well completely recovered, thanks to her."

"You like her, Edith?"

Edith hesitated. "She's got big problems, John Charles. And I think she knows things about Margaret she won't tell me and that bothers me. And worries me. But my heart goes out to her. She's so lost. If a child of mine had lost her way like that I'd want to help. I think Julie may be growing dependent on me. I don't intend to let her down no matter what people think."

"You have a golden heart, Edith," I said. We looked at each other for a moment and I let the deep goodness in her wash over me. I felt better than I had in a long time.

But the feeling didn't last. Hearing Julie's voice on the phone when I called up to make the appointment changed my mood. It didn't get any better when I headed over to the Cully Vet Clinic at five. Because I walked in on something real ugly.

As I drove in, I saw a small, smoky fire. It looked like a heap of rags, burning dangerously close to the door to Julie's apartment. As I approached, a can of paint collapsed into the fire, making a whooshing sound and jetting out gusts of flame. A bunch of teenage boys were beating on the garage door, shouting. They had planks and crowbars and the door looked about to splinter. A tall black locust tree grew up near the garage, some of its branches scraping the roof. This was the tree Asmodeus used to climb in and out of Julie's window and he sat on a branch, leaning over, looking at the boys and spitting and hissing. I got out of my Bronco as one of the boys yelled a string of curse words at the big black cat and flung a chunk of two-by-four at him. Asmodeus sidestepped it easily, then crouched back down and glared at the boys.

"Hey! What's going on here?" I shouted.

"Come out, come out, witch, or we burn the garage down!" yelled the angriest of the boys. It didn't surprise me to see that the shouter was Billy Shelton. He struck the garage door with an iron crowbar. It splintered a little, opening up a gap between the painted boards. The door wouldn't hold up much longer.

"Now, y'all, stop that!" I yelled. "You're wrecking Dr. Cully's property, do you realize that?"

A tall blond boy turned toward me and his face reddened. I realized with dismay that it was Bobby Dunn, Edith's oldest. "We got to get that witch outta there," he said, but I saw shame in his face.

Six strong reckless angry teenagers armed with crowbars

and planks looking for trouble. As they turned toward me, Tiny Beebee waved his two-by-four in my direction. "This is none of your business, Mr. Poe. You better butt out."

I walked slowly and calmly toward them, forcing my face into an expression of puzzlement. "Hey, come on, you guys. Why are you beating on Dr. Cully's garage? This is crazy."

"That witch set her cat on us," Bobby Dunn said. He seemed relieved to have an excuse to stop what he was doing and move away from the door. One good thing. They had stopped battering the door. Even though it meant the attention of six enraged young men had turned to me. I saw a green eye appear in the hole in the garage door. They had trapped Julie in there.

"That so? Why'd she do that?"

Billy Shelton swaggered over to me, smacking his two-by-four against his legs as he walked. "We organized a little surprise for her and that slimebucket cat warned her, she took off, locked herself into the garage, and then the cat turns on us. But she's gonna get her surprise and you're not going to stop us."

"Whatever. Party's over, time to go," I said. "And you guys need to think on what you did to Dr. Cully's garage door."

"Why you protecting that witch?" The third kid I remembered from my dustup on the night Julie picked herbs had come up from behind his friends. The big pale angry one. The one who had twenty pounds on me and acne scars and a mean, ugly scowl. "The cat call you?" I saw he had a bicycle chain wrapped around the knuckles of his right hand. He began to unwrap it and loop it into a big lasso-type ring, which he swung back and forth as he spoke. "I say your party's over and time for *you* to go."

"Don't make things worse for yourself, son," I said softly. "Six guys ganging up on a little girl doesn't weigh more than a hundred pounds soaking wet, it doesn't look good."

"This is dumb. I'm outta here," Bobby Dunn said. "Come on, you guys. Mr. Poe tells Dr. Cully, he's going to hold us responsible for the garage door. I got enough troubles at home without that."

"You wimping out, Dunn? Cause if you are . . . ," Tiny Beebee said. Bobby Dunn looked undecided. I could see that Tiny
Beebee was the leader, but I thought that Billy Shelton's rage
made him more dangerous, and their big friend seemed the
most unpredictable and dangerous of all.

"You going to let a *cat* save that witch twice?" the big acne-
faced kid said.

"Look, Ray," Tiny said. "That cat . . . face it . . . that cat's
not normal. He warned the witch and whenever we have a run-
in with him, Mr. Poe here shows up. Think about that. We
need to take care of the cat, but not now. . . . " He realized that
he was revealing something to me and he stopped suddenly.

"No way. I'm going to get this witch-lover for what he did
to me last time," the muscular kid, Ray, said. He stood about
ten yards away. He swung his loop of bicycle chain and advanced on me.

The other boys stood rooted to their spots by the in-
evitability of what was about to happen. Faintly, as if very far
away, I could hear Bobby Dunn saying, "Hey, Ray, that's dumb,
don't do that, come on. Ray . . . ?"

"Witch lover, witch lover," Ray chanted, his white face
tense, his acne scars like little crevices of dark shadow on his
face. I focused on the chain. I could feel the circle of my attention shrinking in until all I could see was the chain, swinging in
faster and faster gyrations. It had reddish rusted links. I could
hear the sound of his panting breath, the sound of the chain
whistling in the air.

He kept coming. Five yards, now. I ducked and scooped up
a rock the size of a fist that lay by my foot and let loose, aiming
right for the center of his forehead. He sidestepped it, and in
that instant, when he was off balance, I darted in close to him,
under the swinging chain, kicked and hooked one of his legs
with my foot so that he overbalanced and fell sideways. Then
we were both on the ground, I on top of him with a loop of the
chain in my hand. He pulled back on his end. The chain rasped
on my palm and the flesh burned. I held on, but gave him slack
so he'd think I dropped it. Then, just as he thought I'd let go

of the chain, I yanked it back as hard as I could. He yelped and I had the chain and he didn't.

We rolled over each other, he trying to get on top, to bear down with his superior weight, both of us trying to land a telling punch and failing. I could hear him panting, cursing, could smell rage and sweat. Letting him bang on my back with one fist, I bore down on one of his arms, immobilized it, got the chain looped around it. Then, I wrenched away from him, got myself up to a kneeling position, and yanked on the chain. I left myself open while I did it and he twisted up on his knees and socked me in the gut. I felt the air go out of my stomach and I doubled over. The fingers of his free arm scrabbled at the chain on his other arm, trying to loosen it. He struggled to free himself from the chain, gasping with pain, lying in the dirt, kicking out. I got another loop of chain around one of his legs, pulled back, got myself upright somehow. I staggered away, dragging him behind me.

He let out a roar and a string of foul language. I stopped, turned, and saw him doubled over on the ground, blood seeping out of his leg. The tension on the chain had ripped his pant leg, revealing lacerated flesh and a piece of skin hanging loose.

I saw that I had gotten a loop of chain around one of his arms above the elbow and another around one leg and then tangled the chain so he had been pulled into a crouch and I had dragged him several paces along the graveled drive.

I looked at him and he at me. Just like the last time, the fight had gone out of him. His eyes looked like two brown marbles, cold, angry, and unreadable. "You gonna behave if I untangle you?" I said, controlling my breathing and speaking as calmly as I could, though my chest heaved and my legs felt weak.

"Yeah."

"Y'all gonna get the hell out of here and not come back?"

"Sure, right. Promise."

"You give your word on that, Tiny?" I said.

"Yeah," Tiny Beebee said. I handed him my end of the chain and he unwound his buddy and then the whole gang of them headed over to two cars that I saw had been parked on the other side of the garage. Ray limped and left a trail of blood drops.

I heard them get into their cars, slam the doors. Then a window rolled down. "You'll get yours, Poe!" a voice shouted. "Consort with witches and the Devil takes his own. Just wait."

"And tell your witch friend to keep an eye on her cat, 'cause sooner or later he's going to be cat meat," shouted another voice. Then they peeled off in a spurt of gravel and dirt, digging up the grass on the side of the driveway, and drove away down the highway in a blare of squealing tires, hoots and catcalls.

I stood for a moment, waiting for my heartbeat to return to normal, my legs to regain their strength. I could feel the adrenaline surge still racing, but now my anger focused on Julie. Her secrets had to come out. This couldn't go on.

I heard the garage door slide up. "John Charles? You okay?"

I turned in time to see Asmodeus streak down the black locust tree and leap onto her shoulder. She reached up and caressed him, her green eyes focused on me. "You okay?" she repeated. She kept stroking the cat's black fur and it wrapped its tail around her neck. "Come on up, I'll give you some tisane."

"What's this fire?" I said, trying to get hold of myself. I kicked angrily at some ash. The fire had burned down, so all that remained was a small heap of smoking trash.

She stepped around the fire, and opened the ground-level door in the garage. "They set a trap for me. They placed a can of paint on the door lintel. They imagined I would open the door and the can would fall on me and splatter me with black paint. The kind that won't wash off.

"But Asmodeus warned me. I put some cloth on my twig broom and then I put the broom out the door. The can fell upon it and the cloth got soaked with paint. I went out to talk to them but they would not listen. Then one of them set the cloth and paint afire. They tried to take me but I ran into the garage and locked the door."

She climbed the stairs to her apartment and I followed. At the top, she unlocked the second door and we entered. The room was bright, for the sun, sinking low in the sky, shone directly into the living-room window. A faint sickly sweet scent of incense and hot candle wax permeated the room. The sun lit up the shabby sofa, the threadbare rag rugs, the worn flooring and dust motes dancing in the air.

"I'm so lucky to have my own apartment," Julie said. "I never did before. I love the early spring evening here. Soon the Sun God will sleep and the Lady will rise to rule the night. As he departs, he blesses us with his golden light."

What crap, I thought. I hated when she talked like that. With the adrenaline still rushing through my body, I quivered with unsatisfied aggression. I wanted someone to pay for the fear and rage I had felt and for being forced to beat on a kid I had no quarrel with.

"You and I need to talk," I said, beginning to pace the room. I walked to the window and looked out. The ceiling was low. I felt cramped. She fitted perfectly into the little apartment while I felt like a hulking monster. She went to the kitchen area and plugged in an electric kettle. It made a hissing, bubbling sound. I kept pacing the room, looking at her crystal ball, her velvet cloths embroidered with strange designs, her pentagon made of willow branches, her black candles twisted into grotesque shapes. On a table I saw her two ceremonial knives. They lay on a black velvet cloth, their blades razor sharp. Steam began to emerge from the kettle. Julie poured boiling water into a brown earthenware teapot.

"We'll just let that steep," she said in her soft voice. "Can I get you something to eat? I have some special seedcakes."

"No thank you."

"You're still very angry."

"Yes."

"Here. Sit down. Look at this." She selected a smooth green stone speckled with red from a glass bowl of stones. "Just look at it." She handed it to me.

I took her hand and put the stone back in it. "I don't want to look at it," I said. As I touched her skin, my fingertips seemed to burn, and I rubbed them against each other as if to wipe away any residue she might have left there.

"Oh," she said, staring at me. She wore a long shapeless dark green dress. You couldn't see her body, only her white face, masses of black hair, and the gold ring pierced through her nose.

"Please sit down," I said, controlling my feelings with an effort. "I need to ask you some questions."

"Of course." But she did not sit down. She drifted back to the teapot and unwrapped it. She took out two brown earthenware cups without handles, filled them each with steaming brew, and handed me mine. Small leaves floated on its surface and strangely scented steam rose into the air. Because the cup had no handle, I had to wrap my hands around it, and despite myself, I felt the effect of the warm rough earthenware between my fingers and of the scented steam. What I really needed most at that moment was a Blanton's single-barrel, but I took a sip. It tasted like something which should not be in a human's mouth.

"Tell me . . . ," I began.

"Yes, anything." Those green eyes looked at me and I felt their power.

"About Cully. About Cully and Margaret. You were here before she left. You saw . . . "

She sat down on the sofa at the other end from me. Asmodeus jumped on her lap. She began to stroke him, tilting her head down so that all I could see was her thick black hair and a white part running like a scar from the crown of her head to the hairline.

"Rh . . . thrnah . . . ," she said.

"How's that?"

Silence.

"Julie!"

But she had begun to shiver, just like she had been shivering when I had walked in on her and Edith, right before she led us to the ax. I knew she wanted me to hold her and comfort her.

I shoved my hand in my pocket and gripped my talisman. It felt smooth and yielding, and I remembered how white it was, white as Julie's smooth translucent skin. I rubbed it and then I felt it stir and quiver under my fingers.

I yanked my hand out of my pocket and edged as far away from her on the sofa as I could. "Tell me," I said.

She reached out to the side table and picked up her tea mug, her hand shaking, and sipped on it. Without lifting her head, stroking the cat more rapidly, she said, "Margaret said he was changing, drinking, changing."

"Changing how?"

"She treated me so kindly, so good to me, I adored her, John Charles. I loved her with all my heart."

"Changing how?"

"Angry. He'd drink and he'd beat her. She'd run and hide."

"He beat her? Cully? Come on."

"Rage mastered him when he drank. He let in the demon of rage and it beat her. Asmodeus and I told her she had to run away."

"You told her to run away?" Why would Margaret Cully listen to a crazy teenager?

"We were friends. She knew I had the second sight. She knew I had powers. I read her cards. The cards showed rage and a long journey. The Three of Swords meant she must make a change in her life. She had to go away from here. But I never thought a journey meant a journey to the other side, to death!" Julie began to sob. For a moment, I completely forgot my suspicions and doubts about her. For what man can hear a woman sob without wanting to comfort her? The little bit of a thing huddled down over her cat and dissolved into anguish, shaking and weeping. Her sobs seemed wrenched out of her, spasms of grief. And I, cowardly, completely at a loss, I got up and left.

Driving home, I saw Venus, the evening star, pulsing in the deep purple of the early evening sky. I thought I heard Julie's sobs. Get hold of yourself, John Charles, I thought. Remember what your ancestor, Edgar Allan Poe, wrote: observe, remember, analyze. Did I believe Julie? Had Cully lied to me or did the truth lie somewhere in between? Maybe Cully, the worse for booze, lost control when he saw Margaret torturing the animals. He'd surely implied that she'd done that. He had hinted that it was she who had gouged out Cyane's eye and hanged the poor miserable animal. I could imagine how, if Margaret had been cruel to animals, it might enrage him beyond reason. All my observation told me that Julie had been lying, or hiding something . . . or . . . she deluded herself, protecting herself from seeing certain things because she couldn't bear to look. As for her witchcraft talk, I knew I shouldn't let myself be drawn in by it.

I drove into town and parked in front of The Old Forge. I badly needed a drink.

ELEVEN

It didn't surprise me to see Lawrence Cully at the end of the bar, looking the worse for wear, a glass of golden whiskey clenched in his big thick hand. He stared into the mirror behind the bar, past the bottles of scotch and rye and bourbon, morosely studying his reflection. I sat down next to him, and as I did, I realized that I just couldn't believe old Doc Cully had beaten up on his wife. There had to be some other explanation for what Julie thought she'd seen. "Hey, Cully, how ya doin'?" I said.

"Oh, splendid, splendid, absolutely splendid." He had a glass of ice water next to his bourbon glass and he took a deep sip, then wiped the back of his mouth with his hand. "Nothing like spending the evening alone, drinking, thinking about all the stupid things you shouldn't have done."

"I know just what you mean. Want to have some dinner with me? We could drive out to . . . "

"Nope. I just want to stay here and work my way through the bottle, understand?"

"Sure. Why not?"

He had hunched his shoulders, but now he saw that I didn't intend to judge him and he relaxed. Far be it from me to think poorly of a fellow who wants to ease his pain in the time-honored way.

"Mind if I join you?" I said. "I'm not feeling particularly proud of myself at the moment. Tommy, a Blanton's, double, and a tall ice water!"

"How's that?" Cully said.

Tommy brought me my drinks and we both took our glasses over to a booth along the wall. I told Cully what had happened out at his place, and how I'd hogtied the acne-faced kid, Ray. "I keep seeing him hunched over on the ground, bleeding, humiliated, you know?" I said, taking a soothing sip of my Blanton's and savoring the burn. "I remember what it felt like to be seventeen. I must have weighed one-forty soaking wet, six feet, clumsy as all get out, always felt out of place. Whatever I did didn't seem to go quite right. Things would happen and I never understood why. I'd go into black depressions, when I didn't feel good for anything. My daddy used to tell me it was the Poe curse, and I had to pull myself out of it with grit and character, or I'd end up like old Edgar Allan, dead in a ditch at forty."

"Sounds like a real supportive old bugger."

"I guess you could say he lacked parenting skills, but the fact is, he had a point."

"Yeah. Tommy! I had a point when I sent Margaret away. But it wasn't kind. And who knows . . . if I hadn't . . . "

"Cully," I said, leaning forward, looking right at him. "*Why* did you send Margaret away?"

He looked back at me. It was as if I saw his face for the first time. I saw his eyes, the lids heavy, half covering the irises, pale flecked with brown. The whites had red veins running through them, like inflamed forks of lightning. His skin, sallow and glistening as if it were greasy, sagged under his eyes, revealing red rims at the bottom. Deep lines ran from his bulbous nose to below his mouth. And his mouth, moist with bourbon, seemed swollen. He had the face of a serious, troubled drinker and looked as if he had aged ten years in the last month.

"Margaret always wanted something from me, but what? I'd ask her, 'What do you want? What do you want?' but I never understood her answers. Then she got jealous because she saw I loved the animals more than her. Sad commentary, don't you think? Preferring animals to your wife. But they never expect you to be what you're not. They have a dumb helpless goodness. They don't shriek abuse . . . ," he tailed off and swigged down his bourbon. He gestured to Tommy for another round.

I shook my head.

"But no matter how angry she got at me, she didn't have to take it out on the animals, did she?"

"You saying Margaret gouged out Cyane's eye?"

"She wasn't herself, that's the only thing I could think to make sense of how she acted. Maybe she was mad at me and she took it out on them. What do you think, John Charles?"

I didn't want him to know what I thought. "Don't ask me. I don't understand women. At all."

"Give me a break. You got that sexy Marilyn Larue, Edith Dunn looks at you like you're God on wheels, and Julie talks about you all the time."

Tommy brought our drinks and some peanuts. Cully grabbed a handful of peanuts but he didn't eat them. He squeezed them in his hand. Hard. Then he opened his hand and stared at the crushed peanuts in surprise, as if wondering how they had got there. "Margaret and me . . . it had gone old and sour, you know? Everything got dried up and dead between us, and that's the truth. When I saw her hurting the poor creatures, I knew she wasn't herself. I told her to go away, get help, and I'd tell people she went to her folks. She agreed. She knew I was right." He made his fist into a tube and poured the nut fragments into his mouth. The skins of the peanuts stuck to his hand and around his lips and he licked them off. His tongue reminded me of a dog's, thick and wet. "But would you believe it, as soon as she left I started missing her. If that don't beat all. You'd think I'd of been happy not to listen to the whining and bitching and crying. And now I know she's never coming back and I sent her to her death and the quiet is noisier than her loudest carrying on. Who'd want to hurt her? That's what I don't get. If animals could take revenge . . . But I can't see cats and dogs swinging an ax somehow, can you, John Charles?"

He lifted his glass and held it for a moment, staring at me over the rim. I looked back and in his eyes I saw nothing I understood. Then my gaze moved past him, past the crowd of drinkers, to the windows at the front. A tall plane tree stood just outside the front window of the tavern. In the shadows of its high branch a dark shape moved, and I saw the glint of slanted green animal eyes. Asmodeus. But then I saw it wasn't me he watched, it was Cully.

"I heard you beat up on a bunch of teenagers last night," Mrs. Boynton said to me the next morning, the moment I walked into the door of the *Sentinel*.

"Didn't exactly happen like that," I said mildly. I hung up my windbreaker on the coat tree and walked over to the coffeepot. "Buzz in yet?"

"Of course not. Our intern runs on New York City time. Late to late," Mrs. Boynton said, walking over to the coffeepot. "But don't try to distract me, John Charles." She looked right at me, her little black eyes boring into my skull. "You think you can stand up for that Julie but you're wrong. Things are coming to a head. What those boys did at Cully's, okay, it was wrong. But those are sons of influential people. Good kids. You defend that girl against them, people around here won't stand for it."

"By people, do you mean you?"

"Now, John Charles, don't go getting your back up. We need to get that girl to move on. She's a real bad influence."

I took my coffee back to my desk and switched on my computer.

"You know that cat of hers has taken to following Dr. Cully around town? You know what people say about that cat?"

"Hey, I saw that cat last night. Wow, is it strange, or what?" Buzz had come in while Mrs. Boynton spoke and now he joined her by the coffeepot. "You should have seen him. Slinking along the ground like this black shadow, behind Dr. Cully, jumping up on trees and watching him. Real sinister, like the cat is hunting him or something. You know all about hunting, John Charles. Do cats hunt people?"

"It's news to me," I said, calling up my electronic mail to see if the syndicate that handled my columns had gotten any more weeklies to sign up.

"You going to do what I asked, John Charles?" Mrs. Boynton said, coming up behind me and reading off my terminal. Now she, too, knew that another group of regional weeklies had turned me down.

"Not likely," I said. "That girl's not doing any harm to anyone. More the other way round, I'd say."

"She's sexy in an oddball kind of way, don't you think?" Buzz said, giving me that knowing grin young guys think prove they are worldly. Sotto voce he said, "Getting any?"

Mrs. Boynton glared at him. "How are you coming on that article about Mayor Winsome's Charolais bull and how it's improving the breed around here? Lots of folks want to breed bigger beef cattle and they need to know about that bull. You were supposed to have me twelve column inches yesterday."

"Uh, I was hoping to help John Charles on this devil-worship thing. I think there may be a national story in it. Get picked up by the wire services."

"I believe I assigned *you* the story on the mayor's breeding operation. Tomorrow is the deadline. Now I need more words. You can go two full columns. We lost three real-estate ads, so the news hole is bigger. Get on it."

"Okay," Buzz said. He had tried standing up to Mrs. Boynton when he first came to Crowley Creek, but he had given it up as a lost cause.

"And you, John Charles, I want your story on the evils of

witchcraft and the dangers to our young people this week, no more excuses. Quote Fairchild. Give him a little sidebar. And a quote from the Baptist ministers too. Might be a good idea to get a quote from the evangelicals. Be fair."

"How about a quote from the witches and Satanists telling their side?"

"They don't have a side, that's how the *Sentinel* sees it. Make sure that's how you see it. The town is coming together on this, John Charles. I'm warning you, you are either with us or . . . "

"Or?"

"Don't make me threaten you, John Charles. I don't want to do that. You know how things work in this town. We're tolerant and open. But folks here believe in right and wrong. That there's good and there's evil. You get to the line, tolerance starts to dry up. This paper won't survive if people believe we don't stand up for the right. Do you get my drift?"

"But who decides where that line is?"

"Around here, I do," Mrs. Boynton said. She stomped over to her office, went into it, and slammed the door behind her.

I put her out of my mind and got to work. I spent the rest of the day assembling my notes and writing my story about witchcraft and Satanism.

But at five o'clock, still struggling with my story and failing to get what I wanted, I gave it up and headed out into the evening. I drove into Richmond, and by the time I arrived, night had fallen. As I came into the city, I saw the lights on the office towers twinkling against the murky sky. The air glowed with the reflected lights from the city, blotting out the moon and stars.

I went first to the train station and then to the bus station and I talked to everyone I could. I showed them the picture of Margaret I had slipped into my pocket that time I drank with Cully.

But Richmond train- and bus-station ticket takers and jan-itors and snack-stand owners looked at the picture and said it looked like too many people they saw, couldn't say if she'd been at the station the day I mentioned, the day of her disappearance. Didn't remember her, probably wouldn't even if she'd been there.

But when I described Julie, I got a different story altogether. Lots of folks remembered *her* and the big black cat with the green eyes that sat on her shoulder.

Piecing together the bits I got from different people, I had a story, but what did it mean?

I wanted to talk to Edith. I called her from the station at Richmond and asked if she could meet me somewhere for a drink.

"I don't think so, John Charles," she said. She sounded down. "Not unless you want to come out here to the house. I've grounded Bobby and I need to stay home to enforce it. I think you know why."

"Would it be okay for me to come over? Maybe I could cheer you up."

"I guess so," Edith said. "I told Bobby you hadn't said anything about him being with the mob that vandalized Dr. Cully's garage and threatened Julie, but I'm not sure he believes me. He's acting pretty hostile."

"I understand," I said. "See you in about forty-five minutes."

"Have you had any dinner?"

"Uh . . . don't trouble yourself Edith. . . . "

"I'll warm something up for you," she said. "See you soon."

"Rollie Fairchild told me what Bobby did," Edith said. She put a slice of meat loaf, some coleslaw studded with raisins, and creamed potatoes on a plate and set it on the kitchen table. It looked good. I wished she'd offer me a beer, but she didn't think of it and I didn't want to ask.

"Aren't you having anything?" I said as she poured herself a cup of coffee and sat down across from me. Edith lived in a house in "the Farms," the oldest development in Crowley Creek, built between the wars. It had a wide veranda around the front, white siding, green shutters, and dormer windows in the second story. Now the paint had begun to flake and some shingles had gone missing from the roof. Edith's husband had left her for his young secretary, and he often forgot to make his support payments. Money was tight. It hurt me that I had more money than I needed and she would only let me give her what she earned from her work for me, but I understood her pride and respected her for it. And despite the increasing shabbiness and signs of shortage of money, everything always looked spotless and well cared for. The kitchen floor shone, the counters had been polished to a spotless gleam, and pots of red geraniums bloomed on the windowsill.

We sat at an old polished cherry wood table, my plate set on a bright flowered place mat. I always felt happy to be at Edith's, but tonight I saw her face looked worn and tired. No sign of her sons.

"They're in their rooms doing their homework and that's where they're staying," she said when I asked.

"Bobby wanted to go when the kids got rough," I began.

"John Charles, I don't want to hear anything about it. Tell me what you found out in Richmond."

I thought Edith was being too hard on her son. Still, what did I know? I didn't have to raise two teenage boys by myself. She wanted me to change the subject, so I said, "At first, no one at the bus or train station in Richmond remembered Margaret, but when I described Julie, quite a few people recalled her."

"They were together, Julie and Margaret?" Edith said with her back to me.

"From what I found out, it sure looks like that. Talking to different people who saw them, I figure Julie drove Margaret to Richmond in Margaret's car, stayed by her when Margaret bought a ticket to Durham, had coffee with her at a snack stand at the station."

Edith turned to me. "Margaret bought a ticket to Durham?"

"Right. And I saw Margaret's car in Cully's garage, so Julie must have driven it back here to Crowley Creek."

"But Margaret never arrived in Durham. She called her

mother from Richmond saying she was coming, her mother expected her, but she didn't arrive. Remember, I told you."

"Edith," I said, putting down my fork. I'd finished everything on my plate and enjoyed every morsel, but my mood changed and the food felt like a heavy lump in my stomach. "Right now it looks like Julie was the last person to see Margaret alive. And I know for a fact she never told any of this to Sheriff Rumpsey. Rump has no idea that Julie drove Margaret to the station. I doubt Cully knows either. She never said a word about it to me. Did she tell you?"

"No."

"And she knew where to find the ax, don't forget."

"That was Asmodeus," Edith said. "He told her where it was."

"Do you believe that?" I asked her.

Edith got up and poured me a cup of coffee. "Have you noticed something . . . strange about that cat recently?"

"Stranger than usual you mean? Like what?"

"Like that white patch on his chest? I swear he didn't have it before, but the last time I saw him with Julie there it was."

"I don't believe this . . . ," I said half aloud, half to myself. "Just like in the story."

"You mean, where the black cat follows the narrator around and the narrator notices a white patch that gets bigger and bigger?"

"Yes. And the narrator has murdered his wife with an ax," I said. I could feel myself getting angry. "Someone is toying with me. Someone knows that story and is doing things to throw suspicion on Cully and to spook me."

"But how do you make a white patch grow on a cat's fur? What are you saying? You think Julie killed Margaret? That Cully is innocent?"

I didn't answer. I didn't know the answer. Truth to tell, I didn't trust either of them anymore. Both had lied to me. Both had hidden things. And why was Fairchild acting so strange if he wasn't involved in some way?

"Mom, can we make some popcorn? I'm starved. We had dinner *hours* ago."

Jase and Bobby Dunn, Edith's sons, peered around the kitchen door. I saw their two heads, Jase in front, Bobby behind.

Edith sighed. "Boys, come in and say hello to Mr. Poe."

The boys advanced cautiously.

Bobby, the oldest, at sixteen, must look like his father, whom I had never met, because he certainly did not resemble Edith. He had curly blond hair, large clear blue eyes with long pale lashes, and a thin, sensitive mouth. About five-ten, and gangly, several large pimples sprouted from his cheeks. His younger brother, Jase, although I knew to be thirteen, looked more like ten or eleven. A tiny dark-haired kid with an elfin chin, he had his mother's grace of movement and clear, thoughtful, intelligent gray eyes. "Hello, Mr. Poe," Bobby said, not meeting my eyes. "Hi, Mr. Poe," Jase piped in. "Mom, can we make popcorn?"

Something about Bobby Dunn got to me. I saw again that shame and regret I'd seen in his face at Julie's.

"That was brave of you," I said to him, "the way you stood up to Tiny Beebee and Billy Shelton, tried to stop them from going after Julie. And I appreciated the way you told Ray to back off when he came after me with the chain. That took courage."

Now Bobby Dunn met my eyes, and I read resentment and bitterness in his face. "Yeah, sure. A lot of good it did. Now everybody's mad at me." He darted a look at Edith. "I know I should've left when they started acting crazy, but I came in another guy's car. I *should* have left even if I had to walk. Mom's right." He crossed the kitchen to the cupboard and took out a bag of microwave popcorn. "Okay to zap this, Mom?"

Edith had been looking back and forth between us as we spoke. "I didn't know you tried to stop your friends," she said gently. "You didn't tell me."

"Aw, so what. Big deal. It was just a screwup. Things got out of hand."

"I'm sure sorry we helped those goofballs that other time," Jase said.

"Hey, I can call them that, you can't, button up," Bobby said, turning and glaring at his younger brother. "They're still my friends."

"You wish," Jase said. "They order us around."

Edith and I looked at each other.

"Jase, how much do you weigh?" I asked.

Edith stared at me in surprise at this incongruous question, but Jase answered easily, "Fifty-five pounds. There's kids in sixth grade weigh more. Gym teacher says I have small bones, whatever that means."

"Jase is best in his class at gymnastics, that's one advantage of his weight," Edith said, smiling at her younger son. "Jason will be like me, a late bloomer. He'll get his growth spurt in a few years."

"I just bet he's good at gymnastics," I said, looking at the kid.

Jase grinned back at me. "They call me the human pretzel," he said. He did a backbend, then suddenly flipped his legs over his head in a leaping backward somersault. His feet just missed the table. He came upright and cartwheeled out of the kitchen and down the hall. I followed.

"John Charles . . . ," I could hear Edith call. I ignored her.

Jase reached the stairs and—amazingly—walked up them on his hands. I followed.

Down the hall he cartwheeled to his bedroom with me right behind.

He flipped over and onto his bed where he began jumping, as if on a trampoline.

"Come on, stop it, I want to talk to you," I said.

He gave another terrific bounce, so that his head just missed the ceiling, then he settled down into his bed.

"So what did *they* make you do that you now are sorry about?" I said.

The clear gray eyes looked at me. "Guess."

"You went up the drainpipe at the Beebees'. You made pig

footprints. You chopped up her bed and almost chopped her."

"Tiny sneaked down the hall from his bedroom wearing a mask. He did the chopping. All's I did was make the footprints. I made a clay devil foot from my craft set and sqwoodged it up with mud and used that. Tiny was outta there before her parents came in. But she was too scared and it was no fun. Who could know Tiny would go ballistic like that? 'Course, he was careful not to hurt her. You shoulda seen me go up the drainpipe. *Spiderman!*"

"Why did she think you looked like you had horns?"

"We wore devil masks. We just meant to scare her so she thought it was the Dead Souls kids. Tiny wants everyone to think those devil worshipers are wrecking the town. I thought it would be cool. But it turned out dumb. No one blamed Julie and her devil lovers anyway. Guess what. Mommy feels sorry for Julie. She wants her to come over and for us to be nice to her. Can you believe it?"

"Your mother is a very kind person."

"Sure. You don't know her. Like, she grounded Bobby for a month. *A month!* Unreal. And he has to go over and repair Cully's garage door, and pay for paint out of his allowance. Are you going to tell on us about the Beebees?"

"What do you think?"

"You stuck up for Bobby. I bet now he gets reprieved. Would you stick up for me? Mommy will believe *you.*"

"You shouldn't have scared that little Sue Anne," I said. "I can't stick up for that. You have got to pay your dues on that one. But if you confess, apologize, I'll put in a good word."

"Will you tell on me if I don't?" The kid stared at me, those eyes testing me for something.

"I don't know. I have to think about it." Too much was going on I didn't understand. What was driving Crowley Creek kids into these strange escapades? Pretending to be devils. Why?

Jase looked disgusted. "Thanks a lot."

"You can solve it by telling your mom yourself."

But he didn't believe me. He rolled over on his stomach

and put his head into his pillow and his little body looked miserable lying there, all tense.

"Please get out of my room right now," he said, his voice muffled.

I obliged.

Driving back home through the night, I sped past fields, gray in the moonlight, past trees like clouds of dark shadow—the road running ahead, a body of blackness severed by a white line. I passed back through town and saw Cully's pickup parked at The Old Forge. I slowed. Outside in the tree I saw the black shape of Asmodeus. I parked, got out of my Bronco, and walked under the tree. "Asmodeus!" I called softly. "Come down from there, I'll take you home. Come on. Time to go."

The cat leaned over the branch and looked down at me. Now I saw a white patch glowing on his breast, eerie and mysterious. His green eyes studied me. Then he turned his attention back to the window of the tavern. I called him several times but to no avail.

I gave up and went home.

TWELVE

The mayor stood up. "Okay, folks, time to call this meeting to order!" he sang out, his mellifluous voice carrying to the far end of the auditorium without aid of the microphone that sat on the table. He tapped it. "I don't need this thing, y'all can hear me back there?"

A chorus of "yes," "too wells," and "just greats."

"Now, we've called this special meeting at Reverend Fairchild's request, because he has some serious concerns he wants our council to address. I know we're all going to listen real careful to what he has to say. The reverend is famous statewide as an expert in problems like the one we have here and I believe we can learn from him. The reverend's told me he is hoping the council will decide to take action after we hear him out. We've agreed to listen to him and to do it in an open way, right here, so you can all listen too. After he's said his piece, we'll take comments from the floor. I'm countin' on y'all to be calm and respectful. When we've heard your views, your council will deliberate and make our decision. How's that sound?"

Hostile murmurs. Then someone shouted, "We want the witch out!"

"Go ahead, Reverend Fairchild," Mayor Winsome said, sitting down and gesturing magisterially to Fairchild.

Fairchild stood up, holding his Bible. I looked around. Most people were gazing at him respectfully. But Dr. Cully looked pale and anxious, and Julie, at his side, seemed to be shrinking down into her black clothes, as if trying to hide.

"Good people," Fairchild began in his smarmy pseudoloving voice, "as many of you know, I have studied faith and superstition, witchcraft and Satanism, the goodness of our Lord and the evil stratagems of his fallen servant, Lucifer. I'm here to talk to you about these things, to help you understand what is happening in our town. I've discussed my remarks with the ministers from Emmanuel Baptist and First Union. So no special pleading for my church." He smiled to show us this was a joke.

"I'll deal with her, just let me at her!" someone shouted.

"Go Julie! We love you!" An adolescent male voice from the back. I turned and saw a bunch of the supporters of The Dead Souls rock group slouched against the back wall. Boys and girls dressed in black, rings stuck in ears and noses, hair in dreadlocks or partly shaved, they looked like a flock of strange, misshapen, black crows.

Fairchild raised a hand majestically. "My friends . . . ," he began. I hated to admit it, but the man had presence. His blond hair radiant in the stage lights, his eyes seemed to burn with a fanatical fire. "It is my duty to speak to you today, for we have a self-admitted witch among us. Now I have spoken to her, and she has not heard. I have urged her to seek help to drive out the devils within her, but these devils are obdurate, stopping her ears so that she cannot hear. Friends, she is implacable in her ways. I dare not be silent.

"For as it is written in Matthew Ten: Twenty-seven, 'What I tell you in darkness, speak in the light, and what you hear whispered in your ear, proclaim upon the housetops.' No, beloved, I cannot be silent, when I see the Devil at work among us."

Murmurs from the audience.

"You may think that it is not our problem. You may think: Live and let live. But this, my friends, we dare not do. Dare not. Because there is supernatural warfare going on and we are all soldiers in this battle. You may hope to stand silent while the struggle wages on, but this is not permitted. And, thanks be to our Lord, we need not wonder what to do, because the Word is here and we need only follow it." He held up his Bible, then opened it and read in a thrilling voice: "My friends, 'Put on the full armor of God that you may be able to stand firm against the schemes of the Devil. For our struggle is not against flesh and blood, but against the rulers, against the powers, against the principalities of this darkness, against the spiritual forces of wickedness in the heavenly places. Therefore, take up the full armor of God, that you may be able to resist in the evil day, and have done everything to stand firm. Stand firm therefore, having girded your loins with truth, and having put on the breast-plate of righteousness, and having shod your feet with the preparation of the gospel of peace; in addition to all, taking up the shield of faith with which you will be able to extinguish all the flaming missiles of the evil one.' My friends, that reading is from Ephesians Six: Eleven to Seventeen. It tells us that we must fight against the forces of the Devil. We must recognize that—misguided though they may be—tools and victims though they may be—we cannot let the Devil's minions work their wiles among us. We must heed the Word of God. We must follow it!"

"Amen!" someone called out.

"When one among us blatantly rejects our Lord and calls upon the Devil's minions, we must speak out, we must act. For ourselves. For our children. We owe it to our immortal souls!"

Mayor Winsome stood, smiled at Fairchild, and nodded calmly. "Thank you for that reading and your words of wisdom, Reverend Fairchild. Now tell us, what exactly are you askin' for?"

Fairchild turned and pointed to Julie. "The witch must repent of her sins, renounce her demon companions and familiar, and come to our Lord, or she must leave this place!"

The mayor—to his credit—looked uncomfortable. "Well now, I understand your point of view, but how . . . "

"Leave! Julie out! Go go go!" The townsfolk began to chant, drowning him out. It sounded like a ball game, when the spectators are worked up against the away team, except that tonight I heard, in the calls of the crowd, a profound hostility, a sound that caused an ache deep in the pit of my stomach.

The mayor raised his hand and the chant died away to be replaced by a tense, uneasy silence. He surveyed the other members of the council: Mort Beebee, Iris McCain, Jack Tanner, Mary Lou Amos. They sat, looking out over the gym, assessing the mood of the citizens of Crowley Creek, their expressions stony. Then they turned their faces toward Beebee. It seemed he had been designated the spokesman in this charade.

"She ought to go of her own free will," Beebee said. So that was their plan. Beebee nodded as if thinking of this for the first time. "Yes. That's what I think would be best. Why don't we just leave it at that for now, give her a week to think about it? We're reasonable folks."

The other members of the council nodded sagely, as if moved by these words of wisdom.

The mayor turned to the audience. "Your town council wants to let her leave of her own free will, now that she's heard how we all feel," he said. They'd planned it all. Planned to let Fairchild stir up the crowd, then planned to leave it to Julie to get the message.

"Why not take a straw vote?" Beebee said, his sly eyes darting around the audience.

"Good idea," the mayor said. "How many agree with their town council on this?"

A thunderous sound of approval from the audience.

"And how many oppose?"

A silence.

I stood. "The reverend has quoted the Bible to us. But he hasn't given us a single hard fact to show that Julie has caused harm to anyone."

"You opposed, John Charles?" someone called out. "You want the witch to stay in town?"

My fist clenched. The talisman had found its way into my hand and it felt icy and seemed to resist my grasp. "What harm has she done?" I shouted.

Then Edith stood up in her place. "It's a sad day when an entire town turns on a young girl with no evidence," she said, her voice strong.

"That's right," Cully said, his deep kindly voice carrying to the far corners of the room. "She's come among us to help us with our animals, and we need her. We truly need her."

Hostile murmurs. But before their voices could rise up and overwhelm us, the mayor put up his hand. "Good points, John Charles, Edith, Dr. Cully. Good points. Let's not be hasty. Let Miss Julie think on what she's heard. I'm sure she'll make a wise decision. I move this meeting adjourned. All in favor?" He looked at his council then banged a gavel on the table. "Meeting adjourned!"

Julie, Dr. Cully, and I walked out together and Edith came after us, joining our little group. Everyone else left a big hostile space around us. Fairchild came up behind Edith. "Edith!" he said. "I know you mean well, and I understand. Please, we need to talk. Let me give you a ride home."

Edith looked at him. "I am sorry you cannot enlarge your mind and your heart wide enough to make a place for Julie in it," she said. "Tonight I want to ride with Julie." But while her words were firm, I saw the way she looked at Fairchild. She was still attracted, she still respected him.

Fairchild smiled at her. "I know when you think about what you have heard and seen, you will see things my way," he said. They gazed at each other and I felt my heart shrink, and I squeezed the talisman viciously. Then he went on to his car. Edith leaned over and whispered something to Julie. Julie hesitated, then she brushed her hair back from her face and smiled up at Edith.

"Tomorrow, nine-thirty, I'll be by for you. You give her a day off from the clinic. Okay, Dr. Cully?" Edith said.

"You betcha," Cully said.

Edith came over and got in my Bronco. "Take me straight home, John Charles," she said, the animation draining out of her face. She leaned her head away from me, resting it on the window of the passenger's side.

"I don't see how you can stand Fairchild," I burst out.

"Not another word on that subject, John Charles. I'm exhausted. And tomorrow I'm going to take Julie to Richmond for a day off. I'm going to give that gal a special day. Something to help her forget all this . . . *crap* . . . that Crowley Creek is loading down on her." Edith's fist clenched. "I'm going to give that little girl a *wonderful* day, you hear me? Then I'm going to bring her right back here and tell her to stand tall, we're behind her a hundred percent."

"Edith . . . "

"And," she turned to me, "I'll talk to her about what you and I need to know, John Charles, don't you doubt it. I hope that when she sees she can trust me, she will open her heart to me and I will find out what she's hiding, what happened to Margaret. She needs to let go of her secrets. I'll be back around five, give the boys dinner, then call you. Okay?"

I saw that Edith's eyes were wet, she was close to tears. Edith had given her heart to Julie. I just hoped she wouldn't come to regret it.

I knew something serious had happened the moment I walked in Edith's door, around ten the night after the town-council open meeting, and saw her face. She led me into the living room and told me to wait while she checked to see if the boys had fallen asleep. I heard her footsteps going lightly upstairs. Through the sliding-glass doors that opened out onto the patio in back, I heard the murmur of her voice and Jase's in reply. The evening air felt damp and oppressive and I could smell smoke from night fires on the air.

She brought me a bourbon and ice and surprised me by

pouring herself one. Then she sat back in a wing chair. I sat on the sofa across from her. I sipped and waited.

Edith sighed. "It's just so sad, John Charles," she said. "The older I get the sadder I think life is."

"Tell me."

"I gave Julie a beautiful day, I did."

"I'm sure you did, Edith."

"We went shopping in Carytown. I took her for lunch and then I took her to the Jefferson Hotel spa and she had a herbal bath in special scented water. But, John Charles, no matter that I bought her whatever she wanted, she didn't get any happier. Just sadder and sadder, as if something tightly wrapped in her had started to unravel and her sadness came leaking out." Edith ran her hand through her shiny black hair and I saw for the first time thin strands of white around the temples. They shone like silver. I liked them.

"Then, like I told you I would, I took her to Baskin-Robbins. Know what she told me? No grown-up ever took her out for a 'special day' like I was doing. And when I told her to order whatever flavor ice cream she wanted, she looked at me and sort of smiled and said, 'What if I want the black-licorice ice cream?' I said, 'If that's what you like, have it.'

"Then I saw something give way in her. I can't explain it. Like a rubber band breaking. And she started to tell me . . . "

"What, Edith?"

"That girl has had a dreadful, dreadful life. Her mother ran away with another man when she was seven. Her father—they lived in Baltimore—worked in the government, a civil servant, a churchgoing man. But he had feelings he couldn't handle and he started . . . he abused . . . he, goddamn it . . . he *raped* her from when she was eight years old until she ran away last year. She said she felt bad and dirty all the time and didn't tell anybody and pretended it happened to somebody else. Then, in high school, she had a teacher who she liked. She wanted him so much to like her so she said she gave him her body because he wanted it and it made him happy and it made her happy. He fifty years old and she seventeen and she blames herself. Then he got all guilty and tried to kill himself and she ran away and came here. How could she blame herself?"

Edith's eyes bored into me and I shifted uncomfortably on my chair.

Edith took a swallow of her drink. "But Julie says one thing saved her. She got involved with a group of women who were good to her. A coven of witches. They taught her witchcraft and showed her kindness. One night, in a ceremony that Julie talked about with this awe in her face, they gave her a black kitten—Asmodeus. Asmodeus got sick and Julie took him to a vet, followed the vet's instructions, and Asmodeus got better. Since then she says she's studied witchcraft and animals and herbs and that has been the best thing that ever happened to her. She says Asmodeus is her mother and her father and her child and her best friend. She says he never lies to her, never lets her down. He is never disappointed in her and never asks her to change. She says they talk together all the time. He gives her advice. Oh, John Charles, it's so pathetic!"

"Edith . . ."

"Her job at Cully's means everything to her. It's her lifeline after so much betrayal. When her teacher tried to kill himself, her father found out. Her father couldn't stand the idea of her with another man, let alone a man his own age. He turned on her. Before, he'd acted like sex with her was a kind of love. After, he got brutal and violent. Julie couldn't take any more. She said the Goddess and Asmodeus told her to run away. She had nothing. No money, no skills, no pride, no sense of herself, no self-respect. She told me she felt bad, evil even. Worthless. As if the Goddess might reject her and only the Devil would want her. But now that's changing. Now she's curing animals. It's like heaven to her. She's torn, John Charles. She's not stupid. She sees that if she drops witchcraft she might find a place in this town, but she can't do that. She truly believes in it and that's what's holding her together."

"Yes, I saw that."

"But that is not all there is to it. No, I'm sure of it. Something else is eating at her."

"Do you know what it is?"

"I don't. I have to tell you, I'm afraid to find out." Edith saw me start to speak and put up her hand. "But for Margaret's sake, I know we have to try. So I pushed her. I hope I didn't do wrong, John Charles, I truly hope so."

"What happened?"

"You should have seen her, John Charles. First, when she told me all this, I could see it was a great relief to get it off her chest. And when I showed my sympathy, she just let it all out, like a child, confessing to her mother. I could comfort her, well, anyway I did my best. . . . "

"I'm sure you did great, Edith."

"But when I pushed her to tell me what else she was hiding, her skin got real pale. I swear the color went right out of it. I've never seen anything like it, you could see the veins and all. Her eyes went all murky and she wept a river. That girl has another, more terrible secret. I'm sure it has to do with Margaret. She thinks if she tells it she will lose her job, her chance to redeem herself, her chance to work with animals. But the secret is tearing her up inside. She's right on the edge. Well, you know, you've seen her when she starts to shake."

I nodded.

"I couldn't get any more from her. I've read about that kind of thing, fathers and daughters, teachers and students, but I guess I never really took it in. Don't those men understand these girls are *children*? Sure they've got the bodies of women, but they've got the hearts and minds and understandings of children. We've got to protect them, not use and destroy them!"

Edith's eyes burned with anger and pain. "What's happened to us that we use our own children for our selfish purposes? And after all she's been through, what happened yesterday at the town council, John Charles, it's horrible."

"Yes, it is."

"Even Rollie Fairchild, a man of God, a good man, he calls her evil, humiliates her in front of everyone. After all she's suffered. I'll never forgive him."

I got up and walked over to the glass doors and slid them open. Tree branches moved in the backyard. I saw a dark shape in one of them and for a moment I thought I saw Asmodeus's green eyes looking back at me.

"We have to do something, Edith," I said. "No one else will."

THIRTEEN

sure liked that movie. What did you think, John Charles?"
Marilyn said. She looked happy. My Bronco sped along the
interstate and Marilyn tilted down the sun-visor on the passenger side, squinted into the mirror, and touched up her lipstick. We had driven in to Richmond to see a movie, *Waiting to
Exhale*, and then we'd had coffee and dessert at The Olive Tree.
Marilyn had laughed uproariously at the movie, relating to the
story of women who had troubles with their men. But I hadn't
been able to concentrate and now I could barely remember the
film. It faded away like an inconsequential dream as the dark
fields flashed by.

"Earth to John Charles, come in John Charles," Marilyn
said. "You haven't been really with it all evening. Maybe for the
last week or two even."

I didn't say anything.

"You mad at me 'cause I didn't come and sit with you and
Edith and Julie and Dr. Cully at the town-council meeting?"

"Do you think they're right to want to run Julie out of
town? To humiliate her like that?"

Marilyn looked down at her lap. "I don't know what I think," she said. "Something is wrong around here. Folks think it's witchcraft. I run a business in town. I'm not sure I exactly agree, but I don't want to act like I look down on everybody."

"Is that how you think I'm acting?"

"No, no. I'm sorry. That came out all wrong. I know you are doing what you believe."

"Thanks a heap."

"I can think different from you, you know. It doesn't mean I don't care about you."

"I'm sorry," I said. "I didn't mean to jump on you. But I'm all on edge. It's mostly Margaret Cully. I can't stop thinking about it. I can't get my mind around the idea that someone in town murdered her with an ax. Not Margaret. There's no sense to it."

"Poor Margaret," Marilyn said. She unrolled her window a little. I heard the wind rushing by. The Bronco is a noisy car. When you roll down the window a crack, you hear a high, eerie sound. I wished she'd open it farther or close it.

"I can't figure why she'd leave Cully," I said. "She seemed like such a timid stuck-in-a-rut type person."

"I bet she couldn't take it anymore, that's why."

"Take what?"

Marilyn hesitated. "I guess I can say now. She's gone and it's her secret, not his."

"Say what?"

"He beat her, John Charles. That man drank and lost it and whacked her something terrible."

"You sure? I've heard that but it's hard to believe. I've known Cully all my life. He's always been the soul of kindness."

"Maybe. But not lately. Not when he drank. Not after Julie came to town."

"Did Margaret tell you that herself?"

"I did her hair. She tried to comb it over the bruises on her face. She didn't have to tell me."

"Maybe she fell."

"Give me a break. Anyway, I asked her if he beat on her and she started to cry and to say it was the drink and all that crap, so I said to her, 'Don't tell *me.*' You know—hey, everybody in town knows—I threw out two husbands for drinking, fooling around, beating on me. It took a lot of courage but I did it. I told her that. Told her nobody has to put up with it if they don't want to."

"What did she say?"

"She said just what you'd think. How'd she support herself? He would change, he was real sorry. He'd apologized and she loved him and he loved her. He was a good man, da-dah, da-dah, da-dah. You saw how women fool themselves in the movie. Same old same old."

Marilyn sounded cranky. Time to change the subject, which I did. But all the way back to her house, I thought about what she'd said. And after we made love, I lay beside her feeling relaxed and better than I had in a long time, grateful for the straightforward, uncomplicated way Marilyn saw the world. Cully beat his wife. I hadn't been sure if I could believe what Julie told Edith. I hadn't even wanted to believe what Margaret hinted to Edith. But I believed Marilyn. She'd seen the bruises. You couldn't fool Marilyn about things like that.

Cully had lied. Cully beat Margaret. Margaret left him. She got as far as the train station in Richmond. Then she vanished. Obvious next step: Confront Cully. Tell him I know Margaret left him. Get the truth out of him.

Satisfied with this plan, I nestled up to Marilyn's sleeping body, buried my nose into the soft skin of her neck, and fell into a deep mindless sleep.

I pushed Cully's creaky old rowboat out into the creek and clambered in. Cully pulled gently at the oars and we headed downstream, toward Burget's pool, a favorite fishing spot of his. He'd been telling me about it off and on for years. So when

I said I felt in the mood for a day on the water, we'd arranged to give his favorite spot a try and he'd promised I'd be eating fresh fish for dinner.

The old rowboat rode low in the water, though all we'd brought were two six-packs, a plastic grocery bag of bought sandwiches, a net, and a sack of miscellaneous stuff: bug spray, camping knives, rags. I'd stuck my flies in my old outdoorsman hat and he had his favorites pinned onto his fishing vest.

We'd gotten an early start; the sun had not yet risen above the horizon. We headed downstream to a place where the creek widened out. Several smaller streams meandered into it, almost invisible under low-lying branches. Cully took one, barely wide enough for the rowboat.

"I took Julie this way once," Cully said. He hadn't spoken since he'd begun rowing and I was surprised by the tone of his voice. Tense. Troubled. "We came along here and just by Burget's pool she found some herbs she likes. Has to pick them early in the morning, apparently. Quite a walker, that girl. She'll walk five, ten miles through the woods, thinks nothing of it. Might even see her this morning."

I hoped not.

The stream widened into a pool that appeared to be fed by a spring close by. The water looked fresh and fast-flowing, yet I could see promising, quieter spots in the reed pools around the edges where insects hovered over the shadowy surface. We anchored the boat. I tied a fly on my line and cast into one of the pools. Cully did the same. For the first half hour we fished contentedly.

The sky got bluer, the air warmer. I took off my jacket and unwrapped an egg-salad sandwich and opened a beer. Breakfast. "This is the life," I said.

Cully sighed. He took a beer out of a six-pack, popped the tab, tilted his head, and drank. His Adam's apple bobbed as he chugged it down. "One beer just doesn't do it anymore," he said. "Must be grief." He smiled a grim, ironic smile and opened another beer. Then he stretched out his legs, shipped his rod, balanced the beer can on his soft, protuberant belly, and stared off into the distance.

"Can I get you a sandwich?" I said. "We've got egg salad, tuna salad, BLTs, and ham."

"Nope. I'm gonna drink my breakfast."

"Cully . . . ," I began.

He heard something in my tone, turned, and gave me a warning look. "Don't intrude on a man's grief," he said.

His voice sounded false. I think even he heard it, because he gave me a quick apologetic smile. "Some things are best left alone," he said, trying again.

I could see he was on guard. I wouldn't get anywhere asking him about Margaret. I finished my sandwich, crunched up the plastic wrap, and stuck it back in the bag. I picked up my rod and cast into a pool on the other side of the stream. As I reeled in, I said mildly, "Good of you to stick up for Julie at the town meeting. But it made a lot of people angry. You think it will affect business?"

"Don't give a damn." He hadn't started fishing again, he just sat, half lying, his legs stretched out ahead of him, one hand holding the beer can, the other arm dangling over the side of the boat, his fingers touching the water. "They can think what they want. When their animals get sick they need me. I'm the only game in town, vet-wise."

"I have to admit," I said, "that girl gets to me. I wish she didn't, but she does. Know what I mean?"

Cully didn't reply.

"I keep telling myself she's just a kid."

"She's not a kid," Cully said. His eyes were half closed. "She's a woman."

"You think?"

"Keep away from her, you hear me? You've got enough women."

Something in his tone unsettled me. My fingers, in my pocket, sought for my talisman, but then I remembered I had left it at home. Somehow, it hadn't felt right to take it with me, fishing.

To bait Cully, get him to open up, I said, "I think she likes me. . . . "

He sat up suddenly and turned on me. The boat rocked precariously and rivulets pulsed away from us. A glittering pattern of intersecting wavelets agitated the quiet pond. "You keep away from her. *You keep away from her!*"

"Say what?"

"She's mine! I got her, I keep her, nobody else gets any, you hear?"

I stared at him. "You telling me you're . . . "

I saw in his face that he hadn't meant me to know, but rage and jealousy had gotten hold of him and made him careless.

"She wanted it! She practically begged me!"

"What are you saying? A lost, desperate young girl needs work, she'd do anything to get a job, keep it. You can't take advantage of that. Don't you see?"

"What do you know? She loves me!"

"I don't believe this. You slept with her, with Margaret in the house? How could you?"

"Margaret was crazy anyhow. Ever live with a crazy woman? A man needs some sweetness in his life, not just a dried-up old stick."

"I bet it was you drove Margaret crazy. I bet it was you tortured the animals, not her. *You* gouged out your cat's eye, you hanged the cat when it ran away from you and hissed at you."

He had been looking at me with a strange, gleeful grin as I began to accuse him, and it widened when I talked about him driving Margaret crazy, but as soon as I attacked him for torturing animals his face changed. He swelled up, his chest heaved, his eyes narrowed then his mouth opened wide and out came a bellow: "No . . . o . . . o!" The sound of his agonized cry filled the air, echoing outward, striking me like a blow. He reared up, flung himself on me. The rowboat rocked, canted sideways, and dumped us both into the stream.

I got my footing first. The creek bottom felt soft and spongy under my feet, the water reached only chest high. The rowboat had turned upside down. Cully came up behind me, hollering something I could not make out. I splashed to shore to get away from him but he came after me.

I waded out of the stream and up onto the grassy bank. Water streamed off me and sloshed inside my boots. I turned to see Cully, his face swollen and purple with rage, bearing down on me. The man had a hundred and fifty pounds on me, the arms and chest of a professional wrestler and the craft of one too, and he looked absolutely out of his head. I glanced around desperately. I didn't want to fight him. Could I climb a tree? Escape through the underbrush? He had an oar in his hand. He swung it back hard and brought it down toward my head.

I dodged. "Cully! What are you doing? Are you trying to kill me?"

He looked at me and I saw in his face an uncontrolled bottomless rage, a lost self-loathing, self-protecting frenzy. At that moment, I knew I looked into the face of Margaret's killer.

Transfixed by what I saw, unable to move, I heard the whistling air as the oar descended again. Then I saw out of the corner of my eye, a black blur, heard an unearthly hissing sound, and Asmodeus was upon him, striking him full on the chest. Cully staggered back. I collected my wits. The cat clawed at him, shrieking and hissing and Cully fell, his head striking the earth with a heavy thud. Then I heard Julie's clear high call, far in the distance, "Asmodeus! Asmodeus!"

Cully had both arms over his face while the cat hissed and clawed at him. "Asmodeus!" Julie came out of the trees and the cat jumped lightly off his prey. But he did not run to Julie. He stood beside Cully, gazing down at him, his back arched, his tail rigid, pointing upward. "Asmodeus!" Julie said, her tone commanding. The black cat turned to Julie then looked back at Cully. Cully sat up slowly. He brushed at his face. Three scratches ran from below his right eye to the bottom of his cheek, oozing blood, tiny droplets glistening like red beads.

Cully looked at Julie and smiled. I did not understand his smile. Triumphant, warning, the smile of a master to his slave. Julie dropped her eyes. "Asmodeus, I told you . . ." she said, her voice now the tentative everyday one, the one with the seductive cast to it. The cat shook itself as if letting go of something. A writhing motion passing from his head to his tail. Then he loped over to Julie and leaped to her shoulder.

Julie walked down to the stream and waded in. She pulled the rowboat to the stream bank and righted it. She and I waded out and collected what we could find of the boat's contents, which floated in the slow current—the other oar, my jacket, the fishing rods, the bailing can.

"Come on, you two, I'll row you back," Cully said.

"No thanks," I said. "I'll walk."

"Long walk," Cully said.

"Fine with me," I said. I knelt down, picked up my rod, sodden jacket, and fishing hat and then turned to look at them. Julie bailing, using the coffee can, while Cully shipped the oars and organized the contents of the boat. Cully raised up the oars. Sparkling drops of water glistened on the edges of the blades and fell into the stream. He met my eyes. "Nothing you can do about it," he said. "Nothing you can say anybody will believe." He smiled, mocking me, laughing at me, then he turned his back on me and the boat glided slowly downstream, into the shadows.

FOURTEEN

An hour and a half later I stumbled up the back steps and into the kitchen, my clothing sodden, sweat-soaked, my arms and face bug bit and scratched from working my way through the underbrush, my feet aching. I had worked my way back downstream, through the brush, finding my way to old familiar paths, through fields and over creeks I had known since childhood. Every familiar old tree, foxhole, cattle crossing, and swamp seemed alien to me on that walk. The air seemed dull, the sunshine lifeless, the shadows threatening.

Pull yourself together, boy, I told myself for the hundredth time as I dumped my gear by the back door and stumbled up the stairs and along to my bedroom.

"John Charles? Is that you?" Edith, at work in her office. I had forgotten she had come in to work today, even though it was a Sunday. Her ex-husband had her children for the day.

"Be right with you," I called back. "Got to change."

I grabbed dry underwear, a clean pair of jeans, and a T-shirt and padded down the hall, my sopping socks leaving wet patches on the carpet. A hot shower, that's what I needed.

But no matter how long I stood under the steaming water, I felt no better. I got out, dried myself, dressed. The sadness in my heart remained, like a heavy weight. The sense of grief and betrayal. Another piece of my childhood ripped away, floating downstream with the soggy lunch bag full of tuna-salad sandwiches. Hadn't my father told me over and over that I never saw what was right under my nose? Why had it taken me so long to face the truth?

I didn't feel like talking to Edith. The memory of my father drew me to his library. I walked quietly past her closed office door, down the stairs, and into the library. The windows had not been opened, the air smelled musty, of moldering leather and old paper. Of truths written, shut into books that no one opened anymore and no one remembered until it was too late.

I pulled my copy of Edgar Allan's collected works off the shelf and opened it to "The Black Cat." Almost immediately, my eyes fell upon the passage I had been looking for.

Clutching my talisman, I began to read.

> *And then came, as if to my final and irrevocable over-throw, the spirit of PERVERSENESS. Of this spirit philosophy takes no account. Yet I am not more sure that my soul lives, than I am that perverseness is one of the primitive impulses of the human heart—one of the indivisible primary faculties, or sentiments, which give direction to the character of Man. Who has not, a hundred times, found himself committing a vile or a stupid action, for no other reason than because he knows he should* not?

I laid the book down and saw again the face of Cully as he let his murderous self show in his eyes. I picked up the book and continued to read.

> *Have we not a perpetual inclination, in the teeth of our best judgment, to violate that which is Law, merely because we understand it to be such? This spirit of perverseness, I say, came to my final overthrow. It was this unfathomable long-*

ing of the soul to vex itself—*to offer violence to its own na-ture—to do wrong for the wrong's sake only—that urged me to continue. . . .*

I heard a noise and looked up. Edith stood at the door of the library, staring in at me. "What are you doing here, reading in the dark?" she said. She walked across the room and opened the curtains. Sunlight streamed into the room and struck my face, dazzling my eyes.

"John Charles! What's wrong?"

"Come in, sit down, we need to talk."

Edith walked into the library. She was in her stocking feet and her footsteps made no sound. She sat down across from me and looked at me expectantly.

I set my book on the table next to the chair and tried to marshal my thoughts into some kind of order. But they wouldn't settle. I kept seeing images of Cully's face, purple and bloated, his eyes staring, the oar descending toward my head. Then I saw Cully and Julie rowing upstream into the trees, the wake of the rowboat a wide swatch of blackness in the stream. Then I heard Cully say, "Nothing you can say anybody will believe."

"What is it?" Edith said, her voice gentle, concerned.

I still couldn't find any words. She got up, walked over to my chair, knelt down next to it, and put a hand on top of mine. The cool gentle touch of her fingers softened the thick knot of grief and self-reproach in my chest and my mind began to calm.

"Cully killed Margaret," I said. I turned my fingers and held her hand tightly.

Edith didn't say anything. She just looked at me, waiting for the rest.

"It's so like Edgar Allan's story. But then, why not? Edgar just retold an old, old story. One we know happens around us all the time. The story of a good man who drinks, goes bad, beats his wife, then one day kills her. Cully *was* a good man. But he changed. Maybe drinking did it. People say that. I think it's the other way round. Some folks drink to be bad. They want to be bad. They choose to be bad. They drink so it can happen.

That's what Poe wrote in his story and that's how it looks to me. But however he came to it, Cully beat Margaret, he tortured his cat Cyane and he slept with Julie. He's still sleeping with her."

"Lord help us," Edith said. I saw her face change as she absorbed everything I had said and realized the implications. Saw first pity, then disgust, then determination. "We'll tell Sheriff Rumpsey. He'll deal with Cully. We've got to get Julie away from him." She looked at me, wondering, I'm sure, why I sat in my chair talking, rather then rushing to bring the law down on Cully.

"Tell Sheriff Rumpsey what?" I said.

"Well, what do you mean? Tell him what you just said." She gently freed her hand from my grasp and walked back to her chair.

"But why would he believe me? Cully will never admit to it. No one knows where Margaret's body is. If we could find it, we might be able to prove the force used to kill her was greater than Julie could use, but we can't find her body. The ax might be Cully's but no one can prove that. It's just an ax like everybody has. No fingerprints on it. And Julie sleeping with him? You think people in town will blame *him*? They'll say she wanted him and she got him. That she killed Margaret to have him. Look how hard it was for me to accept even that Cully beat Margaret. Only when I saw him change before my eyes. Heard the things he said . . . the terrible things he said. . . . "

"We have to think of something," Edith said, her voice soft. "He can't be allowed to get away with this. He can't."

As soon as she said those words I felt better. "Listen, Edith, the man killed his wife. He has to have left some kind of a trail. I bet if we know more about what happened the night she disappeared, we might get to the bottom of it. After all, we know she arrived at the train station with Julie, bought a ticket to Durham. Then what happened? We should be able to find out."

"Julie knows something. I'm sure of it."

"But didn't you say she's right on the edge? That you

pushed her and you didn't find out what she's hiding and you didn't dare push her any further?"

"It's so frustrating! Why would she be willing to cover for him if he murdered Margaret? She loved Margaret."

"Well, why would she sleep with him? You should see the way he looks at her and the way she cowers."

"I told you, John Charles. That job, working with animals, it means *everything* to her. And face it, she's accustomed to being used like that."

We both sat silently for a moment.

"There's a piece missing," I said. "Something just isn't right with all this."

"You're sure he did it? Killed Margaret."

"No question. Absolutely sure. I saw it in his face. He virtually admitted it. He did it. It's destroying him, but at the same time, he's not sorry. He laughed at me. He dared me to do something about it."

"Do you think . . . no . . . "

"What?"

"Do you think Julie helped him?"

We looked at each other. "Do *you* think so?"

"I just don't know," Edith said. I could barely hear her. "I know she's suffered and she's not very stable and she has some real crazy ideas. But I just don't see her like that. She has such a longing to do good. . . . "

"I'd have said the same thing about Cully. And I'd have been wrong. Don't forget. She knew where to find the ax."

"Asmodeus?"

I didn't believe it. Yet the cat had done some inexplicable things, which I had seen with my own eyes. He protected Julie. When people in town said Asmodeus was a witch's familiar, the proof that Julie was in league with the Devil, I knew what they felt, because I felt it too. But how could a cat have anything to do with murder? And what it had seen, it could never tell.

Thinking about Asmodeus deepened my unease. "Edith . . . "

"She can come stay with me," Edith said. Edith meant well,

but I doubted she could follow through on her offer, considering how Bobby and Jase felt about Julie. Yet I couldn't offer to have her here. I couldn't risk it. Despite knowing Margaret's murderer was Cully, my intuition continued to warn me about Julie and the warning was too strong for me to ignore.

"I'm going to talk to Cully, see if I can't get him to cut her loose," I said. "Then I'm going after him. Find proof he did it."

"How will you do that? You said he laughed at you."

"I don't know," I said. I remembered the way Julie had hunched her shoulders in resignation and shame as she climbed into the rowboat with Cully. I remembered the way Asmodeus had shuddered when Julie called him off Cully, as if he obeyed against his deepest self. "I don't know. But I'll find a way."

FIFTEEN

All night I dreamed of Cully, mocking me, as he rowed away into the shadows. Of Julie's body glimmering white. And of a black cat, his tail turning, winding, larger and more menacing than either of them.

I knew I had to confront Cully. But first I thought I better check in at the office. Perhaps there would be a message from Edith.

As soon as I got in the front door, Mrs. Boynton accosted me. "We need to talk. Come into my office."

I followed her through the doorway and sat down on the guest chair. Mrs. Boynton closed the door firmly, walked around behind her big, old-fashioned oak desk, and sat down in her tall black-leather executive chair. Stacks of paper, file folders, and sheets of numbers covered the surface of her desk. A calculator sat directly in front of her, a ribbon of paper tape extruding from its print head and trailing off over the desk edge and onto the floor.

"I don't need to tell you, John Charles," Mrs. Boynton said. "These are hard economic times. Hard times."

I waited.

"Small towns like Crowley Creek are under threat. New shopping centers, housing developments, can suck the life out of us. People count their pennies. They'll drive fifty miles, shop at a superstore to save ten bucks, and when they do that, they rob their own neighbors of business. It's tough. You know what keeps us alive?"

I sat in the chair, barely listening.

"Spirit, that's what. Belief in ourselves. Belief this is a good place to live and raise our children. Community spirit."

"Right," I said, making an effort to focus on her words.

"Jobs are at stake. People's livelihoods. A town with a history. A town founded by your ancestors, John Charles. Your great-great-great-grandaddy, Montgomery Alexander Crowley, his industry founded this town. You have deep roots here, you have a stake here. You pretend not to care, but you understand."

Despite myself, I nodded. She was right. I *did* understand. I did care.

"I couldn't believe my ears when you spoke out against everybody at the town council. You, Cully, Edith, and Julie against the whole town. Well, I thought, that's just John Charles. He likes to think he's a writer, his own man, a literary eccentric. . . . "

"Hey—hold on. . . . "

"Folks expect a little far-out behavior from you, it's part of your charm, but you went too far that time."

"My charm?"

"It can't happen again, you hear me?"

"What are you talking about?"

"The witch didn't get the message, John Charles. We want her out. We are going to get her out. We're having another meeting and we're going to lay it on the line. Either Julie abandons her witchcraft practices, repents, lets Reverend Fairchild do an exorcism, gets rid of the cat—or else. She's got to go."

"You can't do that. And anyway, Sheriff Rumpsey told her

not to leave town. He has to keep an eye on her until they solve Margaret's murder."

"The sheriff thinks she'll be better off in Richmond. Safer too. It's for her own good. He can keep an eye on her there. And that's where we want her. Out of Crowley Creek. She thinks she has friends and allies here, so she's staying put. You need to let her know she has to go."

"How can you be so sure . . . "

"The mayor has called a town-council meeting for the twenty-seventh. This time the mayor wants *everyone* on side. We have to let that girl know she can't get away with defying us. We need you to speak out, tell her to listen to her elders and betters."

"No way. This is wrong. She may be different, but she hasn't caused any harm to anyone."

"You don't really believe that now, do you, John Charles? I'm starting to wonder if that witch has got to you too."

"It's not in the spirit of Crowley Creek to bully a poor young girl just because she dresses and talks differently," I said.

"Who are you kidding?"

I hated having to defend Julie, when I felt so strongly that there was something deeply wrong about her, but I had no choice. Because I knew who had killed Margaret and I knew it was unjust to put the blame on Julie. But how could I defend her? Not by accusing Cully, that was certain. Mrs. Boynton wouldn't believe me. "What's going on here, it's all wrong," I said.

"You're going to regret your position, John Charles, I promise you," she said.

I wondered what she had in mind. She could be ruthless and I knew from experience it would be a mistake to take her on. But she'd left me no choice. Yet to get Cully I would need powerful allies and it looked as if I had just lost one of the few I might have counted on. It seemed as if forces stronger than any I could muster were directing my steps in a direction I could not foresee or control.

I went back to my desk and tried to work but it was no use. Turning off my computer, I opened the door and went out onto the sidewalk. Rain fell in a fine damp mist. I could see no more than half a block; beyond that people looked like vague shadows. They glimmered into the mist, then disappeared. I walked down the street away from town, moving almost unseen through the haze of raindrops that prickled my skin. I could hear the sound of car tires on the damp pavement but the cars themselves passed by as formless dark blurs. I crossed Main Street and kept walking. Suddenly a small misshapen figure emerged. As we approached each other I saw Julie, with Asmodeus on her shoulder. The cat's green eyes glowed as it stared at me.

"Hello, Julie," I said. My voice didn't sound right.

"I have an invitation for you," she said. She tilted her head up to look at me. Her hair fell back from her face and her large, slanting green eyes, so much like her cat's, stared into mine. Her eyes looked opaque and glassy and for the first time I wondered if the green color came from tinted contact lenses. The thought helped to break the spell cast by the way she and Asmodeus had appeared out of the fog.

"What invitation?" I said. How young she looked. So slight and small, so drab. How could she seem so dangerous and threatening in my dreams? Disgusting, the idea of her and Cully.

"You know the Reverend Fairchild is trying to cut me off from my Powers, don't you?"

"I know he doesn't like what you do and wants to stop it."

"I have to have a special ceremony to hold off his chilling spells. He wants to destroy all my friendly spirits."

"I think you should give all this witchcraft stuff a rest for a while, Julie. It upsets people. Why not do what you do in private? Why rub it in people's faces? It frightens them and they strike back at you."

"I need you, John Charles," she said. She stretched out her hand and tapped my arm, a kind of caress. I could feel her touch burn through my windbreaker. I put my hand in my pocket and sought my talisman.

"I need a strong good male power to hold all the evil male forces at bay," she said. "Please. Just come to my ceremony. I've invited Edith. She is so good. And you are too. Together, you two will protect me from the fate the reverend prepares for me."

What was she up to now? What about Cully? Where did he fit into her crazy way of seeing the world? Better humor her.

"If Edith will come, I'll be there," I said.

"Blessed be," Julie said. Then she stepped into the mist and disappeared from sight.

I continued my walk. Through the mist I heard young voices and I realized I had walked all the way to the school. Lunch break, and kids streamed out of the parking lot. Among the crowd I saw Jase Dunn, just as he saw me.

"Mr. Poe! Hey, Mr. Poe, wait up!"

I stopped walking and waited for him. He loped over to me. "Mr. Poe, we need to talk."

"Sure, Jase, what's on your mind."

"Mr. Poe, are you going to tell Mom about me going in Sue Anne Beebee's window? I got to know."

"I haven't decided. What do you think I should do?" I said.

We walked back toward town. When we got to the little park, we sat down on a bench. Jase had a paper sack in his hand. He reached in and took out a chocolate chip cookie.

"Starting lunch with dessert?" I said, amused. I'd always eaten my cookie first when I was his age.

"I think you shouldn't tell. I said I was sorry. I just can't get grounded now. I'm in the school concert. I play trumpet in the jazz band and I got a solo in the concert. It's in the evening, so if Mom grounds me, I'll miss it."

"Hey, a trumpet player? I'm impressed."

"Don't wreck it for me, Mr. Poe, okay?"

"Why shouldn't I?"

"Look, how about if I tell you a big secret. Would that do

it?" He finished his cookie and removed a peanut butter–and-jelly sandwich from his sack. The sight of it made me nostalgic. As I recalled, I had insisted on nothing but peanut butter–and-jelly sandwiches for lunch for about five years, when I was a kid. Then suddenly I couldn't bear the sight of one.

"What secret?" I asked.

"About Dr. Cully's spooky basement."

"What about his spooky basement?"

Sitting in the park, in the fine spring rain, gave me the feeling of our being alone on an island in a vague, shimmering gray sea. Right in front of us we could see the majestic statue of the Confederate Soldier, holding a rifle. The Soldier had white pigeon droppings on his carved stone uniform cap and broad shoulders, but he still had an air of courage and steadfast idealism, as if he inhabited a realm much less complicated than mine, a realm of pure good and pure evil.

"A while ago we were over there to spy on Julie and we saw Dr. Cully working on this basement room. It's unfinished, you know, and he's, like, renovating it?"

Could Jason Dunn have read Edgar Allan Poe's story, "The Black Cat," and be pulling my leg? Could this be for real, what he was telling me?

"So?" I said, pretending a calm I did not feel.

"So!" Jason said. "Didn't you read 'The Black Cat' story? I know you did, because Mom told me about the story the first time she saw Asmodeus, and I read it then. In the story the bad guy walls his dead wife's body up in his cellar, right?"

"Yes, but . . . "

"So, get this. Dr. Cully was bricking up a wall in the cellar!"

I had to check out what Jase told me. But first, there was Julie's ceremony to get through. She had found an abandoned farmhouse and she explained to Edith and me that she had spent the entire previous night there, "purifying" the site.

She had swept it with her magic broom, sown it with purifying herbs like thyme and rosemary, and burnt incense. Any evil pockets, she assured us, had been neutralized and cleansed. It would be safe to enter. But as we approached and I saw the structure, rotting two-by-four studs on a crumbling cement foundation, floor joists splotched with mold, roofless, kudzu vines and thistles encroaching upon it, I wondered if she had also checked it for structural soundness. It might be "pure," but would the moldering floor joists hold?

The moon, almost full, rode high in the sky, veiled with a nimbus of thin cloud, like a halo. The recent rain had cooled the air and a damp chill emanated from the woods. A light wind rustled the branches and fine drops of moisture spun outward with every gust of air. Beneath our feet, as we followed Julie out of the woods and across the overgrown field to the house, the earth felt spongy and unsubstantial. It adhered to our feet as if sucking us down.

"Why a house?" I asked. "I thought you liked to be outside, in the woods."

"I need a house tonight," Julie said. "I am going to call one of the Dark Powers."

"Why?" Edith said. "I thought you only did white magic."

"The difference is an illusion. I need a Dark Power tonight to tell me how to protect myself against Reverend Fairchild's wiles. He has a whole roaring of them at his beck and call.

"Watch the steps as you go up," Julie said. "They're rotten in the center but the edges still hold."

I noticed that Julie spoke in her special, "witch" voice, clear and commanding. Her words seemed charged with a deeper meaning, so that when she said "rotten in the center but the edges still hold" I heard the metaphoric meaning in her words. Not for the first time, I regretted agreeing to take part in this charade.

Edith stepped carefully on the broken treads. They creaked ominously as she climbed. Once this house had had a wide veranda, with broad steps leading up to it. I followed, the boards bending under my weight.

Inside, we found ourselves on a moonlit platform. The studs, some broken, some intact, no longer supported upper floors or a roof. All had fallen in and been taken away by scavengers. What remained seemed almost like a stage, a decrepit floor around which stood wall studs—broken wooden palings of different heights. A part of one wall still stood, pierced by window holes, its moldy plasterboard pitted and covered with fungus. Julie had placed her altar before this wall and now she began putting out her knives, candles, cauldron, bell, censer, crystal, pentagon, and wands. As she did so, she murmured under her breath, words I could not decipher. They sounded like another language. Asmodeus appeared suddenly, leaping through the window opening. He began trotting around the perimeter of the floor.

Julie had given me a large basket to carry. I handed it to her. She opened it and removed a musical instrument that looked like a xylophone made of varying lengths of bamboo tubing. She placed this on the floor by the altar and ran a mallet over it. An eerie sound filled the air, seemed to shimmer around us, then faded away. Twice more she stroked across the keys. "With this noise I warn You-Who-Listen, we will soon begin— beware," Julie murmured. I wondered if those who listened meant Edith and me or her "powers."

Julie spread a fringed piece of white silk on the floor and directed Edith and me to sit upon it. Once we had complied, she drew from her basket two necklaces strung with pungent seeds. Murmuring something under her breath, she placed these necklaces around our necks. Mine smelled like camphor. I understood from my reading that she must be doing this to purify us.

Julie began to make the magic circle. She sprinkled a trail of herbs in a nine-foot circle around us. As she did, she chanted:

> "Luna, O Luna, hear me,
> Astarte, O Astarte, I call you now,
> Diana, dear Diana, listen!
> Yes, Luna, attend and draw nigh.
> Aphrodite, hear my words,

Oh Athena, my sister, my soul,
Aradia arise,
We await you. Hearken to our call,
Cybele."

Julie lit the censer of incense and walked her circle again, raising her hands and making gestures as if drawing up power and pushing it away. Perhaps because I had read the witchcraft books, I saw the circling swirl of blue energy-light Julie believed she directed from her hands, to create a circle of power to protect us from the opening she would soon make between this world and the Other World. I could hear Edith's breathing, deep and even. As she sat very near me, her arm almost touching mine, I could feel the warmth emanating from her body in the chill damp air. Julie, wearing her black hooded robe, tied at the waist with a band of braided white and silver, a jagged crystal flashing at her breast, stood much taller than usual and moved with a fierce, tense energy. Trails of incense filled the air, circling upward into the darkness.

Julie returned to her xylophone and stroked it with her wand. A sonorous chiming sound reverberated around us. Into this sound, her clear voice rang out: "Fill your minds with the energy of the earth, be ready. I will call upon the Goddess to protect us. Then, when she is present, I will call the Dark Powers to account! I will command them to cease their persecutions, to abandon their master, the Reverend Fairchild, and to return whence they came! I will force them to return to the Other Place, and set guards upon them! Do you understand?"

Edith nodded.

"The Goddess and the Old Ones may speak through me. You will hear their voices and you will know. Do not be afraid. The Goddess will protect me, and no matter how far I travel, I will return before the night is out. Let us begin!"

The moon passed behind the clouds and the circle grew dim. Julie moved to her altar and arranged the items upon it. She touched a knife to the basin of water and murmured something we could not hear. She lit the white and the red candle, chanting softly. She carried a candle to the north side of the circle and lit it. She pressed her hands on the floor. Now I could hear her words. She said: "Powers of the Earth, guard our working. Ground it well." She moved to the east, lit a second candle, placed it on the ground, raised her hands to the air, and said, "Spirits of the Air, Ancient Ones, breathe your sweet breath upon our workings and fill them with the breath of life." She moved to the south point on the circle, lit a third candle, placed it on the floor, and murmured, "O Fiery One, hear my call and guard our workings with your burning power." Then she walked to the western point on the circle, lit her last candle, placed it on the floor, and whispered, "O Spirit of Water, so close here in this water-girt place, attend us, refresh us, renew us, guard us, Ancient One."

She walked to her altar, turned toward us, and tilted her head up. Asmodeus curled up beside her, his black fur blending into the shadows cast by the flickering candles. "Earth! Air! Fire! Water! Hear me! I call you now! Guard us well. Stand nigh to the Doors as I open them. Guard us, watch us, help us, Old Ones."

Julie looked at us. Her face intent. "I am going to call the Goddess now," she said. "You may feel her power, but do not be afraid. The Circle will protect us. Once I have summoned her, the magic will begin. Please, do not move or speak. I have not cut a door, you cannot leave the circle without breaking it, unleashing the Nameless Ones before I am ready. Do you understand?"

Edith and I both nodded, though truth to tell I understood very little and I imagine Edith felt the same.

Now Julie seemed to grow taller. The hood of her robe shadowed her face so all we could see was a white blur and the green glimmer of eyes, narrowed to slits.

"Hear me, Lady, mistress of magic, Queen of the
Night!
Hearken unto my cry, Lady, my Mistress!

I open my heart so you may visit me this Night,
Shadow-maker, Shadow-breaker, your servant cries
out to you!"

Julie stretched her arms upward. I saw that she held the white knife. The silver blade flashed in the moonlight. I felt a chill rise up through my spine and a fine sweat broke out on my brow. I looked at Edith. Her face had grown very pale and her eyes glittered.

Julie spoke, her voice commanding:

"Welcome, Lady! Hear my plea.
He who worships the gods of Death
Seeks to open the Doors.
Chasten him, scourge him, show him your silver light.
Or if it be thy will,
Find him, Bind him, Remind him, Unwind him!
Take the power of spells from his tongue and the lure
from his lips;
O I beseech thee!"

She flung back her head. She opened her mouth and a high keening note, like the thrilling call of a loon, filled the air. The tubes of the xylophone began to quiver sympathetically, so that the air filled with the sound.

Then Julie's face changed. It grew older, colder, harsher. Her eyes gleamed. She spoke in a voice I had never heard her use before—deep, harsh, and vibrant. Asmodeus gave an enormous leap into the air, then he slid under the skirts of her robe. In that strange, deep, hoarse voice, came the words:

"You summon the Lady and at Her word
I appear.
You who bid me silent, first hear my warning.
Before silence, words.
My words are doors. Yea,
My words are curses if not obeyed.

Shall I speak? The Lady guards you. The Ancient
    Ones guard you.
Shall I speak the words of Knowing?"

Now Julie spoke in her own voice, hushed, quavering. "By
the Lady who guards us, speak, Nameless One."
    Again the cold bitter expression transfixed her face. The
harsh voice spoke from her mouth:

"Listen and hearken unto me, son and daughters of Isis!
That which is secret must be unveiled,
That which is hidden must be told.
Blood shed under Isis' light must be avenged,
for the bones of the woman cry out to Her!
Whose blood on the two-headed ax?
Who betrays her lover the hornèd god?
Who opens the gate to the abyss of rage?
Whose evil must we speak aloud?"

A long shuddering sigh passed through Julie's body and she
seemed to wilt. She dropped her head and shook herself. Asmodeus crept into view and lightly leaped onto her shoulder.
Julie reached up a white hand and smoothed her hair. Then,
slowly, as if the strength had drained from her legs, she settled
down cross-legged onto the ground.
    For a moment she sat silent, her head tilted downward, her
hair falling over her face, her breath coming in quick gasps, as
if she struggled for air. Then she let out another long sigh, and
said softly, "Lady, you opened the Door and the Nameless One
spoke the words of his magic knowing." She tilted her head upward, so her hair fell away from her face. Her skin shone white
in the moonlight. Her voice sounded weak, pleading. "But his
words are too hard for me. They tear my heart from my flesh."
She ran her hands through her hair, tugging at it as I had seen
her do before when she struggled with conflicting emotions.
"Lady, do not hold me to his curse of opening. O Lady of the
flowing waters, release me." Her breath rasped in her throat.

"Lady, I cannot do it. Lady, unbind me, I cannot say it. Please, mistress of the gentle rain, pity me." She pointed at Edith and me. "Here—here are those stronger than me. I have brought them to you so that you will free me from this curse the Nameless One lay upon me. By the wand, blade, cup, and pentacle, bind my friends to your service. On *them* lay the task, for the willow bends in the wind, the young sapling cannot hold." Julie stared upward, as if waiting for an answer to her plea.

No one spoke. The candle flames shuddered in the rising wind and I thought I heard the faint chiming tones of the xylophone echoing, blending with the wind.

Suddenly Julie jumped to her feet. She raised her black knife. In the clear resonant voice of the Goddess she said:

"You the father-man,
  You the mother-woman,
  Will you do it?
  I ask you, will you take the burden from my servant?
  For she bends beneath the power of these Old Ones.
  The Secret must be found, bound, reminded, unwound.
  My servant asks your help.
  Do you accept the burden?"

Julie looked at Edith and me. We looked back and saw only Julie, the young woman, not her other personas. We both heard her cry for help. Yet neither of us spoke. The wind grew stronger. I could hear it, like a woman sighing, in the tops of the trees. The candles flickered, the thick chill penetrated into my bones.

Julie stood and clutched the crystal that glittered on her breast. She opened her mouth and gulped in air. "Lady, they do not accept. Lady, the Nameless Ones are here, they are all around me, their curse awaits. Lady, I am alone!"

Suddenly, Julie let out a terrible scream, her mouth open like a black cavern. *"I can't speak it, don't make me! I can't tell the secret! I can't!"* She began to writhe, as if trying to free herself from unseen bonds. "Let me go! Lady, help me! The Dark

Ones have me, they know what I know, and so they hold me. Lady, help me! Lady, I command thee, help me!"

I wanted to go to her. I am sure Edith did too. Her suffering was unbearable to watch. But we were frozen in place by the terror we heard in her screams. She began to sob, and then to sink downward until she lay huddled on the floor, weeping piteously.

Then Edith said. "Julie, you must tell the secrets you hide. No one else can do it for you."

Julie sat up, dried her tears with the sleeve of her robe. Her face, so pale that it looked translucent, lost all expression, as if the soul inside had disappeared. Edith and I sat very still, holding our breaths, waiting.

Julie stood and raised her white knife, pointing at the moon. "I hear you, Lady. So you have spoken and so it shall be." She brought her knife down in an arc, then pointed it at herself and made a ritual cutting gesture, as if she were gouging out her heart. Then she turned and plunged the knife in the cauldron of water. "Leave us, Spirits. By the power of the Lady, I say, return to the Other Place. I have heard. Your words burn in my heart. I attend."

She turned back to us and we saw Julie's face, submissive, tentative, not the transfigured being who had called out into the night. Her shoulders hunched down, as if she carried a weight on her back. The child-woman, lost, frightened, uncertain, gazed at us out of those peculiar green eyes. The candles flickered and the wind blew Julie's hair over her face. She brushed it away, sighed, and straightened up with an effort. Looking wistfully at Edith and me, she said, "I will try. Yes, I will try. Blessed be."

Edith and I let out our breath. I reached for Edith's hand and felt the warmth of her touch as she clutched at my fingers.

"Blessed be," Julie said.

SIXTEEN

Okay, people, can I have your attention—please!" Mayor Jackson Lee Winsome said, standing behind the lectern that had been set up on the school-gymnasium stage. Resplendent in a light tan suit, he had a white carnation pinned to one lapel and his confederate-flags lapel pin on the other. "We have serious business today, sad, serious business. I guess most of you know that a week ago we had a meeting and your council voted to ask Miss Julie Noir to either heed the words of Reverend Fairchild, or if she could not do so, to move on out."

"Right!" "Move on the hell out!" people called from the audience. There had to be sixty people crowded into the seats set up in the gym. The town council sat around the table on the stage and in the front row the powerful people in town—the old powers you might say—Mrs. Boynton, lawyer Prynne, leading members of our oldest and most established families.

The mayor raised his hand and the crowd went silent. "Before we take action, I've said that Reverend Fairchild can give it one more try. Then your council is going to make a final decision. But the reverend assures me that he has the help of a higher power, and that he can accomplish our goals in a godly way. Reverend?"

Fairchild stood up, unfolding a sheet of paper he held in his hand, and walked forward to the speaker stand. He tilted the microphone up and smoothed his paper out on the stand. He looked out over the audience, smiled tensely, then let his face settle into a somber, concerned expression. "Friends," Fairchild said, "Leviticus Nineteen. 'The soul which goeth forth to wizards and soothsayers, I will set my face against that soul and destroy it out of the midst of my people.' " He looked out at us. The room grew silent. You could hear the restless rustling noises of people moving uneasily on their seats.

"My friends, we have been patient, and we have seen the Evil Spirit at work in this town. How much longer will we suffer the witch to move among us? She has invited the Devil onto our peaceful streets, we have seen his works. Look at your sons and daughters! Infected! Corrupted! The sweet innocents whom you held on your knees, now consorting with the Evil One himself." He pointed to the kids dressed in black, the group who had not joined the audience, but lounged against the back wall, leaning indolently, their body language redolent of hostility and rejection. Their partly shaven scalps glowed white in the bright light, contrasting with their dyed black hair, spiked and twisted into strange shapes.

"You wish!" one of the kids shouted. "Screw off," another yelled.

The audience murmured angrily. The disrespect to Reverend Fairchild angered them. Politeness and courtesy are deeply ingrained virtues in this part of the world, and for the young to sass their elders in public seemed to demonstrate the truth of Fairchild's words.

"We warned her but she did not heed," Fairchild intoned. "Now we must protect our immortal souls. Witchcraft is high treason against the Lord God. Those who do not reject this foul practice allow the succubus to fasten upon the body and soul, to grow, to poison everything. We must cleanse ourselves of this evil!" Fairchild stared at Cully. "Leviticus Twenty. 'And the soul that turneth after such as have familiar spirits, and after wizards, to go a-whoring after them, I will set my face against that soul and will cut him off from among his people.' So sayeth our Lord and so we must do!"

I saw that Fairchild trembled. The man believed every word he spoke. He wanted Julie out of Crowley Creek for the good of our souls and for the salvation of his own. He seemed to me to be on the edge of some serious psychological crisis.

Mayor Winsome must have felt Fairchild's anguish and distress. He stood, walked up to the minister, patted him on the shoulder. "Thank you, Reverend Fairchild," he said.

Fairchild stared at him for a moment, then recollected himself, folded his paper, and returned to his seat. "Well," Mayor Winsome said, "anyone else want to address your council on this issue? Now's the time."

Mrs. Boynton stood. "This witchcraft business is dividing our town. Bad for business. We warned the young lady to cease and desist, but she paid us no mind. I say, time for her to move on. Dr. Cully, it's up to you to make it clear to her!"

Mort Beebee nodded. "If I may."

Mrs. Boynton smiled and sat down.

Beebee strolled to the lectern. "A town like ours has to protect itself," he said, in a just-stating-the-facts tone. "We need to identify our problems and deal with them. In business, if you have an employee who is harming morale, you have got to consider the good of the entire organization. You have to terminate the troublemaker. I think that's what's called for here."

I saw lawyer Prynne nodding in the front row, but he was too clever to put anything on record.

Beebee sat down and the mayor regained the lectern. "One bad apple spoils the whole barrel," he said. "It's as simple as that. The witch has got to go. I propose that the council enact a bylaw declaring Miss Noir, as a self-confessed witch, persona non grata. That means, 'not welcome.' Kind of . . . outlawed. Once we do that, I'll ask Sheriff Rumpsey to enforce our bylaw and escort her out of town. And keep her out. Okay? Any further discussion? Not that there's anything more to say. . . . "

I stood up. "What right do you have to tell anyone to leave town?" I said. "This is a free country—or at least it was last time I looked." I sat down. My heart was thumping. I could feel rage rising in me like a fever.

The mayor puffed out like a frog swelling. "Glad you raised that point, John Charles. A free country. Yes, indeed. But a body's got to protect hearth and home. What freedom is there if the Devil is at work? That's our situation here. What freedom do we have with a witch in town, doing black magic on us? Okay, let's call the vote."

"Yes!" "Right on!" "I'd like to burn her at the stake," people shouted out. The audience had grown agitated. I knew they didn't like to see someone disagree when the town had made up its collective mind. They wanted it over and done with. I turned and looked back at Julie. Her head tilted downward so her hair fell over her face and I couldn't see her expression. Cully sat, stiff, his face white, frightened. I thought that, until that moment, they had believed they could ignore what had happened last week. Poor Julie. After her witch "ceremony" she had pleaded with Edith and me to give her time to collect herself. She had been sure she would have that time.

I hadn't taken seriously the seven-day ultimatum the council had given Julie. All I had been able to think about was that Julie had promised Edith and me that soon, very soon, she would be ready to tell us what she had been hiding.

"All those in favor . . . ," began the mayor.

"Wait!" Edith's voice rang out. "This is not right, you know it's not. You're only afraid of her because she's different."

"Right!" "Too different for Crowley Creek!" "A witch, in league with the Devil is sure different!" "You shut up!" people shouted angrily at Edith.

Cully stood up. "This is the gal who saved your animals. Yours," he said pointing to one person, "and yours," pointing to another, "and yours," pointing to a third. "You call that the Devil's work?"

"The Devil has devices and stratagems to fool the innocent, that is how he works his wiles," Reverend Fairchild called out from the stage. "Do not be deceived! The decision is clear. You are either for the living God and His Blessed Son or for their eternal enemy, the Arch-fiend, Lucifer himself! There is no middle ground in this battle."

"I'm going to call the vote," the mayor said to the council. "All in favor? Opposed? Motion carried. Unanimous."

"Hooray! Yes! Right on!" shouted most of the audience.

A rustling noise. I turned and watched as the black-clad teenagers moved away from the back wall and, giving the audience the finger, filed out of the room. As they passed through the door, each in turn spat on the floor. Their slouching gate, their ugly gestures, their defiant and disrespectful demeanor seemed to validate everything the mayor and the council had said.

"I'm glad to see we are all at one on this . . . ," the mayor began, smiling at the audience.

"I'm still opposed!" I called out. "It's wrong. You can't do this." My voice sounded weak and cracked in my ears. I could not believe this was happening, that I had to stand against the entire town, my relations, my lifelong friends. So many in the audience I liked, respected, counted on. I had just cut myself off from all of them.

"I'm still opposed!" With a rush of joy I heard the determined sound of Edith's voice.

"Well, that's too bad," Mayor Winsome said, "but you made your points and the council heard you and we don't agree. We passed the motion. You folks are in the minority here, obviously, why press it? Come on, John Charles, Edith. Now that it's unanimous, why not support your council? For the good of Crowley Creek? No? Any more discussion?"

Silence. The mayor smiled down at all of us. He looked at Cully. "Dr. Cully, the town has a right to know what you plan on doing. We know you're in a delicate spot here. We all see that. But now you know what you have to do."

"God forgive me," Cully said, his voice breaking. "I can't turn her away if she doesn't want to go."

"There can be no excuses!" thundered Reverend Fairchild.

"You are with the Devil or opposed! Therefore, accursed devil," he said, directing his piercing gaze at Julie, "hear thy doom and give honor to the true and living God, give honor to the Lord Jesus Christ, that thou depart with thy works and with thy servant. Depart! Depart! Depart!"

Julie flung up her head and stared at Reverend Fairchild. Then she looked at Cully. "Dr. Cully . . . help me . . . ," she said.

He turned his head away from her.

"Depart by the words of my exorcism, in the name of the Father, the Son, and the Holy Ghost!" cried Fairchild. "Depart! Depart!"

Julie stared white faced at Cully but he would not return her gaze. He neither rejected her nor spoke out in her defense. Julie jumped up from her chair. I saw now that Asmodeus sat on her shoulder, looming larger than I remembered him, the white patch glowing on his breast. Julie stepped out into the aisle, still looking hopefully at Dr. Cully. He raised his eyes to hers. Whatever she read in them caused her to shrink down inside her clothes.

"Witch! Remove hence!" Fairchild called out.

Julie turned and suddenly she bolted, and before I had realized what had happened, she had rushed from the room.

A long silence, then the room erupted into applause, roars of approval. "We did it!" "The power of the Lord's Word drove her out!" "We exorcised the devil-woman!" "When the reverend said those exorcism words, did you see how she ran? That proves she's possessed."

I stood and walked down the middle aisle. As I passed, people grew silent. I could feel their hostile stares. When I reached the last row, Edith rose and joined me. Cully stood as if meaning to join us, then sank back in his chair. This time, Edith and I walked out together, alone. Behind us we heard the town's mocking roar.

I sat in the back of Shelton's finishing my burger. Nobody had spoken to me. Nobody had said "Hi" or "How ya doin', John

Charles?" Nothing but cold stares. The waitress took my order. A high-school kid with acne and a complicated hairstyle, she couldn't look me in the face and failed even to tell me to have a nice day. When I got up to go to the bathroom in the back, I thought I heard people whispering as I passed by. I couldn't even call Marilyn to come round and cheer me up. She had gone to visit her sister in Charlottesville. I figured as soon as she heard the second town-council meeting was on, she'd left town, not wanting to find herself having to choose between me and everyone else. A clever move on her part and I didn't blame her, but it would have helped to see her lovely face across from me right now.

Back in my seat, I felt a cold draft, looked up and saw the front door opening and Cully coming in. He caught sight of me and headed in my direction. Just my luck. The only person in town who would break bread with me was a wife murderer and child abuser.

"John Charles . . . ," he said tentatively, standing by my table. "I need to talk to you."

"Sure, what the hell," I said.

He slid into the booth across from me.

"Some puppies and a beer," he said to the waitress. "A Bud."

I studied him as he waited for his order. His face sagged as if the skull inside of it had begun to melt.

"You gotta believe me, John Charles," he said, "I didn't mean what I said the other day when we went fishing. I just . . . "

He must have seen the expression on my face, because he stopped speaking.

I got hold of myself. What good would it do to let Cully know I had no doubt that he'd murdered Margaret and seduced Julie? Wouldn't it be better to pretend to believe him? The man resented me, was prideful and full of rage. If he thought he had me fooled, wouldn't he be more likely to give away something?

"Jesus, Cully, I don't know what to think . . . ," I said, fixing my face in what I hoped was a confused expression. "Hey, little gal," I called to the waitress, "can I have one of those Buds?"

The waitress gave me a blank stare, then walked slowly toward the counter.

"You gotta believe me," he said again, staring at me, willing me to see things the way he wanted me to see them. "Listen, John Charles. Julie, she's run away. No sign of her since last night when she ran out of the council meeting. She been in touch with you?"

Good God, could he have offed her too?

The waitress brought our orders and set them down without a word. She did it by extending her arms, so that she could stand as far away as possible from us while she served us. Overdoing it. "Nope," I said. "Haven't seen her. And I talked to Edith today. She hasn't heard from her either."

"I checked her apartment. She's taken all her witch stuff. But she's left most of her clothes. I don't think she's left town for good. But the town turning on her like that, they drove her away from me. You saw. Shameful, it was shameful. We've got to find her."

"How come you didn't stand up for Julie? She's worked hard for you, stood by you when anyone else would have taken off."

Cully drank a long swallow of beer, then wiped his mouth. Strange how he did that, almost as if he had started to smile and wanted to hide it from me. Around us the room had grown noisy. The jukebox blared out Emmylou Harris complaining it was hard to keep believin', people laughed loudly, called to one another, and outside you could hear the sound of motorcyclists gunning their motors and racing up and down Central Avenue. The town had to let off steam. Yet the seething energy I felt all around seemed wrong to me, and suddenly it felt like I were seeing everything through the narrow end of a telescope. In the distance Cully's face looked blurred, skull-like. Snap out of it, John Charles, I said to myself. These moods—the Poe curse—would come upon me like someone had cast a spell on me. I told myself the sense that something strange was happening was stress, and I took a long pull on my beer.

"I didn't agree to make her leave," Cully said. "But did you see how she ran when Fairchild said that exorcism? John Charles, what if she really has sold her soul to the Devil? What if that cat—Lord God how I hate that cat—what if that cat really is her familiar spirit? What if . . . everything that's happened really is the Devil's work?"

"You think so? You think you've got a demon in you? That explains the wrong you've done?"

Cully's eyes darted from side to side, as if my gaze, my tone, had pinned him to his seat and he was looking for an escape. "Where is she? Where can she be? What say we go look for her? You've got that second sight, you've always had it. You can find her. . . . " He stuffed a hush puppy in his mouth, swallowed it down with what was left of his beer, and flung a twenty down on the table. "Let's get out of here. This place is getting to me. Come on."

He jumped up and rushed out of the diner. What was he up to? I drank down the few drops remaining of my beer and followed him out to the street.

Outside, night had fallen. It was around eight in the evening, a weekday, so town was quiet. Most folks were at home, except for the crowd making the commotion at Shelton's. Light streamed out of the Dollar Store, but I knew they were just cleaning up after closing.

Cully had begun to walk along the sidewalk. I went after him. He turned and saw me. "We got to find her," he said. He looked up and down the street. "But first I need some serious fortifying." He opened the door to The Old Forge and went in. I went in after him.

Tommy White, my friend from childhood, stood behind the bar. Normally when he saw me, he gave me an enthusiastic smile and started pouring. But this time he looked at me, then turned coldly away without a greeting. It hurt more than anything that had happened yet.

I walked up to the bar and leaned over the shining brass rail. "Aren't you going to say hello, Tommy," I said softly.

"You made your choice, John Charles," Tommy said, not meeting my eyes. "You chose to go against all of us. It's a free country. Just like you said. But you chose wrong. That's all I got to say."

"Well then," I said, my tone easy but my heart heavy in my chest, "all I got to say is, a double Blanton's on the rocks and a chaser of ice water." Behind Tommy's head, I saw the ranks of bottles. I saw the town trophies on the shelf. All so familiar, but maybe because now I was an outcast, it all looked strange. I turned and saw the lithograph of Patrick Henry that hung on the back wall. The old patriot seemed to be pointing at me with reproach.

"Jack Daniel's, double, and a Bud," Cully said. Tommy poured without a word and Cully took the glasses over to a booth in the back. I followed with my bourbon and water. "We got to find her, we can't let her run loose. No telling what she'll do," Cully said.

I didn't know if he feared that Julie might reveal the secrets that were tormenting her, or if she might—in her desperation—do harm to herself.

"If she took her witch equipment, she probably went into the woods to do that witchy stuff she does," I said. "You know, call on the Goddess."

Cully smiled. This time there was no mistaking it. For a moment, I didn't recognize his face. A stranger looked back at me out of his skin, gloating, prideful, triumphant. Then suddenly, he started, paled, and a shudder of terror went through him.

"What's that!" He stared at the bar, at the shelves of bottles, and I followed his gaze. Asmodeus! A black, foreboding mass, crouching on the shelf above the bar, among the whiskey bottles, unmoving. Huddled, as if he had condensed himself to fit on the shelf, yet somehow he looked bigger than ever. But I had looked over there a moment ago and had not seen him.

"I been looking at the bar for five minutes over your shoulder and I never saw that devil cat till this minute!" Cully whispered to me, sweat breaking out on his forehead.

I tilted my head but all I could see of the cat was a vague shape and the gleam of his green eyes. I looked around. It was early for the regulars and there were only four or five people in the bar. No one else appeared to notice the cat.

"That cat hates me, John Charles. He follows me everywhere now. He hisses at me. I'd like to gouge *his* eye out." Cully shifted on the seat, put a hand in a hip pocket, and pulled out a big folding knife. He snapped it open so the long scalpel-like blade shone in the lights. "I'm going to put a stop to this right now, get that blasted cat once and for all."

What was I doing, sitting drinking with a madman, cut off from all my own folks? How had I ended up on the side of rage, and darkness?

"I can't sleep," Cully said, gripping the knife, his face shiny with sweat. "I can't eat, I wake every hour at night, dreaming the most terrifying things I can't remember, and I feel the hot breath of that *thing* on my face and his weight on my heart and I can't move and I know I'm going to die! That demon cat—he's killing me!" Cully lurched out of the booth, the knife in his hand, and headed for the bar.

I jumped up, ran around in front of him, and grabbed his arm. "For God's sake, Cully, cool down. It's only a cat."

Cully tried to push past me, toward the bar. I held onto the arm with the knife. Between my fingers I could feel his arm, rigid like a thick board, muscled, tensed. Cully looked at me, trying to free his arm, then he looked over my shoulder and I felt his arm grow limp and the knife dropped to the floor with a dull, somber thud. "What the. . . . "

I turned and saw that Asmodeus had disappeared.

Cully rushed up to the bar and grabbed Tommy White by the shirtfront. "What the hell happened to that cat?"

"What cat?" Tommy said calmly. "May I ask you kindly to let go my shirt?"

"Say what?" Cully looked down at his big thick fingers, holding a bunch of the cloth of Tommy's white dress shirt. "Oh . . . " He let go.

"Much obliged," Tommy said, smoothing down his shirt.

"The cat, the one that was on your shelf?" Cully said.

We all looked at the shelf. The bottles lined up without a gap. No cat.

We walked back to our table and both of us downed our drinks. Into my mind, unbidden, came a line from Edgar Allan Poe's story, "The Black Cat": "Hereafter, perhaps, some intellect may be found which will reduce my phantasm to the commonplace—some intellect more calm, more logical, and far less excitable than my own, which will perceive, in the circumstances I detail with awe, nothing more than an ordinary succession of very natural causes and effects."

How I needed that intellect "more calm and less excitable than my own." For Cully had read me right, when he spoke of my second sight—only what he did not realize was that that sight could be a kind of blindness. A weakness that allowed me, like my ancestor who had penned those lines, to be so overcome by a sense of what lay below the surface of things that I completely lost hold of what was real.

Or maybe my problem was the whiskey?

For as surely as I saw my own hand wrapped around my tumbler of whiskey, I saw Cully's guilt and his pleasure in it. And I saw his torment. And I saw that he wanted Julie, longed to find her, yet was in terror of her.

And even more clearly, I saw that he mocked me. He knew I knew he had murdered his wife and that I could not prove what I knew, because I knew only with my inner eye. He had begun to torment me and to take pleasure in my suffering. I sat across from a man who had gotten away with murder and it seemed I could do nothing about it.

SEVENTEEN

Perhaps, some intellect may be found which will reduce my phantasm to the commonplace—some intellect more calm, more logical, and far less excitable than my own, which will perceive, in the circumstances I detail with awe, nothing more than an ordinary succession of very natural causes and effects."

I sat in Edith's living room, drinking coffee and listening while she argued her boys to bed. I could hear their angry resentful voices, hers rising in rebuke, theirs arguing back, finality in hers then sullen acquiescence in theirs, then silence. The sounds came in through the sliding glass doors, open to the patio. I heard Edith's footsteps descending the stairs, and muttering from the rooms above.

Edith came into the living room and sat down heavily on the sofa. Her face looked weary, and I noticed lines around her mouth that I had not seen before.

"What's the matter, Edith? Boys giving you a hard time?"

She sighed. "It's rough right now. Ever since their father left, I've had to struggle to get them to mind, but since I spoke

out for Julie, it's been hell around here. To hear them tell it,
I've ruined their lives."

I could still feel the bourbon in my system, though I'd left
Cully drinking and staring at the shelves of bottles at The Old
Forge over an hour ago. I'd taken the opportunity to get away
when he went to the can. Then I'd driven out to his house,
gone into the woods behind it, and searched out the two places
I knew Julie used for her Wicca ceremonies, the one near my
favorite pool, and the abandoned house. No sign of her. She
must have other, more secret places. She might have gone to
them, she might have left town, or Cully might have . . . No, I
didn't believe that.

And although being in the woods had calmed my spirits
somewhat, I still felt a strangeness in the air. Everything seemed
a little off-kilter. The feeling had been coming and going all
evening. I wanted to tell Edith about it. I wanted to talk to her
about everything I sensed. To me, Edith, more than anyone
else I had ever known, represented the calm, unexcitable, logical intellect that my ancestor had appealed to in his story.

"Edith, I saw Cully tonight. He tried to butter me up, tell
me he didn't mean it when he confessed to Margaret's murder,
to sleeping with Julie."

"He's horrible."

"He said Julie had disappeared. And just as I'm thinking,
what if he killed her too? We both see Asmodeus watching us,
huddled up on the shelves above the bar. Right behind Tommy
White. Then we look again and abracadabra the black cat's
gone. It was like a dream, Edith, the way that cat was there and
then he wasn't. I asked Tommy White, 'Did you see it? Did you
see the cat jump down and go away?' And he says, 'What cat?'
Swears there was never a cat on the shelves. Edith, I just don't
get it."

"What don't you get?"

I heard a rustling outside in the garden and saw something
moving across the lawn—a small dark shadow. I walked to the
door and gazed out. The moon came out from behind the
clouds, filling the garden with silvery light. Shadows pooled

under the trees and along the fence line. I stared into them but could distinguish nothing.

I walked back to my chair and sat down. "Cully is mocking me, Edith. Laughing at me. Enjoying how much I want to get him away from Julie, get him for Margaret's murder, and how I can't do a thing! The son of a bitch is going to get away with it!" I banged my fist down on the coffee table, surprising myself and causing my coffee cup to jump in its saucer.

"We have to stop him somehow. There must be a way."

"I wish there were, but Edith, I'm afraid that's a dream." I took the talisman out of my pocket and let it slide from my fingers onto the table. The white light at its heart seemed to pulse brighter as I gazed at it.

"We all dream, that is how we see the truth," Julie said. She came drifting in through the open patio doors. She wore her black witch-robe, with the hood up over her hair so that only a sliver of white face, a gleam of green eyes, and the sheen of her golden nose ring shone out from the shadow cast by the hood. She stood for a moment, her back to the moonlight, then glided over to the sofa and sat down next to Edith.

"Julie!" I said, recovering from my surprise. "I thought I saw something out there." I grabbed the talisman and thrust it back into my pocket.

"I waited for the Goddess to light my path and then she shone her light and then suddenly I heard, coming from this room, the word 'dream,' " Julie said. "That word called to me, so I entered."

"Where is Asmodeus?" I asked. Maybe Julie could explain what had happened at The Old Forge—what her cat had been up to.

"Asmodeus must do our work in the world," Julie said. She pushed back her hood. "But he will return if I summon him."

"Are you okay?" Edith said, her voice gentle. "We've been so worried about you since you ran out of the town-council meeting. Can I get you something to eat?"

Julie flung back her head and ran her fingers through her thick black hair. I saw the curving line of her throat. Her robe gaped so that I could see the swell of small breasts. Despite myself, I remembered her lovely naked body. She sighed. "Yes, please, I am very hungry."

Edith got up. I didn't want to be alone with Julie. "Let's keep Edith company in the kitchen," I said.

Julie smiled knowingly at me. As we walked into the kitchen, she came close up behind me. I could smell her skin. A warm scent of damp earth, of the fragrance of the woods, and of wood smoke. She must have been living outdoors for the last few days. I wished she wouldn't stand so close to me.

Julie and I sat down at the kitchen table while Edith began preparing food. She opened the refrigerator, took out a container, emptied it into a pot, and turned on the heat. "Vegetable soup okay?" Edith asked Julie.

Julie looked at me. "The Goddess spoke," she said. "You heard her. It matters not that Reverend Fairchild calls me devil. For I speak for the Lady."

"Right," I said. She was using that spooky voice of hers. How in the world were we going to get her to tell us what she was hiding? She might hold the secret that would let us nail Cully, but how could we get it out of her?

"I was not ready to come back, but Gomer has had a relapse," Julie said.

"Gomer?"

"The Beebees' setter. I must tend to him."

"But the Beebees treated you like shit, Julie," I said, exasperated. "Mort Beebee was right up there on the stage, goading people into turning on you."

Julie's brows drew together. I had forgotten the delicate way they arched, like the wings of a bird. Her green eyes narrowed in puzzlement. "I don't understand your words. Gomer has done nothing wrong. He is sick and I can help him. While I prayed in the woods, the Lady directed me to pick certain herbs and grasses and to let them dry in the moonlight and to make an infusion for Gomer to inhale. Gomer is at the clinic. I must go there. But I came here first to thank you both for your kindness to me."

Edith handed a bowl of steaming soup to Julie. Julie began to eat greedily. Soup dribbled down her tiny pointed chin and onto her black robe, but she paid no attention, moving the spoon as fast as she could between mouth and bowl. In a few minutes the bowl was empty. She handed it back to Edith, who refilled it.

Edith sat down across from Julie and waited while Julie devoured the second bowl of soup. "You promised to tell us the big secret," Edith said. "The Goddess asked you to and you said you would."

Julie went pale, looked from side to side. Her mouth opened. "Get away! You stop that!" She jumped up, ran to the back door and opened it. Turned back, looked into the kitchen. "Get out! Get out!" she shouted, her voice frantic, her eyes staring at a spot on the wall. She made sweeping gestures with her hands.

"Julie! Pull yourself together," Edith said reprovingly, calmly. "There's no one there."

But I could almost see them, the Dark Spirits that Julie saw, the ones who tormented her each time she came close to telling her last secrets. She made pushing gestures with her hands. "Stop it! Stop it! Lady, help me!"

"Julie . . . ," Edith began.

Julie ran over to the table and picked up her soup bowl and flung it at the wall. "If you try to get me, I will smash you!" she shouted. "The Goddess and I smash what is in our way!" The bowl shattered. China and drops of reddish brown soup splattered on the wall and onto the floor. "I can't, I can't, they gather round to listen every time I begin to speak! They reproach me! They abuse me! Devils! They call me terrible names! I can't! I can't!"

"Julie . . . " Edith reached out to embrace the girl, who trembled violently, clutching at her robe, gathering it around her as if someone were pulling at her.

"You won't get me . . . ," Julie cried, staring at the kitchen wall. "Only these two, only Edith and John Charles can hear the Secret. Not you . . . the Goddess said to tell only them!" She pulled her hood up to hide most of her face and half ran, half stumbled out the back door, down the three steps, out onto the cement walk, around the side of the house, and disappeared from view.

Julie sat on the blanket in Gomer's pen, the old red setter stretched out beside her. She held his head over a basin that steamed, releasing the acrid scent of herbs. "Pet him, talk to him," Julie said gently. Tiny, Travis, and Sue Anne Beebee all cuddled around their dog. Tiny, grim and determined, petted the dog's head gently. Travis stroked his back, his face troubled and anxious. Little Sue Anne petted his hindquarters, her eyes reddened and swollen, her face streaked with tear tracks.

The setter's breath came in ragged gasps. His fur, sweat-soaked and matted, his eyes glaucous.

"Don't die, please don't die, Gomie," Sue Anne said, tears brimming in her eyes. "Julie, don't let him die."

"He's old," Julie said gently, "maybe it's his time."

"No, please, Julie. Give him some of your magic. I'm sorry for what I did, really I am."

"Me too," Travis said, frantically stroking the dog.

Julie smiled sadly. She held the dog's muzzle firmly. The old setter had drawn his lips back from his yellowed teeth, his tongue hung out, furred and whitish looking. Saliva dripped on Julie's hands. Once or twice he seemed to want to bite at Julie, in the kind of spasm you see in old dogs who are losing their faculties. Looking at him, I thought, he would surely die.

"Maybe you ought to let him go peacefully," I said.

All four of them looked up and saw Edith and me standing on the other side of the railing, looking into the pen. "John Charles! Edith!" Julie said, happiness in her voice. "How gracious, how good you are to come." She turned to the Beebee kids. "I was awful just now at Edith's house." She gave a little mischievous smile. "I threw a soup bowl and messed up Edith's kitchen. Can you believe it?"

Tiny and Travis smiled weakly. I looked at Edith in surprise. Who would have thought that the out-of-control teenager we had seen half an hour ago could now be this sensible-sounding young woman?

"Why'd you do that?" Sue Anne asked. "If I threwd a bowl my mommy would wallop me good."

The red setter began to tremble, his gasping breaths grew louder. "You've got to talk to him gently," Julie said to Tiny. She dipped a rag into the steaming herbal concoction, let it cool an instant, then bathed the setter's nostrils. "I might have left it too late, coming back."

"I'm sorry too," Tiny burst out. "I'm sorry we played that dumb joke on Sue Anne to get you in trouble. We didn't mean to scare her so bad. Just save Gomer and we'll stick up for you, I promise. I had Gomer since he was a pup. He sleeps in my bed, he's my best friend in the world."

"Oh," Julie said. She looked at Tiny. "All that rage and deceit. No wonder. . . . " She shook her head. "I think maybe John Charles is right. It's his time. His heart has been broken since the accident, you know. Then, when I went away . . . he counted on me. . . . "

"He's *my* dog!" Tiny said. "Gomer, come on, I love you Gomer, don't die, come *on*, Gomer, you can do it."

"That's good," Julie said. "Tell him you need him." She leaned over the setter's head, her black hair falling down over her face and mingling with the dog's dull, rust-colored fur. In her hand I saw she had a long black string. She began to tie knots in the cord, to press the knots gently to the setter's chest, and to chant in a soft firm voice:

> "I lay this cord on the hurt
>   The hurt comes into the cord,
>   I tie a knot in the cord,
>   So be it.

> "Hurt comes into the cord.
>   Hurt you are trapped in the cord.
>   Twice trapped in the cord.
>   So be it."

The setter lifted his head. His tongue retracted into his mouth. He pushed his nose closer to the bowl of steaming herbs and sniffed. I could no longer hear his breath rasping in his nostrils and it seemed as if the quivering of his hindquarters had lessened. Julie continued to knot the cord and to chant.

> "Hurt comes into the cord.
> Hurt you are trapped in the cord.
> Thrice trapped in the cord.
> So be it."

Gently Julie laid the setter's muzzle in Tiny's lap and stood. She walked away from the dog, who weakly lifted his muzzle and followed her with his eyes, which now looked much clearer. Again she chanted:

> "I take away the cord
> that holds the imprisoned hurt.
> The hurt has come away.
> So be it."

Julie opened the flap and went through it, out into the night. I thought I heard her voice, outside, chanting:

> "I bury the cord in the earth.
> Earth, receive this cord,
> make it earth of earth.
> So be it."

The flap opened and Julie crawled back through it, stood up, and walked slowly over to the setter. The three Beebee kids stared at her with awe and admiration. "He's getting better, look," Sue Anne said, her voice filled with joy.

"Oh, Gomer, come on, *come on, Gomer,*" Tiny said, leaning over and kissing the dog's muzzle, kissing his lips, kissing his nostrils.

The red setter thumped his tail weakly on the floor and

pushed his nose into Tiny's belly. No doubt about it, the dog was recovering. As we watched we saw strength returning to his legs, his tail move more vigorously, the dullness fade from his eyes, his breath return to normal.

"You did this, Tiny," Julie said, looking at him.

The young man looked back at her. All bravado had vanished from his face, which now looked young and vulnerable. "No, Julie, you did it, you saved him with your magic and I'll never forget it, never. None of us Beebees will, right, guys?"

"Right," Travis and Sue Anne said. Sue Anne got up, went over, and threw her arms around Julie. "We love you, Julie," she said. "Forever you're our friend, till death do us part, you hear? And we don't care what *anybody* says about you."

Julie smiled. "Y'all stay and talk to Gomer for a while. I think it'd be better if we keep him here for a few more days so I can give him herbal infusions again. Okay?"

"You got it," Tiny said.

Julie stood up. "I must rest. I have to sleep." She walked slowly, and for a moment I thought she would bump into the railing. But she got her balance and seemed to recover her sight, because she walked down the hall and we heard the door shutting gently as she went out of the clinic waiting room.

After I dropped Edith off, I felt restless. I didn't want to go back to The Old Forge, in case Cully might still be there. And I'd had about all I could take for one day of the cold shoulder from everyone else I knew.

Marilyn. She had been intending to come back from Charlottesville this evening. By now all her friends would have called and told her what had happened at the council meeting. She had probably been trying to phone me. I'd drive by her house. If I saw lights, I'd go on in.

I was in luck. When I went up the drive to her house, I saw lights on in the kitchen and living room. I rang the bell and a moment later she opened the door. "Hi, John Charles," she said, smiling warily at me. "Come on in."

"I hope it's not too late," I said. "I was driving by and saw your lights. Welcome back. I missed you."

I went to give her a hug, but she stepped back from the door, turned away from me, and walked into the kitchen. I followed her. Usually she greeted me with a hug and a kiss. Things did not look good.

"Can I get you something? Coffee? Beer?"

"Coffee's fine," I said. I wanted a drink, but since Marilyn thought I drank too much, it didn't seem a smart move.

She busied herself at the stove, boiled some water, poured me a mug of instant, one for herself. She filled the corn popper with kernels and turned it on. Then she sat down across from me at her kitchen table.

"Did you have fun in Charlottesville?" I asked, taking a sip of my coffee and scalding my tongue.

She ignored the question. "What happened, John Charles? I heard you and Edith went against everybody, and because of that, Cully hasn't fired Julie. People are hopping mad at you guys. I have to say, that was really stupid, John Charles. Why'd you have to be so up front about it?"

"What do you mean?"

"You know as well as I do, there's more than one way to skin a cat. You feel sorry for the little gal, I understand that. But do you think you can do her any good by cutting yourself off from everybody? How in the heck will you help her now?"

"Well, I . . . "

"You don't need to feel guilty, John Charles," Marilyn said, her voice softening. "I saw the way she acts around you, I know those tricks. Some teenage girls are dynamite for older guys. I trust you."

"Thanks," I said. But I was on guard now. I was no match for Marilyn and her amazing understanding of men-women things. Once she analyzed a situation, made up her mind about it, she could be ruthless. She'd dumped me before for drinking too much and acting in a way she thought stupid and it had taken me months to get back on her good side. If I wasn't careful, she would do it again. I didn't want to lose Marilyn. I had never felt so isolated, so alone. She sat across from me, wearing a soft, faded denim shirt unbuttoned enough so I could see flashes of white lace under it when she moved, and the curve of her beautiful large breasts. I wanted her, but it was clear from the cold, irritable look on her face that I was out of luck.

"But you got to look ahead, John Charles. What's the point of getting on the wrong side of the mayor, Mort Beebee, Reverend Fairchild, Sheriff Rumpsey, and everyone else who counts in this town? I bet Fanny Boynton is spitting nails."

"She's not happy," I admitted.

"And I don't get Edith Dunn, either," Marilyn said, watching me as she spoke. "I hear people are taking it out on her kids. They're like outcasts at school because of how their mother acted. Why would she do that to her kids for someone like Julie? It doesn't make sense."

The popcorn began to pop. It rattled in the bin—faster and faster. I knew Marilyn didn't feel much worried about my attraction to Julie, but she suspected the feeling between Edith and me. Mostly she hid her jealousy, but once in a while she let her resentment show, and when she did, it had the perverse effect of reminding me how deep ran the current of my admiration for Edith and my longing for her. How could I have gotten myself into such a stupid, confused situation? Tangled up with three women and not getting what I wanted from any of them.

I heard myself say, "Marilyn, can I stay over tonight?" Dumb, dumb. Marilyn wanted to talk. She wanted me to explain what I had done, to listen to her advice, to promise to consider it, to tell her how much I'd missed her. Instead I'd asked to go to bed.

She looked at me and her face hardened. "Not tonight, John Charles. I'm real worried about this situation. I have a business to run and, to tell the truth, I'm not willing to put it at risk for that dim-bulb teenager. She's got her problems, and I'm sorry about that, but we all have our problems. She needs help. You and Edith, if you want to do her some good, you should get her some serious therapy, not play along with that witch crap like I hear you been doing."

"You saying you're not going to stand by me?"

Her face creased with concern and she leaned over the table and caressed my hand. "No, darlin', don't push me like that. You know how much I care about you. It's just, your good heart is getting you into trouble I can't afford. I think we ought to cool it for a week or two, until things calm down. I'm not like you. I've got to make a living in this town, or I don't eat."

I had no answer to this. I finished my popcorn in silence, kissed her cool cheek. She walked me to the door and I went out into the dark night.

EIGHTEEN

This is a nightmare," Edith said, putting her lips to my ear and shouting.

The screams and jeers of the audience mounted in waves, but the giant speakers drowned them out, swamping us with noise, no longer sound, only vibrations which deafened our ears and throbbed in our bodies. Onstage, the warm-up band, a local heavy-metal group, banged and screamed and gyrated and sweated and swore at the audience, interspersing their "singing" and "playing" with obscene gestures. Their set ended and in a final frenzy they spattered one another with vats of blood-colored liquid and ran screaming from the stage to an approving roar from the audience.

Edith and I had to be the oldest people at this rock concert. Around us young punks, devil-worshipers, heavy-metal fans, most wearing black leather. Some had their hair tortured into fantastical shapes and colors, others had shaved or partly shaved their scalps. They lounged in their seats, or stood on them and screamed, or jumped in place, or crouched down and smoked marijuana in sucking arrogant inhalations.

"Do we dare leave our seats?" Edith shouted at me. Although the warm-up group had gone off, the speakers now blasted out canned music, which consisted mostly of repetitious drum-machine throbbing and squealing electric-guitar feedback.

"I'm afraid to!" I shouted back. "I haven't been this scared since I was in a four-car pileup on the interstate! And The Dead Souls haven't even come on yet!"

Our attendance at the concert had been Mrs. Boynton's idea. I had turned in my article on witchcraft and Devil worship and Mrs. Boynton had not liked it.

"John Charles, what is this supposed to be? I thought you were going to show the dangers of trafficking with all this stuff, not make it sound like a fun fair at the high school," she said, stalking out of her office at the *Sentinel* and bearing down on my workstation.

Leaning over my chair, Boynton held the offending printout in her hand and waved it at me derisively. "I believe your assignment was to show the town the dangers of Devil worship, not write up a wishy-washy summary of the history of old religions."

"I . . . "

"I'm not running an educational publishing house here, John Charles. I'm trying to get out a weekly newspaper and contribute to our community, you know?"

"But a balanced treatment . . . "

"Balanced!" Mrs. Boynton shouted, her face getting red. "Who said anything about *balance*? What ever gave you the idea we published *balanced* stories? What is it, are you catching the Columbia Journalism disease from Buzz or something?"

She began pacing around the room, waving the printout of my story. "We've got Devil-worshipers in this town, we've got a witch dragging us down, business is going to hell in a handbasket. . . . "

She wheeled on me. "You know what Mort Beebee says?"

"What?"

"If you're not part of the solution, you're part of the problem!" Mrs. Boynton proclaimed triumphantly. "Now I hear that Devil band, The Dead Souls, is playing in Richmond this weekend," she said, coming back to my chair and looming over me. "You get on over there and cover that foul desecration, you write it up so people know what's really going on, hear?"

"That's a good idea," I said. Surely the rock concert would not live up to its hype. If I could debunk the rockers as a group of exploitative showbiz manipulators trading in tired special effects, I might be able to distract people in Crowley Creek from this obsession with the occult and evil spirits, lower the temperature in town, ease some of the tension.

Mrs. Boynton was furious with me about my standing up for Julie at the council meeting. Knowing that hardly anyone in town was talking to me, she would have been well within her rights to can me. How does a reporter do his job if no one trusts him and no one will confide in him? But to my surprise, she hadn't said anything about the town's hostility to me. I didn't know why. I even wondered if Mrs. Boynton had a kind of sneaking respect for my willingness to stand alone, though she would never admit it.

So I'd agreed. When Edith heard about my plans to go to the rock concert, she wanted to come. But now, although The Dead Souls hadn't even come onto the stage yet, I feared we'd made a serious mistake.

Edith had tried to warn me. She'd researched The Dead Souls' World Wide Web site and the related chat groups, the "alt" newsgroups. She told me that on-line, you could talk with followers of "black metal" bands who got involved in church burnings, Satanic rites, and ritual murder. Although British bands like Venom were seen as entertainment, Edith's search had turned up more sinister rock groups. The members of Mayhem, Darkthrone, Burzum, and Emperor prayed to Viking death gods and several band members ended up tortured, murdered, or in jail for murder. Edith said she'd found links between the supporters of "black metal" and fascist movements and death cults.

"Most of it is harmless, but if you dig deep enough you find really bad people, John Charles," she said. "They do disgusting things: torture, grave desecration, cannibalism. It's wrong of Mrs. Boynton to try to link this stuff to Julie. It's not the same at all."

But the truth was, neither Edith nor I were sure anymore. Julie herself had said that the difference between white magic and black magic was an illusion. And even though I'm not a religious man, I couldn't help wondering if, without Christianity, you might get confused among the amoral forces, get drawn in by the "Dark Powers," drawn in by your murkier impulses, so that you lost your moral compass and founder. Had that happened to Julie? I remembered how Reverend Fairchild told us that the Bible warned against magicians, soothsayers, witches, and those who consorted with spirits. My own ancestor, Edgar Allan Poe, had tangled with the darkness and not survived, and I struggled constantly against the pull of the casket papers he had left behind.

The seats began to fill up again. We could smell sweat and marijuana and cheap perfume. The lights went down, the canned music faded away, and the stage darkened. Black light came up, illuminating cabalistic designs on the robes of the musicians. Dry-ice fumes rose up from the stage, the smell of incense wafted into the audience, the music grew more intense, the beat faster, louder.

I peered into the smoky fumes and saw the musicians in their appointed positions. The lead singer, Malek Taus, suddenly let out a high, eerie wail. The throbbing drumbeat began to die away and a pinpoint spotlight illuminated him. A tall, powerful-looking man, he wore white corpse makeup and bright red lipstick. All his teeth but the incisors, which had been chiseled to a point, had been blacked out. He had shed his robe to reveal a bare chest, whitened so you could see the blood-red smeared image of the Devil painted upon it. He wore tight black-leather pants, big black-leather combat boots, and silver cartridge bands around his waist and wrists. A vicious-looking dagger hung around his neck.

Malek struck his guitar, forcing out a piercing howl. He

raised a hand and allowed a beat of silence. Then another piercing howl. Acoustic drums began to thrum. Malek grabbed the microphone and sang out:

In nomine Dei nostri Satanas Luciferi exelsit!
"Satan! Satan! Satan lives!" chanted the audience.
"Satan, I command you, come forth!" shouted Malek.
"Satan! Satan! Satan lives!" chanted the audience.
"By the Gods of Hell, come forth and answer to
    your names!"
"Satan! Satan! Satan lives!" chanted the audience.

A black-cloaked figure walked slowly from the back of the stage, emerging from the fading dry-ice fumes. It approached Malek, who grabbed at its cloak, stripping it away to reveal a tall woman, her face white with corpse makeup, long, straight blond hair streaming down her back, naked except for a body-suit made of sparkling black mesh. The audience began to hoot, but Malek scowled and made a gesture and they quieted. The blond woman ran her hands sensually up her legs and over her breasts like a stripper, then she appeared to arch over backward. I stared and saw she had in fact lain down over a black bench.

"She's the altar," Edith said. "They think it's diabolical to use a naked woman for an altar."

Malek struck a reverberating, dirgelike chord on his electric guitar. He leaned over the naked woman, making suggestive gestures with his hands and body.

With a crash of symbols, the music began. Synthesizer chords, drumbeats, a bass three-chord pattern, an eerie metallic electrified violin racing up and down the scale. Malek stalked to his microphone and whanged at his guitar.

"He's reciting the Devil's names," Edith shouted into my ear.

The lights came up on the other musicians. They had thrown off their cloaks. All wore corpse makeup, jeweled swords, tight leather pants. Their chests bare—a few appeared to be bleeding from various wounds—they chanted and gyrated while the audience roared in response:

"Satan! Satan! Satan lives!"

Malek stopped playing, and the other musicians picked up the pace, filling the theater with a reverberating, wailing cacophony. Moving to their beat, he strode over to the naked woman and appeared to plunge his dagger into her side. The audience roared as what looked like black blood pulsed out of the "wound." The woman didn't move. Malek held a chalice in the shape of a skull under the blood, then lifted it to his lips and drank, letting the "blood" drip down his face and onto his chest.

"Blood of woman, die, woman," he screamed, "Blood of death, die, woman! Blood! Dead Souls arise! Satan hear our . . ."

I stood up. "We're getting out of here," I said. I grabbed Edith's hand and we started edging along the seats, past the mesmerized, screaming, chanting fans, some of whom appeared to be cutting their arms and legs with razors. I smelled, real, fresh blood. We made it to the aisle and ran up it, through the lobby and into the night.

Outside we stood on the sidewalk catching our breath.

"Oh, I'm so glad you got us out of there," Edith said.

"Did you see those kids making cuts in their arms with razors?"

"Yes," Edith said softly. "Street kids do it. Sometimes they keep on until they're covered in cuts."

We hurried along the street, to the Bronco parked up ahead. I opened the passenger's side door for Edith. As she climbed up into the car, I smelled her perfume, and her hair brushed my cheek. A feeling of loneliness welled up inside me. I had felt it before when Edith was near. Once she had let me hold her, kiss her, told me she cared for me, but she had regretted it and asked me never to speak of it again. I had accepted her request, though I often wondered if a more aggressive man might have won her over. But it never felt right to me to push past a person's reserve, to push in where you weren't welcome.

I climbed in on my side and started up the engine. "Does Julie do it?" I asked.

"Julie? Cut herself?" Edith said. "No, Julie is too deeply committed to healing. Her Wicca beliefs help her get past that kind of self-hatred, guilt, and despair."

"So that's what it is," I said. I pulled out into the traffic and we drove off, back to Crowley Creek.

The rock concert took place Saturday night. Then came Sunday afternoon, the day of the St. George's bake sale.

St. George's Episcopalian had long tables set out around the small churchyard. Two towering ancient black walnut trees cast a welcome shade, for the day was muggy. People crowded around to buy their favorites: Susannah Gleason's blackberry pie, Madge Baxter's double chocolate brownies, Edith's Toll House cookies.

I walked from table to table, surrounded by a bubble of space. It seemed like no one wanted to get too close to me. A few people greeted me coolly, with a kind of hostile politeness. Most managed to avoid seeing me. I acted as if I didn't notice.

I had come to see Reverend Fairchild. To keep my promise to him to report on the concert. Edith had shown him printouts of her search on the World Wide Web, and the attacks on Christianity on the Satanist sites had infuriated him. I chose to speak to him at the bake sale, because I didn't want people to think I was afraid be out and around, afraid to face up to him.

"Hello, John Charles," Fairchild said. He held a cardboard box full of white and pink sachets of sugar and sugar substitute. "Just hang on there a minute while I bring this over to the coffee ladies, then I'll be right with you."

Halfway over to the coffee urn, Susannah Gleason, Zak's wife, stopped him. "Reverend Fairchild, I hear tell there's news about Margaret?"

I turned to listen.

Fairchild put a hand out and touched Susannah Gleason's arm. A plump, cheerful woman in her late thirties, energetic, hardworking, loyal, she could always be counted on to contribute to a church bake sale.

"I hadn't heard that," Fairchild said, his expression concerned. "I know they've given up looking for her body, and I heard they had a memorial service over at Emmanuel Baptist."

Susannah Gleason darted a look at me and lowered her voice, murmuring something to Fairchild.

"We have no proof, Susannah," Fairchild said. "Remember, Dr. Cully still supports her. As long as he does . . . "

"As long as he does, I guess she has a place in this town," Susannah said louder, not caring who heard. She looked over Fairchild's shoulder at me and her usually cheerful face grew taut. She said, venomously, "As long as *some folks* support her, looks like we have to put up with it. How can you stand by, Reverend Fairchild? With a devil-worshiper in town, witching folks and their livestock. It's not right. You know it's not."

Fairchild patted her shoulder, picked up his box of sugar packets, and adroitly moved past her to drop it off next to the coffee urn. He spoke to a few more people, then came back to me. "You went to the rock concert, John Charles?" he said, looking at me, then licking his lips which I saw seemed dry and cracked.

"Yes. Edith and I went last night."

"How was it? Tell me about it, I'm most interested."

"Bad," I said grudgingly. "I need some coffee." We strolled over to the table where they had set up two tall stainless-steel urns, one for coffee and one for hot tea. They had a row of pitchers of iced tea, and behind them, I saw they were steeping some sun tea in a bucket.

"Bad?" Fairchild said. "What do you mean the rock concert was *bad*?"

I took a deep breath, then let it out. "I guess—you were right about some of it. That concert was worse than just a performance to scare impressionable kids and make money. There

was a lot of dress-up, a lot of posing, but deep down, something
real bad was going on."

"That's right," Fairchild said. He looked at me, his eyes
bright, his mouth twitching. "They call on the Devil, don't
they?"

"Yes, but . . . "

"But what?"

"That's not what matters, it's . . . "

"You're wrong, you're deeply, dangerously wrong,"
Fairchild said. He leaned toward me, clutching his sweating
glass of iced tea. It shook in his hand, and I heard the ice cubes
rattling against the side of the glass. "They open the Gates and
let the Devil in and then he does his work on all the young, impressionable souls they attract with their fame and their
glamor."

I thought of the kids cutting themselves with razors, the
blood welling from the shallow cuts, the crazed frenzy of those
orgasmic cries from the audience, the way the kids shouted,
"Satan, Satan." "I don't think the Devil actually comes, but I
think they manipulate confused, vulnerable kids. Maybe it's just
a difference of words, anyway."

"No, John Charles, listen," Fairchild said intensely. He put
his glass down on the grass. It tipped over and brown liquid and
ice cubes slid out into the grass. Fairchild didn't notice.
"Haven't you seen the same thing happening here in Crowley
Creek? You saw Julie open the Gates during her witch rite, and
now the town is full of evil. It's around us, I know you can feel
it, I know you can." He stared at me and I stared back at him.
His mouth twitched more intensely and he put a hand over the
twitch. "You heard her call the Devil. And that black cat of
hers, that cat isn't an ordinary cat. He's a witch's *familiar*, that's
the form a witch's demon servant takes. Julie can send the black
cat out to do the Devil's work. Haven't you seen him following
Cully everywhere? Never giving the man a moment's peace?
Appearing and disappearing? And Cully doesn't dare fire Julie.
He wants to, but he doesn't dare. Because of Asmodeus."

"Come on. . . . "

"No, *you* come on. You know I'm right. I see it in your eyes. Why won't your mind admit what your heart knows? Everyone says that rock group, The Dead Souls, has songs that call out for death, for murder, for killing, for blood, didn't you hear that?"

"Yes, but . . . "

"And didn't we have a woman murdered right here in Crowley Creek? With an ax? Right after a witch comes to town? And Julie—that very witch—knew where to find the ax? How else do you explain that? We ask her how she knew where to look and she says Asmodeus showed her where the ax had been buried. Well, John Charles? Doesn't that just prove my point?"

I looked away from Fairchild, away from his white twitching face, his gleaming eyes, his trembling hands. And I realized that his voice had been growing louder and louder and that quietly, a group of people had drawn near. Now, all around us, folks were standing, silent, watching us, listening intently, their faces anxious, troubled, doubtful.

"Does she talk to the Devil, John Charles?" Fairchild demanded.

"Well, that depends on . . . "

"Does she commune with Satan? Yes or No? Answer me in the name of our Lord!" thundered Fairchild.

I stood up. Fairchild stood up too. Around us, people backed off, sensing something was about to happen.

"If the Devil is anywhere in this," I shouted suddenly, "he is in you!"

Everyone gasped. Fairchild stepped back in surprise.

Then I remembered Cully. Remembered what Cully had done, and I felt ashamed. Fairchild was misguided, obsessed, while Cully—Cully, surely was evil. But I had no proof. I couldn't accuse him of anything. My certainty drained away.

"I'm sorry," I said miserably. "I shouldn't have said that. But nothing is like you think it is. Julie's in trouble. I can't abandon her." I turned on my heels and walked away. Behind me I heard the murmur of people's voices. The sound of it reverberated in my ears, mockingly, like the calling of a flock of crows, circling high overhead in the spring sky.

I drove home without seeing anything, without thinking anything. I only *felt*. Once I reached Crowley House, I went straight to the library. I drew the curtains then turned on the lamp so it illuminated my reading chair, leaving the rest of the room in shadow. I removed the key from the secret drawer, retrieved the casket from its hiding place, opened it, and feverishly pawed through the packets of papers. My hands had a life of their own. They found a certain packet, untied the tattered pinkish ribbon, selected a sheet of paper. Pouring myself a stiff drink of Blanton's straight, I carried it and the paper to my chair, took a long drink, and began to read.

The strange perversity of the Arch-fiend

In the consideration of the faculties and impulses—of the prime motive of the human soul, our best thinkers have failed to make room for a propensity which, although obviously existing as a radical, primitive, irreducible sentiment, has been equally overlooked by all the moralists. In the pure arrogance of the reason, we have all overlooked it.

It would have been wiser, it would have been safer, to classify (if classify we must) upon the basis of what man usually or occasionally did, and was always occasionally doing, rather than upon the basis of what we took for granted the Deity intended him to do. If we cannot comprehend God in his visible works, how then in his inconceivable thoughts, that call the works into being? If we cannot understand him in his objective creatures, how then in his substantive moods and phases of creation?

Through induction we are brought to admit an innate and primitive principle of human action, a paradoxical something, which we may call perverseness, *for want of a more characteristic term. It is a fact, a motive without a motive. Through its promptings we act without comprehensible object; or, let us say, through its promptings we act, for the reason that we should* not. *In theory, no reason can be more unreasonable; but, in fact, there is none more strong. With certain minds, under certain conditions, it becomes absolutely irresistible. I am not more certain that I breathe, than that the assurance of the wrong or error of any action is often the one unconquerable* force *which impels us, and alone impels us, to its prosecution.*

You doubt me, my descendant? You are certain, I imagine I hear you thinking, that wrong or evil-appearing acts must have a motive? That they are, surely, the misguided acts to which desperation or pain or suffering or folly drive us on occasion.

Yet I dare you, appeal to your own heart. Yes? You have done so? Confess, there you have found the best, the truest confirmation. No one who trustingly consults and thoroughly questions his own soul can deny the propensity in question.

You still doubt me? Imagine.

We stand upon the brink of a precipice. We peer into the abyss—we grow sick and dizzy. Our first impulse is to shrink from the danger. Unaccountably we remain. By slow degrees our sickness and dizziness and horror become merged in a cloud of unnamable feeling. By gradations, still more imperceptible, this cloud assumes shape, as did the vapor from the bottle out of which arose the genius in The Arabian Nights. *But out of this,* our *cloud upon the precipice's edge, there grows into palpability a shape, far more terrible than any genius or any demon of a tale, and yet it is but a thought, although a fearful one, and one which chills the very marrow of our bones with the fierceness of the delight of its horror. It is merely the idea of what would be our sensations during the sweeping precipitancy of a fall from such a height. And this fall—this rushing annihilation—for the very reason that it involves that one most ghastly and loathsome of all the most ghastly and loathsome images of death and suffering which*

*have ever presented themselves to our imagination—for this
very cause do we now the most vividly desire it.*

*You must accept this, my descendant, the more so as the
blood which runs in my veins runs in yours. And if you have
read this far in this missive from beyond the grave, and have
not by now thrown it aside in disgust, I know the motive of
perverseness troubles your soul, as it has mine. And like me,
you struggle to understand.*

*One final word. You, my dear friend, are no doubt, a
stronger and better man than I. You have, perhaps, found the
energy and action to deny this propensity for perverseness. In
the struggle which I so often lost, you who live in a better,
more virtuous era, have triumphed.*

*But before you rejoice in your ascendancy over the cravings
I failed to conquer, consider this:* We might, indeed, deem
this perverseness a direct instigation of the Arch-fiend,
were it not occasionally known to operate in further-
ance of good.

A dull knocking aroused me from my reading. I looked up.
Around me, the shadows in the room seemed to move. A sense
of dread pervaded my body. Again I heard the knock. I got up
slowly and walked to my father's desk, where I set down the casket. I replaced the sheet I had read in its packet, retied the
packet, put it back.

I put my hand in my pocket and drew out my talisman. I
turned it between my fingers, but my sense of dread only increased. I relocked the casket, replaced it in its hiding place, put
the key back in the secret drawer. I walked to the curtains and
pulled them aside.

Standing directly in front of me, almost touching the glass
of the tall narrow window, stood Julie. She smiled at me. I
opened the window.

"Hello, John Charles," she said, in her soft little voice.

"You!" I said.

"Yes . . . I need to talk to you, I'm frightened."

"Why don't you come to the front door like normal people?"

"I'm afraid," she said again. She looked behind her. "Sometimes folks follow me, they want me to leave Crowley Creek, they want to hurt me."

"Yes. I know about that."

"Can I come in the window?"

I opened the casement window wider so Julie could slither through. She stepped into the library, stumbling slightly over her long skirt. She wore a filmy gray skirt, her black-and-purple silk scarf wrapped about her like a shawl. She had on black lace-up boots and a crystal hung around her neck.

"Where's that blasted Asmodeus?" I asked. I tried to speak normally, not to yield to the peculiar feeling that had only grown stronger with her entrance.

"Working," she said smiling. "He has to keep watch."

I walked over to my chair and sat down. Julie followed me and sank down on the floor at my feet. She unwrapped her shawl, slipped it down off her shoulders, and I saw the shape of her small round breasts under her tank top.

"You are my only friend now," she said.

"What about Edith?"

"Not anymore, not after what they just did."

"Who? What? What are you talking about?"

"I can't leave, he won't let me."

I had no idea what she meant. "Who won't let you?"

"Please, you've got to help me."

"Julie, I can't help unless you tell me what you are hiding. You know something about Margaret's murder, don't you?"

She put a hand on my knee. I felt it burn through my jeans. I removed it. She ran her fingers through her hair. "I'm just too scared to. I know I promised, but if I tell . . . "

She had begun that same shaking I remembered from each time I had tried to push her, but I had no patience for it now.

"You stop that!" I said harshly. "If you're going to go into a state you can leave right now, you hear?"

"I'm scared," she said again, her voice faint. But she stopped her shaking. She looked at me, and smiled a small smile, so that I saw those white pointed teeth of hers. Then she took my hand and pressed it on her breast. "Feel my heart, how it's beating," she said, watching me.

Her breast was firm under my fingers. She moved my hand seductively over her breast. I had been aroused the moment I saw her outside and now this . . . she knew how I felt. She kept looking at me out of those green eyes. "It's all right," she said in her soft breathy little voice, "I like you so much. I won't be so afraid if we are very very close, then I can tell you. Then, when I feel you inside me and I taste your breath . . . "

Gently I freed my hand from her clutch and balled her fingers into a fist. I put the fist into her lap and sat back in my chair. "No, Julie. It's not going to happen, not ever. I wouldn't do that to you."

"But . . . You hate me! You think I'm disgusting!" Tears seeped out of her eyes and ran down her cheeks.

"Julie. I am your friend. Friends don't take advantage of each other."

"You want me, I know you do," she said, but her voice lacked conviction. She spoke the words as if she thought herself desirable, but behind them I heard her self-disgust. "Oh, Goddess . . . oh . . . "

"I will wait until you trust me enough to tell me the secret that is eating away at you," I said. "But no matter what, if you tell me or if you don't, nothing will ever happen between you and me. I won't do that." My feeling of dread now suffused my entire body, overwhelming lust, overwhelming curiosity, overwhelming the sadness I felt when I looked at this lost, confused young girl. She raised her hands again to her hair and I saw that her wrists looked fragile enough to snap like a dried branch.

"You need never fear telling me anything," I said to her. "You can trust me."

She looked up at me. She opened her mouth. Nothing came out.

Then she turned away, wiped her eyes with her hand,

wrapped her shawl around her shoulders, and slipped out through the window. I watched as she crossed the lawn and entered the woods. Once she had disappeared from sight, I sighed, took my glass over to the shelf and refilled it. I took a deep, long drink and felt the whiskey burn going down.

NINETEEN

Sunday night found me home, alone. I rounded up some left-over rice and boiled shrimp from the refrigerator, chopped some celery and peppers, and fried the whole mess up in hot oil, sprinkled red pepper flakes over it, took a cold beer, and ate sitting out on the back patio, watching the sun sink slowly behind the trees at the end of the lawn. The fading light illuminated the undersides of the leaves so that they glowed in the darkness, and the shadows of the hickory trunks looked like long black bars on the grass.

I brooded about how I had sent Julie away, made her weep and feel disgraced. It had seemed the right thing to do at that time. But maybe it was just cowardice. Hadn't my father told me over and over that I ran away from things? In the back of my mind I might have been remembering how *The Malleus Malefi-carum* claimed a man could become a servant of the Devil if he had congress with a witch.

Servant of the Devil? I thought of Cully and I felt rage rising in me, pressing on my chest. Secure in his position in town, abusing Julie, mocking me, and not a thing I could do about it.

He had murdered his wife, and it seemed like an aura of wickedness was growing and spreading out from him, corrupting everything. Yet I could not think of a way to bring him down.

Then I remembered what Jase had said about Cully's basement. That was one thing I could do. Check out the Cully cellar. Next: Go over to Edith's, find out what was going on over there, find out what Julie meant when she said Edith could not still be her friend. Better than sitting here, sliding into a bottle of Blanton's.

When I got to Cully's, I saw five cars parked in his driveway, and another one drove in behind me. Among the cars, I recognized the mayor's glossy blue Windstar minivan, Mrs. Boynton's white Cadillac Seville, and the Beebees' black Mercedes. Not the people I would have expected Cully to invite over. I pulled my Bronco off the driveway and onto the grass so they could get by me.

It had grown dark. The moon, three-quarters full, looked pale yellow and the sky a deep navy blue sprinkled with faint pinpoints of stars. A dog barked and then another then a bunch of them. The tree frogs kept up their insistent, ominous clamor. I walked along the side of the house to the addition that housed the vet clinic then around the back. The dogs stopped yapping, and as I stepped around the corner of the house, I saw Julie come out crawling, headfirst, from one of the dog-pen flaps. She stood up very slowly and walked away without seeing me. She crossed the yard silently, walked to the garage, opened the door, and went up to her apartment. A moment later I saw her shadow, a dark shape at the window. Now I felt it, stronger than ever, the aura of evil that seemed to emanate from the Cully house.

I continued around the building. The kitchen window slid open and I heard a loud chortle. Mayor Winsome, laughing, but he didn't sound very happy. At the end of the house I saw concrete steps going downward to a cellar door. Beside them stood a pile of logs, and a smaller pile of split wood. I went down the stairs. I smelled newly split wood, damp concrete, mold, earth. At the bottom of the steps I found an old door, the paint peeling, the knob loose. I turned the knob and the door opened into darkness. Strong fumes of paint, Poly-Fil, brick dust, mortar, and plaster brought tears to my eyes. I reached around the opening, found a wall switch, and flicked on a light. Before me I saw a basement room under renovation. Three walls newly plastered. The fourth bricked up with old brick so cleverly that it seemed to have been there always. But the fresh pointing and the pile of old bricks in the corner said otherwise. It looked as if someone had prepared this wall for a coat of plaster, meant to cover the brick. An old door rested on a pair of sawhorses in the middle of the room. On it I could see paint cans, a sack of plaster, sponges, trowels, renovation magazines, a bucket, and tools. Under it, a bag of mortar.

I entered the room. Beneath my feet, new subflooring. At the far end of the room, a door. I crossed, opened the door, and looked into the unfinished part of the basement. Off in the distance I could see an oil furnace, an old coal chute, potato bins, a washer, a dryer, an ironing board, and laundry tubs. The floor was concrete, oil-stained, and damp. The walls sweated moisture and the room reeked of damp and mold.

I went in and looked around. I came back out and inspected the renovated room carefully. No signs of an old fireplace. No signs of anything untoward. Just a basement room. Yet despite the innocuous smell of chemicals, the meticulous workmanship, the texturized plaster treatment, the room sent a chill up my spine and my mouth went dry.

Suddenly I felt the dark power of Edgar Allan Poe's tale, "The Black Cat," filling the basement room, and for a moment I seemed to see the woodpile, the crumbling bricks, the damp plaster, which, in the old tale, had witnessed the hideous moment—when the enraged murderer raised his ax against the black cat and smashed it down upon his wife's skull. The present grew dim, and the past, with all its evil rose up around me. I shivered violently. The room seemed to grow dim, the floor porous—as if it might give way under my feet.

Pulling myself together with an effort, I turned off the light, went out, shut the door behind me, and mounted the stairs.

I walked quietly along, hugging the side of the house so I could not be seen from the kitchen window. Lights blazed out from the window and now I heard the saccharine tone Mrs. Boynton used when she tried to persuade, then the confident sound of Mort Beebee's voice. Their familiar voices helped me to recover from the shock I had felt in the basement room.

I could have walked right up to the kitchen door and invited myself in, but I didn't. I kept walking along the side of the house until I got to the dog pens. I opened the flap to the pen Julie had come out of and crawled in.

Once inside, I smelled dog and the strong scent of one of Julie's herbal concoctions. I stood up just as I heard a scrambling nose, than saw a dark shape rush at me and felt paws strike my chest, hot breath on my face. "Down, boy, down, boy!" I said, raising my knee and pushing Gomer off. My eyes adjusting to the dim light, I saw the old red setter, his tail wagging madly, coming at me again eagerly. I reached out and pushed him down gently, petted him. "Hi there, boy, how ya doin'? Feeling better, aren't you? That's good, that's good. . . . "

He licked my hand, snuffled around my trouser legs, pressed his nose against my thigh. "You sure are better, boy," I said to him. "I thought you'd had it, but Julie saved your bacon, no doubt about it. Did she tell you her secret? I bet not. But no matter how bad she feels, she comes by to bring you your herbs, doesn't she? A woman who loves animals like she does, can't be all bad, don't you think? Yes? That's what I think. Can we let her down? No sir, Gomer, we can't do that. No matter the dark shadows around her, we can't use and abuse her, we can't treat her like those other men did, can we, Gomer? We'd break her heart, wouldn't we? And she's had it broken enough, poor thing, you can see it in her eyes. You did your part by getting better. Now we've got to do ours."

Gomer clearly agreed. He wagged his tail and trotted over to a basin steaming in the corner and sniffed at it. He came back to me and rubbed his grizzled muzzle on my trousers again to be petted some more.

I spent a few more minutes patting Gomer and telling him

some of the things that weighed on my mind. Strengthened, I walked along the corridor and quietly opened the connecting door that led into the back hall. My sneakers made no sound as I moved along the hall toward the kitchen.

"I just don't get you," I heard Mayor Winsome's voice coming out of the open door. I flattened my back against the wall and sidled over to the doorway. If anyone came out, they'd see me. I took a quick peek.

Cully sat at the chrome-trimmed Formica-topped kitchen table, his back to me. Around the table I recognized Boynton, Winsome, Beebee, Fairchild, Grissom, the minister from Emmanuel Baptist, and Iris McCain, a big shot on the town council. It looked to me like a deputation.

"You can't go on like this," Winsome said, his voice agitated. "We got all the sympathy in the world for you, boy, Margaret dying like that. But you had no business letting the witch come back here after Reverend Fairchild drove her out. After we passed an ordinance against her. The town won't stand for it."

"She's a bad influence," Iris said. I didn't know Iris well, but I knew her well enough to realize that she could be a loyal friend or a vicious enemy if she took against you. "I can't believe you'd go against what's best for Crowley Creek if she didn't have some hold over you."

"We'll all help you," Fairchild said.

I couldn't see Cully's face, but he sat slumped in his chair, as if exhausted. They had a pitcher of iced tea in the middle of the table and a bowl of potato chips. Everyone had a glass of tea and Cully now picked his up and drained it, then poured some more.

"I don't need your help," he said. "I didn't ask for it."

"You've got to send her away for good, that's all there is to it," Mrs. Boynton said. Her voice had that commanding tone I knew so well. The tone that let you know that arguing was pointless, that she had the power and would use it any way she had to to get her way.

Cully stood up so suddenly his chrome-and-vinyl chair

flapped backward and crashed to the floor. He pushed back from the table with his hands, rattling it so that tea slopped over the surface. "I didn't invite you here!" he shouted. "This is my kitchen and my home and you are no longer welcome. People don't tell me what to do in my kitchen. . . . "

"Now calm down there . . ." Jackson Lee began in his most ingratiating voice.

"Out! I want y'all out! Right now!"

"Well, if that's how you're going to be . . . ," Iris began.

"Now look here . . ." Beebee said in his business-is-business tone.

"Out!" yelled Cully. "Y'all ought to be ashamed, ganging up on a penniless, homeless girl who wouldn't hurt a fly and just loves animals. You got crazy ideas in your head, you see ghosts and spirits, that's your problem. Your problem, you hear me? People can't handle their teenagers, business is bad, spirits in town are low . . . you looking for someone to blame? Blame yourselves! Life is full of trouble and sorrow. You know that! I know that! Who are you kidding?"

He was panting, pacing the kitchen, and they stared at him, mesmerized by the force and passion in his words.

"In the name of our Lord . . . ," began Fairchild.

"Our Lord!" shouted Cully. "Since the time of our Lord weak people have looked for scapegoats and that's what y'all are doin' and you know it. I won't have any part of you. I won't turn on a little gal who trusts me. Do what you want to me. Whatever you do can't be any worse than what's already happened. Now get out of my house!"

They pushed their chairs back and got up slowly. I backed down the hall and slipped into the animal clinic, went down the hall out the side door. As I came around the corner of the house, I saw the deputation hurrying out the front door. Without a word they got into their cars and one by one they drove away. Cully stood in the front door, framed by the hall light, watching them go. Now the only car parked outside was my Bronco.

"John Charles? You out there?" Cully called.

I walked back toward him.

"You too?" he said, peering out into the darkness.

"I just came by and when I saw their cars I didn't want to come in. That group's not too keen on me right now," I called back to him.

Cully stared out at me. "I can't see you. Come into the light, boy."

I didn't move. I stood there. "What are you up to, Cully? Why won't you cut Julie loose? You know what's going on between you and her is wrong."

"Wrong?" Cully laughed. It was a terrible laugh, a laugh full of rage and despair and a kind of pleasure I didn't understand. "Wrong? You don't know anything. And you won't find out anything either. Why don't you go see your friend Edith?" He laughed some more. "Wrong?"

Still laughing, he turned and shut the door behind him.

I drove over to Edith's. I rang the bell and waited. No one came. But lights shone out from the windows on both the ground floor and the second floor. I rang again. No answer. I walked over to the garage, opened the side door, peered in, and saw Edith's Taurus. She had to be home. I walked around to the back door, rang the back doorbell and waited. Again, no answer. I opened the screen door and tried the back doorknob. Unsurprisingly, it opened. Most of us in Crowley Creek still don't lock the back door when we're home. I stepped in.

"Edith? Anybody home?" I called out.

The kitchen smelled of soup and baking. A pan of fresh brownies lay on a rack on the counter. "Edith?" I yelled as loud as I could. "It's John Charles! You here?"

"John Charles? That you? Hold on. . . . " Her voice sounded very faint. I heard footsteps approaching, then Edith came into the kitchen. Her face looked worn, deep circles under her eyes, lines graven around her mouth. Her hair, usually so shiny, hung limp around her face.

"Edith! What's the matter?"

"Sit down, John Charles," she said without meeting my eyes. "I've been meaning to call you, but to tell the truth, I couldn't face it." She collapsed into a chair. "I just couldn't face it."

"Edith, you look terrible. Can I get you something?"

"A coffee would be good," she said.

I poured her one from the Mr. Coffee on the counter and brought it to her. Then I stood behind her and put a hand on her shoulder. "What couldn't you face?" I said gently.

"Maybe I'd rather have a glass of wine," she said, surprising me. "There's a bottle of Chardonnay in the fridge." She put a hand up over mine and pressed her fingers down onto mine. Her skin felt hot and dry. I stayed there for a moment, enjoying the feel of her flesh, then went around and got her wine, poured myself one without asking, and sat down across from her.

She picked up her wineglass. "Trouble," she said. "Big, big trouble."

I looked at her.

"It's Jase. Someone attacked him."

"Oh God, Edith. Is he okay?"

"Physically. On his way home from school, someone jumped him, blindfolded him, tied him up. They dragged him into the woods. They . . . "

"Oh, Edith." I got up and went around and pulled her up from her chair. I put my arms around her and held her. She wrapped her arms around me and hugged me back and for a moment I could hear her heart beating in her chest, feel her breath on my cheek. How good it felt, her body fitted against mine perfectly. She belonged in my arms. I knew it and I am sure she knew it too. Warmth flooded through me but she tensed and pulled away and I heard heavy footsteps. I looked up to see a heavyset man in his early forties coming into the kitchen. He had thinning curly blond hair, pale blue eyes, a bloated face, and I disliked him instantly.

"Rob," Edith said, "this is John Charles Poe. John Charles, this is Rob, my ex-husband."

"What's he doing here?" Rob said, glaring at me.

Edith sighed. "Sit down, Rob. We're having wine. Would you like a glass?"

"Uh, sure. Sorry, Poe. I'm not at my best right now." He slumped into a chair. Edith got up and poured him a glass of wine. He slurped at it, dribbling some down his chin. "Goddamn, I get my hands on whoever did that to Jase, I'll kill him, I swear I will."

"Mommy . . . I just throwed up again," said a weak little voice. Jase Dunn shuffled in. He wore a baggy Baltimore Orioles T-shirt, white Jockey briefs, and sport socks. Vomit stains trailed down the front of his shirt.

"Oh, darling," Edith said, jumping up. "Come on upstairs, we'll get you cleaned up."

Jase caught sight of me. "Hi, Mr. Poe," he said, looking at me. "Did you hear what Julie did? They, like, kidnapped me, her and Asmodeus, and made me eat cat food. Isn't that disgusting? I am *real* POed. I'm maybe, like, poisoned. I keep throwing up."

Edith looked at me directly for the first time since I had come to the house. Now I saw that our embrace had been a kind of good-bye. "I'll be right back," Edith said. "I just want to get Jase cleaned up and back in bed. He needs to rest. Jase, honey, do you think you could keep down a brownie? I made your favorite double fudge kind."

Jase's face was flushed. "I don't think so, Mommy. My tummy feels weird." He scuffed back out the door, dragging his feet so that his socks made a slithery sound over the kitchen tile floor. Edith followed him out.

"Bastards," Rob Dunn said. "Why would they attack a little boy and force cat food down his throat? Then they cut a chunk of his hair off and cut his fingernails and took the hair and fingernail bits away. That's got to be crazy. Sick. Wacko." He put his head in his hands. "Edith should keep a better watch on my boys. She shouldn't be out working. She should be home. Boys need their mother."

"I don't follow you there," I said. "How would her being

home stop kids from grabbing Jase on the way home from school? What's her working got to do with anything?"

"You got any kids?" Dunn asked me.

"No, but . . ."

"Then shut up. You don't know what you're talking about. Women have all the trump cards in this country, you know that? They get the kids and there's not a damn thing you can do about it. They don't raise them right, they don't listen when you tell them what to do, and you have to sit back, powerless, and watch your kids being screwed up, know what I mean?"

I could feel myself getting angry. I knew for a fact that Rob Dunn had left Edith and the kids for his secretary, gone off to live in Roanoke, was way way behind in his support payments, and hardly ever came to see his boys. When he did take them he spoiled them and tried to turn them against Edith, by criticizing her discipline. He let those boys down over and over. But now here he was, upset, and I guess he had a right to be. I hated seeing him in that kitchen, acting like he still lived there. I hated what I'd seen in Edith's eyes, that she had pulled back from me in some fundamental way.

Edith came back into the kitchen and sat down.

"How's he doing?" Rob said. He sounded sad and frustrated and helpless. "Should I go sit with him for a while?"

"That would be good," Edith said. "He's so happy you're here. Why don't you play cards with him? He likes that."

"Sure," Dunn said, brightening. "Good idea." He got up heavily and went out and I heard his footsteps going up the stairs.

"Edith?"

"Look, John Charles, I don't know that it really was Julie. Some people came out of the woods dressed like she dresses, long black robes, hoods covering their faces, and for sure Asmodeus was there. They pinned Jase down and forced cat food down his throat. Or something disgusting they said was cat food. They cut off bits of his fingernails and some hairs and said they would use them to cast a spell on him. They said they did it to increase the power of the Goddess in Crowley Creek. John

Charles, you know I can't help Julie now. It would hurt Jase too much. I have to put my children first."

Then, for the first time that evening, Edith looked right at me. Her clear gray eyes asked my forgiveness. "I have to put my children first," she repeated. "They come before everything else."

"Before you, yourself, Edith?" I said. Never had I seen more clearly how deeply she cared for me, so that my grief over her words boiled around inside me and mixed with my joy in discovering that the intensity of her feelings matched mine. Surely, sooner or later, she would have to admit to what she felt?

But it seemed that I didn't understand.

"Yes, absolutely, my sons come first," she said, and then it was as if a shutter came down over her eyes and I looked into a face now cold, forbidding, unmovable. "Stay away, stay away," said her cold eyes, the tight line of her lips, even the narrowing of her nostrils. "Please, don't make it harder," her eyes said.

"I am sorry about abandoning you now when you need me," Edith said. "I am desperately sorry I will have to hurt Julie— she's so fragile—but that's what I have to do."

"You mean I'm all alone now?" I said. "You are going to the other side, like everyone else in town who has turned against Julie?"

"Yes," she said. "That's exactly what I mean."

She turned her face away from me, but not before I saw her tears.

TWENTY

That night I couldn't sleep. I lay in bed, staring out the window into the branches of the oak tree, which shook and cast muddled shadows onto the floorboards. I had raised my window open as wide as I could and a damp, cool wind blew into the room, smelling of night. Outside I heard an owl hooting and, very faint and far away, the bark of a fox. Then I heard a car go by with a rush of tires on asphalt and I wondered if the driver might be headed away from his old life to a new one and I wished I could just jump into my Bronco and drive away from Crowley Creek and from this omnipresent sense of dread, and from everything I had become.

Finally I got up, put on a pair of jeans, an old flannel shirt, and a pair of sneakers, slid my talisman into my pocket, and padded down to the library. I poured myself a Blanton's, took the glass and the bottle, and went out through the kitchen doors onto the patio.

The night air felt damp and heavy on my skin. High above, the three-quarter moon sailed through thin streamers of opalescent cloud. Behind it the sky seemed very black, yet the air around me shimmered in the pale cloud-filtered light. I looked up and saw the black shape of a bat coasting on an air current, then it dived on outstretched wings into the woods beyond the lawn. I sat down on a chair, pulled up another, put my feet on it, and leaned back and listened.

All around me I could hear the sounds of the night. Beneath the croaking of the tree frogs, I heard baby birds in their nests and field mice and squirrels rustling through the underbrush. Night predators were on the prowl. I drank my whiskey and listened harder. Now I thought I heard whispers from the woods, as if the animals were trying to speak to me, trying to tell me secrets I needed to hear. Pouring myself another glass of bourbon, I sipped. As the whiskey took hold, I felt sure that any minute I would understand the voices about to emerge from the rustling of the wind in the branches.

Then the hair rose on the back of my neck and gooseflesh prickled on my arms. Asmodeus came out of the woods and bounded toward me, his green eyes glowing, his tail upright.

"Julie? Julie!" I called into the dark night. No reply.

I realized that Asmodeus had come alone. Had he turned his malevolent attentions to me?

He trotted up to me just as I swung my legs down from the chair. He rubbed up against me, lifted a glossy black paw, and touched my leg. He jumped on my lap, arched his back, looked at me with those luminous green eyes, and I could feel his claws pierce through my jeans, scratch against my skin.

As if he spoke aloud and I understood, I heard: *I am not here to guard you or to threaten you. I am here because She needs you. It is time for you to know what you need to know. Come.* He jumped down, strode a few paces on stiff legs, then turned to look at me. *Come, come along, there is no time to lose.*

I drained my bourbon, set my glass carefully on the table next to the nearly empty whiskey bottle, and followed Asmodeus. A huge cat shadow bounded after us, so that it looked as if a void, a hole in the earth, was our companion.

Asmodeus moved through the woods along the path I knew so well. He leaped lightly over roots and fallen branches, but kept casting backward glances to assure himself I still followed. We reached the creek and Asmodeus picked up speed, running along the bank. We were headed in the direction of Cully's. We had gone about a mile when Asmodeus vanished.

A moment later I reached the spot where he had disappeared and saw a narrow path leading away from the banks of the creek, deep into the woods. Asmodeus crouched there, waiting for me, his tail curled, lashing slowly back and forth. *Hurry, hurry,* he seemed to say.

I followed him along the path and soon I smelled wood smoke—green wood—and heard the faint crackling of burning tinder. The trees thinned and we entered a small glade.

Julie sat before a tiny fire which burned in a circle of stones. She had piled green wood on her fire, so a tall column of smoke ascended into the moonlit sky. She had dressed completely in white, a white robe wrapped with a silver cord around the waist. A wide silver band held her dark hair off her face. A large jagged chunk of crystal hung on a silver cord around her throat and sparkled in the firelight. Asmodeus ran up to her and jumped onto her shoulder. He glared at me, the pupils of his green eyes black vertical bars, like gates into a darker world.

"John Charles," she said softly, "you came. . . . "

I did not know if I were dreaming or awake. I walked slowly toward her, then sat down on the soft, moss-covered earth. "You have something to tell me?" I said.

She threw a handful of powder on the fire and a faint acrid smell filled the air. I breathed in the fumes. Again she threw powder into the fire, and again I breathed in a pungent scent that caught in my chest and rasped in my throat.

She raised her head and looked at me. Her green eyes and the eyes of Asmodeus moved, merged, separated, came together again. I felt the whiskey in me, the night air on my skin and heard the sounds in the wood as if they were in my blood.

The cat-woman opened its mouth. Tiny white teeth and a pink raspy tongue made a sound I did not understand.

Again it spoke, but again its sounds made no sense. My head was swimming. The trees leaned inward and the glade became smaller. A cone of light seemed to fill the air, and looking up I saw silver smoke swirling into shapes that I could almost—but not quite—recognize. Shadows moved on the dark mossy ground.

I can't let this happen to me, I thought. Whatever it is, I have to see past it. I reached into the fire and pressed my wrist to a burning ember.

The glade widened, the cone of light dimmed and vanished, and the being across from me separated into Julie and her cat. I stood up.

"Julie!" I said.

She tilted her head upward to look at me. "Yes, John Charles?" she said in an obedient, toneless voice.

"I want you to be strong now, be very strong."

"Yes, John Charles."

"I want you to choose the right way, the hard way."

"Yes, John Charles."

"Let out the secret that is poisoning your heart."

Slowly, gracefully she stood. Looking across the fire she slid her hand into a fold of her gown and took out her black *udjat*. At the same time I reached into my pocket and found my white one. I reached over and handed it to her. She pinned the white talisman on her robe. She hung her own around her neck and hooked the chain around mine so that the jet black eye and the white moonstone eye looked back at me together.

"I saw it, John Charles. I saw Margaret's murder."

"Tell me."

"You need to know the whole story of it."

"Yes."

"When I came to work with the animals, I saw that Dr. Cully wanted me. He was a grievous, sad man, dying inside and he thought that making love to me would bring him back the life and youth he felt draining away. To me, it seemed a small thing to do for someone who was so kind to me. But it was a lie I told myself, for soon I found that the Goddess was angry with me for misusing her gift. Still, it seemed that Dr. Cully was very big and I was very small and I did the best I could.

"But when I got to know Margaret better I saw that I had done a terrible wrong. Margaret felt the lies all around her, and when Dr. Cully looked at me and wanted me, she felt it. When she spoke her suspicions, he told her she was crazy. He told her the true was false and the false was true and everything grew sour and ugly. Margaret had been kind and gentle, but now Dr. Cully and I had filled the house with dark energy and lies and Margaret grew fierce with rage and Dr. Cully swelled up with rage and they fought and he beat her. She screamed and she shouted and she accused him of things. Then she saw what she was becoming and she knew she needed to go away.

"But when she spoke of leaving he told her she was a crazy woman—she imagined everything—she caused his cruelty and madness. He shouted there was nothing between him and me. And the angrier she got and the angrier he got the more he delighted in using my body."

Julie wiped her hands across her green eyes.

"And so the bands of Margaret's trap grew tighter and tighter around her and it seemed that only I could loosen them. I thought: If I tell her the truth she will be able to leave him. So I gathered up all my courage"—Julie looked up at me and smiled—"what little I had then, so little. And I read her tarot cards. I told her the truth and I told her to leave him, that he was now deeply mired in his lies and his self-deceit and his desperate selfishness and he would drag her down if she stayed. She grieved to be betrayed but she felt relieved to learn that she had not been going mad. She cried herself out and then I took her to the station in Richmond and helped her buy a ticket. She kissed me and thanked me and went out to the train.

"But then we saw Dr. Cully. He had followed us. He took Margaret aside, pleaded with her, talked her out of getting on the train and he drove her back home in his pickup. In Richmond he said sweet, kind words and he promised to change. But as soon as we got back to the house he started to drink and to talk the way he had before and Margaret started to shout at him and call him names and abuse him for having sex with me. He went down to the cellar to chop wood and she came after him on the stairs shouting at him and calling him terrible names. I followed to try to tell them both to stop. He got to the bottom of the stairs and Margaret came after him and he turned to her and started shouting at her and Asmodeus jumped at him and he swung the ax at Asmodeus and struck Margaret. The ax sank into her head. Blood spurted up a geyser of red. Asmodeus screeched like a devil from hell. Margaret fell on the cellar floor, her head broken open, blood draining out, her eyes empty, her skin pale as wax."

Julie slid down onto the ground and folded her hands in her lap. She stared into the fire. "I told Dr. Cully we should call the police. I would tell them it was an accident and then I would leave Crowley Creek. I couldn't stay with him anymore. There we stood, both covered in blood and I saw he wanted me more than ever.

"And then I found that my evil acts had to be paid for. Dr. Cully told me no one would believe me. He had an old fireplace in the wall in the cellar. He put Margaret in there. He grabbed me and mushed my fingerprints on the bricks around her. He bricked her up in the wall. He told me then that I had to stay, to do what he said, to be his lover forever, or he would say I killed Margaret and nobody would believe me and everybody would believe him. And he laughed and then he made me lie down on my stomach on the bloody floor. He got on top of me and took me from the back, hard, so it hurt. I let him do it. We were both covered in blood and brains when he did that and he really liked it. He banged me against the cold cement floor, against the brick grit and into Margaret's blood. Then he got up laughing and walked out. Asmodeus and I lay there in the blood, cold coming up into our bones and we smelled rot and mold and brick dust and hardening mortar and congealing blood and we thought we would die right there.

"But Asmodeus told me I couldn't die. I had work to do. And he promised me he would watch Dr. Cully. So I got up and went down to the creek and I bathed and I purified myself and I prayed to the Goddess to help me. The Goddess told me that help would come, to be patient and strong and wait.

"Dr. Cully ordered me to clean the basement room so not a spot of blood remained and to hide the ax. I obeyed. I cleaned the room and I buried the ax. Then Dr. Cully started plastering the other walls and he put in a new floor in the basement. He filled the room with the fumes of paint so when they searched with dogs the dogs couldn't smell anything but paint. They couldn't smell Margaret. I don't know why he hasn't plastered over the wall where Margaret is." She looked up. "Really I do know why."

"Why?"

"Because when he left the night he bricked up Margaret I removed some bricks and mixed soft beeswax and honey in with the mortar. So there are eight bricks that won't dry. You can take them out and see into the cavity where Margaret's body is rotting away. So he keeps having to remove them and re-mortar them. And then I remove them and put in my magic mortar and it never dries. It's making him crazy, that those bricks won't settle. I can pull them out whenever I want.

"But what good would it do, John Charles? If the sheriff finds Margaret's body, he'll find my fingerprints and not Dr. Cully's. He'll think I did it. Everyone in town but you thinks I did it now. Dr. Cully won't let me leave him ever because he wants me and because he's afraid of what I know. And I can't leave because he will say I murdered Margaret."

"Oh, Julie," I said. Terror and disgust and grief and pity filled me and I put my arms out and gathered her in. She nestled in my arms like a kitten, like a child, and I patted her and comforted her as if she were my daughter.

"You believe me!" she said.

"Yes. I believe every word."

"You'll help me?"

"Yes."

"And Edith? We need her too."

Edith. Would she believe this story? Would it change anything for her?

"I don't know what to do, John Charles."

I took her gently by the shoulders and stood her away from

me. "Come on, you're coming over to my house. We'll call Edith. I think when she hears the truth, Edith will stand by us."

Asmodeus had been looking back and forth between us. He leaped off down the path. Julie smiled at him. Carefully she heaped damp earth over her fire, extinguishing it. Then she and I set off down the path after Asmodeus.

TWENTY-ONE

I went into the far guest room and threw a couple of sheets, a pillowcase, and a light blanket on the stripped bed. I showed Julie the nearest bathroom, then went back down to the library to call Edith.

But when I picked up the receiver, I realized I could not remember her telephone number, a number I knew as well as I know my own. My head felt thick and heavy, the outlines of objects in the library blurred until they faded into the thick air. I slid open a window and breathed in deeply.

I couldn't understand it. Julie and I had walked over a mile back from the glade to my house. By now, the whiskey I had drunk would surely have worked its way out of my system. Then I remembered the powder Julie had thrown into the fire and the way images had shifted after I had inhaled it. Could my memory of her revelations be some kind of a drug-induced dream? Maybe Julie had not come home with me, maybe she had not really made that wrenching, horrifying confession, maybe I had dreamed it all. The room began to move around me, the colors blurred and I thought I heard whispered voices telling me to forget what I had heard, to push away the dark shadows and return to my normal life.

I went up to my room, shut the door, flung myself onto my bed without removing my clothes, and immediately fell into a troubled, stuporous sleep.

I awoke the next morning to the gurgling of the pipes. For a moment I didn't understand. The shower, who could be taking a shower? Outside the sky looked milky white. The sun must be just over the horizon. I sat up and watched the world take form in the pale morning light. Objects in the room came into focus: my rubbed-cherry dresser with the tilt-back mirror, the worn, rush-seated ladder-back chair with my jacket thrown over the back of it, the white curtains at the open window. My head felt clear and light, my body strong and fit.

Then I saw I had on a clammy sweatshirt and a pair of jeans, hardened mud on the cuffs, and had fallen asleep on top of the quilt. Why? With a rush of dread, I remembered.

Julie. Her terrible story. Could it be true or had I dreamed it? The memories had a dreamlike quality. Hadn't I seen Julie turn into a cat?

I put my hand in my pocket. My talisman was gone. I felt a throbbing pain in the inside crease of my wrist and lifted my arm to look at it. I saw a large burn blister. It had an uneven shape, like a small animal with an arched back and a long curved tail.

I showered in my own bathroom, dressed in clean clothes, and went down to the kitchen where I found some aloe cream and put it on the blister. Outside the kitchen window, the sky shimmered with diffuse white light, as if the sun sought and failed to break through. I made a pot of coffee, checked my watch. Seven. Edith would have been up for at least half an hour. She was an early riser. I picked up the phone and called her. As I dialed, Julie came through the kitchen, carrying a small bag. She had wrapped a towel around her thin body and was barefoot. She smiled, waved at me, and passed out through the kitchen into the backyard. I watched as Julie walked across the patio, then down the lawn toward the woods.

"Hello?"

"Edith?"

"Hello. That you, John Charles?" Her voice sounded tired and distant.

"Sorry to call so early."

"It's okay." The voice she used was courteous and polite, like you'd use with a stranger. It surprised me how much that hurt.

"How is Jase doing?"

"He's better. Thank you for asking." Then her voice warmed a little. "I've calmed down too. I don't think it was Julie who hurt him. I got him to tell me the story again. It sounds like there were two of them, and I think they were bigger than she is. Jase was scared and he saw what they wanted him to see. Someone wanted me to blame Julie. Someone meant to turn us Dunns against her."

"Are you going to let them?"

"Oh, John Charles, I don't know what to do. I truly don't."

"Edith, Julie saw Dr. Cully kill Margaret."

"What!"

"Edith, can you come over? She's here. She needs to talk to you."

"Lord, I just don't know. . . . "

"Edith. I think you should. You've always lived by your principles. What will you be teaching your boys if you back off when you are threatened? Isn't it best for them to learn that sometimes you have to stand alone for what you believe in?" My heart beat as I said these words. Who was I to preach about principle to Edith, whom I so admired and respected? But this time I thought she was wrong. She shouldn't let a threat make her run, even if the threat was to her children. In the end, surely kids learn by the way we lead our lives. And I believed she'd let her concern for Jase blur her clear sight. I thought she needed to hear it from me.

A long silence followed my words.

"I think you are right," she said very softly. "But, you know

I want to see you. That could be mixing me up. Making me forget what I owe my kids. I feel empty not seeing you."

"Me too."

"My children still come first. It's hard. . . . "

"I know it's hard. Look, come over. Talk to Julie. Listen to her story. Then decide, okay?"

Edith sighed. "Today is Jase's first day back at school since it happened. I'm going to drive him and pick him up so he doesn't have to go in the car pool with other kids. He's not ready for that yet. I'll come by after I drop him off."

"I can hardly wait to see you," I said to her.

"Oh, John Charles," she said. Her voice was as warm as a lover's hand touching my cheek.

I watched for Edith. When I saw her drive up I opened the door, and as soon as she was inside, I put my arms around her and held her and she wrapped her arms around my back and pulled me close. But neither of us said anything. I think we were both afraid to.

I invited her into the kitchen, poured her a coffee, and then called Julie to come downstairs.

Julie had come back from wherever she had gone. When I told her Edith was coming over, she had nodded but said nothing. And when I told her she would need to tell Edith what she had told me she had closed her eyes and pressed her fists hard against her heart as if to hold it inside her chest. "She'll despise me," Julie had whispered. "She'll think I'm lower than a snake's belly."

"I don't believe that," I said, hoping I was right. "But we have to tell her and hope for the best."

Julie swallowed. "So be it," she had whispered. Then she had rushed upstairs to the room I had given her and I thought I had heard her, off and on for the last hour, chanting up there.

Now Edith and I waited for Julie. She came sidling into the kitchen, Asmodeus trailing after her. She wore her droopy black jumper over her black tank top, multiple earrings in her nose and ears, and her tall black lace-up boots. Her hair hung over her face. She walked with her shoulders hunched. Now that I knew her secret, I saw how that walk of hers had told the story of her fear and humiliation, not the evil I had imagined.

"Hi, Julie," Edith said. Edith smiled a normal cheery smile, as if she could not feel the waves of emotion emanating from Julie. How did she keep so calm?

"Uh . . . hi," Julie said, not looking at Edith.

"I'll make you some herbal tea," I said to her. "We have mint and lemon spice."

"Mint. I'll make it," Julie said. "I like it to steep."

"Sit down, Julie," I said.

She sat.

"Tell Edith," I said.

Julie opened her mouth. Nothing came out. She started to shiver. Edith rose from her chair to go and comfort her. "No, Edith," I said. I stared at Julie. "Stop that. Tell her," I said.

Julie stopped trembling. My conviction seemed to flow into her. She straightened up, her mouth firmed. She began to speak.

When Julie finished telling her story, her face was wet with tears and Edith was crying too. Edith got up, walked around the table, put her arms around Julie, and hugged her. She rocked her back and forth, murmuring words of comfort to her, the words you say to a hurt little child. Over Julie's shoulder Edith's face looked at me, grief stricken, appalled.

"What are you going to do about it?" I said to Julie.

"What?" Julie pulled away from Edith and stared at me.

"You going to let him get away with it?" I said.

"But what can I . . . "

"Have you ever read Edgar Allan Poe's story, 'The Black Cat'?"

"No. . . . "

"Well, let me tell it to you, tell you how the cat unmasks the murderer. Then you and I and Edith are going to think of a way to bring Lawrence Cully down. We're going to plan it and we're going to do it, you hear?"

"Oh, John Charles," Julie said, in her tentative little voice, "I don't think I could. I . . ."

"Yes, you can! And you will. Now listen."

An hour later, Julie had gone up to her room to commune with the Goddess and Edith and I went out to the garden.

"You think it's a crazy idea, don't you?" I said to Edith.

"I'm afraid it is, John Charles," Edith said. "You're expecting too much of Julie. She's not very strong. She's had a tough life and just to survive has used up most of what God gave her. She's not going to be able to carry out such a complicated plan. At least I don't think so."

"I think you're wrong."

"She runs away into her witchcraft rituals and her fantasies. She'll do it again when things get tough. Look at everything that happened to her at Cully's. Look how she stayed there after."

"You said you'd help. You acted as if you believed we could do it."

Edith sighed. She sat down on the iron bench and let her arm dangle over the back. The bench backed on a flower bed. Edith reached out behind her and plucked a spray of mock orange. The tiny green leaves had begun to unfurl. She began pulling the leaves off and letting them flutter to the earth. "I'm afraid I agreed because I want to be with you and I want to make it up to you, for shutting you out yesterday. I will never forgive myself for that. I will never forget the look on your face when you said, 'You mean I'm all alone now?' "

"It's okay."

"No it's not, and you know it's not. And you know what else? This plan will put Julie in terrible danger. It *could* work the

way we think. Or Cully could turn on Julie. He must be beside
himself, knowing she wasn't home last night. He'll guess she's
over here. You could be in danger too."

"Cully's not going to hurt me."

"What makes you so sure?"

"And Julie knows she's at risk. But she has always been at
risk. Nothing's changed. I think Cully is too sexually besotted
with her to hurt her."

"I can't believe you believe that. That's the kind of feeling
that turns to murderous rage faster than any other. Especially
when she starts telling him no."

"You could be right about that."

"I am right."

The phone rang. I got up and went inside and answered it,
picking it up on the fifth ring.

"John Charles? That you?"

"Yes." It was Cully and he didn't sound happy.

"I can't find Julie. She's taken off again. She's not there, by
any chance?"

"No, I haven't seen her," I lied.

"Oh yeah?" He didn't believe me. Where Julie was concerned, his instincts told him every man lied. "Well, if you see
her, tell her to get back here. We have seven sick animals in the
small animal clinic, I have house calls to make. I can't manage
without her. This is the time of year when a lot of baby animals
are at risk. I've got to go out this afternoon. Tell her to get
home. And, John Charles . . . "

"Yes?"

"Keep your hands off her, you hear? I'm warning you, she's
mine. If I find out . . . "

"Cool your jets," I said mildly, forcing myself not to speak
the words that boiled up inside me, not to let out in my voice
the fury I felt. "I'll send her home if I see her. Bye now." I replaced the receiver in its cradle as gently as if it were an egg
going into a basket. Then I slammed my fist into the wall so
hard I tore the skin. "Son of a bitch! We're going to get you!"

Julie came into the kitchen. "Was that Dr. Cully?"

"Yes. I told him you weren't here."

"I better go then," she said.

"I'd give you a lift, but it's probably best no one sees you in my car."

"I'd rather walk anyway," she said, smiling up at me. Her smile, no longer seductive, trembled slightly and I saw how frightened she was. Could Edith be right? Had we put too much of a burden on Julie? But it had been her idea, most of it.

"Let me walk you through the woods, then," I said. "I still feel a little funny after last night and the walk will help me clear my head."

"Okay."

Julie and I walked out into the garden. "I'm going to walk Julie back to Cully's," I told Edith. "We'll go through the woods."

Edith frowned.

"What's the matter?"

"I don't know. I feel real uneasy all of a sudden."

"Don't worry. We'll be okay." Julie and I walked down through the garden, through the gap in the hedge, through the blackberry bramble, and into the woods. For a small person, she walked quickly and she seemed to know the way as well as I did. I heard a rustling noise and Asmodeus appeared suddenly, jumping from a low-lying branch to the ground, then onto Julie's shoulder. "Oh, Asmodeus, hello," Julie said. "I missed you dear, dear friend." She stroked his back as she walked. He purred and rubbed his side against her cheek.

The path meandered along Crowley Creek. Insects buzzed and high overhead I saw a hawk circle, then stoop and plummet downward. After about two miles we came to a path leading away from the creek. Julie turned to me. "I always take this way back to Cully's," she said. "I'll be okay now."

Asmodeus suddenly went tense, flattened down against her shoulder, his tail rigid and pointing downward, his ears forward, his whiskers quivering, like alert antennae. I could not hear birdsong now and the buzzing of insects seemed peculiarly loud. "I'll go just a little farther with you," I said.

She headed into the woods and I followed. The path went around a bend. I heard a whooshing noise. Julie screamed. Then she screamed again. Asmodeus hissed. I rushed forward to see Julie struggling on the ground as if in the clutches of a formless, giant monster. Then I saw she had triggered a trap. A rope net had fallen on her and she struggled under it to free herself. But what was that sound, a sinister rattle, and that shining coil? I looked and saw to my horror, caught in the folds of netting with Julie and Asmodeus, a giant rattlesnake, its head and tail lashing frantically, its forked tongue spitting in and out of its open jaws. Brilliant diamonds shone upon its scaly skin. It reared back, its head preparing to strike Julie. I grabbed a rock and smashed down on its head.

"No, John Charles, don't hurt it!" Julie shouted at the same moment.

"Shut up!" I struck again. The snake shuddered and writhed, then subsided, its coils relaxing, although it continued to writhe reflexively for several more seconds.

"I had to," I said, pulling the netting away from Julie and Asmodeus. "Didn't you see? It was about to strike."

"You killed it, poor thing," Julie said.

"Think straight! Someone set a trap for you. We hardly ever get rattlers around here. Someone put that snake in the rope trap and someone pulled it just as you came through." I looked around rapidly. Perhaps that someone had stayed near to see if they had succeeded? "Quiet, listen!" But we were both still panting and our breath was loud in the close air. We could hear nothing else. All around us the underbrush, shadows; Julie's attacker could be anywhere, could be watching, could have slipped away. We would never find him. "You've got to smarten up, Julie. You've got to be careful and watch out for yourself. Stop worrying about 'poor' snakes and start thinking!"

"Don't be angry, John Charles. I'm most grateful. It's just, it hurts to see one of earth's creatures destroyed."

My breathing had returned to normal but adrenaline still coursed through me. I would feel much better if I saw Julie just once get angry, vengeful. Her passive sweetness drove me crazy.

I walked Julie to the place where the woods gave way to the open fields around the Cully property, then watched from the shadow of the trees until she got to the house.

Would she be safer there? Who would know better than Cully how to handle a rattler and use it to set a trap? Who better than he could get hold of one? Surely I had led her right into danger. To the house of a murderer. But wasn't that the plan?

After all, where would she be safe? Everyone in town was out to get Julie. Many must know she used this path to get down to the creek. I'd heard from several people about her witchcraft practices. The descriptions sounded accurate enough to suggest that someone had been detailed to spy on her. The trap could have been set by anyone.

If the rattler had stung her, she might have died, or she might have made it to the hospital. In either case, she'd be out of the way. Or could Cully have planned to find her and "save" her?

Sighing, I made my way back through the woods. No way to know who had done it. I had shouted at her, but what braver thing could anyone do than go back into the house with a murderer and a plan to unmask him?

And one thing seemed clear: Someone wanted to harm Julie. Our plan had just gotten even more dangerous.

TWENTY-TWO

The next evening I dropped by Cully's on the pretext of finding out if Julie had turned up. I found Cully in the small animal clinic, setting the leg of a tiny poodle.

The poodle must not have been anaesthetized because I heard its high-pitched, frenzied yapping as soon as I entered the reception area. But as I walked along the hall, the barking stopped. The sound had come from behind a door at the end of the corridor of open pens. I opened it to see a white-tiled, windowless room with medicine cabinets around the walls, a deep sink at one end, and a table in the center. Julie held the little black dog in her arms, pressing a herb-scented compress gently on its nostrils while Cully completed fixing a cast to its leg.

"Hi, John Charles," Julie said in her faint, tentative voice, looking up as I opened the door.

"Hey, close that door," Cully said. "Hang on, we'll be out in five minutes."

I closed the door, went outside, and sat down on the front step. In the dim light cast by the lamp at the end of the driveway, the yard looked overgrown. The lawn hadn't been mowed in a long time. White clover heads and yellow dandelions pushed up through the tufts of grass. Under the oak trees, bare patches had filled in with crabgrass, thistle, and the broad, saw-toothed leaves of dandelion. Insects buzzed around the beam from the porch light and I moved into the shadows to avoid them.

"Nervy little things, toy poodles," Cully said, coming out the front door with a six-pack in his hand. He sat down beside me, pulled a bottle of Bud out of the pack, and handed it to me. "Owners went to Vegas and left the dog with neighbors who couldn't care less. One of their kids stepped on him."

I didn't say anything.

"So, how's it been over at your place?" Cully said.

"What do you mean?"

"Uh . . ." Cully took a swig of beer. "Hear any, uh, strange noises in the night?"

It took all my willpower to sit there talking normally to Cully. It felt so strange. He looked more like himself than he had for a long time. His hair neatly combed over his bald spot, his chin clean shaven. He still wore his vet's smock over his jeans, which looked new and very clean. At that moment everything about him reminded me forcibly of the man I had known and trusted all my life. Yet my skin prickled at his nearness and I felt queasy with the knowledge of who he was and what he had done.

"Strange noises?" I said, drinking down at least half my beer.

"Julie came back yesterday morning and she sure perked me up," he said, looking at me and smiling a smug smile. "She missed me."

I felt sick to my stomach. The man saw what he wanted to see. Or he liked to boast. Or both. "What strange noises?" I said.

Cully downed the rest of his Bud. A dark shape raced across the front lawn. Cully started, paled. "What was that?"

"Just a coon," I said.

"Oh. For a moment there . . . You remember that time we saw Asmodeus at The Old Forge?"

"Uh-huh. The time we thought we saw him, you mean."

"We saw him!"

"We'd had a few. . . . "

Cully rubbed his eyes, took another bottle of beer out of the pack, and popped off the top. "You're saying we imagined it? We *both* imagined it? That doesn't make sense."

"You know," I said, "sometimes when I've been drinking, I see things . . . it's like I see forms of things when really all that's there is feelings, fears . . . know what I mean?" I eyed him covertly to see how this went over.

"Don't know what the hell you're talking about," he said, swigging at his beer. "I saw a cat sitting in the bottles on the shelf at The Old Forge. You did too. And last night I heard this howling from the basement. Right under my den, you know? I'd fallen asleep in my La-Z-Boy watching the late-night movie, like I've done every night since Margaret left. I thought for sure it was Asmodeus, but Julie swears Asmodeus was with her and quiet. Fact is, I been hearing this howling off and on."

"Think it's Asmodeus?"

"I know the sounds cats make and this god-awful sound is nothing like that. But Asmodeus is not your ordinary cat, so it could be. Julie says it's . . . "

"What?"

"Forget it."

"No, come on, what does she say?"

Cully laughed. How horrible the sound of his laugh had become. Manic, prideful, empty. "She says it's a devil after me." He laughed again. "You heard about the 'devils' that attacked Sue Anne Beebee? Bunch of kids. You hear about the 'devils' that attacked Jase Dunn? Same kids. If teenagers in town want to scare one another with devil stories, fine by me. Maybe it's teenagers howling in my yard."

"You think that's what it is?" I said.

He handed me another beer. "Yep."

I took a deep swallow. The wind came up and passed over the long grass so that white clover heads and yellow dandelion tops bent as if a hand had pressed them down. The clouds broke apart and the rim of the moon emerged, casting a cold beam of light across the lawn. Suddenly, from deep within the house came a piercing high wail, like the sound of a woman in pain. The sound began as a thin, extended high note as if someone had drawn a bow viciously across the catgut strings of a violin, then it rose until it vibrated, and trembled and filled our ears with an almost unbearably painful shriek. Just when I thought my eardrums must shatter, it quavered, diminished, and died away. It took all my willpower to sit there as if nothing had happened.

"Hear that?" Cully said. He had gone pale, broken out in a sweat and he clutched his beer bottle. He seemed to be holding his breath. The sound came again, starting as a thin ribbon of a scream and rising to an anguished, outpouring of suffering.

The light came on in the garage, the window opened and Julie called out. "Dr. Cully! Dr. Cully! Are you okay?"

Her last words were drowned out by the scream issuing from the cellar. This time it went through my body, vibrating along my nerves, causing almost unendurable pain, like a drill on an exposed nerve. Still I kept my face placid as if I heard nothing.

The window closed and a moment later Julie appeared at the garage door and came toward us. "Dr. Cully, are you okay?" her voice sounded soft, seductive, concerned.

"You heard it, Julie? John Charles? What the hell was it?"

I shook my head. "Sorry, didn't hear anything, except maybe a little scratching sound from the cellar."

"Well, I heard it," Julie said, her voice quivering. "I'm afraid it is an evil spirit, a vengeful evil spirit. And only *we* can hear it."

Cully flushed. Dark red rose up his neck and flooded his face so that it looked purple with blood. He jumped up and flung his beer bottle down on the front step. It shattered, jagged pieces of glass flying off in all directions. One just missed me. "Shut up! Shut up!" His voice hoarse and rough, sounded as if it could barely escape from his throat. "Don't you dare say that, you hear? You watch your mouth or you'll have more than evil spirits to worry about. I'm warning you!"

He leaned toward Julie and for a moment I thought he would strike her and I started to rise. But he turned and stumbled, bumping first against the wall and then against the door, as if blind. He reached out a hand and fumbled for the doorknob, finally got his nerveless fingers around it, thrust open the screen door, and hurtled himself into the house. The front door and the screen door banged behind him.

Julie and I looked at each other and smiled.

But why had we smiled? What we were up to was serious business, dangerous business. And the person most in danger was Julie. Even before we'd begun to carry out our plan, someone had set the rope trap on her favorite path through the woods. Now that our plan had started, more people would get spooked and Julie's situation could only become increasingly dangerous. So perhaps I shouldn't have been surprised at what happened next. After all, I knew how everyone in town had turned their face from Julie.

The next day, sitting at my computer at the *Sentinel*, and listlessly trying to make a "good news" story out of the developer's decision not to proceed with Stage Two of Laburnum Estates (just a postponement until real estate picks up, etc.) I heard Mrs. Boynton's heavy tread crossing the floor toward me.

She peered over my shoulder at the screen. "Shame about the Estates," she said. "Lots of folks were counting on the business the construction would have brought in. Not goin' to help real-estate prices either, those unsold houses in Stage One. John Charles, got a minute?"

I nodded and followed her into her office. She shut the door behind me, fished out a piece of paper from a pile on her desk, and handed it to me. "Have a look at this."

I took the paper. On it someone had typed on an old, manual typewriter:

The Lord Speaketh thus:
"There shall not be found among you anyone that useth divination, or an observer of times, or an enchanter, *or a witch.* For all that do these things are an abomination unto the Lord. And because of these abominations the Lord thy God doth drive them out from before thee." Deuteronomy 18: 10–12
"Thou shalt not suffer a witch to live." Exodus 22:18

"What's this?" I said.

"It came in an envelope, with cash, and an ad order," Mrs. Boynton said, taking back the paper. "The sender included a note. It says he wants it to run for the next two weeks, in a prominent place in the classified section."

"We can't print that," I said, looking at Mrs. Boynton. "It's an incitement to violence—maybe to murder."

"It's like I've been telling you," Mrs. Boynton said. She did not sit down in her chair, but stood with her back to me, looking out the window into the scrubby backyard behind the *Sentinel* building. "Things are getting real ugly. I agree about not publishing that thing, even as an ad, even though it's paid for. Because it's meant to be nasty. Folks won't be fooled. After all, the Devil can quote scripture to serve his own ends. No, the way I see it, printing this won't do the town any good. And it's not the kind of copy folks expect to see in the *Crowley Creek Sentinel.*"

"I agree."

"But it's not that easy." She turned toward me. "We don't print it, whoever wrote it is just going to get madder. We can't even send the money back. No return address. Know what I think?"

"What?"

"They're going to start taking it out on her direct. The

troubles that girl's had are about to get worse. Cully has to cut her loose or he'll go down with her."

"He said people will always need a vet."

"Maybe. But they don't need a witch."

"You saying someone's going to hurt her?"

"Look. Most people in town are decent folk. But not everyone, know what I mean?"

I did.

"You care about that gal. I can't figure out why, but you stood up for her. What's done is done. You made your choice."

"And I appreciate you keeping me on when hardly anyone in town is talking to me." Hard to believe, Mrs. Boynton had stuck by me when Marilyn hadn't.

Mrs. Boynton made a face, didn't meet my eyes. "Don't count on it," she snapped. Surprised, I realized she was embarrassed by her own loyalty. "The point here is, you want to do something for her, get her out of town, out of harm's way. She stays around, she's going to get hurt. This ad, it's just a straw in the wind."

"You been hearing things?" I said. I sat down in the visitor's chair. Mrs. Boynton sure was acting strangely. I couldn't figure it. Normally bombastic, combative, hostile, today she seemed uncertain. She twisted the ad-copy paper in her hands.

"There's a group of people after that girl. Someone's going to get hurt, hurt bad. It's got to be stopped." I saw that the ad copy she had been crumpling in her hand had been torn to shreds. "I don't know what's happening to folks! It's like they're going crazy. They won't listen to reason. They see the Devil's work and you can't talk to them anymore." Her eyes narrowed as she stared at me. "It's bad for business," she said.

I wondered what Mrs. Boynton would think if she knew about Edith, Julie's, and my plan. What we had underway would make the situation worse. Bring things to a head. But it had to be done.

A knock on the door. Buzz stuck his head in. "John Charles? Phone for you. It's the witch, I think." He winked at me. Buzz still saw the whole Julie/Devil-worship feud as a giant joke. He thought we all were a bunch of dumb rednecks, the kind of people who believed the special effects on *The X-Files* were real and saw UFOs flying over the fields. Sometimes I admired the certainty he had about what was real and what wasn't. But at least Buzz hadn't turned on me. I had to give him that.

Mrs. Boynton waved at me. "Go talk to her," she said. "Tell her she's in danger. She'll believe it if *you* say it."

I crossed the big room where everyone waited to hear what I would say to "the witch." Buzz leaned back in his chair, his legs stretched out, a soda can balanced on his stomach. The other staff ostentatiously stared at their desks or tapped the odd key on their keyboards. Not very convincingly.

"Hello?"

"Hi, John Charles." That breathy voice. "I've got to talk to you. I need to come into town and get some things for the clinic at Dilbey's Hardware. Could you meet me at Shelton's in, say, ten minutes? I'm taking Dr. Cully's pickup, so I'll be right over."

"Sure."

"See you soon," she said, and hung up.

Mrs. Boynton stood in the doorway of her office.

Four faces stared at me.

"You still her friend?" Buzz asked.

"She has something she wants to tell me," I said. "I'm meeting her at Shelton's."

"Jeez, might as well walk into a nest of hornets," Buzz said, admiringly. "Meet with the witch where everyone in town can see you do it. You been smoking something? Think you'll walk outta there alive?"

"Remember what I told you," Mrs. Boynton said.

I grabbed my jacket and got out of the office before anybody else could give me advice.

The moment I sauntered into Shelton's, a sudden silence descended on the place. You could hear the chink of dishes from the back and the steam hissing out of the deep fryer. But not a word of conversation. Faces turned and watched as I walked to the back. This time no waitress came to take my order. So after a moment, I got up and went behind the counter and got a clean coffee mug, walked over to the coffeepots on the warmer, and filled one for myself. I put down a dollar bill on the counter and walked back to my booth. Everyone stared at me and no one spoke. The silence stretched out, then someone laughed nervously and people began to talk softly to one another, their voices much quieter than usual. Bunny Shelton came out from the kitchen, glanced around, caught sight of me, frowned, then walked slowly over to my table.

"Sorry, but I'm going to have to ask you to leave," Bunny said.

I looked at her without speaking. She tried to hold my eyes, but she couldn't. "Well, okay," she said. "One cup of coffee, but that's all. Then you're outta here. . . . " She saw my expression and lowered her voice until she was practically whispering. "Come on, John Charles. It's for your own good. People are so upset, so angry, it's better not to do anything more to stir things up, you know? Please?" I had never seen her be anything but tough, never seen her plead. She looked frightened. "Nobody knows what's happening," she whispered to me. "Things are going bad."

"Sorry, Bunny," I said, clearly, politely, so everyone could hear. "But I think I'll just finish my coffee, if you don't mind. I'm waiting for a friend."

Her face went hard. "Have it your own way, but you're a fool." She walked back to the counter, grabbed a rag, and began angrily swabbing away at the counter.

The door opened and Julie came in. She wore her purple-and-black fringed shawl wrapped around her and pinned with her *udjat*, her thick hair tumbled down over her face, and you could see her nose ring gleaming against her pale skin. She smiled at me and walked over to the counter. "Hi, Mrs. Shelton. Can I have an herbal tea? Chamomile, please."

Bunny Shelton looked at me. She opened her mouth, I am

sure to tell Julie to get lost. I started to get up. She must have seen something in my face because she shut her mouth, turned to the shelf behind the counter, and picked up a mug.

"If you wouldn't mind, Mrs. Shelton, could you put the bag in first and the hot water on top and let it steep for a few minutes?" Julie said.

"Now you listen here . . . ," Bunny began.

"Just do it," I called out to her. Bunny pressed her lips together and turned her back to find a tea bag. Julie came over to me and sat down. She looked thinner than I remembered. Dark purple patches stained the skin under her eyes.

"You look tired," I said to her.

She smiled. "It's the howling. We heard it off and on last night. Then in the middle of the night Dr. Cully came to get me and I wouldn't let him in. He's trying to act like he doesn't care but I can see it's getting to him. It's tricky. I can't push him too far, or he'll turn on me and that will ruin our plan. So mostly I just act frightened. So far, so good."

I picked up a spoon and stirred my coffee. Over at the counter I saw Bunny Shelton tear the foil package off an herbal tea bag and put the bag in a mug. Then she opened the spigot on the boiling water and let some into the mug. She put the mug on the counter. Someone turned on the jukebox. A few people went up to the counter to ask for their orders; service in the coffee shop had come to a virtual standstill. For a moment I couldn't see Julie's cup, too many people crowded around. Something about the sudden burst of activity in the tense, funereal atmosphere of the place set my alarm bells ringing. I got up, walked over to the counter, eased my way into the little knot of people standing by the counter, and took Julie's tea.

I brought it over and handed it to her, then I turned away to watch the action around the counter. It had a strange, staged look. Or could that be me imagining things again?

I turned my back on them and sat down across from Julie. She wrapped her hands around her tea cup and sniffed at it. Then set it down without drinking.

"I hate to say it, but I think we should get out of here," I said. "I think something bad's about to happen."

"It already has," Julie said calmly.

"What do you mean?"

"Here, smell this." She handed me her mug. I sniffed. It had that boiled-laundry smell of herbal tea.

"What? I don't smell anything."

"Oh? Well someone's put baneberry in this tea. I can smell it."

"Baneberry? What's that?"

"It's a poisonous plant. It grows all over the place, like a weed. Probably they steeped the roots and put a few drops into the tea when no one was looking, while it was on the counter. This place is glowing with an evil aura. I felt it the moment I walked in." She smiled. "Ill-willing from everyone except for you, of course. You felt it too. I saw you watching them around the counter. Someone must have done it then. Put poison in my tea."

"Baneberry? Poisonous? Could it . . . kill you?" My palms had grown moist, my face felt stiff. Could someone have tried to murder Julie right before my eyes? For the second time?

Julie picked up the mug and cautiously sniffed at it. "Maybe it could kill me. I'm kind of weak right now. Hard to say. Or maybe just make me real sick so I'd have to go to the hospital, have my stomach pumped out. Either way, I'd be out of here, which is what they all want."

I grabbed the mug and walked over to the counter, held it up, and looked around. "It's not going to work, you hear?" I shouted. "Ask yourself, who is the evil person around here!"

Everyone turned to stare at me. Their faces white in the fluorescent light, unsmiling. Some looked puzzled, some confused, some angry. But all hostile. I walked behind the counter and poured the tea down the sink. "What's happening to you people?" I shouted.

I walked over to Julie. "Come on, let's get out of here."

She got up and followed me, and as we slammed the door I heard a sudden roar of voices, as if people's tongues had been suddenly loosed, and from within came the sound of their voices, their harsh laughter, rising and threatening as thunder.

I kept Julie company while she went into Dilbey's Hardware and bought some nails and mortar and a dozen large rattraps. "Why the rattraps?" I asked.

Julie consulted a list, her tiny pink tongue protruding from between her white pointed teeth as she concentrated. "What? Oh, this is Dr. Cully's list." She gave me a sidelong look and smiled. "He's decided the screaming he hears at night is rats. He thinks we've got rats in the cellar."

I frowned. "Does he really think that?"

"That's what he says."

Julie waited patiently at the checkout counter until her purchases had been rung up. I took the sack of mortar, the bag of nails, and the traps and we went outside to the pickup.

Twilight. We stood for a moment looking at the sky, watching as the sun sank out of sight and the last streaks of blood red faded away into darkness.

Julie sighed. "I feel kind of woozy. I think I shouldn't of breathed in the baneberry-tea steam. I need to go into the woods and get some comfrey root or coltsfoot to clear my respiratory system."

"I don't think you should do that, Julie. That's just what folks would expect, that after you'd sniffed up something bad you'd go down the path behind Cully's into the woods to find some curing herbs. Someone set a trap for you there once. They might again."

Julie frowned. "I'd take Asmodeus with me, he could warn me of a trap. But he's working. I don't know. . . . "

"Is Asmodeus okay? He's not frightened or anything?"

"Asmodeus trusts me and I trust him," Julie said. She looked at me as if to say that I should trust her to walk in the woods, and I felt ashamed.

"How about if I go with you?"

"Okay."

I followed Julie out to Cully's. She drove the pickup right into the garage. I came after and parked in the driveway. As I got out of my Bronco, Cully opened the front door and came out. I saw that he had been drinking. His face looked flushed and he walked very carefully, as if his world had gotten unsteady. "Julie? Did you get everything?"

"Yes, Dr. Cully," Julie said.

"John Charles, have a drink with me," Cully said.

"Well, I don't think . . . "

"Come on, boy, don't be a stranger. Go on in. I'll be there in a minute." I went around to the back as if to go in the kitchen, but instead I stayed just out of sight around the corner of the house.

"I heard it again, while you were gone," Cully said. "Where's your damned cat?"

"Asmodeus? I don't know. Maybe out hunting mice. Or those rats?"

"Don't toy with me, girl!" Cully said, raising his voice. "That sound. You know what it is."

"It can't be Asmodeus in the cellar, Dr. Cully. You and I went down there and looked and we saw nothing. And I know Asmodeus. He doesn't sound like that."

"You lie!"

"Dr. Cully, someone tried to poison me with a baneberry infusion this afternoon."

"Say what?"

"I need to go for a walk, get some curative herbs. John Charles is coming with me."

I peered around the house. Cully stood, facing me, but he didn't see me. He looked far beyond me, over the fields into the woods beyond. "You going walking without your blasted cat to guard you?"

"I guess I have to."

"Well, I've got to talk to John Charles. You go on ahead and I'll send him along as soon as we're done talking."

To my dismay, she nodded. She took a deep breath, coughed, took another breath, and began to walk slowly away, in the direction of the woods. I sprang up the steps to the kitchen door, and when Cully came in, he found me pouring a Jack Daniel's from a half-empty bottle on the kitchen counter.

"Julie says someone tried to poison her," Cully said, coming into the room and collapsing onto a kitchen chair. "I tell you I feel like poisoning her myself if that would help me to find her blasted cat. Thing's gone completely crazy."

"How's that?"

Cully shook his head. "Sit down. Take a load off."

I sat down, despite the feeling that I shouldn't, that Julie might be in danger and I should go to her.

"Witchcraft," Cully said. "You believe in it?"

I mumbled something and picked up my glass of bourbon.

"When you work closely with animals," Cully said, "sometimes things happen. Things you don't understand. And I can't deny it, that girl has powers." He turned to look at me, his face gray in the bright kitchen light. "I think she's tryin' to turn those powers against me, John Charles." He stared hard at me. "I won't have it, hear? I won't sit back and let her do that to me."

"You saying you believe in witchcraft?" I said derisively. "Come on, Cully. You're a man of science. It goes against the laws of physics."

"To hell with the laws of physics. I'm telling you, John Charles, I won't stand by while she turns her black magic against me."

"Maybe you need to call a minister over, exorcize your house or something." I stood up. "I've got to be going. I'm worried about Julie out there in the woods alone when so many people are out to get her."

Outside the sky had grown dark, so I could no longer see the backyard, only faint shadows moving over the ground. "Do you have a flashlight I could borrow?"

"Sure thing," Cully said, a sudden smile flashing over his face. An ugly, triumphant smile that disappeared so quickly I thought perhaps I had imagined it. He opened a kitchen drawer and handed me a big rubber flashlight. I tested it, then downed my Jack Daniel's and headed out the back door. "I need to be sure she's okay," I said. "I've got a bad feeling she shouldn't be out there tonight."

"I wanted you to stay, see if you hear it," Cully said. "Starts at dusk, every night, the sounds make your blood run cold."

Just as he spoke we both heard it. That same transcendent wail, a sound of pain, grief, like someone being tortured. "That's it! Hear it?" Cully said, staring at me, his eyes glistening.

But I shook my head. "Nope. Don't hear a thing. Sorry."

Before he could reply, I swung the back door shut, bounded down the stairs, and loped off after Julie. As I headed away from the house, I heard it again, that piercing, unearthly sound, as if the earth had opened and the Devil's cruelty had been loosed upon the world.

TWENTY-THREE

The flashlight sent a tunnel of white light into the woods, showing up the columns of tree trunks, which seemed to march ahead of me like ranks of soldiers on guard. Insects attracted to my flashlight swirled in front of me in the beam like smoke. In my mind, the unearthly howling I had denied to Cully echoed, as if I heard it still, so loud and so terrifying that it seemed to drown out the night sounds of the woods.

I could not track Julie in the darkness. I had no way of knowing where she would turn off the path, but I blundered on. I remembered that smile of Cully's. Why had I let him distract me from staying by her side? I had thought he might be ready to reveal himself, to confess, but I had been wrong. A serious mistake.

I swung the flashlight up, to the left, to the right, as I walked, so that the moving beam seemed to cause the trees and underbrush to rotate around me.

What was that? A cry? A choked-off cry? I stood still, listened, held my breath. Now I could hear it behind the cacophony of the tree frogs. "John . . . John Charles . . . "

I shone the light directly ahead and speeded up my pace. The path curved gently to the right. "John! John Charles . . . " I directed my light into the trees, in the direction of the call, and saw a narrow, lightly trodden path. I turned down it. Now I could hear a thrashing sound. I began to run.

I came upon Julie, lying on the path, something horrible attached to her leg. Bent over, she seemed to be struggling with the thing, gasping with pain. I knelt down by her and saw a rusted contraption sunk into her ankle. Her foot hung awkwardly and blood oozed out from where the metal had pierced through her boot.

"I think it's a bear trap," Julie gasped. "A very old, very evil trap."

"Didn't old Dilbey used to have one of these hanging off his top shelf in the hardware store?" I said as I reached for the trap and carefully began to pull at it.

"Watch out," Julie said. "It has vicious claws. If you open it, it could spring on you." Her face, drained of blood, glowed white in the diffused moonlight.

I got up, found a fallen branch, and using it, I carefully pried open the teeth of the trap. Julie's breathing was shallow. She looked as if she were going into shock.

"I think—my ankle—it's broken. I'm sorry. I should have been more careful, I know I should. Oh . . . I'm so . . . sorry. . . . "

"Don't apologize!" I snapped at her. "It's not your fault. None of this is your fault. Come on, we have to get you some help. I don't want to leave you here alone. You're going to have to hop on my back and I'll carry you out."

Gasping with pain, she rolled over onto her knees. I squatted down and she put her arms around me. I handed her the flashlight. "Light me out of here," I said to her, and we set off back down the trail, me bent over and she clinging to my back.

"I put that trap out for Asmodeus," Cully said.

"How could you!" Julie gasped.

"Never meant for you to get hurt," he said, smiling that empty smile I had grown to dread. "Let me set your ankle, you won't have to go into Richmond. I have everything I need in the clinic."

"No! Stay away from me," Julie said. "How could you want to hurt Asmodeus?"

I could see that Julie cared more for her cat's well-being than for her own. She accepted that Cully might want to do her harm, but not that he would dare to harm a cat.

"That cat is after me. He's driving me around the bend," Cully said. He stood at the doorway of his house and watched as I set Julie down in the passenger seat of the Bronco.

"I'm taking Julie to the hospital to have this looked after," I said. "You're not touching her."

"I put the bear trap out for that damned cat," Cully repeated. "I don't know what got into me. I never meant anything to happen to Julie. Come on, honey," he said, looking at her, "you know I wouldn't hurt you." His voice sounded flat. I had taken off my windbreaker and put it over Julie. Now I started up the Bronco. I unrolled the passenger window and glared at Cully. "I know you set that trap for Julie, and I am going to prove it."

Cully ignored me. "Julie! Julie, honey, you don't buy that, do you?"

Julie gave him her passive, slavish smile. I held my breath. "I don't know what to believe anymore," she said in her tiny, little-girl voice. Then she turned away and slumped down in the seat.

"Don't turn on me, Julie. I'm warning you . . . ," Cully called out.

I started up the Bronco.

"Nobody will believe you, remember that!" Cully shouted. "I can do what I want!"

My stomach boiling, I rolled up my window, backed up, then made a big loop, driving over the grass, and peeled out down the driveway. In the rearview mirror I saw Cully standing in the lighted doorway, staring after us, smiling.

* * *

At the hospital, it took a long time to get Julie's broken ankle set. While I waited, I called Sheriff Rumpsey, told him what had happened, and asked him to meet me back at Crowley House. He agreed. Then I called Edith.

"Cully thinks she's trying to work black magic on him," I said to Edith. "I think he's right on the edge."

"Well, we did want to spook him . . ." Edith said.

"Yeah, but I didn't think it would play out like this. Maybe we got led astray by Edgar Allan Poe's 'The Black Cat,' " I said. "Edith, in the old story, when the bad guy is spooked by the weird howling, he tries to kill the cat. But Cully is after both Julie *and* the cat."

"That trap—he just wanted to hurt her, not kill her, right?" Edith asked.

A nurse wheeled Julie into the emergency waiting room. "I have to go now," I said. "I'll drive Julie back to my place. You meet us there."

"But I searched that cellar," Sheriff Carter Rumpsey said. "I had the bloodhounds down there."

We sat in my kitchen at Crowley House—the sheriff, Edith, Julie, and I. I had put out coffee and cookies but nobody seemed interested. The sheriff acted suspicious and doubtful. He suspected he was being manipulated and lied to by people on the wrong side of the mayor and the council and he had no intention of letting himself be snookered.

"The cellar reeks of paint and plaster," I said. "Would they scent a body walled up in the cellar with such strong smells to hide it?"

Rumpsey shifted on his seat. "I'm no dog expert, but those handlers . . . "

"No dog could smell anything with the fumes down there," Julie said.

"It had to be Dr. Cully who set the traps," I said. "He's after Julie because she suspects him of killing Margaret."

"So she says," Rump said, then he looked at Julie, sitting tense in the kitchen chair, her head tilted forward so her hair covered most of her face. She looked like a small child, her face hidden with shame, her shoulders rounded—like she might be about to burst into tears. "No offense meant, ma'am," Rump said, clearing his throat.

"I saw that antique trap hanging from the top shelf in Dilbey's Hardware every day of my life," I said. "I'm a hunter, but I never knew what it was."

"Dr. Cully knew it was a bear trap. He showed it to me the first time we went in there together," Julie said. "He told me how the world was a better place now that we don't use traps like that anymore, traps that make animals suffer." She tilted her face up and I saw how sad her face looked. I thought she grieved over how Cully had changed.

Rump looked at me and raised his eyebrows. His expression said, Why should I believe this crazy teenager? A witch and all. . . .

"What can it hurt to search Dr. Cully's house one more time?" Edith asked.

"I got to tell you, John Charles," Rump said, "folks in town are saying you are under the spell of that wi . . . pardon me, ma'am . . . of Miz Noir, here. People don't trust you now that you've gone against the town. To search Cully's house just 'cause you and Miz Noir ask me to— No, I don't see it."

"You remember my son Jase was attacked?" Edith said.

"Yes, I do, Miz Dunn. But I believe that was Billy Shelton and his friends. These kids want to turn the town against Miz Noir and against that gang of Dead Souls rock fans. Teenage troublemakers, is all. Billy Shelton told me the Dunn family should be punished for standing up for the witch."

"I agree with you there, Rump," I said. "I think the teenagers in town have been feuding, the jocks against the black-metal types. The break-in at my house, the attacks on

Sue Anne and Jase have all been part of that feud and have nothing to do with Margaret's murder."

"I think so too," Edith said. "Julie's just been a kind of lightning rod and scapegoat for the tensions in town."

Rump nodded slowly. Our agreeing with him on this point seemed to relax him and I thought he might be a little more open to listening to us about Dr. Cully.

"But, Rump," I said, leaning forward, looking him right in the eye, "something's gone terribly wrong with Cully. You only have to look at the man."

"Drinking problem," the sheriff said.

"Right, but that doesn't change the facts—his behavior is more and more suspicious." I could see Rumpsey wasn't buying it. "Now he claims he hears screaming and yowling from the cellar. I think that's his guilty conscience."

"Is that right?"

"Why don't you ask him?" Julie said in her soft little voice. "I bet he'd be most happy to let you look in the cellar."

I remembered Cully's pride. Julie understood him better than any of us. She had reason to, of course.

"Okay, okay. If it'll make you folks feel better," Sheriff Rumpsey said. "But if he agrees to let us look around, and we search down there and don't find anything, I want you all, John Charles and Edith, to take this little gal to Richmond and find a place for her there, till things calm down here. Okay?" He looked pleased with himself. Certain there was nothing to find in Dr. Cully's basement, he figured he had backed us into a losing position.

Edith and I looked at each other, exchanging in our looks our fear that Julie had deceived us in some way we hadn't quite grasped. But before we could respond, Julie spoke. "We agree, sheriff," she said.

"Why sure! Sure!" Cully's voice boomed out of the phone so loudly Sheriff Rumpsey had to hold it away from his ear. "Come on over right now!"

The sheriff, standing by the phone in my kitchen, looked at Edith, Julie, and me. "Got to round up my deputies, so say, an hour?" Sheriff Rumpsey said into the telephone. "What's that? John Charles and Julie? You want them there too?" He looked at us and we nodded. "Done deal. See you later, then, Doc," Rump said. He hung up the phone and studied us all for a moment. "I guess the doc has a pretty good idea you put me up to this. He sounds dead sure we won't find anything and he wants you all there to see he has nothing to hide." Rump shook his head. "I get the feeling I'm being played for a fool here, John Charles, and I don't like it. What's this about the doc thinking you talked Miz Noir here into coming to stay with you? She staying with you?"

"Well, uh . . . "

Rump frowned. His face went hard and cold. "I don't know what you've been up to, John Charles, but I have to tell you, I don't like it. I don't like it one bit."

He picked up the phone to call in for his deputies. Edith, Julie, and I looked at one another. If our plan didn't work, it now seemed clear, we wouldn't get a second chance. Cully would be home free, would get away with murder, Julie would be exiled, and Edith and I would be outcasts, forever, in our own hometown.

TWENTY-FOUR

Cully looked better than he had in months. Beaming, he welcomed us to his home. "Julie, honey!" he said, smiling, as I helped Julie down from the Bronco. They had put a cast on her ankle at the hospital, and loaned her a cane. She picked her way with difficulty up the front stairs and into the house.

"Welcome, welcome all! Come on in. Can I get you something? Sheriff, a cup of coffee? Iced tea? John Charles, like a bourbon?" He wore a white doctor's coat and pristine new sneakers. His face freshly shaven and pink. As he shook my hand vigorously, I smelled cologne and mouthwash. He led us into his kitchen. "Have a seat, folks. What can I do you for?"

"You're looking well," I said to him, uneasy at this change in him.

"Had a good night's sleep last night. Feel like a million dollars today. Glad to have Julie back too," he said. "That strange noise I've been hearing—that's been keeping me awake—not a sound of it last night. First good night of sleep I've had in days. Sure you won't have anything?" he said, turning to Rump and his two deputies.

"I'm sorry to trouble you like this . . . ," Rump began.

"No trouble! No trouble! Glad to have the chance to set your mind at ease. I understand, people start rumors"—he gave me a look—"you got to investigate. Just doing your job. But I'm in control here in my house. I know what's going on. No question. If someone hid Margaret's body here, I'd know about it. Didn't happen. So go on, look, you have my full permission."

My uneasiness increased. What was he up to? Then I remembered Edgar Allan Poe's story, "The Black Cat." In the last scene, the murderer had been full of confidence, certain that his crime was so well hidden it could never be discovered, delighting in his cleverness. Maybe our coming had cheered Cully up. He thought he would outsmart us. He believed he would have no problem demonstrating his innocence and so would completely undermine any chance I might have to get the police to take my suspicions of him seriously.

"Sheriff," I said. "Read him his rights."

"Well now, I don't see the need, John Charles," Rump said. "At this time, he's not a suspect. Of course that might change at any time, then I would certainly . . . "

"Sheriff!" I said.

Something in my voice got Sheriff Rumpsey's attention. He stood up, pulled a laminated card out of his pocket, and carefully read Cully his rights about remaining silent.

"Sure, sure," Cully said magnanimously, almost before the sheriff had finished droning away. "I understand. I definitely do. Let's get this show on the road."

We all stood up and Cully led us on a tour through the house. We saw the upstairs bedrooms, the downstairs, the vet clinic. The house had a dusty, dreary, abandoned air and smelled of stale sweat and booze. But it all seemed very innocent and slightly sad. The only signs of habitation in the renovated house were in Cully's den, where beer cans and fast-food take-out boxes spilled out of the wastebasket. Sheriff Rumpsey and his deputies searched the closets, under the beds, the bathrooms, and the attic crawl space. They looked with a halfhearted air, as if going through the motions, frequently glancing at me as if to say that they hoped *this* would satisfy me and get me off their backs.

We finished up the tour back in the kitchen. "See? Nothing," Cully said, smirking at me.

"How about the cellar?" I said.

"The cellar!" Cully cried. "Terrific idea! How could I forget the cellar? Follow me, folks."

We trooped out the back door and around to the cellar steps. Down the steps we went with Cully chattering manically. He opened the door at the bottom and we were momentarily overwhelmed by a gust of new paint and plaster fumes.

"Renovated it myself, and did a great job, if I do say so. Did that new kind of texturized plaster, you know? First I laid on old brick, left over from when our house burned down, then fresh plaster on top. Sound workmanship. Sound." He tapped the wall vigorously. "Any job worth doing, worth doing well, is what I always say."

The deputies huffed down the stairs after the sheriff and looked around the room. They followed Cully, still chattering, into the back room and we could hear them walking around, with Cully talking nonstop, pointing out the coal chute and other places they might search.

Meanwhile, Julie, trailing behind the deputies, hobbled halfway down the stairs. Just as Cully came back through the door opening onto the unfinished part, her cane slipped from her grasp and clattered down the stairs into the renovated room.

Cully bent down with a little laugh and retrieved it. Julie sighed and settled down on the top stair, watching us all through the open door.

"So? Seen everything?" Cully said, the cane in hand.

The small basement room reeked of paint and plaster. Edith stood in a corner and the sheriff and his men stood in the center, looking around with very little interest.

"You've been most cooperative, Dr. Cully," Sheriff Rumpsey began. "We sure do appreciate it. We know how hard this must be. . . . "

"Think nothing of it!" Cully crowed, his eyes glinting as he darted glances of triumph at me. "Proud to show off my home improvement project. You satisfied then, Sheriff Rumpsey?"

"Yes, I guess so," the sheriff said.

"Sure of that? Anything more you want to see? Just ask! I've got no secrets!"

"No, no, that's okay, let's go men . . . ," the sheriff began.

"Outstanding workmanship," Cully babbled, "glad to have the chance to show it off." He waved Julie's cane. "Look here." He tapped the brickwork of the unplastered wall with Julie's cane. "Solid construction. Good, old-fashioned workmanship." He tapped harder on the wall. Harder and harder.

Then, suddenly, as if in answer to his tap, a sound, muffled and broken, like the sobbing of a child, issued from behind the brick wall. It swelled into one long, loud continuous scream, inhuman—a howl—a wailing shriek, half of horror and half of triumph.

Cully started back, dropping the cane on the floor. He staggered to the other side of the room, his face suddenly dead white, his eyes starting, perspiration springing out on his brow. For a moment, everyone remained motionless, staring at the bricked wall.

Then the sheriff and his deputies fell upon it, scrabbling at the bricks. They hardly noticed Julie hobbling to join them, pulling away at five or six bricks at the top of her reach.

As she did so, a piece of the wall fell away and we saw, in a brick niche, a huge black cat, a luminous white patch on its chest, its fiery green eyes staring at us. Asmodeus. Then, out of his red extended mouth issued the most horrendous bloodcurdling cry I have ever heard. It rose into the air, filling the room with its intense, demonic, high-pitched ululations.

The sheriff grabbed a crowbar and struck frantically at the wall beneath the cat's niche. The bricks fell away. The corpse of Margaret, decayed, clotted with gore, the head a seething mass of maggots, stood erect before our eyes and a gruesome stench flooded the room, blotting out the fumes of paint and plaster. Safe in his brick niche, Asmodeus wailed in triumph and in retribution. Cully covered his eyes, staggered, then stumbled against me.

"Speak!" I shouted at him. "Asmodeus wants you to tell! Now!"

"Demon cat! Demon cat!" Cully cried out. "God forgive me, it was the cat I meant to kill, not Margaret! I swear it by the archfiend! It was you, cat, *you*! You, the devil who had to die!" He turned to Julie, who sat upon the stairs. Her eyes met his and she smiled.

His back to the wall, cowering as far away as he could from Julie and her cat, Cully shouted, "You, you seduced me into murder! You made me kill Margaret. It was you! You the demon black cat! You who damned me to hell!"

TWENTY-FIVE

D arling Asmodeus, I love you," Julie said, holding the black cat to her breast and caressing its soft fur tenderly. The cat pressed against her, purring, looking gratefully at me as if to say, she's safe now, we saved her.

We sat at a table in Shelton's—Edith, Julie, the mayor, and I—me drinking beer, they drinking iced tea, and all of us holding court. Spreading the word. The word that Cully had confessed to Margaret's murder. Sheriff Rumpsey had a proper confession now, repeated after Cully had been cautioned a second time. Of course Cully was still blaming the black cat for everything, but this was not a defense likely to go down well in Crowley Creek.

But did he really mean the blame for Julie? Perhaps he blamed her and the town still would?

"I want y'all to know that John Charles here wouldn't give up until we found that body and Cully confessed," the mayor told everybody. "We owe him an apology, we most certainly do."

"Not until he repudiates the witch and her craft!" sang out

Fairchild. I hadn't seen him enter, but now he closed the door behind him and came into the café.

Around us, the townsfolk had been chattering to one another, sharing their astonishment over the events of the day before, the day when Cully had been unmasked and taken away to be charged with manslaughter. The charge might have been murder, if Julie hadn't insisted that his deadly ax blow had been intended for Asmodeus. Hard to accept that she still wanted to help Cully, that her tenderheartedness endured despite all that the man had put her through. Folks turned to see Fairchild come in and repeat his tired accusation. But before anyone could reply, the front door burst open behind him and in rushed Tiny, Travis, and Sue Anne Beebee, their parents bringing up the rear.

"John Charles, I believe Crowley Creek owes you our thanks . . . ," Mort Beebee began, not noticing Fairchild. Sue Anne, dragging Gomer behind her on a leash, flung herself upon Julie and Asmodeus, hugging them joyfully. "Julie! Julie! Lookit Gomer. A hunnerd percent well! You did it. You saved him. You and Asmodeus and your magical powers!"

"Now just a moment, young lady," Fairchild thundered. "The Devil's work, evil spells . . . "

Sue Anne twisted away from her embrace of Julie and tilted her face upward to stare back at Fairchild.

"She's not evil, Reverend Fairchild," Sue Anne said in her high, little-girl voice. "She's full of love for the little creatures, just like our Lord. She sacrifices herself for them."

A silence followed these words. Fairchild looked thunderstruck.

"You thought she did bad things. Everyone thought she killed Mrs. Cully. But we was wrong. And when you're wrong you have to apologize and ask forgiveness, that's what I learned in Sunday school."

"But . . . the Devil is in her and in her familiar, that demon cat," Fairchild said weakly. The steam seemed to have gone out of him. He looked back and forth between Sue Anne and Gomer, the old dog wagging his tail enthusiastically, and Julie, embracing her cat and gazing tranquilly back at him. Then he lowered his eyes.

"Julie, Sue Anne, they're our children, Rollie," Edith said. "We need to care for them and help them, not denounce them." She pitied him, but I could see that her infatuation was dead. My heart lightened.

"Well I think she stinks!" Billy Shelton said. "Say what you want. She's a witch, she has weird powers, and she doesn't belong in Crowley Creek."

"Oh, shut up," Travis said. "Why not let her be? Who cares anyhow?"

Billy hesitated a moment, averted his eyes, and shuffled back into the kitchen.

Mort Beebee insisted upon shaking my hand. He gracefully thanked Julie for saving Gomer. Barbara Jane Beebee leaned over and kissed her. "You don't know how much the kids love that old dog, honey. We are so grateful for all you've done."

"So, Jackson Lee, looks like we'd do best to put up with having a witch in town," Mort Beebee said to the mayor. "Got to put all this conflict and commotion to rest. Bad for business."

"Mrs. Boynton says I might be able to get a job in the new crystal and unicorn shop that's going in on Central Avenue," Julie said. "I won't be able to work with animals at the Cully Vet Clinic, 'cause the clinic is closed, but I'll help animals whenever I can."

"My suggestion, be businesslike," Mort Beebee said. "Charge for your advice. That'd help you get along here. Remember, folks don't value what they don't pay for."

"Oh? I haven't noticed that," Julie said in her innocent voice.

"Mort, we have to be going. Come on, Travis, Tiny, Sue Anne," Barbara Jane Beebee said, leading her brood toward the door.

"Bye, Julie," Sue Anne called. "Come over anytime and play with Gomer. And remember, we love you."

"A pillar of the community, the Beebees," the mayor said

contentedly, watching the family leave. "Good folks. Sound. So, John Charles," turning to me. "Looks like you're the hero of the day. Where's Marilyn?"

I poured the last of my beer into my glass and drank it down. "Marilyn and I are giving it a break," I said.

"Now, don't take it against her that she didn't stand up for you," the mayor advised me. "You were pretty far out of bounds there for a while. In my opinion, you deserved what you got, acting like you thought you knew better than everybody." His genial mask slipped a little. "Who woulda guessed things would work out the way they did? Who woulda guessed the witch and her cat would unmask Dr. Cully and solve Margaret's murder? Marilyn just acted sensible."

"Sure, sensible," I said. Now that the dark confusion, the heavy sense of impending doom I had been living with for weeks had dissipated, I could feel the hurt of Marilyn's easy abandonment. She had apologized, but when I looked at her shrewd, pretty face, I felt a lack of something in our relationship, and though I missed her and still wanted her, I thought it would be a long time before I could forget that she hadn't been there when I needed her. I understood. I didn't hold it against her. I just didn't want to see her for a while.

"It appears a lot of people in town miscalculated," Edith said. I could see she, too, would have trouble forgetting how the town had been willing to accept Margaret's disappearance and blame the subsequent troubles on Julie. "Don't forget, people in town tried to harm Julie."

"Well, the vet admitted he set the net trap and the bear trap for her," Mayor Winsome remarked. "The rattlesnake was a pet he'd just got."

"Glad I killed it," I said.

"But someone else, someone put poison in her tea and sent nasty letters to the *Sentinel*," Edith said. "You think we should just forget that?"

"Live and let live, that's what I believe," the mayor said, getting up ponderously. "Got to say hello to a few folks." He began to move from table to table, shaking hands and sharing with people their now rapidly growing view that they had all known the vet was up to something, that he had got what he deserved when the witch turned on him and used her powers to unmask him.

"I know," Edith said to me, "Rollie stirred people up to ugly things like the poison and the hateful letters. But he acted out of his beliefs."

"Do you really think so?" I asked Edith.

"Yes, I do."

I turned to look at Julie, who sat tranquilly, sipping her herbal tea and petting her cat. Was she just an emotionally fragile young girl with a love of animals? What explained the dark power that both Fairchild and I had reacted to so strongly? And that cat. . . .

"How did you get Asmodeus to go in and out of that brick niche?" I asked her.

"The niche was separate from Margaret's hiding place," Julie said. "I created it before the bricks had set. It connected to an outside vent. When you and Edith said we should try to spook Dr. Cully, like in Edgar Allan Poe's story, it seemed the best way. Asmodeus was okay. The niche had plenty of fresh air and he only went in of his own free will. He had to mourn Margaret. He loved her."

"Why was Dr. Cully so chipper that last day?" I wondered. "He'd been going downhill and then, when we brought the sheriff over, it was like Cully had gotten a second wind. I was real surprised when I saw him acting so brazen."

"I think the one night of silence let him believe he was in control again," Julie said. "He felt he was back on top, then when he struck the wall with the cane and heard Asmodeus howl, so unexpected, the evil spirits in him startled and the truth slipped out."

"He blamed you, you know," I said. "He believes your arrival brought demonic spirits which came to possess him and lead him into evil."

"I know he thinks that," Julie said sadly.

"But he embraced the spirit my ancestor called 'perverseness,' " I said, thinking aloud. "He stood on the edge of the abyss and he flung himself over just because it was wrong."

"You could have embraced the same spirit," Julie said. "But you refused it."

Edith put out her hand and I clasped it tightly. Her fingers felt warm twined in mine and the sadness I felt seemed to dissipate, as if her hand were a poultice on a wound.

"You refused the Dark One," Julie said. She stroked her cat with soft, repeated, sensual caresses.

"Did I?" I said. "Did I?"

I looked out through the window of Shelton's. In the sky behind the village, I saw a circle of black crows and I thought I heard them call to me from the distance.